KAY L. MOODY

WRATH&
CRYSTAL THORNS

FAE AND CRYSTAL THORNS 5

Wrath & Crystal Thorns
Fae and Crystal Thorns, #5
By Kay L. Moody

Published by Marten Press
3731 W 10400 S Ste 102, #205
South Jordan, UT 84009

www.MartenPress.com

Cover by Angel Leya
Edited by Deborah Spencer and Justin Greer

ISBN: 978-1-954335-29-5

ALSO BY KAY L. MOODY

Fae and Crystal Thorns
Flame & Crystal Thorns
Shadow & Crystal Thorns
Blade & Crystal Thorns
Curse & Crystal Thorns
Wrath & Crystal Thorns
Standalone: Nutcracker of Crystalfall

The Fae of Bitter Thorn
Heir of Bitter Thorn
Court of Bitter Thorn
Castle of Bitter Thorn
Crown of Bitter Thorn
Queen of Bitter Thorn

The Elements of Kamdaria
The Elements of the Crown
The Elements of the Gate
The Elements of the Storm

Truth Seer Trilogy
Truth Seer
Healer
Truth Changer

Visit **kaylmoody.com/beauty** to download a bonus story,
Bargain of Power and Beauty, for free.

CRYSTALFALL
Amberglow Marshes
Mushroom Patch
Emerald Lake
Diamond Isles
Gilded Labyrinth
Gemfields
Celestine Meadow
Forest of the Wraiths
Rubyrise Mountains
Crystalfall Castle
Goldvein Mountains
Lifespark Tree
Pixie Grove
Mortals Camp
Valley of Beryl
Sapphire Falls
Crystals Caves

1

THEY NEEDED A PLACE TO hide. Chloe leaned in closer to her dragon's scales, urging the creature toward a small clearing in front of a dense forest. With night falling, the golden gleam of the tree trunks wasn't as noticeable as their gnarled, skeletal frames. A slight chill hung in the air as all the dragons behind her landed in the clearing beside the forest.

Chloe and the other Golden Shields had just managed to escape Crystalfall Castle after Julian's crown and magic were restored to him once again. They were still reeling from the consequences of that stunning revelation. Julian was the king they'd been searching for. Julian, their greatest enemy. And now he had unimaginable power.

Doing her best to forget about that, Chloe glanced back at the other dragons. Shivers ran through their enormous wings as they landed on the black soil of Crystalfall. The creatures gazed at the forest ahead of them through narrowed eyes. Tension reverberated through Shadow's body, enough that Chloe could feel the dragon shaking beneath her. Despite the dragons' hesitation, Chloe did what she knew she must. Grabbing onto Quintus's hand, she slid down her dragon's back until her feet landed on the ground.

One of the Shields had given Quintus a coat to borrow. He had removed his shirt to stop the blood from the cursed wound in his side before Chloe had finally healed it, but that shirt had been left at the castle. Now Quintus wore a simple coat made of coarse wool with wooden buttons fastening it closed.

Golden tree trunks stretched toward the sky in front of them, almost like claws. Each tree stood so close to the next that it would take effort to trudge into the forest. No paths lined the ground. They would simply have to climb over tree trunks and through thick branches to get inside.

But they needed a place to hide.

The Forest of the Wraiths frightened their dragons too much for the creatures to enter. The wraiths inside the forest would want memories from anyone who walked its paths. It was unlikely any of the Golden Shields would get a good night's rest, but what choice did they have?

With her eyes straight ahead, Chloe prepared to speak loud enough for all the Golden Shields to hear. "Leave your dragons here and follow me. We will sleep inside the forest tonight."

She didn't dare look back to watch anyone's reaction. Considering the eerie light and the spine-tingling chill the forest gave off, the Shields may have been even more afraid of the forest than the dragons were. But even that was better than how Quintus stood at her side.

His face held no expression. His arms hung loose and despondent. He said nothing. He probably felt nothing. The pain of the defeat they had just experienced had stricken his heart so hard that all feeling had probably vanished. Now his eyes looked dull and without sparkle. Without life. He only moved when Chloe directed him.

Her own heart twisted at his state, but she couldn't think about that right now. She couldn't think about Julian or what he had just gained by getting his magic back. She could only think of the forest.

Get inside. Get safe.

Forcing her feet forward, she moved into the damp, oppressive air of the forest. Layers of powdery dust covered every branch and rock, giving a stale, lifeless quality to the air. And yet, she moved on.

The Golden Shields trusted her to lead them. Maybe she didn't have any hope to inspire them with, but she could at least be steady and sure with each step she took.

As they entered the forest, Mishti came to walk at Chloe's side. Mishti's midnight blue tunic had been ripped on the end near her left hip. One of the leather arm bracers she so carefully oiled every night had been sliced almost all the way through. The damage was probably too great to repair unless Quintus used his crafting magic to do it. Mishti's thick dark hair was still braided, but nearly half the hair had come loose.

Holding tight to the sword hilt hanging at her hip, Mishti turned toward Chloe and spoke under her breath. "What are we doing here?"

A small movement in one of the branches caught Chloe's eye. She consciously turned her gaze away from it, desperate to keep moving forward no matter what. "Remember how the wraiths wouldn't tell us anything about the king? Remember how they seemed to hate him? I thought maybe the king hates them too."

Mishti raised one eyebrow. "You think Julian will avoid the wraiths and that we'll be safe here?"

It took effort to answer with any sort of assurance, but Chloe did her best. "I doubt this is the first place he'll come looking for us. And if we go to any other court, we might put that court and those people in danger. I thought it would be better to stay in Crystalfall and go somewhere he would not think to look."

Several moments passed while Mishti stared straight ahead, but eventually she nodded. "This is a good plan. Well, a good enough plan."

Good *enough*. That summed it up perfectly. It wasn't good. It certainly wasn't great. But it would do well enough for now.

Chloe turned her gaze toward Quintus for half a breath, just enough to make her trip over a dusty tree root. The leather strap holding her wooden foot against her leg slid down, nearly pulling the foot off completely. She managed to take an awkward step and push her leg back into place without the foot falling off.

But she couldn't get the look of Quintus's eyes out of her mind, no matter how she had secured her foot. His eyes were dismal and dark and ready to give up. She swallowed, forcing herself to continue the conversation. "Besides, we might get information while we're here too."

Mishti folded her arms in front of her chest before she answered. "For a price."

And both of them knew if the information came from their wraith friend, Chandril, then it would mean Mishti was the one who would have to pay that price.

Ludo caught up to them, rubbing at his left elbow with one hand while his voice stayed suspiciously silent. His blue-and-red eyes raked over the forest, a tiny shiver rocking through his shoulders. His lips trembled at the sight of the trees around them.

Only a moment later, one of the other Golden Shields, Batu, tripped over one of the skeletal branches of the forest. Ludo released the elbow he'd been rubbing and used his arm to catch the man before he could fall to the ground. Batu nodded in thanks, careful to not say *thank you*, since such words would make him magically indebted to Ludo. In return, Ludo placed a hand on Batu's shoulder and offered the tiniest smile.

"Cheer up," Ludo said in a voice barely above a whisper. "I have been to this forest before, and I survived. It might look frightening, but it can still be a shelter for us."

The words immediately brought a grim frown across Mishti's lips. She glanced through the side of her eye at Chloe before tilting her head back toward Ludo. "You know things are bad when Ludo stops complaining." Though she whispered, Ludo's fae hearing probably still heard every word. Mishti swallowed before she continued. "I don't know if I've ever heard him offer words of comfort before."

Chloe's gut twisted at the thought. In previous fights against the Zeakriesh, Ludo had complained and suggested they give up even when death seemed inevitable. The fact that he didn't now…

Her vision suddenly blurred as tears filled her eyes. Squeezing her eyelids shut, she flopped onto the ground and studied a pearlescent white pebble sitting in the black soil. It served no purpose except distraction, but maybe the others would let her pretend it meant something. After another moment of examining the pebble, she stood.

At least she had blinked the tears away. Tightness still ached inside her throat, but she could ignore that. "We will sleep here for the night."

Miraculously, her voice didn't falter as she spoke. It gave her just enough courage to continue. "Do not speak to any of the wraiths. They will claim to grant your wishes, but I promise, the cost of granting that wish will not be worth it. If any of them attempt to speak to you, direct them straight to me."

No one said a single word after that. They simply nodded and dropped to the ground. Usually, they slept on sleeping mats with warm blankets Quintus had crafted for them, but all those mats and blankets were back at their camp in the hills of

Crystalfall. No one said anything about that, though. They all must have known as well as Chloe did, they'd have nothing but the ground to sleep on tonight.

Quintus sat down with his back against a gnarled tree trunk. His elbows rested against his knees as he stared ahead, looking at nothing in particular. He didn't seem to notice how a large knot in the tree dug into one of his shoulder blades.

The first wraiths found them soon after. Unlike the first time Chloe had entered this forest, the wraiths did not approach them right away. Their translucent bodies blended in with the shadows. Their lithe, wispy frames made it difficult to see them sitting on tree branches and hiding behind bushes.

Each wraith had glowing eyes in a different color that stared at Chloe and her companions. But the wraiths did not approach. They did not offer to grant any wishes. Instead, they stayed back and watched.

Despite their silence, she could practically feel their questions in the air. Last time Chloe was here, she, Quintus, Mishti, and Ludo had been asking about the king. The wraiths told them nothing now, but they clearly still wanted to know what had happened. Even with no words spoken, she could see the questions in their glowing eyes.

Did you find the king? How much power does he have? Did you defeat him? Did you lose?

As much as the wraiths clearly wanted answers, they must have feared them even more since none of them approached. It wasn't until Chloe started clearing away a spot on the soil to sleep that Chandril finally came.

His long fingers hung at his side, slightly longer than a mortal's fingers. His blood-orange eyes glowed brighter than any other wraith around them. But he looked different. Even more different than the last time she had seen him.

He had always had dark skin, but it used to be so translucent, she could practically see right through him. But now it looked more substantial. It still had a see-through quality to it, but one that only came through at certain angles. And he was definitely taller because now he stood slightly taller than her. When they had first met him, he was at least a head shorter, just like all the other wraiths, but now he was nearly as tall as Quintus.

Perhaps getting memories from Mishti was turning him into something more than a wraith. Was it possible he was turning fae?

His voice still came out as chilling as she remembered. He stared straight at Mishti and asked, "Did you kill the king?"

"Kill him?" A cold laugh sputtered from Chloe's lips. "If we had known who he was, we *would* have killed him."

Guilt darkened Chandril's blood-orange eyes. Faerie itself had prevented him from giving them the name of the king. He had only been able to tell them Julian knew where to find the king, not that Julian *was* the king.

Chandril's eyes narrowed at Chloe. He reached for Mishti's arm, tracing a finger over the slice in her leather arm bracer. "What happened then?"

The strangest look entered Mishti's eyes then. Her face always looked stoic with only the tiniest hints of emotion shining through. But with Chandril standing close, stroking her arm, the hardened expression she always wore dropped away and true vulnerability shone in her eyes. She took a step closer to him with her gaze dropping to the ground. "He has the crown now."

Chandril's hand stopped moving at once while the rest of his body went rigid. When he spoke, his voice had tightened. "The crown? The crown of Crystalfall?"

When Mishti nodded in response, Chandril grabbed onto her arm and held tight, as if that might change her words. But of course, it didn't. He gritted his teeth before asking a final question. "Does he have his magic too?"

"Yes." This came from Ludo who shook his head and stared at the ground.

Dropping his arms to his sides, Chandril closed his glowing eyes. "We are doomed then. Doomed."

"Don't say that," Chloe said with a snap. Of course she felt the same way. They *all* felt the same way. But nobody needed to say it out loud.

Chandril turned back to Mishti, taking her braid into his hands now. He touched the pieces of her hair that had come loose from the braid and tried to tuck them back into place. "How did he get the crown?"

"He tricked us," Chloe said.

But it didn't matter because Quintus chose that exact moment to speak his first words since they'd entered the forest. His voice was scratchy and heavy and thicker than ice. "We gave it to him." He dragged both hands down his face and released a huff that felt like a knife to Chloe's chest. So much pain in his words. In his face.

Quintus shook his head as dread crept in around them. "We *gave* him the crown."

Anger flashed in Chandril's eyes. He turned to Mishti. "You said you needed to find the king in order to save Crystalfall. I thought you were going to kill him."

"We didn't know Julian was the king." Chloe stepped toward the wraith. "We thought the king would be able to stop Julian and save the court."

At that moment, Chandril and every wraith surrounding them hissed. The chilling sound filled the air and caused Chloe's stomach to flop over on itself.

Chandril narrowed his eyes and spoke in a voice more harrowing than any Chloe had ever heard. "Do *not* speak his name in our forest."

The other wraiths jumped off their tree branches and out from behind the bushes they'd been hiding behind. Their translucent skin and spindly long fingers paired a little too well with the predatory stances they all took. Each of them suddenly looked like they wanted to rip the heart out of Chloe.

Quintus jumped to his feet and wrapped his arms around Chloe from behind until her back was pulled tight against his chest. He was probably staring down every wraith, attempting to meet their predatory eyes with a frightening gaze of his own.

As usual, Mishti seemed awakened by what should have scared her. She turned to Chandril, staring at him like she had never trusted anyone until that moment. "Why do you hate him so much?"

Chloe had been wondering the same thing, though she was in no position to ask.

The question startled the other wraiths enough that they all turned to look at Mishti. With her braid still in Chandril's hands, she looked at him carefully. "Why do you fear him?"

Anger still flashed in the other wraiths' eyes, but Mishti's words wiped it clean from Chandril's. He was instantly subdued.

After a deep breath, he said, "There is much to explain." He glanced toward the edge of the forest. "But we should go deeper into the forest before I say any more."

He beckoned their group forward and everyone followed without hesitation, even the other wraiths.

Maybe Julian had his magic and power back. Maybe Crystalfall and Faerie was in more danger than ever. But maybe, just maybe, they'd finally find a way to defeat him this time. Maybe with the right help and with the right information, they'd finally have a chance.

CREAKING FROM THE GOLDEN BRANCHES filled the heavy air. Each step brought Chloe and the others deeper into the Forest of the Wraiths. Unease twisted in Chloe's gut, tension growing thicker with each moment that passed.

Chandril's lithe frame seemed to flicker for a moment as he turned back toward her. "Prepare yourself now. I do not have some secret way to defeat the king of Crystalfall. I am simply going to explain why he has already won."

Her belly filled with dread, but she did her best to ignore it. They already knew they had little chance. They already knew the wraiths had given up. But *she* wasn't going to give up. Not yet.

Mishti stomped forward a little more vigorously, perhaps trying to find some hope to hold onto like Chloe had. Ludo's face looked glum, just like the other Golden Shields, but all of them kept walking forward. That had to mean something.

And Quintus… he kept rubbing his arm and wrinkling his nose. No hope at all lay in his eyes. His face still had no expression at all, as if even frowning would take too much out of him. At least he didn't need Chloe dragging him forward to keep him walking anymore.

After only a bit farther, they had reached the heart of the forest. She assumed it was the center, anyway, considering they had just come upon a tree much larger, much thicker, and much more frightening than all the others. Something about it seemed as undead as the wraiths.

Shadows enveloped them as they stepped carefully toward the tree. The dark night sky turned nearly black above them.

By now, several other wraiths had joined them. Chloe didn't notice the other wraiths until Chandril stopped, and she bent to remove her wooden foot.

The day had required much physical activity, and the end of her leg was sore. While she rubbed the aching muscles, she glanced around at the two dozen or so wraiths around them. Their translucent forms blended into the shadows so completely, she could only see them when they moved. That probably meant even more wraiths stood nearby that she hadn't detected. The thought sent a shiver down her spine.

Chandril directed the Shields to sit, and they all found spots on golden tree roots or patches of green pearl grass strands. Just as Chloe got settled, Quintus sat close enough to her that their hips brushed against each other. His arm rested on the ground behind her back, creating a barrier between her and anything that might reach her from behind.

Once everyone got settled, Chandril nodded. "Now that we have reached Undulle Tree, I will tell you what I know."

A wraith with short blonde hair and a silky skirt stepped toward Chandril with one eyebrow raised. "We should not help them unless they give us a memory." She leaned closer to him and lowered her voice. "You know that is our way."

Sitting taller, Chandril looked at her and then out at the other wraiths, making it clear he addressed all of them. "We will not take a memory for this. If they want to defeat our common enemy," his nose twitched before he continued, "our *greatest* enemy, then we will help them without taking anything in return."

Chloe had time to put her wooden foot and boot back on before the other wraiths finally started nodding in agreement. At least they eventually agreed. Clearly, they'd do anything to get rid of their king.

With that realization at the front of her mind, she turned straight to Chandril, ready to finally get some answers. "Why do you hate him so much? The king?"

It took an extra thought to stop herself from saying *Julian*, the name they so deeply despised, but she managed to fix it at the last moment.

Chandril's entire face flinched. "He *stole* our magic. We use memory elixirs to take memories from people so we can live those memories in our minds. But *we* only take memories that are offered. We never take them without a bargain."

Ludo pinched his eyebrows together. "So Juli—" He stopped in the midst of saying the king's name as the wraiths surrounding him all started to hiss. But then he cleared his throat and continued. "So the king takes memories without a bargain?"

A tight energy continued to fill the air after the wraiths' hissing, but Chandril answered. "He does worse than that. He takes memories and then he mutilates them until he can extract the energy from them, which he then uses for himself. He stole our knowledge and magic, and he perverted it for his own purposes. Memory magic belongs to wraiths. No one else should be able to wield it."

By the time Chandril finished speaking, he was practically spitting the words from his mouth.

Each sentence tugged at Chloe's mind until a memory of her own surfaced. She reached for the leather bag that had been on her shoulder only a few moments ago. "I remember reading about this."

Plucking the king's journal from the leather bag, she placed it onto her lap. She'd done the same thing dozens of times before. They'd gained valuable information from that journal. But as she reached now for the worn cover, disgust shook her hand.

Julian was the king. He was the one who had written every word in this journal. Though she had learned that truth already, it kept hitting her in all new ways. Her nose twitched as she began flipping through its pages, doing her best to touch it as little as possible.

It didn't take long to find the passages she remembered. She read them with all-new eyes, knowing now Julian had been the one who wrote them.

It took three more memory elixirs and three more lost memories, but I finally re-created a memory elixir of my own.

For a while, I thought I might never figure it out, so I attempted to extract energy from other Faerie items. The balance shards that can turn mortals into fae had the most power, but their instability and destruction caused me to give up on them almost as soon as I started.

I also tried extracting energy from trophies, which are also called tokens, but mine were never powerful enough. I even tried getting energy from stories the way the Swiftsea fae do, but that failed miserably.

Memories are the only viable option. My experiments will continue this evening.

Tightness filled her throat as she scanned the words, the puzzle pieces still coming together in her mind.

Her eyes narrowed as she asked, "When you say he turned the memories into energy for himself…"

"The energy gives him life," Chandril finished.

Mishti sucked in a sharp gasp at these words, almost like she'd been punched in the gut. Her arms tensed as a sickened look hardened in her eyes. "*He* took our memories."

Squeezing her hands into fists, Mishti shook her head slow and then faster and faster. Her jaw clenched hard, forcing her to speak through her teeth. "That's how he keeps himself alive. It's been over a hundred years since Crystalfall was destroyed, but he's still alive and looks only a few years older than the rest of us."

It took a moment before Chloe realized what Mishti was saying. Once she did realize, Chloe gulped hard. "You told me you have missing memories from when you lived with Ansel. That you and the other mortals would forget some of the things that happened to you."

A hard puff of air escaped Mishti before she nodded. "All this time I thought I forgot things because they were too painful, but it never made sense *all* of us had lost memories we couldn't account for. He probably took memories from Ansel too, making sure the fae never questioned why he had lived so long."

Though melancholy had consumed Quintus since they escaped the castle, a new look entered his eyes now. He was thinking. Trying to figure this out with them. Chloe allowed herself to believe it meant he hadn't given up completely.

Staring deep in thought at a white pebble on the ground before him, Quintus spoke in a subdued tone. "But he had no magic while in Ansel's home. When my father destroyed Crystalfall, Faerie blocked his magic from him so he could not use it. That was why he needed the crown. To get his magic back. How could he have turned memories into energy without magic?"

Mishti shook her head, despair nearly swallowing her eyes. "He *did* have magic. It just wasn't his own magic."

Everyone near Undulle Tree turned to stare at Mishti. Even the wraiths didn't seem to understand.

But Ludo just slapped himself on the forehead. "Of course! The king used Ansel's gemstones. Ansel used blood magic to capture magic and store it in gemstones. The king must have used the gemstones to convert memories into energy."

"I *hate* this." Mishti glared at her hands as she clenched and unclenched them into fists. "I helped keep him alive. I lost memories without even knowing it, and all to keep a madman alive long enough for him to defeat the only true family I've ever known."

When she finished speaking, she covered her face with her hands and groaned.

Everyone else seemed to be filled with that same energy. Resentment. Several other Golden Shields groaned. A few of them even laid down and curled themselves into balls. It must have hurt knowing they'd been violated just to keep their greatest enemy alive.

Mishti's complaint caught Chloe in the heart, especially the very end of it. At nearly the same moment, she, Quintus, and Ludo all seemed to catch each other's eyes. They must have noticed the same words Chloe had.

A moment later, Ludo raised a teasing eyebrow and smirked at Mishti. "Ah, so I am *family* to you now, am I?"

Her eyebrows flew upward, and she punched him in the arm. Considering how Ludo's body shifted, she must have hit him hard.

He gave a short chuckle in response.

She folded her arms over her chest as she glared. "How do you know I was talking about you?"

Ludo lifted one shoulder in a shrug. "Who else would you be talking about?"

"Perhaps me," Chandril said through a hiss. He bared his sharp white teeth, which actually weren't all that sharp anymore, and slinked his thin frame forward until he sat directly in between Mishti and Ludo.

Ludo rolled his eyes, which only made Chandril hiss again. Ludo waved his hand casually. "You have no need to be jealous, if that is what you worry about. I am sure she thinks of me as a brother, nothing more."

Tilting his head to one side, a pronounced smirk lifted one corner of Ludo's mouth. "Although," he said in a long, drawn-out tone. "Now that I know you see me as a brother, I can finally rest easy knowing any threats you make against me are empty."

Mishti scoffed at that. "I might have killed my real brother, so don't assume you're safe."

A little too much hate filled her tone. In a gesture that seemed far too gentle for a wraith, Chandril put his arm around Mishti's shoulders. She remained as stoic as ever, but the smallest hint of pain flickered in her eyes.

"Might have?" Ludo asked. His teasing tone had vanished, speaking only with concern now.

Chandril glared. "Do not ask her about it again."

The exchange had started sweet with Mishti accidentally admitting she saw the rest of them as family. Then it turned amusing, but now it had reverted to what the rest of this day had been. Gloomy. Hopeless.

"Forget about that," Batu said in a huff from behind them. "What are we supposed to do about the king? How can we possibly defeat him when he's already taken so much away from us?" He shivered as he said those final words.

Most of the other Shields had lived in Ansel's house just as Mishti had, and they must have lost memories to Julian too. No wonder hopelessness suffocated the air around them. But Chloe wouldn't let it stay like that. When hope was nowhere to be found, they'd just have to make some of their own.

"Yes," she said, sitting up straight. "So he's been stealing memories and will continue to do so to keep himself alive. Just because he won't die of old age doesn't mean he'll live forever." Her statement held just enough intrigue to capture the attention of those around her. She waited until most of them glanced toward her before she continued. "We can still kill him, right? We just need to make a plan."

Chandril released a laugh completely devoid of humor. "You already forgot what I told you earlier. The king has already won."

Leaning closer to him, Mishti turned her eyes toward his face. "Why are you so certain about that? What do you know?"

Shaking his head, Chandril let out a heavy sigh. "There is a magic ritual so obscure that almost no one in Faerie knows of it. The ritual requires blood and sacrifice. If the king performs this ritual, he will become immortal in the same way as the high fae. He will not need memory magic to keep himself alive, though he can still be killed the way high fae can be. *However,* the ritual will also afford him even more power than he already has. He will be able to steal power and magic from any fae he stands near. He will be able to steal magic from Faerie itself."

Quintus spoke again, his voice even more dejected than the last time he'd opened his mouth. "I have never heard of such a thing."

Pity sent creases across Chandril's forehead. "I assure you, it *is* real, and he intends to complete the ritual. Your life is in more danger than anyone."

The tiniest fleck of gold sparked in Quintus's brown eyes as he narrowed them. "Why?"

"He needs blood to perform the ritual," Chandril answered. "He needs so much blood that a mortal like him— even with his magic—would not survive. But he does not have to use his own blood when he can use his son's instead."

A knot formed in Chloe's chest, sending a sharp pang through it. "The king can use Quintus's blood for this ritual?"

Chandril's blood-orange eyes glowed as he nodded. "And killing his own son will count as the sacrifice the ritual requires."

Ludo huffed grumpily. "I have never heard of this ritual either. Maybe it truly exists, but if we do not know of it, why should we assume the king knows of it?"

Unfortunately, Chandril had an answer. "A scale from a dragon is needed for the ritual too, and the dragon must belong to the ruler of a court. Of course, only one such dragon exists in all of Faerie, and that is King Severin of Fairfrost's dragon."

Chloe's heart jolted. Without thinking, she clenched her fingers so fast it partially tore a page from the king's journal. While unclenching her fist, she turned to glance at Quintus. He was already staring back at her.

They had seen King Severin's dragon in Crystalfall. They had wondered why King Severin would be there.

Now they knew.

Chandril nodded at the two of them knowingly. "I doubt King Severin knows what the Crystalfall king plans for his dragon. It is more likely the king of Crystalfall lured King Severin here under false pretenses. But whatever he said to get King Severin here, one thing is clear. The Crystalfall king knows about the ritual, and he plans to perform it. He will kill his son and gain unimaginable power all at once."

Chloe clutched her chest. That knot inside it throbbed and burned.

It hurt. It hurt knowing what Julian planned and how it might affect her beloved. Where could she possibly find hope in all this?

But even as an oppressive gloom sank into her pores, she found a tiny bright spark she could hold onto. All this time they'd been fighting, and they'd never even known who their true enemy was. But now they had something they'd never had before.

They had Julian's plan. For once, they had a chance to get one step ahead of him instead of always being behind. And with that information, they just might be able to stop him.

Once and for all.

3

CHLOE TOOK A DEEP BREATH, and asked the wraiths, "What else do you know about the ritual? What other ingredients are needed? What else can we do to stop the king from performing it?"

Every wraith around them turned away from her when she asked. So, of course, she turned to look Chandril directly in the eye.

He shrugged, and then he too looked away. "You know enough."

She tipped one of her eyebrows upward. "What if I give a memory?"

"No." Both Quintus and Mishti said the same word at the same time.

But Chloe wasn't about to back down just because her beloved and her best friend were overprotective. "If this is the only way to defeat the king, I think it's worth a memory, don't you?"

Mishti scowled, which probably meant she agreed but didn't want to admit it. Quintus just slumped his shoulders even more and let out a heavy sigh. His face went back to having no expression while his eyes looked duller than ever.

But… none of the wraiths offered to take Chloe's memory. A few of them even took a step backward. When she looked one wraith in the eye, about to offer a memory again, the wraith shook his head and took a step back.

Chloe's mind whirled, trying to understand their behavior. Was it possible they didn't know anything more than Chandril had already told them?

Finally, a wraith with glowing purple eyes spoke in a whisper from the shadows. "What knowledge you need, Faerie itself will provide."

Oh, wonderful, just what she needed. And extremely cryptic response that didn't help or reveal anything. Unfortunately, such a response meant the wraiths probably *had* already told them everything they knew. If Chloe and the other Golden Shields were going to learn anything else about the ritual, it was clear they would have to figure it out on their own.

That might have seemed doable, except the wraiths refusal to give more information had turned the mood grim.

Quintus glowered. The small golden glints that had been in his eyes earlier had completely vanished now. "Chandril is right. My father has already won. We should leave this court and find some place to hide. He will likely find us eventually, but if we are clever in our hiding, we may be able to prolong that."

"No." Chloe checked her boot to make sure her wooden foot was securely in place. And then she stood. "We are not leaving this court. Crystalfall is a court for misfits, for anyone who needs freedom and safety. For anyone who needs a home."

Sofia stared bitterly at the ground in front of her. "That's what we promised when we became Golden Shields." She then reached for the golden chain mail piece attached to her dress. "But if we cannot fulfill that promise, then Crystalfall is no longer a court for all."

Silence hung as thick as the shadows of the forest. Chloe knew the right words would have the power to change the tone surrounding her and the others, but what could she say to inspire everyone? What would be enough to peel away the dread that had so thoroughly encased her fellow Golden Shields?

"Yes, it is." Chloe stood taller, looking purposefully into each Shield's eyes before turning to the next. "Crystalfall has *always* been a court of misfits, even before the king ever got here. It has always called to those who needed somewhere new to live."

A few faces in the crowd turned a little less bleak. Mishti sat forward, hanging onto Chloe's words more than any of the others. Fire burned in her eyes, as warm as the hope rising in Chloe's chest.

Infusing her tone with as much conviction as she could muster, Chloe continued. "We don't promise safety and freedom to all who enter Crystalfall simply because we think it sounds nice. We do it because Faerie *needs* us. Faerie itself needs warriors like us who can make this court what it was meant to be."

That ember inside her chest grew until it filled her every limb. All around Undulle Tree, several Shields gained peace in their expressions. If she wasn't mistaken, a few of the wraiths even looked calmer. They wanted this court she talked about.

They wanted Crystalfall to be a haven for all, including themselves.

She lifted her wrist, showing off the pieces of golden chain mail wrapped around it to form a bracelet. "We are the Order of the Golden Shields. Should we give up just because the king beat us in a single battle? Just because he has a plan? He may have power, ingenuity, and ambition propelling him, but we have something stronger than that. We have a purpose, a purpose more important than anything *he* has ever done. Are we going to run and hide and leave Crystalfall or are we going to defend and protect it like we promised?"

Mishti stood with a start, nearly dropping the sword that had been on her lap. "I will *not* run and hide," she said while sheathing her sword. Then she reached up for the three golden earrings she wore, each one made from the same golden chain mail Chloe's bracelet had been made from. With her fingers on the earrings, Mishti continued. "I will keep defending this court until the king is gone and Crystalfall is safe again."

She stood and eyed the faces surrounding her. "Who else? Who else will keep their promise to protect this court?"

Ludo's blue-and-red eyes pulsed with color as he got to his feet. "I will. I will fight to defend Crystalfall, not as a fae, but as a Golden Shield. Because that is what Crystalfall is. Not a place for just fae or just mortals but a place for all."

A few others stood then, Sofia and Batu among the first. Even Chandril stood, quickly closing the distance between himself and Misthi.

But not Quintus. He sat as slumped as ever, his gaze pinned to the ground. He wouldn't look at Chloe. He wouldn't look at anyone. When he finally spoke, his voice broke over the words.

"I do not know if I can fight." His head dropped more until his chin fell to his chest. "I may make things worse, not better."

Chloe had been waiting for this. She'd known it would be coming from the moment they left the castle, from the moment they realized Julian was the king. Raising an eyebrow, she put her hands on her hips. "Why, because you failed to kill the king when we had him captured?"

Surprise lifted Quintus's gaze, causing him to nod before he had even realized he had moved. "Yes."

She shook her head, lowering her hands back to her sides. "None of us knew who he was. He tricked *all* of us. That wasn't your fault."

Quintus scowled. "But he is my father. I should have recognized him."

"How were you supposed to recognize him when he wore a glamour the only two times you saw him knowing he was your father?"

A crease appeared between Quintus's eyebrows. "Well, then I should have *felt* his blood or a connection to him or something."

Chloe tilted her head to the side. "That's not a thing fae can do, is it?"

"It could be," Quintus said, lifting his chin high. "Maybe."

"Not unless it is their greatest magic," Ludo said from behind Chloe. "But Quintus's greatest magic is in crafting, so no, that is not something he could do."

Nodding, Chloe continued. "You couldn't have known who he was. None of us could have known. He made *sure* of that."

"Chloe's right." Mishti spoke in a ruthless tone that had a strangely steadying effect in this conversation.

"But…" Quintus looked from one edge of the forest to the other, clearly trying to reach for more imaginary reasons he wasn't good enough. With a huff, he crossed his arms over his chest. "My father has beaten us many times. You said we should not give up just because he beat us in one battle, but he has beaten us in *many* battles."

Chloe glanced down to catch his gaze. "And yet, we're all still here, as ready as ever to fight back."

"He has more power now," Quintus said, though he had loosened the arms around his chest.

She shrugged. "And we have more resolve."

"*And* we have dragons," Sofia said with a surprisingly cheerful smirk.

Batu nodded, courage growing in his expression. "We were able to capture the king and take the castle because of our dragons."

One of the Shields who had been sitting, now stood. Hilda took a deep breath and reached for the golden circlets she wore. "We only had to flee the king because he took us off guard. Now that we know his plan, we can be more prepared and won't be surprised like that again. We *do* have a chance."

"Exactly." Chloe turned back to Quintus and reached a hand out to him. "We needed you in every battle we've fought so far, and if we have any chance at all of beating the king, we'll continue to need you each step of the way. The *last* thing you'll do is make things worse. I'm certain you'll lead us to victory instead, as long as you are still with us."

The final sentence did it. A hint of a smile curved his lips upward. Suddenly, he was staring at Chloe with the same fire in his eyes as she felt burning in her chest. He grabbed her hand and got to his feet. When he stood, he stood tall. "I am always with you, Chloe. Always."

With her hand still held tightly in his, he lifted his other hand into the air and shouted, "We fight for freedom. We are Golden Shields!"

Many others repeated his final words, shouting them as they punched the air. Every Shield that had been sitting now stood, determination blazing in their eyes. It had taken a few moments, but their little group was ready to fight again. All of them.

Remarkably, four wraiths came out of the shadows and stood with them too. The wraiths enviously eyed the small golden circles each of the Shields had. Perhaps they wondered whether they might be allowed to join the order. If so, the answer would be a clear *yes*. No such questions were asked though. Instead, their presence must have meant they agreed with the order's purpose.

When Quintus had first brought Chloe to Faerie, this fight had been about mortals versus fae. But now, the fight had become something so much more important. Now one side fought for power strong enough to destroy all those who would oppose, and the other side, their side, fought for a place they and others could call home.

A wraith with a full skirt, glowing red eyes, and sharp black teeth stepped out of the shadows and into the clearing with the rest of them. She glanced around with narrowed eyes until her gaze landed on Chloe.

"I cannot tell if you are fearless or if you are foolish to believe you have a chance against the king. Perhaps you are unaware, but he is the one who *destroyed* this entire court. He left us wraiths in limbo while we continued to exist, even when the court around us did not. You do not have as much power as him, no matter how many fight with you."

Chloe's stomach curled in on itself at the imagery those words created. It had never occurred to her what Crystalfall was like for the wraiths while it didn't exist. It must have been very strange indeed for these creatures who were neither dead nor alive, and as such, could not be killed.

After a hard swallow, Chloe finally managed to respond. "Maybe we don't have as much power as him, but there is something we have."

Her gaze jumped to Quintus, hoping he might have an encouraging look for her. Luckily, he delivered a wide smirk that gave her all the courage she needed to finish.

Turning back to the wraith, Chloe said, "We have the audacity to *try*."

The wraith's eyebrows rose, and a slight smile emerged on her face for a moment, as if she could not stop it before it appeared. With a shrug, she turned and addressed their entire group. "We wraiths do not believe you will succeed, though we will not stop you from trying. You may hide from the king in our forest for tonight, but you must leave after that."

Her red eyes glowed as she turned back to Chloe and nodded. And then she and the other wraiths disappeared into the shadows of the forest.

Mishti raked her gaze over the ground. "I guess we should choose our sleeping spots now."

"Um." Chloe cleared her throat and had to take two deep breaths before she continued. "There is one last thing we should do before sleeping."

Questioning eyes stared back at her. Even Quintus didn't seem to know where this was going. Her belly twisted and her heart squeezed, but she couldn't say *nothing*. It would be hard, but this needed to be said.

She let herself swallow once more and then she forced the words from her lips. "I think we should take a few moments to remember Jansher." Her gaze dropped to the forest floor as the weight of it sank in. "He was willing to guard our greatest enemy for us, and he died because of it. I know we cannot change what happened, but I think we should at least allow ourselves to honor him."

Many Shields nodded, some had already started crying. It hurt to remember how Julian had not just tricked them, but he had also killed one of their strongest members in order to get the crown and his magic back.

Once Chloe's invitation was out, the others immediately took her up on it. Soon, memories were shared of how Jansher had loved wrestling and how he was distractable and how he was a good friend. They laughed. They cried. It hurt, but it was needed. They needed to remember him and how empty it felt without him.

After they had talked and talked and had nothing left to say, they finally chose spots on the ground and settled down for the night. Despite the pain, it was good to be reminded everything was more bearable when they were together. They said nothing more to each other as sleep overtook them, but they didn't have to. Yes, they had just experienced great defeat at the hands of a powerful enemy, but at least they still had each other. And with each other, one thing was abundantly clear.

Julian hadn't won yet.

WHEN DAY DAWNED, CHLOE STRETCHED and scanned the area around her. The Golden Shields had made it through the night by hiding in the Forest of the Wraiths. They had survived. And now they needed a plan. Everyone woke up slowly and got ready even slower. A few more tears were shed for Jansher. Ludo conjured food for them, but he reminded Chloe his supplies would soon run out. After all her inspiring talk about not leaving the court, it seemed they might have to leave Crystalfall in order to get food.

Quintus used his crafting magic to fix clothing and bracers and boots of the Shields that had been damaged in the fight the day before. He even crafted himself a new coat and pants that were a rich dark green. Soon, it was time to go.

But as their group trudged through the shadowed forest to leave it, Chandril fell into step at Chloe's side. He glanced in every direction before finally speaking to her in a low whisper. "Golden tables can be summoned."

She jerked her head toward him, which caused several wraiths from the shadows to look in her direction. Based on how Chandril had carefully glanced around and lowered his voice, he probably didn't want the other wraiths knowing he gave this knowledge freely, without a memory.

Brushing her fingers through her hair, she tried to play off the head jerk as if she had gotten her fingers stuck and moved her head quickly to force a knot from her hair. Once the other wraiths turned away, she kept her eyes straight ahead, as if she didn't even notice Chandril walked beside her.

But then she whispered back. "How?"

Chandril sighed throwing a longing glance toward Mishti. "It has been so long, even we wraiths do not remember. We only eat dust, not food, so we have no reason to hoard that knowledge."

Possibilities filled Chloe with this new revelation. If a table could be summoned, they could hide anywhere in Crystalfall. They would not have to return to their old camp, where Julian would certainly have spies or soldiers or both.

They could still leave the court, but only if they needed help. They wouldn't have to leave for basic necessities like food.

But how could a table be summoned? She knew of only two tables. One stood where the mortals had first camped in Crystalfall and one stood in the castle. What did those two places have in common?

Her heart sank once that question filled her mind because an answer came soon after. Julian. Julian had lived in both those places. He had ruled in Crystalfall Castle back before the court got destroyed. And he had lived in the mortals' camp when the court had first been re-opened. Had he summoned both tables? As king, was he the only one who could?

Scrunching her mouth into a knot, she turned to Chandril. "What if the king is the only one who can summon a table?"

"No." A gleam appeared in Chandril's orange eyes, which appeared more alive than she had ever seen them. "That is one thing I remember for certain. The tables were here before the king ever stepped foot in Crystalfall. You do not need *him* to get a table. You just need magic."

As they had nearly reached the edge of the forest, she set those words at the back of her mind to consider later. For now, they needed to focus on making a plan to defeat Julian.

Narrowing her eyes, she stared at the gnarled trees at the edge of the Forest of the Wraiths. She'd been walking with Chandril, but now they had reached the edge, he stepped away from her and moved closer to Mishti. Quiet words moved between them, but they spoke too low for Chloe to hear. Eventually, Chandril turned around to walk back into the forest.

By the time the rest of the group had caught up and prepared to exit the forest, Mishti's eyes had turned watery. No tears had fallen yet, but she kept having to blink to keep them from falling.

Clearing her throat slightly, she steeled her expression. "Chandril is going to stay here to try and get the other wraiths to help in the fight. He believes it will be better if he tries to convince them while the rest of us are not here."

Ludo playfully elbowed her as he walked by. "It seems our hardened soldier has feelings after all."

She threw him a glare even sharper than any of her many weapons. But once he laughed and walked past, a light smile played on her lips. She leaned in close to Chloe and said, "My real brother never cared about me enough to tease me like that."

Chloe responded with a smile of her own. Even she, who had grown up with a good family, could appreciate just how much it meant to have friends so close she considered them family.

On sighting the Shields, the dragons that had been resting outside the forest flapped their heavy wings in greeting. Chloe rushed over to Shadow, rubbing her golden scales with swift strokes and inhaling her metallic scent. It had only been one night, but she had missed her dragon greatly. Shadow's blue wings flapped in response to her touch, causing sparkles as the light caught the gem-like sapphire blue of her wings.

Quintus moved in front of the dragon, throwing small bits of bread for the creature to catch in her mouth. He must have saved the bread in his magical pocket for just this occasion. Each of his throws got sharper and more angled, but Shadow still managed to catch every one.

After releasing a small chuckle, Chloe climbed onto Shadow's back. Once atop the dragon, she spoke loudly enough for all the Shields to hear. "We are heading to Rubyrise Mountains next."

Now that his chunk of bread was gone, Quintus scurried up Shadow's back to sit at Chloe's side. "When did you decide that?"

"This morning. I asked my magical book where we should go, and it simply showed me a map of Crystalfall. But Rubyrise Mountains looked a little more sparkly than everything else, and they're far away from the castle, so I thought maybe it was a sign." She tilted her head toward Quintus, doing nothing to hide the hesitation that probably filled her face. "It should be easier to hide in the mountains too, right? There will probably be more places to hide than the hills where we were before."

Quintus ran a hand over Shadow's golden scales as he considered. If he had answered too quickly, it would prove he would have agreed to anything she said whether it was a good idea or not. So, she appreciated he thought before answering. Eventually, he nodded. "I agree that mountains will be easier to hide in than hills. And my father will probably not think of looking for us there since we have never been there before. He may still find us, but it should keep us safe for a while."

With that, Chloe urged Shadow to fly up and into the sky. With her leading the other dragons, they flew to Rubyrise Mountains.

Instead of taking a straight route over the celestine meadow and the castle, Chloe directed her dragon to fly over the many rivers at the edge of Crystalfall. Then, once they had nearly reached the black caves full of golden sparkles, they flew over Pixie Grove and finally to Rubyrise Mountains.

A sparkling mist surrounded the towering peaks of the mountains. Their slopes were adorned in black soil mixed with red rubies that sparkled in the sunlight. Golden and emerald trees and jeweled bushes and wildflowers dotted the lower parts of the mountain, but Shadow flew directly toward the top where only the soil and rubies were. The jagged ruby rocks were bathed in the fiery glow of the sun, casting breathtaking red and gold hues onto one another.

The air was infused with a sweet scent of lemon and vanilla. The dragons began to descend swiftly and found their way through the peaks. They landed on a wide mountain ledge more than large enough for all of them to set up a camp. The edge of the ledge ended in a steep cliff.

Just as the dragons were landing, Chloe distinctly heard Mishti call out to her stormy blue dragon with its clawed and scarred wings.

"Wonderful flying, Temper." Mishti leaned in, resting her cheek against the chipped and bent scales of its neck. "Wonderful."

Since Mishti's dragon sparked with electricity every time it moved, it didn't seem very smart to rest one's cheek against its scales. Then again, choosing the most dangerous, most angry and scarred-looking dragon hadn't seemed very smart either, and it had worked out fine.

When electricity did zing through the scales next to Mishti's cheek, she simply chuckled and slid down off her now-landed dragon's back.

Once Chloe slid off her own dragon, she used her chin to point toward Mishti's stormy blue dragon. "You named her *Temper*?"

With a smile, Mishti reached back and touched a hand to the enormous creature's belly. "I named *him*. And yes, *Temper* seemed appropriate."

Chloe nodded in response. Shadow's name had come to Chloe easily, and in a moment, she had known it was right. The same thing must have happened to Mishti with her dragon. How many of the other mortals had already named their dragons too?

Chloe dropped to the ground and reached for her wooden foot. Her leg had ached more than usual during the ride, but a little rub would help with that. It didn't happen very much anymore, but as she sat and kneaded her muscles, she wondered what life would be like if Portia hadn't chopped off her foot.

She had gone nearly all her life without having to remove a wooden foot before going to sleep and without having to find it as soon as she woke each morning. And now, those little things had become so ingrained into her routine it almost seemed strange to imagine a life without them.

Then again, she couldn't deny wearing a wooden foot instead of a real one did make life more complicated. And occasionally more painful. At least Quintus had that piece of wood from his home in Bitter Thorn. At least he was a master craftsman and could carve her a new foot to wear.

"Are you okay?" Quintus dropped one knee to the ground at her side, staring fervently at her foot and the end of her leg.

"I'm fine. My leg just needed a little massage." She slipped her leg back into the leather strap, reattaching it easily.

Because of the bond she shared with him, he must have known at least some of the pain she felt. His gaze turned to her face while worry wrinkled his forehead. "You have been doing that more often lately. More than you used to."

It had severely traumatized him when she'd needed to chop the end of her leg a second time in order to re-heal the improper healing she had done when Portia had first chopped off her foot. He must have been afraid she might have to do something similar again.

With her foot securely in place, she stood and attempted her most reassuring expression. "That's only because we have been busier lately. Once we defeat Julian, I'll be able to give my feet the rest they need. Or maybe I'll just get stronger with all this extra walking."

The worry creases in Quintus's forehead became deeper.

She waved him off. "Forget that. Right now, we need to strategize."

It took some instructions and some maneuvering, but soon the dragons formed a circle around the outside edges of the clifftop where they had landed. The Golden Shields then gathered in a large circle directly in the middle. Red light cast over their faces from the rubies in the soil.

Once everyone was settled, they all looked to Chloe, waiting for a plan she still didn't have. Clearing her throat, she attempted to appear courageous. "Before we plan how we'll go up against Julian next, we need to figure out, what do we already have that we can use?" A heavy silence filled the air while she prepared to speak again. When she did, some of her courageous tone had dwindled. "And what do we still need?"

No one said anything at first. They all just stared at her, expecting her to have the answers. She hated that she didn't.

After another few moments of uncomfortable silence, Ludo finally spoke. "We have us." His blue-and-red eyes looked far more red with all the rubies on the mountain peak. "We have three dozen Golden Shields, and we are fierce when we need to be."

"And we have our dragons," Sofia added. The woman glanced back at her dragon whose scales resembled faceted crystals in pale pinks and yellows. The dragon kept stretching its limbs or tapping the ground. Just like Sofia, the creature didn't seem capable of sitting completely still.

"And we have your magical book," Mishti said, her fingers slowly rubbing the hilt of her sword. "Perhaps it can give us information about the castle or about the ritual Julian is planning to do."

Feeling her eyebrows tip upward, Chloe nodded. "That's a good point. And if it doesn't tell us that, maybe it will at least tell us how to summon a golden table so we can eat."

The prospect of food sent delight through several of the eyes around her. Sitting up straighter, she asked her other question a second time. "And what do we still need?"

Quintus rubbed his chin thoughtfully, though he said nothing.

Sofia drummed her fingers against her knee for a moment before she said, "We need to stop Julian from performing the ritual. If we don't..."

"Julian will be too powerful for anyone to defeat," Batu finished for her. "Our only chance is to defeat him *before* he can do the ritual."

Mishti nodded, unfazed by this truth. "The ritual needs ingredients, I assume. If we can find out the ingredients, we might be able to stop Julian from gathering them."

"We already know two ingredients," Chloe said. "We know a scale from King Severin's dragon is needed, but Julian has probably not taken it yet since the dragon is still here in Crystalfall." Her heart was too heavy to mention the other ingredient, but it didn't matter because Quintus said it for her.

"The ritual also needs blood and sacrifice. I am meant to offer both of those." Anger laced his voice, which was better than the bitterness Chloe expected.

"Then we also need to protect Quintus." Batu sat forward narrowing his eyes as he thought. "Quintus is heir to the throne and will rule this court well... as long as we get rid of Julian first."

"But those can't be the only ingredients, right?" Sofia asked, her fingers now twisting a strand of hair over them.

"Of course not." Ludo turned to Chloe expectantly. "Ask your book. See if it will tell us what other items are needed."

Sucking in a breath, Chloe reached into her leather bag and retrieved the magical book. Her fingers gripped the cover a little too tight as she whispered into it. "What is this magical ritual Julian plans to perform?"

Holding her breath, she opened the book and started flipping through its pages. But nothing new appeared on the parchment before her. She found information on castles and crowns on herbs and medicines on many things she had read so many times before.

Before giving up, she tried another question. "What ingredients does Julian need for his sacrificial ritual?"

But again, the book gave her nothing new. No blank pages, no scrawling handwriting with exactly the information they needed. Just pages and pages of interesting facts about Faerie that were useless to them now.

"We will find out the ingredients another way then." Quintus put a hand on Chloe's back, offering reassurance just when she needed it. Suddenly, he sat up straight. "King Severin probably knows something. If we sneak into Crystalfall Castle, we might be able to get information from him about the ritual or about what else my father has planned."

Ludo groaned loudly at this announcement. "You want us to waltz into the home of our enemy? Should we hand Julian the weapons we want him to kill us with too?"

A smirk tilted Quintus's mouth upward. "He would never expect us to enter the castle without trying to attack him. We might be able to sneak in and out without him ever knowing we were there."

"And if he does find us," Mishti said as she reached for a small dagger hidden under her tunic, "I'll be sure to stab him with every single one of my daggers."

Chloe couldn't help but smile. Grumpy Ludo had returned along with heroic Quintus and frightening Mishti. Now they just needed Chloe, the mastermind, to find a clever way to make their idea work.

That she could do. Yes, they would waltz right into the home of their enemy, but if they were smart about it, they could do it stealthily and get the information they needed without anyone getting caught.

The order of the golden shields and their dragons stayed on Rubyrise Mountain for only one day before they prepared to move once more. Their next destination of Crystalfall Castle was essential to learn the rest of the ingredients Julian needed for his ritual.

Unease rolled like a shiver among the Shields as they climbed atop their dragons and departed the towering red-and-gold-hued peaks of Rubyrise Mountain. They had entered the castle before, but they all knew it would be different now that Julian had the crown. He was finally reconnected to the magic he'd once had, the magic he had used to destroy an entire court. Even sneaking in, this would be more dangerous than any of the other times they'd entered the castle. They only had a few weapons, their dragons, and hope and determination in their hearts.

Atop their dragons, a sparkling river flowed beneath them, which then changed to a large mountain range with copper peaks. Soon, the ruby red spires of the castle came into sight.

"Prepare to descend," Chloe shouted to the others. But just as the words left her mouth, Shadow suddenly reared back. A guttural cry erupted from her throat. What had happened? Was she injured?

Even with her focus on her own dragon, Chloe still noticed, from the corner of her eye, the other dragons flew to the same distance as Shadow, but then suddenly reared back with strangled cries.

Chloe reached for the harp string reins, which she barely ever bothered to use anymore, since Shadow always followed her commands now. But even with the reins tight in her grip, she couldn't convince Shadow to fly any closer.

Quintus sat at Chloe's back as usual. He leaned to one side and smoothed a hand over Shadow's golden scales. "What is wrong? Why will she not fly forward?"

"I don't know." Chloe bit her lip and glanced around the area. Every Shield wore the same expression of confusion mixed with worry as she felt. And every dragon hung hovering in the air, apparently unable to fly forward anymore.

Ludo and Mishti both rode atop Temper. The stormy-blue scales of the creature crackled with electrifying zaps that increased in speed.

"There must be a barrier enchantment," Chloe finally said.

"Barrier enchantments cannot be hidden completely from view. Even if they are mostly invisible, a shimmer of some sort should appear once they are touched. Though…" Quintus leaned in close to whisper in her ear, fear lining the words. "We have encountered a barrier with no visible shimmer before."

Ignoring that for a moment, she waved to get everyone's attention. "Follow Shadow. We're all going to land back there and figure out what to do next."

Once she directed Shadow backward, she could feel tension release from the dragon's muscles. They should be able to get to the ground, as long as they didn't try to get any closer to the castle.

"Do you remember the invisible barrier?" Quintus asked. "It was in Bitter Thorn when the iron poisoning was so strong it stopped us from getting to Bitter Thorn Castle."

"I remember," Chloe answered. She focused on the ground where Shadow would soon land. "But this is not because of iron poisoning."

"How do you know?"

Chloe huffed, wishing she was a little more sure of herself. "I already healed Crystalfall and the rest of Faerie from iron poisoning. It shouldn't be possible to infect it again."

He gently reached for her shoulder, then spoke in a tender voice. "What if it *is* possible? What if my father found a way with his new magic?"

"He didn't." She leaned heavily on her dragon's neck, refusing to consider that possibility. "He probably just found a way to make a barrier enchantment that doesn't shimmer."

"I suppose that is also possible."

She couldn't tell if Quintus believed an invisible barrier enchantment was actually possible or if he was just choosing to not argue.

Either way, they soon landed on a patch of green pearl grass strands at the base of the copper mountains. The Shields slid off their dragons, instinctively forming a circle as they had back on Rubyrise Mountain. But once all the mortals and fae had gathered, the dragons immediately slumped onto the grass, as if completely exhausted. Soon, they began to snore heavily, their bodies heaving up and down.

"Why would they all fall asleep like that?" Chloe blinked at the enormous creatures as startled as she was troubled.

"They've never done anything like this before," Mishti said, staring at her dragon. She glanced back toward the castle, which looked much smaller from this distance. With her eyes on the castle, she reached for her sword hilt and glared.

"Our best weapon, and they all decide to fall asleep? What chance do we have now?" Ludo said gloomily.

Shifting the leather bag on her shoulder, Chloe stared at the ground. "Quintus thought perhaps it's because of iron poisoning. We *did* meet a barrier somewhat like this back in Bitter Thorn before I healed the land."

Both Ludo and Mishti's heads snapped up to stare at Chloe. Their expressions looked as harried as she felt.

"No." Quintus stepped carefully toward Shadow, who slept only a few feet away. "I changed my mind. Iron poisoning only stopped us from going forward, but this made all the dragons sleep."

He tilted his head while placing a hand to Shadow's golden scales. With a start, he turned back to Chloe. "I think you are right. I think this is magic. Julian knows the dragons are the best defense we have. He must have found a magic that repels them and forces them to fall asleep."

Ludo wrinkled his nose at the snoring creatures all around them. "How long do you think they will sleep?"

Quintus shrugged. "I do not think they will sleep forever, especially now that we are farther away from the castle. But even still, we should not wait to enact our plan. My father will be even less likely to expect us inside the castle if we cannot get there on our dragons. This is the perfect moment to sneak in."

"But how are we supposed to get to the castle without our dragons?" Sofia had one hand on the pale pink scales of her dragon as she turned to look at Chloe and Quintus.

"Ludo and I can open doors that lead inside the castle," Quintus responded.

Chloe nodded. "We can split into two groups. Actually, we should split into three groups. Sofia and Batu, you stay here with ten others. The rest of us will go through the doors into the castle."

The Shields nodded, accepting her direction without hesitation. It still seemed strange to have their unquestioning support when all these people knew just how useless she was in a fight. But then, they also knew how *useful* she was when making plans. One of these days, she'd stop thinking of herself as useless in a fight and start remembering fights weren't the only place to be useful.

Shaking that thought away, she selected those who would stay with Sofia and Batu to look after the dragons.

Then she and Quintus chose how to split the rest of the group into two. She and Quintus would lead one group and Mishti and Ludo would lead the other. Once divided, they decided to walk on foot as close to the castle as they dared to see if they could learn anything.

On foot, they traveled past the copper mountains and into a forest of golden trees with emerald leaves, they did their best to step lightly and make no noise.

They didn't dare get too close to the castle, but after a bit of walking, they managed to get past the spot where the dragons had gotten stuck. That proved whatever had stopped the dragons wasn't iron poisoning, since the barrier created by iron poisoning had stopped all of them, including the mortals and fae. The invisible barrier around Crystalfall Castle must have been made specifically for dragons then.

When they got as close as they dared, Quintus's face tilted upward. With furrowed brows, he studied the sky around the castle. "Look."

Chloe, and nearly everyone around them, followed his gaze. At first, the sky looked normal. Well, as *normal* as it could look in a court made of gems and jewels. But then she tilted her head to the side. Parts of the air *did* look a little more sparkly than usual. After staring hard, she finally saw what Quintus had already noticed.

Several small floating glints filled the air around the castle.

"I see it," Mishti said, her eyes as squinted as Chloe's. "Are those… crystals?"

It hadn't been obvious before, but once Mishti mentioned crystals, Chloe suddenly realized exactly what floated in the air. She nodded. "I think it's the celestine crystals that grow in the meadow beside the castle. Well, the dust from crushed celestine, to be more accurate. There's only a bit of it though, and it's somehow been evenly dispersed throughout the air."

She stared at the glints for another moment, then immediately reached for the bottom of Quintus's coat. He was far too preoccupied by her sudden touch to stop her from lifting the coat. Soon, his chest was bare while she held the coat high up to his shoulders.

By then, he managed to cough out a reaction. "*What* are you doing?" His voice came out breathy and hot and entirely uncontrolled.

The corners of her lips twitched into a smile, but she ignored the question and touched the leather necklace he still wore under his coat. A sparkling celestine crystal hung at the end of that necklace. She had used it to heal the cursed wound he had gotten from Julian. The wound may not have been permanently healed, but somehow, she knew the celestine crystal would keep the wound at bay. It made her glad to know he still wore the crystal around his neck.

Nodding to herself, she dropped his dark green coat until his upper body was covered again.

"Chloe," he said in a low rumble. "What was that about?"

His voice still came out a little too breathless. If they weren't busy with a mission, she might have slipped into his arms.

Instead, she glanced upward and studied the floating crystals in the air once again. "Some herbs—belladonna, for instance—can be medicinal in small doses but lethal in larger doses."

She spoke the words absently, not really sure if they were for herself or for the others.

Mishti pointed her chin upward. "You think those crystals are lethal?"

"I don't know," Chloe answered. "Probably not, especially since they only seemed to affect the dragons and not us. And there isn't much crystal dust in the air anyway, but maybe the crystal behaves differently when it's crushed as opposed to solid. Maybe the crushed crystals made the dragons sleepy, but again, why only them and not us? I don't know what it means. I'll have to research more when we get back to Rubyrise."

With a grin, Ludo pulled a small glass vial from his pocket. "You are lucky to have a friend who loves collecting things. Having a few crystals to test should make things easier, I assume."

"Yes," Chloe said with a nod. "Much easier."

But Ludo had stopped listening. With a swift jump that sent him much farther into the air than any mortal could ever go, he managed to gather several small crystals from the air around the castle into the vial. His blue-and-red eyes shimmered as he held the collected sample out to her. "Done."

"Good." She took the vial and tucked it into her leather bag.

"Did you notice the castle?" Mishti asked. She jerked her head toward the castle, which looked the same as it ever did.

But then Chloe sucked in a small breath. "He fixed it."

A knowing look filled Mishti's eyes. "Yes. When we came here just a few days ago, the entire castle had been split apart. Even the soil at the base looked dull and leeched of color. But now it looks as good as new."

Quintus looked like he was going to be sick. "He fixed it quickly. I know he has magic, but… maybe he has even more power than we realized."

Touching a hand to Quintus's shoulder, Chloe spoke in a softened tone. "Elora and Brannick fixed their castle quickly once Faerie was healed of iron poisoning, remember?"

"Yes, but they are the High King and the Queen of the highest court. No other ruler in Faerie should be as strong as they are."

Chloe gulped hard, lowering her hand away from Quintus's shoulder. Maybe he was right to worry, but what could they do except what they had already planned?

"Ludo," Chloe said, turning to the Fairfrost fae. "Start putting glamours on everyone to turn us invisible."

Mishti cleared her throat and stood a little more rigidly than she usually did. "We will need a way to communicate once we get inside the castle."

"We can speak through our doors," Ludo said without thought. But then his nose scrunched. "No, that will not work because the doors would stay in one place, and we need to walk around."

"Plus," Mishti said raising one eyebrow. "How are we supposed to hide a huge swirling tunnel? Your glamour can turn us invisible, but it can't hide a door."

"I have…" Quintus frowned, clearly still upset about how quickly Julian had repaired the castle. But after a little head shake, he dropped his hand into his pocket. "I have something that will work. I crafted them last night. I already gave one to Sofia and the others who stayed with the dragons."

He pulled out several small smooth stones, each a different color. He handed Chloe a brilliant smooth ruby stone and then handed a sapphire stone to Mishti and an opal stone to Ludo. Quintus kept the smooth emerald stone for himself, then handed out the remaining ones to the other Shields. There weren't enough for every person to have one, but at least half of them got one.

Once the stones had all been passed out, Quintus held his emerald stone up for all to see. Once he had everyone's attention, he held one arm out in front of himself and then placed the stone atop his coat sleeve.

"When the stone is not touching either of your hands, nothing happens." He then plucked the stone off his sleeve and held it in one hand. Bringing the stone close to his mouth, he then whispered into it. "But when you hold it, everyone else who touches a stone should hear the voice in their ears."

Chloe gasped at the sound of his words. Not only because she heard the words directly in her ears as if he whispered less than an inch away from her, but also because his voice did not seem to come out of his mouth either.

It was as if the stone took his voice from his mouth and transferred it straight to her ears.

Quintus grinned as similar gasps worked through their group. With the stone still at his lips, he whispered again. "If you whisper into the stone, your voice will also be silent when it leaves your lips. It will only be released to all those who hold a stone."

With a flourish, he dropped his hand to his side, still holding fast to his smooth emerald. "But if the stone is away from your mouth, your voice will come out like normal and be heard like normal. The other stones will not receive it, but you will still be able to hear from anyone else who speaks into a stone."

"Remarkable." Chloe turned her ruby stone over in her hands with her eyes growing wider the longer she looked at it.

He lifted one shoulder in a shrug, as if crafting such things were a normal occurrence. "I call them whispering stones."

"These will come in handy," Mishti whispered into her sapphire stone.

Just like with Quintus's voice, Chloe heard the whisper in her ear while Mishti made no sound at all from her mouth.

Quintus turned to look at everyone. "I recommend we keep the talking to a minimum since everyone who has a stone will be able to hear all communication. Only a few of us should talk—Chloe, Ludo, Mishti, and me—unless there is some sort of emergency."

"Excellent. These will be perfect for communicating inside the castle." Chloe turned to Ludo. "Finish glamouring everyone to be invisible, and then we'll be ready to go."

Ready to enter the castle of their enemy, gain information, and hopefully, come out alive.

6

Knowingly walking into the fortress of their enemy took all Chloe's strength. She held her breath, taking the last step that led her inside the walls of Crystalfall Castle. The moment she stepped through, an invisible Quintus pulled her around a nearby corner. She recognized his rugged scent and the feel of his hands on her. He must have waved his hand because a moment later, his door vanished.

"The other Shields are over here." His voice sounded directly in her ear, so he must have used the whispering stone.

He had gone through the door first, the other Shields in their group came next, and she had gone through last.

Once safely around the corner, Quintus whispered to her quietly. "There were guards patrolling just as I stepped through my door. I do not believe they saw it or any of us, but we need to be careful."

"How many guards?" she whispered into her smooth ruby stone. It was strange speaking words and hearing no sound leave her lips.

"I saw three, which is no cause for alarm." His tone changed to a tighter one. "What *is* alarming is these were people we have never seen before. *New* people."

Thoughts erupted in her mind like an explosion. New people? A few of Portia and Julian's soldiers had escaped after their last fight when it became clear their side had lost. Yes, those people had all run away, probably to other courts. But who else besides mortals would work for Julian? How had he found new guards already? How had he done that *and* repaired the castle?

Tension broke out across her forehead and at the back of her neck. Ice seemed to prick at her pores, turning her thoughts darker and wilder. But she had learned giving in to such thoughts was never productive. Sometimes she couldn't turn the dark thoughts off no matter how she tried, but right now, she had a great deal to distract her.

They had come with a plan, after all.

"Let's go," Chloe said, reaching blindly for Quintus's invisible hand. When she found it, he squeezed it gently, offering the comfort she desperately needed.

Once they began moving forward, Quintus spoke into his whispering stone. "Everyone in our group has entered the castle, and so far, we have avoided detection. We are on the move. What of your group?"

Mishti's voice sounded in Chloe's ear, even though Mishti was on the opposite side of the castle. "We had a small scuffle when we first entered, but we are all inside now." After a heavy pause, she continued. "Julian has fae guards. *New* guards. These are people who have never worked for him before."

Chloe's stomach flopped over on itself. She heard Quintus gulp at her side.

Tugging Quintus forward, she pulled her whispering stone to her mouth. "We saw the same, but we will have to talk about it later. We need to stick to the mission right now."

A dozen Golden Shields walked down the glittering hallway with her and Quintus. They couldn't get distracted when they had work to do.

They turned a corner, and Quintus grabbed her around the waist to stop her from taking another step.

Four guards with pointed fae ears marched down the corridor. Slinking backward, Chloe tried to become one with the wall behind her. It didn't matter if they were invisible. If they weren't careful, the fae still might sense their small group.

Just as the fae walked past them, one of them turned and sniffed the air, as if he had noticed something. Her heart thundered in her chest as the guard sniffed again.

The other three fae turned to him in confusion. Just then, the sniffing fae turned until he looked toward Chloe, Quintus, and the other Shields.

She held her breath, but she couldn't hide the sound of her beating heart. It pounded so fast, the guard, with his fae hearing, might be able to detect it.

One of the other guards poked the sniffing guard. "What is it?"

All at once, the guard stopped sniffing and shrugged. "I must have caught dust in my nose."

They moved on, but Chloe couldn't breathe again until Quintus wrapped an arm around her shoulders.

"This way," he said through the whispering stone. "We will go in the opposite direction of those guards. Hopefully we do not meet up with them again."

Luckily, it didn't take them long to find a large open courtyard near the outer edge of the castle. The debris and rubble from their last battle had been removed. Gleaming golden walls towered around them, looking even more magnificent than ever. Even the faint scent of mildew and dust that had once lingered in the castle had now disappeared. Now the air smelled of rich vanilla and lush gardenias.

Before they could cross the entire distance of the courtyard, a group of a dozen fae entered it. They walked far enough away that Chloe and the other Shields would be safe from detection, but still. A *dozen* fae? And they weren't even dressed as guards.

Some fae wore bright dresses with bold flower prints. Others wore navy blue suits with gray shirts. A few fae wore silk tunics and pants and smelled of cinnamon. The very last fae had an opulent brocade dress encrusted with opals. She carried a curved axe as she glanced around the courtyard.

Even though she hadn't visited the other courts recently, Chloe still recognized clothing from the courts of Swiftsea, Mistmount, Dustdune, and Fairfrost. Not only had Julian already recruited this many fae, he had also found them from several different courts.

Once the fae had passed through the courtyard and they were not in danger of being discovered, Chloe whispered into her ruby stone. "We just saw over a dozen more fae, and they wore clothes from at least four different courts."

"Four?" came Mishti's quick response, directly in Chloe's ear.

"Who is joining him?" Ludo asked through his whispering stone. "They may not remember he destroyed an entire court, but they know he is the one who nearly destroyed the rest of Faerie with iron poisoning."

"I do not understand why they would join him," Mishti said. "What does he have to give them?"

"Forget that. We need to continue with our plan." Quintus whispered harshly through his stone. Then he grabbed Chloe's hand and began moving across the courtyard again.

The hairs on the back of her neck stood on end. Each time she allowed herself to think of the fae and of how much Julian had already accomplished, her steps faltered. Soon she hesitated at every step. Fear gripped her limbs, making it a chore just to keep walking.

But finally, they reached the area they had been hoping to find since they entered the castle. In the stable yard and chained to the ground with a thick golden chain was a beautiful dragon with pastel hues.

King Severin's dragon. If it was still here, there was still a chance Julian hadn't gotten the scale from it he needed. If they helped the dragon escape, then they could leave the castle and worry about all the fae they'd seen inside it. They might not even need to speak with King Severin. The dragon was sleeping, which worried Chloe after what had happened to the other dragons, but she tried to hope they could simply shake it awake.

Both Chloe and Quintus tiptoed toward the sleeping creature, but then they stopped with a start. Standing right behind the dragon, just out of their sight until now that they'd moved close enough, was King Severin of Fairfrost.

Heavy blue and white brocade covered his tall form. White fur embellishments trimmed his collar and the end of his sleeves. He wore a crown with icicle-like tines that shimmered in every color of the rainbow.

He stood next to a female fae with blonde hair and ice blue eyes. Her attire looked as magnificent as his, but it also included an opulent necklace of opals and light blue gems.

The Fairfrost king stood close to the female fae and spoke to her in hushed tones. "You know I do not trust him, Tindra, but what choice do we have?"

The female—Tindra—opened her mouth to speak. From the farthest reaches of her mind, Chloe vaguely remembered these two. King Severin was the king of Fairfrost of course, but Tindra was his beloved, who had once worked in Fairfrost Castle as a researcher. Chloe's sister, Elora, trusted these two.

And it boded well that King Severin didn't trust *him*, who was probably Julian.

"Perhaps we could ask Queen Elora for—"

Whatever Tindra was about to say, it got swallowed up when Chloe accidentally knocked into a small vase, which clattered to the ground.

King Severin gasped at the unexpected noise, but Tindra moved straight into action. She threw one hand out, silver sparkles erupting from her fingertips. The magic moved too fast for Chloe to dodge. Once it touched her, the glamour keeping Chloe invisible fell away, turning her visible once again.

Now Chloe gasped.

Quintus appeared half a breath later, already putting one arm in front of her in a protective stance.

"Who are you?" King Severin demanded. "Does King Julian know you are here?"

Fear trickled down Chloe's spine, turning her limbs to ice. At least the other Shields were still hidden. Quintus must have removed the glamour from himself so he could protect Chloe, but the others would be safer while still invisible.

When Chloe said nothing, King Severin pulled an axe from his magical pocket. He glared at her and then at Quintus. "Tell me who you are and why you are here, or I will bring you to King Julian myself."

With fear gripping her so tightly, all Chloe could do was gulp.

7

RAISING ONE HAND WITH THE palm open, Chloe tried to appear as non-threatening as possible. "We are not here to fight."

Such a claim would have been more believable if Quintus hadn't just pulled a spear from his magical pocket.

"Then what are you here for?" Anger laced King Severin's voice. "Are you spies? Tell us!"

"We are not spies." Chloe spoke in her gentlest tone, one her mother had taught her to use once people started yelling. A healing voice, her mother had always said. And as Chloe knew, healing had a way of calming anger.

Tindra raised an eyebrow, perhaps noting how Chloe's tone had changed.

After a quick breath, Chloe continued. "I am Queen Elora's sister. My name is Chloe."

Both Severin and Tindra glanced at each other in surprise. Immediately, Severin dropped his weapon, his face open and calm.

But Tindra simply narrowed her eyes. A researcher like her must have known better than to believe without question. "You are mortal. Mortals can lie."

Lowering her hand in defeat, Chloe let out a sigh. Maybe it had been naïve to believe she could calm them so easily.

But then Quintus spoke. "*She* is capable of lying, but I am not. Chloe *is* Queen Elora's sister. And Chloe is also the one who healed the iron poisoning in Faerie. If you care at all about our land, you will listen to her."

A light sparked in Tindra's eye at the sound of that. "*You* healed Faerie?" She stepped a little closer. "Did you have to go to each court to heal them individually?"

It took a few eye blinks before Chloe registered the question. "Uh, no. I only had to heal one spot, Bitter Thorn Castle, and then I used magic to heal the other courts by imagining it in my mind."

"Magic?" Tindra's eyes turned even brighter. "But you are mortal."

And then Severin's jaw clenched tight. "King Julian is also a mortal who has magic. Are you his spy?"

"No." Chloe's hands flew upward, trying to dispel any thoughts that she might be working with Julian.

His voice raised as he took a step forward. "You still have not answered my first question. Why are you here?"

Afraid someone might be attracted by his raised voice, she once again adopted her healing voice. "Before you caught us, I heard you say to Tindra that you don't trust *him*. Were you talking about Julian?"

The Fairfrost king and his beloved immediately exchanged glances. They probably didn't want to share that information. Why would they? In war, trust had great limits.

Instead of answering directly, King Severin simply said, "Continue to speak."

Chloe lifted her wooden foot and rubbed it against the back of her opposite leg. She'd have to choose her next words carefully. Things could go very wrong if Severin chose to alert Julian to their presence. It was probably best just to tell him everything. But how much of it would he believe if he never knew Crystalfall had once been destroyed? He probably thought it was a brand-new court, not an old one newly restored. Either way, she'd explain as much as she could.

"We don't trust Julian either. In fact, we know much about the evil deeds he has done. He cares only for power and glory and does not care who he crushes to get it. He would destroy entire courts if they stood in his way. That puts us in perilous danger. *All* of us."

The final sentence came out slowly, deliberately, with her eyes fixed on King Severin. She didn't dare try to explain how Julian had already destroyed an entire court and taken away all memory of anyone who knew of it. But hopefully Severin would understand Julian truly was powerful enough to commit such an atrocity.

Severin and Tindra glanced toward each other, sharing a look no one besides them could understand. After a beat, Tindra gave a tiny nod. Severin nodded back and then turned to look at Chloe once again. "I have not spoken to King Julian much, but already he seems both manipulative and ambitious." A nerve ticked in his jaw before he continued. "My father and sister both proved those two traits make a dangerous combination."

"Why are *you* here?" Quintus asked suddenly. He had lowered the end of his spear to the ground with the tip pointing toward the ceiling, so it no longer hovered in an attack position. But he had not put it away completely. "*We* are here to stop Julian. To find a way to defeat him. But he asked you to come here, am I right? Why did you? Did he offer you something?"

Hearing those words, Severin lowered his gaze to his feet. "My court is not producing food like it once did."

Tindra continued where he left off. "It is because Queen Alessandra, the previous Fairfrost ruler, damaged the magic of our court when she imprisoned the sprites. But she stole magic from other courts, which helped to mask the problem."

Severin nodded sadly. "At first, we did not even notice, since some of her stolen magic lingered to alleviate the problem, but the true consequences of her actions are finally affecting us all. We no longer have enough food for the people of our court."

Quintus gripped his spear. "Did the king offer you food or did he offer you magic that would restore the food in your court?"

"Both." King Severin shrugged. "It seemed like too great a promise for what he asked. I should have known better than to trust him."

"Is that why you *don't* trust him?" Chloe asked. "Because he asked for so little and gave so much?"

"Yes," Severin said. "He asked only for few fruits from our trees and then later he asked for a protective enchantment to be placed over the castle, one that would stop dragons."

"Fruit?" Chloe shook her head. Did that mean Julian *didn't* know about the ritual? Had he not brought them here to get a scale from King Severin's dragon? Or had he simply lied about his true purpose so he could get the scale without them knowing?

It only took a small look upward to answer that question. The pastel-hued dragon behind King Severin clearly had a single scale missing just under its left wing. Considering how the leathery skin beneath it appeared raw and bright red, the scale must have been removed recently.

So perhaps Severin didn't know the true reason he'd been brought to the castle. Julian must have assumed, correctly, that Severin would come to Crystalfall by using his dragon. And Julian must have taken the dragon scale at some point without Severin realizing it.

"What was that look?" Tindra asked. She stared at Chloe, her eyes narrowed. "You just realized something. What was it?"

Chloe gulped and her gaze flicked to Quintus for a moment. He stared at her for less than a breath before he glanced up at the dragon. She could see in his face the moment he found the missing scale. His face fell as a hot exhale escaped his mouth.

Turning to face forward again, she found both Severin and Tindra's faces zeroed in on hers. But it hurt now to have to proclaim the truth. "Julian didn't care about your fruit. He probably never needed it. He only lured you here with promises because he needed your dragon."

Tindra and Severin jerked their heads toward the pastel-hued creature behind them. They must have seen both Chloe and Quintus stare at the same spot because their gazes soon locked onto the missing scale.

"A scale is gone," Tindra said in a whisper.

Severin didn't seem bothered though. Instead of being worried at all, he released a small chuckle. "If the king thinks he can train dragons the way my father did, he will be sorely disappointed. That trick will not work now that this dragon has left Fairfrost."

Quintus took a step back, his eyebrows high on his forehead. "*That* is how King Pavel trained the Fairfrost dragons? By removing scales from his own dragon?" Disgust twisted through his words.

Severin responded with a solemn nod, displaying just how barbaric he found the action. "Yes, and then he placed the removed dragon scales into different dragons. But as I said, that will not work anymore."

"Unfortunately," Chloe said, her voice wavering a little. "Julian does not plan to use the dragon scale to train another dragon. He is planning to use the scale in a ritual that will make him immortal. The ritual will also give him power unlike any Faerie has ever known. He will become more powerful than even High King Brannick."

Shock swept across Severin's face, which settled very quickly into acceptance. "I knew I never should have trusted him. I would kill him now except I have seen his magic. He is already more powerful than me. It would be pointless to face him when he would defeat me easily."

"Have you heard of this ritual before?" Tindra turned toward him in surprise.

"I may have. If it is the abomination of a ritual I am thinking of, then I heard of it through my father. During his life, he always sought to gain more power, no matter the cost."

"What do you know of the ritual?" Chloe stepped forward. "Anything you can tell us about it may help us defeat Julian. We will do anything to stop him if we can."

Severin glanced toward Tindra before responding. "I will need to go back to Fairfrost to look through my father's things. I may not be able to find any information, but if I do, I will send you a message with a sprite."

He threw another glance toward Tindra, which she responded to with a nod. Without another word, they both climbed atop the pastel-hued dragon that was still sleeping.

"What are you doing?" Chloe shook her head. "You can't leave."

"Are you going to try and stop us?" Severin asked with a raised eyebrow.

Tindra wore the same incredulous look as her beloved. Even Quintus appeared confused. But Chloe just gestured above.

"You said you created a barrier enchantment that blocks dragons, remember? Isn't that why your dragon is sleeping? How are you supposed to leave while that enchantment surrounds the castle?"

Tilting her head to side, Chloe examined the air carefully. Questions spewed from her mouth before she even thought to consider whether it was likely Severin might answer them. "Did you make the enchantment out of celestine crystals? How does it work?"

Both of Severin's eyebrows lifted upward. He was impressed by her questions. Hopefully that would make him want to answer. Luckily, he did respond. "We have celestine crystals in Fairfrost too. When crushed, they release magic that acts as a signal, if you know what to look for. Dragons are naturally drawn to these signals, but if there is too much crystal dust, and it is all spread out, it confuses their natural navigation systems."

From his side, Tindra nodded. "It confuses their navigation systems, *and* their minds get too busy trying to read the signal that it makes them sleepy."

That made sense. But it still didn't answer Chloe's first question. "But then how is your dragon supposed to escape the enchantment?"

Severin smirked as he pulled a celestine crystal from his pocket. It was slightly bigger than a thumb and fit in the palm of his hand. "You think I would create an enchantment to block dragons without a way for my own dragon to get past it? King Julian may have deceived me, but even I am not that stupid."

After that, Severin crushed the crystal in his hand and held it high above his head. In a flash, his dragon's eyes snapped open. Its wings started flapping before Chloe could say anything else. Apparently, the conversation was over. They would learn nothing more from the Fairfrost king and his beloved today. Severin and Tindra might find something useful about the ritual after they returned to Fairfrost Palace, but they clearly weren't going to wait around for Julian to manipulate them anymore.

But *how* had that crystal awakened his dragon? And how was it getting past the enchantment? The crystal Severin crushed had *certainly* looked like celestine, but how could the same crystal that confused the dragon's navigation system also be a way past the enchantment? Chloe was missing something, but in that moment, she couldn't figure out what.

Soon, Severin, Tindra, and the dragon were gone. Their one chance to gain more information had led to nothing. They hadn't stopped Julian from getting the dragon scale, and they still knew nothing more about the ritual.

What were they supposed to do now?

The answer came almost immediately after in the form of a familiar face and a golden and emerald crown.

Julian.

He strode toward them. He must have seen the dragon fly away and came straight to the stable to see why Severin had gone. And now, Chloe and Quintus came face to face with their greatest enemy once again.

8

CHLOE'S HEART STAMMERED AS SHE stared at Julian. Madness filled his eyes. The crown on his head glinted with sharpness, looking almost as ominous as the king's expression. He laughed his hair-raising and wild laugh.

And then he spoke in a voice that sent a chill down her spine. "I love when people fall right into my hands. I didn't even have to go looking for you, and now, I can kill you."

His body whirled into action. He drew a long sword from behind his back and charged toward Chloe. Quintus, who had been standing at her side, immediately yanked her away. She and Quintus slammed into a wall because of how fast he'd yanked her. But the sharp pain from hitting the wall was far less than what she would have endured if Julian's sword had sliced through her.

Once again, Quintus had saved her life.

Julian huffed and pivoted on his heel until he faced the pair of them again. As before, he raised his sword, aiming for Chloe's chest.

With a wave of his hand, Quintus glamoured himself and Chloe to be invisible. He'd kept hold of her hand and held on tight to it before dashing forward. He moved just in time to miss another of Julian's sword swings.

Though they were invisible, Julian knew they were still there, and he had clearly not given up on killing them.

At least the other Golden Shields with them were still glamoured to be invisible. Whether that would help them or not, they would soon find out.

Quintus held tight to Chloe's hand and ran as fast as his fae legs could carry him. Luckily, he could move much faster than his mortal father. Once they left the stables and re-entered the castle, he spoke into his whispering stone. "Meet back in the same hallway where we first arrived. I will open a door and take us back to the dragons."

Mishti responded a few moments later. "Do you want us to meet you in that hallway? I'm not sure I know how to find it from where we are now."

"No!"

Both Chloe and Quintus spoke into their whispering stones at the same time, uttering the same word.

Chloe dropped her stone hand and let Quintus finish the explanation. He continued to run as he spoke. "I only meant those in our group. We ran into Julian. Everyone needs to leave the castle immediately. Ludo, open a door and take your group back to the dragons now. The rest of us will follow when we can."

"Understood," Mishti said through her stone.

It didn't take long before Chloe and Quintus got back to the hallway they'd started in. It would take the other Shields much longer to get there since they didn't have fae speed like Quintus. But at least they were invisible, and Julian had never seen the other Shields. As long as they moved quietly, they should be able to get back without any detection.

Quintus had dropped Chloe's hand. Their glamour keeping them invisible was still in place, but she could hear him pacing the golden hallway. His stomping footsteps set her heart skittering every time they touched the ground.

They didn't wait long, but it felt like hours. It felt like days. Quintus's pacing kept increasing in speed until he was nearly jogging back and forth over the floor. But suddenly, he stopped.

"I hear them." He spoke in a whisper but without his whispering stone.

Chloe strained her ears and soon heard pattering footsteps. She wouldn't allow herself any relief until she found out for sure those footsteps belonged to Golden Shields and not to the new fae soldiers walking throughout the castle.

But only a moment later, they heard a quiet whisper from one of the Shields in their group. "We're all here now, I think. You might need to remove the glamours before we know for sure."

A whoosh of magic fluttered through the hallway, and soon, every Shield from their group stood before them.

Now Chloe let out her sigh of relief.

It came too soon. The moment the sigh left her lips, Quintus stumbled back as if he'd been yanked backward. It soon became clear that someone, maybe even two someones, were holding him from behind and wrestling him to the ground.

Julian's fae soldiers must have found them. And they must have used their trick of glamouring themselves to be invisible.

Quintus kept trying to pull himself out of their grasp. He even tried to wave his hand to open a door, but his hand was immediately slapped against the floor, where he'd never be able to use it for magic. Judging by the wince across his face, the invisible soldier must have been stepping on Quintus's hand to keep it against the ground.

The other Shields acted, lunging forward to help Quintus. But as soon as one of the Shields moved, an invisible force stopped them. Soon, so much movement filled the hall, it was difficult to keep everything straight.

Just then, Julian's wild laugh ricocheted against the hallway walls. There may have been more invisible assailants in the hallway, but Chloe took the moment to do what she did best.

She hid.

Ducking behind a large chair, she did her best to move quickly and silently. With any luck, she'd escape the attention of any other soldiers.

Just as she slipped behind the chair, Mishti's voice sounded in her ear. "Our group has left the castle, and we're back with the dragons now. Where are you?"

Panic laced her words, even though she had clearly tried to speak in her usual stoic tone.

With her hand shaking nearly out of control, Chloe managed to bring her whispering stone to her lips. "They found us. They have Quintus on the ground. His hands are immobilized so he can't do any magic. He can't open a door. The other Shields tried to help, but…"

Her voice shook even harder than her hands. She gripped tighter to the stone, afraid it might slip from her grasp. No matter how she tried, she couldn't finish her sentence.

Julian stepped around the corner then. His malicious eyes scanned the hallway before his lip curled in disgust. "Remove all glamours. I want to see everyone."

In a flash, glamours dropped away, revealing two dozen fae. It had taken five of them to pin Quintus down, and even then, they clearly struggled to keep him down. The other soldiers kept the Shields back.

"Should we return to the castle to help?" Mishti's voice sounded in Chloe's ear again.

It sounded more like noise than words. Closing her eyes, Chloe focused on what her friend had said. She wasn't trying to think of an answer. Not yet. For now, she could only attempt to process the question.

"Chloe?" Mishti asked again. "Should we come?"

"I don't know." Chloe's voice shook, tears already pooling in her eyes. She was grateful for the whispering stone because it muted the short sob that escaped her lips. "I don't know if you should come back; you might get trapped with us. I don't know what to do."

Another sob escaped her then. She had to pull the whispering stone away from her mouth because now she needed to wrap her arms around her knees and hug them tight to her chest.

She needed to think. She needed to make a plan.

The Golden Shields had started fighting again. Quintus managed to throw one of the fae off him. They were good at this. They wielded weapons and protected themselves naturally while she cowered in the corner behind a chair.

No. She shook her head to reinforce the point to her mind. She *wasn't* cowering. Just because she had a different skill set didn't mean she was useless. The other Shields were good at fighting, and she could trust them to stay alive despite an attack from Julian.

But while they fought, they needed her to be useful in her own way. She needed to use her mind to find a way out of this.

The skin at the back of her neck still prickled. Her heart still beat too fast, and she still had to hug her knees to her chest just to keep herself from losing all control. But that was okay. She could still think.

Weapons clanged and whooshed through the air. Magic erupted and slammed into people. The sounds washed over her while her mind spun. How could they escape this? Quintus had done his best to fight off the fae pinning him down, but even more fae had entered the hallway now.

It was clear they wouldn't be able to escape through a door. What they really needed were their dragons. The hallway they fought in was positioned by a large window big enough for all the dragons to enter through. Their bodies would damage the castle walls, but they'd still be able to get in. And they'd blow fire and snap their sharpened teeth at any fae who tried to stop them.

If only the dragons could get past the celestine barrier, they'd have the perfect way out.

Think, Chloe. Think! It was no use daydreaming about the dragons since they couldn't get past the barrier like Severin's dragon had. She needed to find an actual solution.

But her thoughts got interrupted when a flying sword knocked against the chair she'd been hiding behind. It clattered to the ground, and Julian flicked his gaze toward the movement.

In an instant, he caught sight of her. His entire face twisted with wild delight. "*There* you are." He had a Golden Shield by the throat with one hand and a knife poised to kill the woman with his other hand, but he immediately dropped her and stepped toward Chloe.

A tilted smile stretched across his lips as he plucked an axe from the ground. His gaze stayed trained on Chloe as he lifted the axe to attack.

"No!" Quintus screamed, his body fighting against the seven fae now holding him down. Even with so many of them, Quintus still nearly freed himself.

Julian smiled wider at his son's reaction, a laugh bubbling in his throat as he moved closer and closer to Chloe. By the time he reached her, his tilted smile had turned to a treacherous sneer. He threw the axe, aiming it right at her chest.

But even with seven fae holding him down, Quintus managed to free his hand for the tiniest moment, just long enough to send a blast of magic.

The golden sparks that erupted from his fingertips hit the very tip of the axe blade. It didn't drop the weapon to the ground, but it did shift its course. A moment later, the axe slammed into Chloe's upper leg.

Pain exploded through her, hot and fierce. She gasped and felt certain she would never breathe again.

Quintus shouted something, but the pain was too great to process anything. Tears streamed down her cheeks as she let out a strangled yelp.

Julian snarled, clearly upset his weapon had missed its mark and failed to kill her. He turned back to Quintus with a hateful glare. And then Julian said, "You forget I no longer need weapons to cause injury."

Crackling emerald and purple magic sizzled out of his fingertips like lightning. It hit Chloe harder than the axe had and sent unimaginable pain through her entire body. Her breathing stopped completely. She coughed once, but then couldn't cough again because she had no air.

Her chest heaved, trying to suck in air. Nothing was coming. Black spots broke out through her vision. Despite the breathing issues, the pain fracturing through her was more than anything she had ever experienced before.

Blackness closed in at the edges of her vision. Quintus was shouting again, filling the entire hallway with the sound. A strange blue shimmer entered her vision.

It wasn't something she could see. With so much pain, she could no longer perceive the world like she usually could. Instead, she got the distinct impression this was not something she could currently see, but something she had previously seen.

And then it came to her. A way for the dragons to get past the barrier.

Suddenly, she gasped hard. Air filled her lungs as a bright clarity hit her even harder than the pain. Somehow, she didn't know where the strength came from, her hand lifted to her lips.

She hadn't dropped the whispering stone. That in itself was a miracle she couldn't focus on because she only had a moment or two before she'd pass out.

Pressing the stone to her lips, she whispered what might be her final words. Instructions to get the dragons past King Severin's celestine enchantment.

Another blast of sizzling magic hit her then. Her entire body shook and crumpled to the ground. Her vision went pitch black.

More grunts and weapon clashes filled the air, but she couldn't make them out. The little consciousness she had was drifting away.

And then it was gone.

9

DARKNESS FILLED THE SKY WHEN Chloe blinked open her eyes. It took more effort than she expected to grasp onto consciousness. Tiny rays of light reached up through the horizon, suggesting day would soon dawn. A blanket had been wrapped around her, which provided both warmth and stability.

Pain like a sharp knife sliced through her leg when she tried to move to a sitting position. A tight moan escaped her before she could stop it. The sound prompted footsteps that hurried toward her.

"Chloe." Quintus dropped to his knees at her side, his voice filled to the brim with concern. "Are you awake? Are you okay?"

His arms wrapped around her, the strength in them holding her safe and secure. It prompted a memory of those same arms around her just before she lost consciousness. Along with the memory of the arms, she remembered weapons. Danger. Julian.

With a gasp, she tried to sit up again. Pain shot down through her leg like thousands of hot needles. Despite the pain, she managed to force out a sharp whisper. "What happened? Julian was there. Did he… Did we…"

"We are safe." Quintus held her tighter, doing his best to keep her still so as not to move her leg again. "Everyone got away thanks to your ingenuity."

After planting a soft kiss on her temple, he helped her get into a sitting position while keeping her limbs as still as possible. Somehow, he knew just where to touch so the pain wouldn't be as intense. Once sitting, she could see sleeping mats arranged in a large circle with Golden Shields atop them. Most of them were still asleep. The dragons formed a circle around the outside, protecting their group while they too slept.

"My ingenuity?" Her memory was still fuzzy from the pain and from losing consciousness. There had been a battle. Julian had tried to kill them and nearly succeeded. The noises came straight to the forefront of her mind. The grunts, the clashing of weapons, the crackling of magic. But how had they escaped?

Her eyes scanned the landscape again, noting they no longer camped on top of Rubyrise Mountain. A field of glittering jewels stretched across the landscape. Even in the darkness, the gems twinkled.

"Where are we?" she asked.

"In the Gemfields at the edge of Crystalfall. The dragons awoke, but they were still tired, so we thought it would be best to land closer to the ground instead of up in the mountains."

"The dragons?" She felt a knot form in her forehead from how deeply she furrowed her eyebrows. She had no memory of the dragons helping them escape. She shook her head, trying to make sense of it. "But what about the barrier around the castle? How did the dragons get past it?"

A smirk lifted Quintus's mouth, as if he couldn't tell if she was teasing him or not. "Do you not remember?"

When she shook her head, his smirk fell away.

Then, he answered gently. "You realized King Severin got past the enchantment because the signal from the crushed celestine in his hand was far more concentrated than the tiny bits of crushed celestine in the air. With a strong signal to focus on, his dragon was able to awaken and get past the barrier around the castle."

She nodded, slowly remembering how she had realized all this during the fight.

He continued. "Once you explained it through your whispering stone, Mishti and Ludo got celestine crystals from the meadow and were able to awaken our dragons and get past the barrier to rescue us."

Chloe would have nodded again, but the pain in her leg caused her to wince instead.

Without another word, Quintus turned to dig into a bag. Hearing scattered items and small papers, she knew it was her leather bag he dug into. A moment later, he held a wide glass jar on the palm of his hand and removed the lid.

The herbal elixir's scent filled the air. Her nose detected dewdrop moss and sunlight berries along with some sort of fern she couldn't name. Lavender had been added with olive oil as the base.

Instinctively, she knew this concoction would provide powerful healing, but she had not made this elixir. Had Quintus? How had he known what ingredients to use?

He must have seen the question in her eyes because he gave an answer without her having to ask. "Your magical book gave us the recipe for this. Ludo already knew where to find the ingredients, so he managed to open a door and gather them quickly. Mishti prepared the elixir while I..."

Pain etched across his eyes as he trailed off.

"While you did what?" Chloe prompted.

He swallowed and locked his gaze tightly onto the glass jar. "I tended to you. I had to arrange your leg and stop the blood. You had two broken bones."

His gaze lowered to the ground and his voice dropped to a whisper. "I am surprised you do not remember it. You were…screaming so much."

Her eyebrows flew upward. "Was I?" He seemed concerned she couldn't remember, but considering the pain she must have felt, she was oddly grateful to have no memory of it.

"How did you know what elixir to make? The book has hundreds of different remedies."

With a twitch at the corner of his mouth, Quintus rubbed the back of his neck. "The book spoke to me, the way it speaks to you. It did not work at first, but then…" He gave a tiny shrug. "I screamed at the book that you were dying, and suddenly, the exact elixir we needed appeared on the page."

She raised one eyebrow. "Really? It told me nothing the last time I tried asking."

Lowering the glass jar, Quintus wrapped his hand around hers. "The book was very forthcoming once it realized the danger you were in. It even told me how to summon a golden table for food, which Ludo and I did after you finally fell asleep." His expression brightened into a smirk. "I think Faerie itself likes you more than you realize."

Warmth pooled in her belly at the sound of that. For how little information Faerie gave her when she wanted it, it was nice to think Faerie *did* want to help her after all.

Quintus picked up the jar again and stared at it a little more closely than necessary. "I have been massaging this into your injury throughout the night, whenever I woke up. But now that you are awake, you can use your healing magic to heal yourself."

The significance of his words didn't hit her until another shot of pain erupted through her leg. Her upper leg bone had been broken, as well as the lower one. But if her upper leg had been broken, and if he'd been massaging the elixir into her leg…

Suddenly, his fixed stare at the glass jar made sense. How far up her leg had he massaged? Heat bloomed in her cheeks, fast and hot.

He shifted to face her, immediately sensing the change in her. "I kept you as covered as possible," he said quickly. And then his voice turned more gravelly. "I did not take advantage."

Heat spread all through her face, down her neck, and through the rest of her limbs. Her face must have been bright red. Despite that, she dropped her head onto his shoulder and leaned into him. "Thank you."

"Chloe." His voice came out scolding the moment he heard those words, which made her indebted to him.

But she just shrugged. "You told me *sorry* twice, remember? By me thanking you, that just cancels out one *sorry*. Right?"

He huffed and then shook his head. "I would still prefer if I owed you two favors, but fine." Then tension filled his body as he turned toward her. "Can you heal yourself now? I do not want you to suffer any longer."

A smile lifted her lips as she took his hand and closed her eyes. Just like when she had healed his cursed wound back at the castle, the healing needed came to her mind easily. She did not have to remember the correct herbs or the exact healing process. Instead, elixirs and remedies and healing came to her mind, as if put there by Faerie itself.

It only took a few moments. When she opened her eyes and tried to move her leg again, it shifted without any pain at all.

Seeing the movement and the lack of reaction from Chloe, Quintus let out a deep breath of relief. "Finally." He reached for his chest and closed his eyes.

But as he sat in relief, memories from the battle washed over her. She'd only given the barest instructions through the whispering stones before Julian had gotten to her. Mishti and Ludo had put a lot of trust in Chloe to try her idea of crushing large celestine crystals, even though it had probably sounded a little crazy.

"I have never been so scared in my life," Quintus said suddenly, cutting into her thoughts. Strain filled his voice.

She turned slightly, her chin grazing the upper part of his chest. A mild lavender scent lingered on his coat, which she inhaled deeply. Even with her head down, she could feel when Quintus shook his head.

"He had you pinned to the ground, ready to kill you. His fae soldiers had me immobilized, and I could do nothing but watch him hurt you. I have never felt terror like that before. I have never felt so *powerless*. How can I forgive myself for how he hurt you?" His voice broke. "I cannot. Not ever."

Chloe trembled at the sound of his words. When he ached, she did too. If he suffered, she suffered.

She wanted to remind him it was not his fault, but that was pointless. If the roles had been reversed, she would have felt just as awful as he did. Still, she couldn't do nothing while he suffered.

Turning her head upward, she caught his eye. She could feel how tension still gripped the muscles in his shoulders. With her gaze on his, she wrapped her arms around him.

"It's fine now. We all survived. I'm safe. Alive." She murmured against his neck as she continued to hold him tight. He pulled his arms around her, but his body remained tense. She could feel how his biceps kept bulging and relaxing in quick repetitions. But as she continued to assure him, his body began to relax, and his heartbeat resumed its regular pace.

He held her for a long while after that. They didn't say anything to each other, simply dwelling in the embrace. Though it had caused them both to suffer, they could at least be grateful they had walked out alive after their first battle with Julian now that he had the power of the crown.

Streaks of dawn continued to color the sky. A few of the Shields started stirring in their sleep.

Quintus kissed her on the forehead and then stood. Next, he moved toward a small stream of water, dipping his hands in and using the water to wash his face. His dark skin almost seemed to glow in the early daylight. She had long since stopped trying to prevent herself from falling more in love with him. That was impossible. But she did have to congratulate herself for falling for the most beautiful man she had ever known.

"Chloe." Mishti sat up with a start from a nearby sleeping mat. The young woman's long black hair had been braided so tight, not even sleep had disturbed the strands. "You're awake. How's your leg?"

She whispered the words as she scrambled from her sleeping mat and came to Chloe's side.

"It's fine," Chloe said, reaching for her wooden foot and securing it in place. "Quintus heard me wake, and I was able to heal myself the rest of the way."

"How long have you been awake?" Mishti glanced over at Quintus over by the stream. Her gaze rose up to the sky, probably noting the light on the horizon.

Chloe forced herself to her feet before she answered. "Not long."

After she uttered those words, her legs shuddered, and she nearly lost her footing. Mishti grabbed her by the elbow and managed to help Chloe balance. Concern sent a crease between Mishti's eyebrows.

A loud growl erupted from Chloe's stomach just then. Her legs might be sore, even after being healed, but she could ignore that. First, she had a much higher priority to worry about. Reaching both arms around her stomach, she scanned the area around them. "Quintus said he and Ludo were able to summon a golden table."

The statement came out as more of a question than anything.

Mishti released a soft chuckle and pointed to a spot just past the dragons. "Over there. It is good to see you acting like yourself again."

Ludo woke by the time Chloe got to the table. She took hold of a plate and requested her food. Soon, a steaming pile of eggs, fish, and bread sat in front of her. Ludo got to the table just as she started shoveling the food down.

He raised an eyebrow. "Should I be offended that you enjoy this food so much more than any I have ever conjured for you?"

Without missing a beat, she responded. "Should I be offended that you didn't ask about my leg?"

He chuckled in response and grabbed his own plate. "I am glad to see you up and moving again. I am even more glad you found a way for us to escape that fight with Julian."

The rest of the Shields began waking and getting food and washing up. Many of the Shields came to ask how she was feeling after the night before. She appreciated their concern, but oddly felt a little guilty at making them all worry so much.

It was also strange to have so many people anxious about her welfare.

They would need to get together soon and figure out what they had learned, if anything, and what they would need to do next. But for now, she needed to think and to rest. Finding a grassy patch with soft jade grass strands and sparkling amethyst flowers, she settled down and looked inside her leather bag. Should she reach for her magical book or for the king's journal? Which had a better chance of supplying the information they needed?

No answer came, and her mind quickly wandered. She scanned the camp for the one who was continually in her heart without her permission. It only took a moment to find him among the dragons, standing directly next to Shadow.

Quintus had his hand on the creature's neck, stroking her scales. His lips moved, as if speaking, but Chloe was too far away to hear the words. Without any prompting, his earlier statement to her came to the forefront of her mind.

I have never been so scared in my life.

Her hand moved, nearly of its own accord, until it spread over her chest directly above her heart. That she could be cared for with such intensity never ceased to awe her. That he cherished her, even with her weaknesses… It made her feel powerful instead of weak, strong instead of useless. Even with a wooden foot and scars and immobilizing fear, he still believed in her as much as she believed in him.

Her heart swelled, but she forced herself to look back inside her leather bag. If she wasn't careful, she'd spend far too long daydreaming about Quintus. At least now she could make a decision. Reaching inside, she grabbed her magical book.

The leathery richness of the cover glided against her fingertips while her mind spun with ideas. She opened the pages, which still had nothing new on them. But for some reason, she kept finding the pages she had already read many times before twice as interesting as they'd ever been. Even simple remedies that she clearly understood suddenly made sense on a deeper level than ever before. As books often did, these pages thoroughly entranced her, making her forget the rest of the world entirely.

After reading over half the book, a figure appeared at her side. Her gaze stayed fixed on a paragraph she had to finish, but she recognized Quintus's voice once he spoke.

"When are you coming back to Crystalfall?"

Her eyes narrowed, but she managed to finish her paragraph before she glanced up. "What are you talking about? We're already in Crystalfall."

"No," Quintus said with a chuckle. He sat down on the grass next to her. "*You* disappeared into the book realm where you forget completely that I exist. When will you be coming back?"

She smiled and took one last glance at her book before finally giving him her full attention. "I guess I needed a distraction after that battle yesterday. But it's been long enough. We need to decide on a new plan."

If the Golden Shields were intent on treating her like a leader, then she needed to find a way to lead them to victory. The last thing she wanted was to let them down.

10

CHLOE STARED AT THE MAGICAL book in her lap, allowing the wandering thoughts in her mind to come together and form something clear. She leaned into Quintus, who immediately drew his arms around her. Thinking came easier that way.

"Julian acted different yesterday," Chloe started. "I thought about how many times we have encountered him. He almost always pretended he wanted us dead, but there were also times he would carefully make sure we didn't actually get injured. I'm certain that was because he needed the crown, and he knew he'd only get to it through us. But now? Now he *truly* wants us dead."

"I noticed that too." Quintus's fingers had been slowly tracing up and down her arms, but now they tensed. "There is more to it though. My father knows what *you* mean to me. He knows you care for me in return. And he knows how much it would hurt me to lose you."

Her heart squeezed tight before she could answer, but then devotion flared in her chest. "If he thinks I merely *care* for you, then that's his biggest mistake. I don't just care for you. I love you. And we aren't going to let him take me away from you, just like we won't let him take you away from me."

He pulled her closer, his arms holding her both tighter and more gently than before.

She turned her nose to his neck, breathing in deeply to inhale his intoxicating earthy smell. "We can defeat him. Together."

"Yes," he said, pulling away just enough that he could look her in the eye. "We will stop him. He hurt you while I watched, powerless to do anything." Determination and fury made the golden specks in his brown eyes sparkle like stars. "I know I lost hope after we learned the king's true identity, but I will not wallow in pain any longer. I refuse to let him get the upper hand again. I will not allow him to hurt you anymore."

No words could embody the emotion inside her just then, so she simply reached for his hand and intertwined her fingers with his.

He spoke again, even more determined than before. "I used to be afraid something was wrong with me because I came from him. I was afraid I was destined to turn out like him. But I realized, I get to make my own choices. I do not have to be like him if I do not want to be." His fingers squeezed hers. "And because of you, I know exactly *how* to be a better person. And a better person is what you deserve."

His eyes shone bright after that, and his face drew closer. Her heart thumped, and her gaze fell to his lips. She moistened her own lips in preparation.

But just as her eyes started fluttering closed, he said huskily, "Not now." He swallowed hard. "If I kiss you now, I do not know if I will be able to stop."

She withdrew from him a fraction, ready to counter that maybe it would be better if he didn't stop. Her entire body filled with desire. Fire lit inside her, and suddenly she realized that maybe *she* wouldn't be able to stop either.

"Okay." Was that her voice? It came out so hoarse and breathless. She had to clear her throat before she could continue. "Let's make a new plan then. Did anyone find out any other ingredients needed for the ritual while we were in the castle?"

It took nearly all her willpower to pull her gaze away from her beloved and look down at the book in her lap instead.

"No, but we learned the name of the ritual. King Severin sent a sprite while you were sleeping. The ritual is called Bloodstone Convergence." At least his voice was just as hoarse as hers had been.

Nodding, Chloe took her book in both hands and spoke in her clearest voice. "What is Bloodstone Convergence? What are the ingredients needed? How is it performed?"

The book had given them nothing the last time she asked, but maybe it would be different now they had the name of the ritual. She really hated to think they might have gone to the castle and nearly gotten killed for nothing. But if the name of the ritual helped them, then maybe it had all been worth it.

Nothing happened for five excruciatingly long heartbeats, but then, the corner of the page started curling. The curl continued until the page flipped over, all on its own. Soon, the pages started turning faster. Golden sparks of magic shot out from the spine, showering her in a warm light. Finally, the pages slowed and stopped until the book had opened to a blank page where a scrawling handwriting started writing out two words.

Bloodstone Convergence.

"This is it," Chloe whispered, her heart beating faster again, this time from adrenaline. Of course she had wanted to believe the book would give them the answers they needed, but part of her hadn't actually believed it would.

But now the words to the ritual sat on the page before them. Both she and Quintus leaned in, devouring each word carefully.

This sacrificial ritual has only been attempted once, and it led to the death of the person performing it because not all conditions had been met. It must be performed under a moon and outside a Faerie castle. The following ingredients are needed:

A scale from a creature bonded to the ruler of a Faerie court

Blood of the one who wishes to converge

Opposing branches of life and death

An instrument of creation

Sacrifice of a body or a limb

After reading over the ritual twice, Chloe held her place in the book and got to her feet. "We need to tell everyone about this."

Quintus nodded without hesitation. Together, they gathered the Golden Shields and told them everything they had learned from the book. Chloe even read the words inside the magical book aloud so everyone could hear the exact words written.

Ludo kicked at the ground after she finished reading. "I see now how Quintus can be used for both the blood and the sacrifice. He truly will die if we are not careful to protect him."

Mishti absently pulled her dagger in and out of her leather arm bracer. "But the last person who tried to perform this ritual died. Maybe Julian will die too."

It seemed too hopeful to dream of, but apparently Quintus agreed. He stood at Chloe's side and pointed to the book. "I think I know why the last ritual failed. This book says the ritual must be performed under a *moon* and outside a Faerie castle.

But Faerie has no moon. Not except this one." He gestured toward the crescent moon tattoo under his eye.

Ludo threw his hands into the air. "Oh, so you can provide the moon too? Once King Julian captures you, he will have everything he needs to succeed."

"Or maybe he will fail and die since Faerie has no moon," Quintus said tersely.

Chloe studied the words more carefully. She had forgotten Faerie had no moon, but that didn't make any sense. The ritual was clearly a Faerie ritual. It had to be performed in front of a Faerie castle, so it had to be performed in Faerie. The other ingredients came from Faerie as well. Her eyes narrowed. "Perhaps it is metaphorical. Or perhaps it's a riddle. Or maybe it just means there needs to be something that represents a moon."

Mishti raised an eyebrow. "You think Julian knows about the moon and knows how to include one in that part of the ritual?"

After letting out a long breath, Chloe finally answered. "I think we have underestimated Julian before, and it would be unwise for us to do it again."

Silence fell among them. Batu glanced up, nodding as the impact of what she had said dawned on him. He was likely thinking of the many times Julian had twisted their actions for his benefit. Batu rubbed his elbows to ward off a chill, probably from fear.

"What do we do now? Can we stop him from gathering the other ingredients?" Mishti's serious face had turned even more stern.

Chloe bit her lip and turned her gaze downward. "We might be able to, but I have to confess, I have no idea what *opposing branches of life and death* means. And *an instrument of creation* could be anything. He may have all the ingredients already. Everything except Quintus."

"Let me read that again." Quintus stood closer to Chloe, glancing over her shoulder to see the magical book.

"Even if he finds a moon, the ritual still must take place outside the castle." His head tilted to the side. "While I was taking care of Shadow earlier, I kept wondering why my father needed an enchantment to block out dragons."

Mishti removed a loose stitching from her midnight blue tunic as she glanced upward. "To keep *us* out, obviously."

A flicker of understanding sparked in Chloe's head. "No, because otherwise he would have just done a barrier enchantment. Instead, he needed an enchantment that specifically blocked out the dragons."

Quintus's mouth curved into a smile. "Exactly. He wanted us to be able to enter the castle, but only without our dragons. He is afraid of them."

"Of course he is," Ludo said as a small shiver shook through his shoulders. "Have you seen Temper? That thing could swallow us all whole in one gulp if he wanted to."

"And Shadow has already nearly killed Julian a few times." Chloe closed her book and dropped it into her leather bag. "He knows exactly what she's capable of."

Mishti dropped her arms to her sides, her expression skeptical. "This is our plan then? To use the dragons?"

Ludo scoffed. "If we use them the same way we have before, the king will be able to defeat them once he has an army. And since we have already seen numerous new fae at his castle, it will probably not take him long to gather that army."

"We will not just *use* the dragons," Quintus said with a cunning smile. "We need to train them. We must ready them for battle and teach them how to defeat an army. Then we will have something my father has never seen before. Then we will have a chance."

Sofia picked at the golden circle attached to her clothing. "How are we supposed to train dragons? Does anyone here have any idea how to do such a thing?"

"I do." Mishti stood a little taller, her face determined. "I've had to train elephants for battle before, so I know a little about working with wild animals."

"You don't have to—" Chloe started.

"I want to," Mishti said even more determined than before. "For once, I can provide good training and good strategy to a side that actually deserves to win."

Nodding, Quintus stood tall and addressed everyone. "We may not have a solid plan yet, but once we have trained the dragons for battle, we will be stronger than ever. And whatever we must face, we will do it together."

Chloe could barely keep herself from smiling. Not only did they have a new plan, she could also see Quintus had meant it when he said he had come out of his despondency and was now willing to fight Julian with everything in his power.

After a few brief instructions on what everyone could do to make this new camp a little more permanent, they dismissed and divided into their individual tasks.

Settling into a spot near the sleeping mats, Chloe sorted through a small pile of gems that some of the other Shields had gathered. She found the gems that would make the best arrowheads. Then she passed them along to Quintus, who had piles of golden sticks and branches. He used his crafting magic to make new arrows and spears for them to fight with.

Energetic chatter broke out through the camp as they all performed their various duties. It felt good to have a clear purpose again, and it felt even better to be completing tasks that would help them accomplish that purpose.

When the sun started dipping toward the horizon, everyone stopped and gathered around the golden table to eat. Once Chloe finished her food, Quintus stood and stretched his hand toward her. "You have been sitting for too long. We should take a walk."

Without hesitating, she grabbed his hand and stood. Her stiff knees proved he was right about her sitting too long. They headed toward a nearby stream, following it as they walked deeper into the Gemfields.

Hand in hand and in comfortable silence, they walked as the setting sun cast colorful shadows across their skin. Acres of gorgeous glittering fields sprawled out ahead of them filled with brilliant colors. In what seemed like almost no time at all, they had walked so far, their camp looked like a small smudge on the fields.

"Should we head back?" Chloe had been staring over her shoulder but now she turned back to her companion.

Quintus looked carefully at her face, perhaps noting the beads of sweat collecting at her temples. With a smile, he said, "No, we should rest here for a bit. If we need to return to camp quickly, I can simply open a door."

Sighing with relief, Chloe flopped onto the ground. "I would love a rest. I did not realize how far we've walked."

Sitting beside her, he stared deeply into her eyes. "Do you have enough strength to return?"

Her cheeks burned as she attempted to cover her face. "I know I have the strength of a gnat. It's embarrassing how easily I get exhausted."

He shrugged in response. "It is probably because you are mortal." His head cocked. "Then again, Mishti is also mortal."

Chloe huffed. "Mishti had a completely different upbringing than me. She is a warrior, and I am a healer."

Unexpectedly, Quintus leaned in, gazing into her eyes deeply. "And you are also my…" Quintus voice trailed off, and he swallowed. The heated look he had given her caused her heart to accelerate. Her mouth had suddenly gone as dry as paper. She had an idea of how he intended to finish that sentence, but she wanted him to say it out loud. Why had he stopped?

An awkward silence stretched between them then. He had promised to do better at trusting her, and he had completely stopped being angry at her. But maybe their bond still needed a little longer to heal.

He kept opening his mouth, like he wanted to say something but wasn't sure how. She waited for him to speak, but nothing came out.

When the tension in the air became thick enough to touch, she could bear it no longer. A simple sentence with no expectation might get him talking. She gestured ahead, and said, "These fields are beautiful with the sun setting over them."

"Yes." He offered a single word in response with nothing more.

The urge to smack him and demand he say what was on his mind flooded her, but she had a feeling that wasn't the right approach for this moment. Perhaps he pondered on the depth of the words that had been cut short in his throat. He had already told her many times that he loved her, so why would it bother him to say it now? But maybe something had changed. Maybe he had finally realized just how problematic their love was.

A mortal young woman and an immortal fae. Even if she lived a long mortal life, she *would* eventually die. And maybe he had finally come to understand just how painful that would be, no matter how wonderful the years before then were.

If that's what he didn't want to talk about, then she wouldn't force it out of him. She didn't want to talk about it either. She didn't even want to think about it. They needed a lighter topic to discuss.

Opening her mouth, she brought up the first lighter topic she could think of. "I saw you with Shadow earlier. You seemed to be comforting her. Is she okay?"

"She is now," he said, staring out at the fields. "She was skittish throughout the night because you were unconscious when she took you out of the castle and then you were screaming once we landed. I had to let her know you were awake and okay. She is very protective of you, you know."

Chloe laughed. "She reminds me of someone."

Quintus did not even smile. He stared straight into her eyes with an intense expression that made her mouth go dry again. "That someone is even *more* protective of you."

He did it again. Her heart pounded in her chest while his one little look set her insides on fire. How could he affect her so greatly with one touch, one look, even with one single word?

"Come here." He opened his arms, welcoming her into an embrace. She complied immediately and closed her eyes as she felt a calm flow through her body.

They were going to be okay.

Their mortal and immortal problem was far from being solved, but as long as they were together, they were going to be okay.

11

ONCE NIGHT FELL, THE TRAINING of the dragons began. Without the heat from the sun, they could train longer and need fewer rests in between. They flew their dragons out to the middle of the Gemfields, away from their camp.

Mishti knew a great deal about warfare. Her time in the mortal realm had taught her helpful techniques and strategies, but even wild beasts like elephants were not the same as training dragons.

The creatures flew in a V formation naturally whenever they flew together, but getting them to fly in other formations proved to be difficult. Communication was a problem too, especially for the larger dragons like Shadow and Temper. At least now they had the whispering stones.

It would take several strategies and a lot of practice to have the dragons trained enough to fight like an army.

At the moment, dragons and Shields alike had frayed nerves. Tension was so high, the air crackled with a palpable sense of unease. When they had entered Crystalfall Castle and used their dragons in battle earlier, the creatures had sensed the danger and instinctively protected their riders. But without any true threat, the dragons refused to cooperate. Everyone got more frustrated the longer they worked.

Batu's dragon with silver and teal geometric patterns coloring its scales thrashed and roared. The creature flapped its heavy wings while Batu tried to regain control of it. But the dragon simply descended and threw Batu to the ground. Mishti encouraged him to try again, which he eventually did. But he wore a heavy glare while he did it.

After what felt like hours of training, the Golden Shields mounted their dragons and struggled to keep them flying in the circle formation Mishti had wanted them to practice.

On the ground, Chloe stood next to Shadow and rubbed the scales of her neck. Quintus stood on Shadow's other side. They had been training on and off with the others, but since Shadow always did everything Chloe directed, the training came easier for them. She had taken a break from this formation to give the others more chance to practice.

Quintus cupped his hands over his mouth, trying to give orders to the riders above. Despite everyone's determination, the circle formation had slowly drifted back to a V with the dragons completely ignoring all directions, even when the riders used the reins that had trained the dragons in the first place.

Moving to Shadow's other side, Chloe caught Quintus's eye. "I think the problem might be their bonds."

He lowered his hands from his mouth and turned to her with a question in his eyes.

She gestured upward. "At first, Shadow followed the command of anyone holding her harp string reins. But then she started listening to me even without me touching the reins."

Chloe paused for a moment to give more emphasis on her next words. "And then she stopped following my commands and did whatever she thought needed to be done to protect me."

His gaze trailed upward to the dragons refusing to follow their riders' commands. He understood at once what she implied.

She shook her head. "The only way they'll be able to train properly is if they create a stronger bond between them and their dragons. Rider and creature need to understand each other, see each other, trust each other. Without that bond, we might be wasting our time."

Quintus groaned, probably because he knew she was right. But it had taken work for her to build the bond with Shadow. It had taken dangerous battles and time they didn't have.

He pinched the bridge of his nose. "Are the dragons useless to us then? Can we only use them as we have, but never train them to do more?"

"We don't need to give up so easily." Chloe did her best to bolster him after the trying practice that had seemingly gone nowhere. "The dragons are still our best chance at defeating Julian."

Quintus swiped a hand across his brow and then flicked away the sweat it had gathered. "I know, and I am not giving up. Perhaps I just needed to complain a little."

The dragons flew to the ground then, many of them throwing their riders off as soon as they touched the ground. Temper had crackles of electricity zinging across her scales. One of the bolts caught Mishti just as she jumped off the creature, causing her body to jolt.

Chloe gasped at the sight, but Mishti caught her balance easily after the electricity shocked through her. She clenched her jaw and squared her shoulders.

When Mishti glanced back at her dragon, Chloe expected the young woman to glare or yell or maybe pull out a dagger. Instead, Mishti wrapped an arm around the creature's neck and rubbed the scales vigorously. She spoke words to her dragon too, and judging by the expression on her face, they were gentle words, not angry ones.

Soon after, Mishti left the dragon and approached Chloe and Quintus. "This has proved to be an enormous waste of time."

"There is no time in Faerie," Ludo quipped from behind her.

She rolled her eyes as he joined her and the others.

Quintus tilted his head. "Chloe has an idea."

"What is it?" Mishti had started to pull a dagger from one of her leather arm bracers, but her hand froze as she turned expectantly.

"It's the bond," Chloe explained. "Each rider needs a stronger bond with his or her dragon before they'll start following all commands. Everyone has trained their dragons, so the creatures will protect their riders in a moment of danger. But there needs to be more trust between dragons and riders before the dragons start following all commands."

Mishti nodded slowly, then glanced back at her dragon. "How do we deepen the bond?"

Chloe shrugged. "I don't know. I didn't do it on purpose with Shadow, so I'm not sure how to recreate it. And Shadow saved me from several perilous situations before the bond truly strengthened between us. But if everyone has to experience perilous situations with their dragons before we can train them, we might not be able to train them before we have to face Julian again."

Mishti's thick dark brows furrowed as she considered this.

"Can we forget the training for now?" Ludo said through a whine. "I am tired. My arms might fall off if I have to grab onto any more reins."

Chloe, Quintus, and Mishti released identical chuckles at the thought of that.

"It *is* late," Chloe said.

Mishti nodded. "I will tell everyone the training is done for tonight. The dragons are tired so they should be willing to bring us back to camp without much complaint."

Chloe and Quintus climbed atop Shadow and waited for the other dragons to begin flying. Luckily, Mishti had been right that the dragons were happy to head back to camp. They had worked hard and must have been exhausted.

Once in the air, Quintus came in close behind Chloe, straddling his legs on either side of hers. "Are *you* tired?"

"Not really." She leaned into him until her back met his chest.

"Good." He wrapped his arms around her waist and spoke into her hair. "I want to show you something."

Anticipation raced through her veins, which only heightened as she felt every subtle movement from Quintus behind her. He removed his arms from around her waist and took hold of Shadow's reins.

Wherever he planned to take them, she could only guess the experience would be magical.

12

Shadow flew over the gemfields of Crystalfall, carrying Chloe and Quintus closer to Rubyrise Mountain. Quintus held fast to the dragon's reins, guiding her carefully over the landscape.

The chirpings of jeweled birds were the only sounds piercing the night as they flew. Anticipation raced in Chloe's heart. Shadow slowly began lowering, leading them to a secluded valley nestled between the towering ruby and golden mountains of Rubyrise.

Excitement surged through Chloe's limbs as Shadow landed, and they climbed off her back. But even though they had landed, Quintus must have had a specific spot in mind because he took her hand and led her through a cluster of golden trees. The scent of lilacs was stronger here, pairing perfectly with the subtle scent of vanilla that seemed to be everywhere in Crystalfall.

"What is it you wanted to show me?" She turned toward him, narrowing her eyes.

His eyebrows popped upward for a moment, mischief dancing in his expression.

The night wind hummed as it blew around her, rustling her dress against her skin. When they reached the bottom edge of Rubyrise, she rested her free hand on a golden boulder with deep red veins, using the grip as support as they walked around it.

Darkness had fallen completely, making it difficult to see the landscape around them. She managed to see well enough to walk without tripping, but she couldn't admire what was likely a gorgeous valley of jeweled flowers and magnificent bushes made of gems.

Just as she regretted not being able to see, her hand intertwined with Quintus's began to warm. Glancing down, she saw a shower of golden sparks drift out from their clasped hands. When she looked back to Quintus, the mischievous look in his eye had doubled. The corners of his lips twitched as he clearly tried to hold back a smile.

She mockingly glared at him. "You still haven't answered my question. What did you want to show me?"

"Something beautiful." With that, Quintus raised their intertwined hands, and the golden sparks shot high above them. Instead of disappearing into the night, each spark grew until it became as large as a fist. Once large enough, each light stopped moving and hovered in the air, filling the sky just above them with dozens of glowing lights to illuminate the area.

Now she could appreciate the beauty of this valley. A tapestry of vibrant jeweled flowers blanketed the sloping hill in bold hues of red, orange, yellow, and purple. Dazzling streams with sparkling blue water meandered through the valley. The gentle bubbling of water felt like a song, harmonizing with the rustling emerald leaves that blew in the night wind.

Closing her eyes, she listened more carefully to the spectacular sounds. Though she had always loved playing the harp, she hadn't thought much of it since coming to Faerie. Considering the land had been in danger, and her life had been in danger nearly all the time she'd been there, it wasn't as if she'd had much chance to think of harp playing. Survival had always been a higher priority.

But hearing the magical sounds of this landscape made her miss the way music had once filled her every day.

"Are you thinking of music?" Quintus had his hand in one pocket as he stared at her carefully. Before she could register any surprise at his knowing her thoughts, she instead noticed how the crescent moon tattoo under his eye had turned completely golden. It sparkled and shimmered as brilliantly as the jeweled flowers surrounding them.

"I was." She tilted her head to the side. "How did you know that?"

He smirked and shoved his hand deeper into his pocket. "I tried to send you thoughts of music through our bond. I was not sure it would work, but apparently, it did."

"Through our bond?" That revelation filled her mind with far too many questions for her to bother speculating on what he was pulling from his pocket. If he could send her thoughts through their bond like that, could they talk through their bond too? If their bond strengthened, would they someday be able to have conversations entirely in their minds?

The thoughts vanished when he finally pulled out the object from his pocket. It was proof fae had magical pockets because he had retrieved an entire harp from it. He set the stunning instrument on the ground in front of her and then pulled a stool from his pocket next.

Her fingers ran over the gleaming wood at the pillar of the harp. He had carved intricate scrolls and books and pots of ink, but that was only on one part of the pillar. A little lower there were herbs and crystals and potions. He had taken all her favorite things and immortalized them in the wood.

And he'd embedded polished gems inside the carvings, each one gilded to emphasize the shape. There must have been a shimmering mineral inside the protective varnish on the wood because it gleamed like an opal in the golden light.

"This is the most beautiful harp I have ever seen," she whispered.

A wide grin curled his lips. Concentration etched lines across his forehead as he raised his hand into the air. "I have one more trick." He shifted his hand, as if about to wave it in a circle, but stopped suddenly. "Hopefully this works."

His face turned to even deeper concentration, and he finally waved his hand in a circle.

A moment later, a simple melodious tune drifted from the harp, the strings plucked by nothing but magic.

"This is..." She swallowed. He had put so much thought into this. And energy. When had he crafted an entire harp without her noticing? And with all the plans against Julian, how had he managed to find a moment to share something so special with her? She pressed a hand to her mouth, too overcome with emotion to speak. After swallowing hard, she managed to finish her thought. "This is perfect."

He was perfect. How had she ever lived without him? How had she ever believed her life could be complete by staying in the mortal realm? It was clear more than ever they were meant for each other and that nothing could keep them apart.

With the simple tune from the harp filling the valley, Quintus offered a sheepish smile. "I know the song is not as intricate as one you could play, but my magic could only do a simple one like this."

It was remarkable he had been able to get the harp to play on its own at all. She reached for the pillar again, her fingers running over each of the gilded carvings. "I cannot believe how beautiful this is."

Her fingers itched to reach for the strings, eager to play anything, even though it had been so long since she practiced. But music had always brought her solace and to live so long without it had caused an ache in her heart.

Quintus cleared his throat. He had probably seen her eye the strings. "I know you have not been able to play since coming to Faerie, but I crafted this so you could play again once…"

He trailed off, but then a determined look filled his eyes. "Once we defeat my father and save Crystalfall."

The ache in her heart immediately filled with a flood of warmth. Seeing Quintus confident again brought her joy like nothing else could.

After clearing his throat, he turned his gaze downward. "There is something else I need to show you."

He gestured to the ground and they both found a spot on the strands of jade grass. Once seated, he pulled out the sketchbook he always had with him. Carefully opening it to a specific page, he then handed her the book.

Curiosity raced through her limbs, which only heightened once she saw what had been drawn on the page.

A crown. A beautiful, intricate crown fit for a queen.

But this was not the crown any of the current Faerie queens wore. So what was it then?

Quintus stared at his hands. "The crown my father wears, the crown I crafted, it is not…" He shook his head, as if trying to find the right words. "It is not right. There is something wrong with it."

Her eyebrows jumped up her forehead. "There's something *wrong* with it? But we saw what happened when Julian wore the crown. It gave him his magic back. It accepted him as king. So far it has worked the way all other Faerie crowns work."

"I know, but..." Quintus gestured toward the drawing of the beautiful crown in his sketchbook. "This is the Crystalfall crown. I don't know what that means, but I know it is true."

"This?" She turned her gaze back to the sketchbook. "But this is a woman's crown."

"I know." He shrugged, looking even more confused than she felt. "But this is the crown of Crystalfall."

Thoughts shot through her mind, all moving too fast to make sense of any of them. But then one pulled forward, pushing the others away.

"Your mother," she said in a whisper.

His face flinched, but then he gave a nearly imperceptible nod. "I had that thought too. It does not make sense that Faerie would choose a mortal to rule one of its courts. I know my father forced himself to be ruler somehow, but I wonder if it was meant to be my mother, not him."

His mother had originally come from Bitter Thorn, but then again, everyone in Crystalfall had originally come from a different court. And his mother had lived in the castle and knew the court well. Perhaps Julian had used her magic to make his crown. Or perhaps *she* made the crown, and he stole it before she could ever wear it. If anyone was *meant* to be the ruler of Crystalfall it made far more sense it was a fae and not a mortal.

"Do you think we should take the drawing to her?" Chloe asked.

Quintus flinched even harder, shaking his shoulders when he did. "I doubt she will listen. She refused to come with us when we met with her before. Why would she help us now?"

As much as she hated to admit it, Dyani, Quintus's mother, might *not* be willing to help them. Crystalfall was the most beautiful and most magical of any court. It was the court that opened its arms to both fae and mortals, but that wouldn't matter to Dyani. Not when Julian, her greatest nightmare, reigned in terror over the place. It had been clear in their last meeting she still feared him greatly.

But they had to save Crystalfall, and maybe that meant they needed her. The odds of getting her to face Julian again seemed insurmountable, but maybe she'd be more willing if they showed her they had a clear plan.

"We should go to her." Chloe reached for Quintus's hand. "We must see if we can convince her to help us now that Julian has his magic back."

His nose wrinkled while he gave no indication of a response.

She took a deep breath before continuing. "If she was the one who was meant to have the crown, then she might be the only one who can defeat him."

"I came to the same conclusion," Quintus said in a miserable voice.

Chloe squeezed his hand. "We have to try."

He looked sick for a moment, but then he stared at their clasped hands and nodded. "For you, I will try, but only if we must. I can do it with you by my side."

A smile lit under his lips, which she fully expected to bloom into a true smile. But then the fierceness in his face dimmed until it was gradually replaced by a somber expression. The change in his demeanor caused unease to sprout from every pore in her skin.

"What is it?" She shook their intertwined fingers, as if that would shake him free of the gloom that had overtaken him. It worried her how his eyes had turned so sad in a matter of moments. It didn't take long for her to know why.

"Julian wants you dead." The flat tone of his voice sent her thoughts into spirals. A thousand things had come to her mind at seeing his gloom, but none of them went along with what he just said. She didn't know if she should be relieved he was concerned for her or worried he couldn't accept something so obvious.

Since she had no idea where this statement had come from, she did her best to comfort, though she didn't know if it would help. "Of course, he does. He wants all of us dead. We're the only ones who have a chance at stopping him."

Still, relief did not brighten Quintus's eyes. "No, it is more than that. He wants *you* dead. I keep replaying in my mind that battle in the hallway of the castle. I keep seeing how he looked at you in a way he did not even look at me. I finally realized why." He reached out to touch her cheek.

The music stopped playing then. The wind stopped blowing, and even the babbling stream seemed quieter than before. It was as if everything in Faerie had stopped moving and the only thing that throbbed with life was his thumb moving slowly up and down her cheek. His hand on her skin. The only thing she could think about. The only thing that mattered to her. Only him.

"Why?" she finally whispered, her voice as breathless as if she had been running for miles.

Sadness gripped his eyes completely. Even though his touch on her skin continued to remain tender, it could not bring her comfort with his eyes like that. "He knows I am in love with you. He has seen it. And now he wants you dead. Of course, he wants *me* dead too, but he wants to kill *you* first because he knows how much it will hurt me to lose you." Quintus lowered his hand away and stared hard at the ground. "He wants me to suffer before he kills me. He wants my heart dead before I actually die."

Even if Chloe wanted to look away from the glints of gold in his eyes so she could digest these words, she wouldn't have been able to. The intensity in them called to her, drawing her in through the power of their bond.

He loved her.

He would feel dead if he lost her.

This wound was painful enough on its own, she didn't need to make it any worse. But the words came out from her mouth of their own accord. She could not stop them. "You know I will die someday, even if not by Julian's hand. No matter how long I live, I am mortal, and…"

Sound caught in her throat as her voice broke. She couldn't finish the sentence. She could barely even breathe.

In response, Quintus pulled her tight into his arms. He held her firmly against his body and squeezed harder than he usually did. Energy shivered through his limbs, making his hold on her more desperate than ever. He held her as if he'd drown if he let go.

"I cannot do it, Chloe," he whispered into her hair. "I cannot lose you. Not now. Not ever."

"I tried to tell you." Her words came out stretched thin, accompanied by a pool of tears that started slipping down her cheeks. "I tried to stop you before it was too late." She buried her face in his chest, hoping he'd hold on just a little tighter, as if that embrace might save them both.

In silence, they held on, breathing, crying, trying not to think about the future they could never avoid.

Eventually, they let go, knowing they needed to return to camp to get some sleep. He put the harp and stool back into his magical pocket. With a wave of his hand, the golden balls of magic in the air that had given them light vanished.

They continued holding on to each other as Shadow flew them back to camp.

But just as they were settling onto their sleeping mats, Quintus whispered words just for her.

"Maybe there is a way to turn you immortal. Another way besides the shards." He pulled his blanket up to his chin, then looked at her with fierceness in his eyes. "Maybe we can find it."

Of course the logical part of her brain rejected his statement. Such a thing couldn't be possible. It would never happen. He never should have fallen in love with her in the first place. But the idealistic part of her brain, the part that wanted what he wanted just as much as he did, fully accepted the idea. Why not? Once they defeated Julian, Quintus would be king of Crystalfall. Or maybe his mother would be. Might the next ruler have enough power to make Chloe immortal without her having to use a shard? It was almost impossible. But perhaps it was just a tiny bit possible too. If Quintus wanted to believe it was possible, then she would believe it too.

13

THICK MIST WOKE CHLOE FROM her sleep. The sky was still gray, waiting for the light from day to dawn. A shimmering mist usually sat over the Gemfields, but this mist felt different. It had a pulsing energy and a sharp prick when it touched the skin.

She sat up with a start, instinctively reaching for her wooden foot. Other Golden Shields began sitting up next, many of them rubbing a hand over their arms, as if trying to wipe something away.

Quintus glanced upward suddenly. His heightened fae senses must have picked up some sound the rest of them had missed.

But once Chloe followed his gaze, she soon discovered what had woken everyone. All heat immediately drained from her face.

Quintus lunged from his bed, throwing an arm over Chloe to protect her. He must have known that would do no good, though.

A huge cloud of dark green and purple magic had erupted in the sky, not far from their heads. The strange cloud shimmered at its edges with emerald magic. The entire cloud suddenly shook slightly, as if the clouds were about to drop buckets of rain on them.

"The king. He did this." Quintus clenched his jaw, his arm still over Chloe as he glared at the magic above them.

As much as she loved that his first instinct was to protect her, his arm would do nothing against a cloud of magic. And anyway, the Shields saw her as their leader. They needed her to think of a way to escape without being hit by the magic. After putting on her foot, she ducked under his hand and stood to get a closer look at the cloud.

When Sofia caught sight of the pulsing cloud, she screamed. The remaining Golden Shields awoke at the sound, and so did the rest of the dragons. No one could miss the hysteria and fear in such a scream.

Shouts and exclamations filled the air as everyone's gaze followed Sofia's trembling finger as it pointed toward the sky.

"What is that?" Ludo stared at the cloud while scurrying out of his bed to stand up. His short hair shook as he jerked his head in all directions, trying to look at the cloud from several angles. He glared harder and harder the longer he stared at it. "Is this a memory cloud? Like the one King Julian used to make everyone forget Crystalfall?"

Mishti rolled her eyes at him. "Just keep glaring at it, Ludo. I'm sure that will help."

Ludo ignored her as his face shifted from a glare to one of dread. His hands dropped to his waist. He began to rock his body side to side, his eyes still on the green and purple cloud hovering ominously above them. "We are finished. How can we ever defeat him if he takes our memories? We are done for."

"Stop talking, Ludo," Chloe said sharply. "Unless you have something useful to say." Authority rang through her voice as she moved to stand directly beneath the middle of the cloud. His outburst of panic would do none of them any good. At the moment, she needed everyone to be composed, or silent at the very least, while she figured out if Julian had truly sent the cloud, why it was sent, and how long they had before it would fall and envelop them with its magic. So far, it had done nothing but hover above them, which piqued her curiosity. Why hadn't it done anything yet? But just because it had done nothing so far didn't mean it would stay harmless.

As Ludo had mentioned, Julian had created a memory cloud in the past, just before he destroyed Crystalfall. That memory cloud made everyone in the court, including Ludo, forget the identity of the king. And Ludo had lost so many more memories after that, even forgetting where to find his own brother. He had only recently found his brother again, and clearly, the fear of losing memories again was more than Ludo could bear. Even though she told him to stop talking, she had to admit, he was right. If any of them lost *any* memories right now, they might never be able to defeat the king. They might not even remember who he was.

As the gazes of the Golden Shields turned to her, waiting for her to say something, for her to say anything, her stomach rumbled with unease. She already knew the truth. All of them did.

Julian *had* sent the cloud. But what could they possibly do to avoid it?

She stood a little taller, trying to examine the sparks of emerald magic inside the mist.

Mishti came to Chloe's side. The young woman smoothed out her midnight blue tunic and spoke under her breath. "What do you suggest we do?"

Rather than answer, Chloe rushed to her sleeping mat to grab her leather bag. Once she had it, she frantically dug through it for her magical book.

Putting her right hand on the rich leather cover of the book, she closed it and spoke aloud. "If this is a memory cloud that will steal our memories, how do we destroy it?"

She waited for the book to send sparks of golden magic everywhere before the pages would start flipping on their own to give them the answers they needed.

But the book did nothing. She even opened it and waited an extra moment.

Still nothing.

It stayed unmoving in her hands, as if nothing more than a regular book.

Biting down the fear rising through her, she urged herself to remain calm. Then she glanced at the cloud before turning once again to her book. Maybe there had been too much desperation in her voice. Maybe she had rushed the words too much. Maybe she had asked the wrong question.

She closed her eyes, her chest expanding and then contracting as she inhaled and exhaled heavily. When she felt calm enough, she spoke again. "How do we counteract the effects of this magical cloud?"

But still, as if the book was purposely being stubborn, it remained motionless, refusing to give her any answer at all.

Why did the book only help sometimes and not every time she needed it? Did it *want* Julian to win? Her fingers gripped around its spine as she glared at it.

A shadow fell on top of the book, and she knew before turning that Quintus had come to her side. She bit her lips to stop them from trembling, but it would not hide the panic in her eyes. When magic started crackling within the cloud above, complete helplessness overtook her.

"The book won't help. It gives no answer." She slammed the book shut, only barely stopping herself from admitting she had no idea what to do.

Quintus looked at her then. So did the rest of the Golden Shields. They stared at her expectantly, waiting for her direction. She could not feed fear to them. She could not.

He put his hand on her shoulder and squeezed it reassuringly, as if he understood the fear she tried to suppress and how she was torn between her feelings and her duty as a leader. "Maybe it knows we can fix this ourselves."

Ludo pouted and shoved both hands into his pocket. "What? Are we supposed to know what to do just by looking at the cloud? That did not work out for the people who encountered Julian's last memory cloud, if you recall. That cloud fell down on everyone in Crystalfall, including *me*, making them forget everything about the king. And soon after, he destroyed the entire court."

"Is it even possible to stop it?" Batu asked, tension darkening his words.

"Why hasn't it descended yet?" Mishti asked. "Didn't Julian's other cloud move so fast no one could avoid it?"

That was the same question that kept turning over in Chloe's mind. Was it something about their group? Was it a different sort of cloud? Scratching a nail over the threads in her dress, her mind spun.

Why had the cloud not descended yet? Or maybe that was the wrong question. Maybe the cloud simply hadn't descended because it was still building energy. Maybe Julian assumed they'd all still be asleep since day hadn't dawned yet and never thought they'd be able to stop the cloud before it descended. Instead of focusing on that, she needed to focus on why the cloud was there.

If they were all about to lose their memories, maybe the real question she needed to ask was, what was stronger than a memory?

Finding the right question was the trick to opening the closed door in Chloe's mind. As she scanned through her memories, her mind spun faster, almost too fast for her to follow. As least her mind was busy. That made her feel a little less useless.

Her head jerked to the side until she caught the gaze of the Fairfrost fae. "Ludo, when you slowly regained your memories of your brother, what helped?"

He started making a face at her but then seemed to realize how desperately she was trying to help. He stopped then and took a moment to think before he answered. "Seeing objects, items from our past. But what good will that do when everything that could help is right here and will all be touched by the same memory cloud?"

Ignoring his question, she asked another one. "Why did seeing things help? What happened when you saw them?"

His harried expression made it clear he thought this questioning was useless. Luckily, he still answered. "I felt things that did not make any sense. My emotions did not match my surroundings."

"You *felt* things." A grin tugged at her lips. "So feelings lasted longer than your memories? Excellent."

And now she was ready to spring into action. She dashed across their camp until she stood at the other end of it, directly across from Quintus. Then she reached her hands out, stretching them toward the two closest Shields. "Everyone, clasp onto each other's hands until we form a circle."

A few eyebrows raised and a few heads tilted, but everyone still complied with her request.

Quintus stared at her through narrowed eyes from across the clearing. His eyebrows furrowed, making it clear he was upset in some way. Hopefully it was just that he wished he could hold *her* hand because soon enough, he'd understand why she had chosen this spot so far away from him.

With everyone in position, she spoke confidently. "We are all going to stand here together and think of why we need to save Crystalfall. Let the emotions flood your mind. Think of why you became a Golden Shield. How will it feel to bring freedom and safety to this court?"

All around the circle, she could see expressions become serious as the Shields focused on these feelings. Just as they started, the cloud above began crackling even louder. Sparks of emerald magic shot from the thick billows above them. Her stomach twisted into a knot.

"Is it happening?" Sofia asked, her voice so thick that fear had clearly lodged like a boulder in her throat.

"I think so," Chloe said. "But we can beat it."

Her eyes locked onto Quintus's, who stood directly across from her. She spoke loud enough for everyone to hear, but at their core, the words were meant mostly for him. "I don't know if this will work, but I know you and I share a magical bond."

The moment those words left her lips, she felt the star tattoos under her eyes begin to tingle. "Maybe our bond can amplify our own emotions. And maybe if we are all touching like this and focusing hard, our emotions altogether might be enough to counteract the memory magic."

Before she finished speaking the sky grew darker, even though the sun had just started rising. The cloud lowered. It was nearly upon them. The Golden Shields visibly trembled.

Chloe took a deep breath and attempted to infuse her words with more determination than she felt. "What is the purpose of the Order of the Golden Shields? Freedom! Safety! Home!"

A hum of agreement went through the crowd. Heat prickled through her tattoos. At least the bond with Quintus seemed to be strengthening. Hopefully it would be enough to overcome the cloud. "Our emotions are what make us who we are. Our feelings can keep our memories inside us. Say these words with me. Freedom. Safety. Home."

Everyone closed their eyes and opened their mouths. Together they repeated the words in unison.

"Freedom. Safety. Home."

The cloud began to descend.

"Louder," she shouted. Again, they repeated the words.

"Freedom! Safety! Home!"

Emerald and purple mist surrounded her, enveloping her with a cold and prickly sensation. But as the chill closed in around her, one part of her body began to rise in temperature. Her hands suddenly felt hot, as if she had caught a fever. Her heart leapt. It was working.

But even as that thought entered her mind, confusion set in. *What* was working? What was she doing?

"Freedom! Safety! Home!" The words left her lips with conviction, but *why* had she said them? What did they mean?

A cloudy magic surrounded her with crackling bursts. The strange mist was cold. She didn't like it.

"Freedom. Safety. Home." There it was again. She said the same three words, but why? And why were other people saying the words too?

Her fingers twitched, gaining the surprising awareness that she was holding the hands of two different people. In fact, all of these people were holding hands. They all stood in a large circle. But why?

"Freedom. Safety. Home."

The words came out weaker this time. She'd had so much conviction the first time she said them, but how could she have conviction now? She didn't even know what the words meant. But still, she said them.

It lasted for less than a breath, but a flicker of something stirred in her heart. A feeling. Something about why these words mattered. About why they needed to be said with conviction. She had to say them again. Maybe then she would understand why they were so important.

"Freedom. Safety. Home!" The last word she shouted, and she didn't know why, but she knew it felt right. It would work. It had to work.

Her head cocked to the side at that thought. *What* had to work? What was she doing? But that flicker in her heart stirred again. And this strange cloud around them had started to gather back together. It began lifting back into the air. Perhaps it had finished what it came to do. But that meant the real work had only just begun.

Whatever *that* meant.

But even though she didn't understand why, her heart called to her to say the words again. *Louder. Stronger. Don't give up.*

"Freedom! Safety! Home!"

A few of the people around her had started whispering the words instead of shouting them. But when she spoke with such determination, their heads snapped up. Their eyes brightened. When she shouted the three words again, everyone joined in, even louder than before.

Warmth spread in her cheeks as a soft tingle pricked the skin under her eye. And then it started.

Quintus.

She gasped and looked ahead, finding him standing directly across from her. The crescent moon tattoo under his eye glowed with sparkling golden magic. When she caught his gaze, he stared at her strangely.

She shouted the words again, and everyone joined in. "Freedom! Safety! Home!"

A tear started trailing down her cheek. She remembered Quintus. He had lost his home because his father had destroyed it, but that didn't matter because she would be his home now. They had found strength in each other.

"Freedom! Safety! Home!"

That was all it took. One last chant of those three words, and the rest came rushing back to her. The Golden Shields. Julian. Crystalfall.

As the memories flitted into her mind one by one, the cloud around them rose higher into the air. It stopped crackling, it stopped pulsing with energy. But it didn't go away. It hovered above, but it did not attempt to descend again.

Everyone in the circle started murmuring.

I forgot everything. I did too. But I remember now. Do you remember? Do we all remember?

They did remember. Every last one of them. Apparently, their memories had pushed the cloud away, not allowing it to work its magic on them. Chloe and Quintus's bond had amplified the emotions of everyone in the circle, and the emotions had helped them reclaim their memories.

But the cloud had not disappeared. It still hung over them, casting an ominous shadow over their camp.

They attempted to fly away from it on their dragons, but as Chloe guessed it would, the cloud followed them. They returned back to the Gemfields with a new problem to overcome.

They had kept their memories, but how could they get rid of the cloud completely?

Considering how it churned and sparked, Chloe had the feeling it was building up energy again. That meant they would be safe for a while but not forever.

Their chant and the emotions had worked to save them this time. But before the cloud descended again, they needed a way to get rid of it forever.

14

EVEN THOUGH THE CLOUD HOVERED above, everyone did their best to ignore it while Chloe tried to think of a solution for it. They still had a lot of work to do in preparation for battle. Most of the Shields worked to create more weapons for the stash. Others found clever ways to use the jeweled landscape to create sparkling armor. Mishti led a small group of Shields out deep in the Gemfields where they tried to deepen their bonds with their dragons.

Chloe sat in the middle of camp with her useless magical book on her lap. It still refused to give any answers, not even any hints, on how to deal with the cloud.

They needed a solution soon.

Hilda, a Shield with red hair and a quiet temperament, approached Chloe

Chloe assumed the woman was simply taking a rest and mostly ignored her as she studied the book in her lap.

Why didn't Faerie give more answers through the book? A heavy thought hit her then. Maybe the book didn't know. What if Julian's magic was so depraved that even Faerie itself didn't know how to defeat it. That seemed a little too harrowing with the cloud still hovering above. But maybe what Quintus had said was true. Maybe the book simply knew Chloe had the resources to discover the answer on her own and wanted to let her figure it out.

Her lip curled at that thought. Maybe it helped her grow to figure these things out, but maybe she was sick of growing. Why couldn't things just be easy for once?

Focusing again, she sifted through her mind, anxious to remember anything that might help her. She had strategized, discarding one idea after another but nothing seemed to be what she needed. Nothing.

Sighing loudly, she glared at her book. Weariness from so much thinking sank into her blood. It wasn't fair that she could be so tired when it was still morning.

"In times like this, I wish I had a special skill besides being a swordswoman," Hilda said softly.

At first, Chloe didn't process the words. She'd been too immersed in her turbulent thoughts. But the woman shifted slightly, trying to catch Chloe's gaze.

"What?" With a start, Chloe snapped her head upward. "Did you say something, Hilda?" A lock of blonde hair fell across Chloe's eye. Irritation sprung inside her when it blocked her vision. She dug into her leather bag and pulled out a ribbon, which she then used to tie her hair into a quick bun.

"Not really," Hilda said, softspoken and shy. "I was just talking out loud. It's nothing you need to worry about."

Chloe didn't like the excessive remorse in the tone of the other woman. She had once thought her own desires and needs were less important than those around her. She wouldn't let a fellow Golden Shield feel the same.

"I want to hear. I didn't realize you were talking to me before, but I'm listening now." She offered a smile to the woman. "Don't ever think you are insignificant."

Hilda's pretty black eyes shined, and it was clear Chloe's words had hit something in her.

"If you insist," Hilda said with her gaze drawing downward.

"I do." Despite knowing Julian's cloud of magic would probably descend upon them again, Chloe did her best to focus on this conversation. "What is it you were saying?"

As a leader, it wasn't enough for Chloe to reassure the woman. She also had to make her see she meant every word she said. That was the only way to build a tangible connection.

Hilda wrung her hands in her lap, her necklace made from a strand of the golden mail bouncing slightly against her neck. She finally looked at Chloe.

"I said that in times like this, I wish I had a special skill besides being a swordswoman. If I did, maybe I would be able to help you find a way to get rid of the cloud."

Chloe felt her brows furrow in surprise. "But being a good swordswoman is still highly valuable to our group. I have seen how you fight. You have helped us out of many tough spots."

Hilda shook her head, sending wisps over her shoulder. "I know, and I am happy to help fight. It's just that everyone seems to have other skills too. You are good with healing and strategy. Quintus is good at crafting and fighting. Ludo has magic and is good at finding things. Mishti knows battle strategies and intimidation. I wish I had at least one special skill like that."

"But you are very good with a sword, and that should not be ignored. I may be good at healing, but I am woeful at fighting. You've seen it. We all have our strengths and our weaknesses. At least you're better than Ludo at staying positive." Chloe said the last bit in a teasing tone, hoping it would set the other woman at ease.

As expected, soft laughter left Hilda's mouth.

Chloe continued. "In truth, I am certain you have other skills too, but maybe it has been difficult to discover them since we've been constantly moving and fighting. Once we settle down someday, your own unique skill will likely come."

Hilda grinned wide at the sound of those words. Her reaction made Chloe smile with satisfaction but then Chloe's lips straightened into a mild frown.

During the course of the conversation, something, something so light it had yet to take form, had slipped onto her mind. She couldn't quite catch it yet. Unease took hold of her as she tried to grasp the thought, causing goosebumps to coat her skin. Hilda must have known Chloe dove deep in thought again because the woman gave a short nod and trailed away.

Once alone, Chloe ran her fingers over the green pearl grass strands around her. They glittered and swayed in the wind and felt strangely soft under her hands.

A thought tugged at her mind. It spun and twisted. It was coming to her. Or at least, it was *trying* to come to her. That she was sure of. But she could not make sense of it. Not yet.

Waves of frustration washed over her. Maybe Quintus could help. She scanned the camp and found him sitting on a golden boulder crafting arrows and small throwing knives. His fingers moved deftly over the objects. Concentration lines etched in his forehead while magic glowed out from his hands.

The work took effort, but his skill probably improved with each new weapon he crafted.

Suddenly, she froze. Finally, she could make sense of the thought spinning and twisting in her subconscious.

Hilda's words had brought the idea forward. Her wish had been sincere and harmless, but even more important, it had given Chloe the answer as to why Faerie hadn't helped them yet.

I wish I had a special skill like that.

That's what the woman had said. And now it all made sense. Chloe shoved the book into her leather bag and ran across camp toward Quintus. Adrenaline pulsed through her so high that her wooden foot felt as natural as her real foot.

Quintus glanced up as soon as he noticed her moving toward him. He smiled at her approaching form but worry soon overtook his brown eyes.

He stood, dropping the knife in his hand without even seeming to realize it. "What happened?" He took a step toward her. "Are you hurt?"

"No." She glanced down at herself. Had she been running off balance? She hadn't noticed doing so, but maybe the adrenaline had covered it up. "Why did you ask that?"

He stared at her carefully. "Your face is…worried. Are you worried?"

She gestured upward at the cloud while raising one eyebrow. "Of course I'm worried."

His gaze locked onto hers and her tattoo prickled. Warmth spilled into her cheeks, and suddenly Quintus's expression changed. "You are excited?"

She tilted her head to the side. "Did you just use our bond to figure out what emotion I'm feeling?"

"Why are you excited?" he asked, ignoring her question completely.

Luckily for him, she *was* excited. Much too excited to care about how he'd used their bond. In fact, she filed the memory away so she could try doing the same thing the next time she couldn't decipher his thoughts.

But now, she said what she'd come here to say. "I figured something out."

His gaze flicked upward before turning back to her. "About the cloud."

Pride rushed through her veins as she smiled. "Yes."

A half smile lifted his lips. Then he sat back on the boulder, this time leaving room for her to sit next to him.

She quickly sat, then said, "I think you were right. I think Faerie knows we can figure out this cloud problem by ourselves."

His pointed ears perked toward her. "Do you know how?"

She took a deep breath before continuing. "Julian stole the memory magic from the wraiths. It's magic he shouldn't be able to wield. It's not *his* magic. So I think the only way to defeat it is by using *our* unique traits. We need to use our own special skills to destroy the cloud. Since those traits *do* belong to us, they should be stronger than the magic that does not belong to Julian."

Quintus raised a single eyebrow after hearing that, and nothing in his expression seemed to agree with her idea. Instead, the incredulity in his eyes made the idea seem ridiculous.

She squirmed on the boulder next to him, suddenly certain he would begin to laugh.

Instead, he glanced up at the cloud and stared at it intensely. After several breaths, he finally spoke. "It could be possible."

That wasn't the sweeping approval she'd been hoping for, but at least he hadn't laughed at her idea.

After a moment, he sighed. "It does seem a little farfetched to me, but I have learned to trust your ideas. In fact..." He turned his gaze to his hands. "I think I may be able to craft a vessel that can trap the cloud inside it. It is one thing to create a vessel and another thing to trap something inside it, much less a cloud. But maybe with some other unique traits in our group it could be possible."

She scrunched her nose in thought. "I wonder how my healing skills might help. I don't know of any concoctions that can suck a cloud into a vessel, unfortunately."

He stared at her with a hope in his eyes that she did not deserve. Through their bond, she could feel what he did not say. He believed in her. He seemed certain she could figure something out. She did have a vast and deep knowledge of herbs, even of Faerie herbs now that she had read her magical book so many times. How could that knowledge be useful here?

"Are there herbs that can weaken enchantments? Or herbs that can enhance memories?" Quintus asked, still staring at her with far too much belief in his eyes.

Not wanting to disappoint him, she searched her mind for an answer.

"Shadowblain blossom can weaken the effects of harmful magic. It usually works against magic that injures the body, but I think it might work." She frowned as she thought more about it. "I don't think it will be enough on its own though."

"You and I were not the only Golden Shields who stopped the cloud from enveloping us earlier," Quintus said. "Perhaps we need others too."

She nodded at his gentle reminder. "True. I will look for more herbs as well. Even the celestine crystals might help. And I'll have to skim through my book to see if I can find any remedies for enhancing memories."

He touched her cheek. "You never cease to amaze me."

Heat trickled through her face and into her neck. She brought his hand to her lips and kissed it softly before rushing back to her spot across camp. Hopefully she had filled his stomach with flutters as much as he had done to her.

Shadowblain blossom and a vessel to trap the cloud. They had a start. Now she just needed to find the other things they needed before the memory magic descended upon them again.

15

IT TOOK SOME RIGOROUS SEARCHING, but Chloe managed to find two different herbs that could enhance memories. Those combined with the shadowblain blossom and the celestine crystals would make a powerful tincture. Hopefully it would be strong enough to counteract Julian's memory cloud.

As nightfall neared, she refused to rest. The tincture took all her attention. Now that her bond with Quintus had been healed, she could have made the tincture in her mind and used the magic to administer it, but for this particular problem, it seemed best to create the concoction in real life.

Ludo, using his magic in finding things, took her to gather the memory-enhancing herbs and the celestine crystal from the meadow near the castle. They moved quickly, making sure they didn't get caught. Once back at camp, she found an ancient alchemical method in her book that allowed her to distill the herbs in dragon tears. That preparation gave her a larger quantity and made it more potent.

Now the only thing left was to wait for the sun to set. Sofia had made an off-hand remark about how this sort of ritual felt like one that was best done at night. Maybe it wasn't a special skill to know such a thing, but it was probably worth it to wait until night, just in case Sofia was right.

Luckily for them, the cloud continued to pulse as it built up more energy. By Chloe's calculations, the cloud wouldn't try to descend again until day dawned the next morning, so they should have enough time to do the ritual before the cloud descended again. Then again, there was no time in Faerie, so she could never be sure about such a thing.

Quintus spent the day working on the vessel he planned to craft. He had started with a drawing in his sketchbook. But since he worked on the other side of camp, she hadn't been able to check his progress while she worked on the tincture.

Just as she finished it up, Mishti came to Chloe's side. The young woman stared at the two large buckets holding the magical tincture. She raised an eyebrow at them.

Guessing the question Mishti had not asked, Chloe said, "I distilled the herbs with dragon tears, which makes their medicinal properties more potent. That way I have a lot more liquid to work with than just a small vial."

Mishti gave a noncommittal nod, so Chloe still had no idea if that was actually the reason Mishti had raised her eyebrow in the first place.

She dug her toe into the ground and cleared her throat, both odd for Mishti, who usually showed no signs of discomfort. When she spoke, even her voice sounded a little timid. "Ludo said you need our unique skills to defeat the cloud. You are using your healing ability, Quintus is crafting, of course, and Ludo helped you find things."

Mishti stopped talking, but it sounded like she wanted to say more. The end of her last sentence cut off short, as if she intended to tack on another sentence, but silence followed instead.

"Yes." Chloe said the word slowly, still not sure what to make of this conversation.

Mishti's gaze dropped to the ground. "Do you need any of my unique skills?"

"Oh!" Suddenly Mishti's unease made more sense. Chloe glanced down at the buckets of tincture and then up at the cloud. "I'm not sure. Did you have anything in mind?"

Mishti shook her head gloomily. "No, I just wanted to contribute. I thought it might be nice to help in a way that didn't require hurting anyone. But I guess I don't really have any skills besides that."

"You have other skills besides fighting. You have lots of other skills."

Mishti raised an eyebrow. "Name one."

"Uh." Chloe's mouth hung open as she desperately tried to think of something. Anything. Of course Mishti had other skills. But, of course, when she needed to name them, Chloe's mind had gone completely blank.

Waving a hand through the air, Mishti reached for both of the buckets. "It doesn't matter. It was a stupid thought. Quintus said the crackling inside the cloud is increasing and the sun is setting so we should probably get started."

But though the young woman picked up the buckets and shifted her face to its usual hardened expression, Chloe could tell her friend still hurt. It must have been frustrating being so good at fighting and killing when Mishti longed to be good at anything else.

No matter how she tried, Chloe could think of nothing comforting to say. Her mind was still too anxious about getting rid of the cloud, leaving no room for Mishti's predicament.

She wouldn't forget this, though, Chloe decided. After the ritual, after they got rid of the cloud, she'd talk to Mishti again.

Together, they'd make a whole list of all the special skills Mishti had.

Once they reached Quintus, they found him still crafting the vessel. The bulk of it was smooth yellow glass that had so much shine, it was more likely crystal than glass. A seam around the center had been sealed with a decorative line of melted gold. Quintus had carved small designs into the gold that made the vessel beautiful enough for a throne room.

He never could craft something just for function. He always had to make his creations beautiful too. This vessel fit right in with the glittering court of Crystalfall.

"Almost finished," Quintus said as they approached. He worked on the hinge of a door where the cloud would be able to enter the vessel. His magic created a rubbery substance around the edge that would stopper the door and prevent any wisps of cloud from escaping once they shut it inside.

Now that she stood close enough, Chloe realized the vessel was much larger than she expected. The oval-like shape could fit her entire body if she bent in half at the waist. Her eyebrows bounced up her forehead. "That is quite large."

"So is the cloud," he replied without missing a beat. His gaze stayed fixed on the door, making sure the hinge still worked even after he had added the rubber.

She glanced toward the horizon where the sun had nearly set. "Have you been working on this all day?"

It had taken her all day to complete the tincture, so she wasn't complaining. But considering his skills with crafting, she would have expected him to finish sooner.

A twinge broke across his face before he answered. "I started with a wooden vessel. I used a tree from Bitter Thorn, and I hand carved it." He shook his head. "But it was not right. It was not large enough, and it was too heavy. Everything about it felt wrong, though it took me most of the day before I finally gave up."

Stepping closer, she brushed her fingertips across the crystalline surface of the vessel. It truly looked magnificent.

"I started over with yellow gems from the flowers out there." He gestured out toward the fields surrounding them. "Everything is going much smoother now. It will not be long before I finish."

"Interesting." Chloe tapped her chin. "I suppose since the magic was created in Crystalfall, perhaps it needs to be defeated by Crystalfall."

"What about fire?" Mishti cut off the very end of Chloe's sentence and blurted out her question in a rush.

Both Choe and Quintus jerked their heads toward her in surprise.

"Fire?" Chloe asked.

"Yes." Mishti nodded, an almost-smile forming on her face. "That could be my special skill that isn't fighting. I'm very good at making fires. And aren't clouds made of water? Surely a fire could help to dissipate the cloud."

Quintus froze long enough to roll his eyes and then try to hide that he had rolled his eyes. He immediately turned back to his work, leaving Chloe to deal with the suggestion.

Chloe wanted Mishti's idea to work. She really did. So it pained her to respond. "But Crystalfall has no wood. Everything is made of gold or jewels. How are we supposed to make a fire with no wood?"

Instead of looking defeated, Mishti beamed. "See, this is exactly my special skill. You don't need wood to make a fire, you just need fuel. Remember the glass jars we used to carry that had iron mixed with fuel at the bottom? We made them so we could injure any fae who came near us. That was *my* idea. I'm sure we have something around here we can use as fuel. Or I can conjure something using the golden table. Once I'm ready, we can use the fire along with everything else."

"Let's try it." Chloe forced her voice to sound as excited as possible. "Hurry though. We are almost ready."

Mishti broke into a run immediately, dashing across camp toward the golden table.

As soon as she was out of earshot, Quintus threw Chloe a skeptical glance. "You think fire will help?"

"I don't know," Chloe said. "But Mishti wanted to use a special skill to defeat the cloud too, something besides fighting. How could I tell her *no* when she was so anxious to help? And anyway, maybe she's right. Fire can evaporate water and clouds are made of water, so maybe the fire will help."

He gestured at the churning, crackling cloud above them. "*That* is not made of water. It is made of magic."

Chloe huffed with a frown. "Fine, maybe the fire won't help, but it's not going to hurt either, will it?"

"I guess not," Quintus responded. He turned back to his crafting, making a few final adjustments. After staring at it for a moment, he gave a sure nod. "This is ready."

Though he was finished, he stared at the crystalline vessel, carefully running one thumb across the surface. His gaze roamed over the entire object, probably checking that everything had been built as it should.

Watching him work on the vessel reminded her of when they sat in the black caves after she had shown him her foot had been chopped off. He had crafted a foot for her then, a foot made from the only wood that remained from his home that had been destroyed. Just like then, he put great care and attention into his creation. And also just like then, the item he had crafted had the potential to save her.

"How heavy is it?" As an object that was big enough to fit her entire body, she doubted anyone would be strong enough to carry it except him.

To her surprise, he passed it into her hands.

With a gasp, she braced herself for the weight of a boulder. Even the buckets carrying her tincture were too heavy for her, and Mishti had to carry them. But it turned out, she had no need to brace herself. The vessel felt even lighter than her magical book. She nearly lost her balance from her change in stance, expecting a much greater weight.

He chuckled and flashed her smile. "Lighter than you expected?"

"Much." Now she lifted the vessel a few times, still amazed she could move it so easily.

Taking it from her, he used his chin to point toward the center of camp. "We should get set up and begin as soon as possible. I do not like how much noise the cloud is making."

She agreed and moved swiftly to the center of camp.

When they moved in, the Golden Shields around them started forming a circle around the edge of camp like they had done when they first encountered the cloud. Hopefully, it would not be necessary to chant like they had already done, but it was wise to be prepared just in case. Light began disappearing down the horizon. Soon, night would fall completely.

While Quintus held the vessel, Chloe directed Batu and Hilda to pour the tincture inside through the open hinged door. Once all the liquid was inside, Chloe closed and locked the door, checking the rubber seal to be certain it would hold.

She gave a slight nod to Quintus, and he began swirling the liquid around until it coated the entire interior surface of the vessel. Just as she finished, Mishti barreled forward with Ludo on her tail.

"We're ready," Mishti said. She held up a glass jar that had a small portion of fuel sloshing around the bottom of it.

Ludo began pulling jars from his magical pocket. Each one held a bit of fuel at the bottom. "We have enough for everyone."

"Good." Chloe smiled at her friends as they passed out the jars until every Shield held one. She had gone most of her life feeling like all her skills were useless. Even if the fire might not help, she refused to make Mishti feel useless in this moment.

Without another word, Chloe and Quintus stood side by side and held the vessel between them with clasped hands.

Silence fell upon their camp as they all waited for something to happen.

A fierce crackle broke through the emerald-and-purple cloud, filling it with electrifying sparks. The items were set in place, now all they needed was a little magic.

Holding onto Quintus's hands with both of hers, Chloe closed her eyes. Somehow, even without looking, she knew he did the same. It took another moment of concentration, but then magic sparked at her fingertips. She opened her eyes again to see shimmering golden magic gathering around their clasped hands at the bottom of the vessel.

At the same moment, they lifted the vessel until it nearly touched the undulating mass above them. The golden magic at their fingertips began to heat up the yellow crystalline vessel. Soon, emerald green wisps erupted, flowing from their fingers as easily as the golden sparks.

Chloe closed her eyes and imagined a bottomless pit sucking an enormous amount of energy into its center. She thought of each herb and crystal inside her tincture, calling on their properties to counteract the cloud.

When she peeked through one eyelid, a pang went through her heart.

It wasn't working.

The cloud hadn't budged. Even worse, it descended faster now. It had moved past the very top part of the vessel, but it hadn't gone inside it. She and Quintus had to lower their hands to keep the vessel underneath the cloud. But it still wasn't working.

"It's time for the flames." Mishti turned to Ludo with her face as serious as ever. "Use your magic to strike the stones against the flint."

Ludo nodded, snapping his fingers. The moment he did, tiny sparks of light flashed inside each of the glass jars the Shields held. They must have each had tiny pieces of flint and stone inside, which Ludo struck with magic.

The sparks of light immediately burst into flames when the embers dropped into the fuel at the bottom of the jars. Soon, every jar had flames that licked out from the surfaces. The combination of so much fire brought warmth through their camp.

At first, the fire did nothing. The tincture did nothing.

"Should we move in closer?" Mishti asked, a subtle tremble in her tone.

"Yes, good idea. Let's try." Chloe let her mind spin as the Golden Shields moved in closer. It probably wouldn't help, but it might give her enough time to think of another idea. And she still refused to let Mishti's effort go unappreciated.

But as the Shields moved closer, a remarkable thing happened. Just as Quintus had predicted, the flames had no effect on the magical cloud. The flames did, however, seem to change the air around the cloud.

Since the air itself was invisible, it took Chloe a moment to work out what was happening. But her years of studying books had taught her many things. One thing she remembered distinctly in this moment was that hot air moved higher than cooler air.

With the flames heating the air all around the cloud, that air moved upward. And by doing so, the cooler cloud started moving down. First it was only a wisp, but then a little more.

It was *working*.

The cloud above them began to rumble, as if heralding a thunderstorm. It shook and swayed and, little by little, began falling *into* the vessel. The heat helped, but it appeared a little more magic would still be needed.

Chloe imagined again a bottomless pit sucking energy inside it. Squeezing her eyes shut tighter, she did her best to concentrate even more. Blackness enveloped her gaze with her eyes shut tight, allowing her to imagine. Magic continued to pulse from her fingertips, but then they started vibrating. It must have been the vessel that shook them.

Someone exhaled sharply behind her, which sent her eyelids flying open. After only one moment of seeing, her heart leapt in her chest.

The cloud had turned into a heavy torrent of energy. It twirled so fast she could only see its motion and not its shape. It pulsed and undulated, emanating a powerful, almost palpable force that seemed to defy any constraints. Energy reverberated through the air like the hum of a thousand voices. Emerald leaves rustled around them, reacting to the intensity in the air.

Then, as if the tincture had a magnetic force, the emerald-and-purple cloud still remaining outside the vessel immediately got sucked inside in one smooth, whirling motion. Quintus acted quickly, slamming the door on the vessel shut and locking it into place.

His arms shook from exertion as he forced the door to close. Afterward, the vessel shook violently. Would the beautiful yellow glass shatter and explode all around them? But Quintus held his hand tight over the door he had crafted. His eyes fell closed, probably to concentrate.

Taking a deep breath, Chloe kept one hand under the vessel to hold it in place. She sang Quintus's praises in her mind for crafting something so light, otherwise her one hand would not have been enough to hold it.

Once her other hand was free, she stretched it out and laid it over Quintus's so both their hands could hold onto the locked door. Golden magic shot from their hands as soon as they touched. The magic spread over the entire vessel and then it spread through the air in the camp.

The vessel continued to vibrate vigorously, but they held it fast.

She'd been too focused on the cloud to see much of anything else, but a few gasps of wonder from the other Shields caught her attention.

With her hands still in place, she glanced around at the others. Following their gazes, she soon turned to the darkened night sky.

The golden magic from her and Quintus had soared over all the Gemfields. Not only that, it also created a maze of glittering magic in the air. Such beautiful intricate patterns danced in the sky that it made her catch her breath. It was as if the entire place, the *entire court*, had become a kaleidoscope of golden magic. The fields, the trees, the mountains all seemed to have golden sparks bursting through them. And in the sky, it almost looked like stars twinkled. Of course, that would have been impossible since Faerie had no moon and no stars, but *something* had clearly changed.

Could that be possible? Had the magic of their bond done something to Crystalfall? If so, was it a welcome change... or a dangerous one?

16

No words could explain how brilliant the night-darkened court looked. Chloe could have stared at it forever, but with a vibrating vessel in her hands, she easily managed to turn her attention away from it.

Her gaze turned back to the glass filled with the crackling emerald-and-purple cloud. Then she studied the area around them, anxious to find any stray wisp that might have escaped. But there was none.

Mishti's idea with the fire truly had worked. They'd needed all four of them after all. Chloe's tincture, Quintus's vessel, Ludo's magic in finding things, and Mishti's fire. They'd even needed the other Golden Shields standing by and offering unwavering support. Combined with Chloe and Quintus's bond, all their special skills had saved them from Julian's magic.

The vessel eventually stopped vibrating and slowed to gentle pulses. She and Quintus were able to move their hands away from the door, and it held to keep the cloud in place.

"What…" Quintus trailed off as he looked upward. His eyes widened impossibly as he gaped at the sky above. "Chloe, it… Did you see…"

"I know, it's beautiful. It looks like the entire court is filled with our magic."

"No, not that." He tapped her arm, not quite hitting in the right place because his gaze was still fixed above. "There is a…"

He apparently still lacked the ability to finish a sentence, but he stopped batting her arm and moved until his fingers brushed across the skin under his left eye. He had touched his moon tattoo, which sparkled with golden magic.

But why had he touched the tattoo? The question felt like a jolt in her stomach, forcing her gaze upward once again. In a flash, she saw what had Quintus stammering. In fact, she was shocked he'd been able to form any words at all. Her stomach jolted harder, twisting inside itself.

Her mouth hung open completely as she stared at the impossible sight.

Right there in the night sky, just above where Julian's cloud had been, a moon surrounded by a constellation of stars shone like a polished pearl. The yellow crescent moon cast a gentle golden glow over their camp. Each star adorned the sky with brilliance.

"You brought a moon to Faerie." Ludo spoke in a hushed tone, filled with equal amounts of awe and fear.

Chloe turned to Quintus again. Did he fear this new development? Or was he awed by it? Julian's ritual needed a moon, and now, thanks to their magic, Faerie had one. It should have filled her with the worst sort of fear. But even though Chloe knew that, she felt deep in her gut magic like this might bring more good than harm. Logic told her Julian had gained a victory with the presence of the new moon, but her heart told her this victory was all theirs.

Quintus's fingers kept poking the moon on his face, which shined just like the moon in the sky. Shock covered his expression so completely, she could not tell if he felt positive or negative emotions for the new moon and stars.

Using the same trick he'd used on her earlier, she concentrated on their bond and attempted to decipher the feelings in his heart. It only took a moment to find them.

Fear. It sat there along with the shock, but something even bigger enveloped it. Excitement. Courage. Though he clearly had not expected this change, he did feel it was mostly positive. He felt the same strange peace she did then.

"What does it mean?" Quintus finally peeled his gaze away from the sky, immediately locking it onto the stars under her right eye. His eyebrows bounced at the sight, probably because her tattoos had turned golden and sparkling just like his.

Her eyes narrowed as she thought. "You said once a moon is a mortal symbol."

"Yes." He leaned toward her eagerly, as if she must have known the answer already.

An answer she did not have, but she did have a guess. "Perhaps our magic has marked Faerie to be a haven for mortals. Maybe our moon and stars in the sky mean this place is meant for both mortals and fae."

"But it only happened because of my father." His chin dropped to his chest. "It was a reaction to his magic, not an attempt to make Faerie safer."

"It was an attempt to make Crystalfall safer for us." She gestured to the dozens of Golden Shields around them. "For all of us."

"Maybe this was meant to be all along." Batu stepped forward, a look of conviction on his face.

"That's what I was thinking too," Sofia said from beside him. "Why else would you have moon and star tattoos on your faces? Maybe this was always bound to happen, and Julian's cloud just happened to be the thing that unlocked it."

It was a beautiful thought. The tattoos had come after Chloe and Quintus were bonded together. Perhaps from that moment on, their fates had become forever intertwined.

Back when they became bonded, they hadn't even known Crystalfall existed. But even then, the court had been calling to Quintus. He was heir to this court, and he'd clearly always been meant to save it.

Maybe by bonding herself to him, Chloe had made herself destined to save the court too.

Quintus stared intensely at nothing in particular while Batu and Sofia's ideas must have been turning in his mind. It took a moment, but he eventually gave a short nod.

"And maybe it also means a sky can have no moon and no stars or it can have both a moon and stars, but it can never have one without the other." Quintus gave Chloe a look once he finished speaking.

She knew exactly what he was trying to imply. He couldn't bear to live without her, so he was trying to believe this magic meant she had turned immortal. Sadly, she instinctively knew that was not the case. If she had changed that much, she would have felt it. But she wasn't about to crush his belief when he hoped so deeply. She could break the truth to him later, after they had saved the court from Julian.

Mishti stared at the sky as a small chuckle left her mouth. "Julian tried to pull us apart. He tried to make us forget each other. Instead, he made this court even more of a home for all of us. I think the moon and stars prove this is where we belong."

Chloe's throat bobbed as she swallowed hard. They were right. All of them were right, except probably Quintus. No matter what the moon and stars meant, one thing was clear.

Julian had tried to defeat them, and he had failed. Now they were more capable than ever at destroying all his plans.

But this sweet moment did not last. Of course it didn't. They should have known trouble would be close behind.

Quintus and Ludo turned with a start, both looking in the same direction at the other side of their camp.

With their gazes leading her, Mishti must have found the source of whatever had caught their attention.

They all must have heard something, but of course, Chloe hadn't noticed it. She never seemed to notice sounds until it was too late.

Mishti withdrew her sword from its sheath in one fluid movement. Her feet barely skimmed over the jade grass as she ran, leaving behind a rustle of wind in her wake. Quintus sprang into action next, following Mishti and quickly speeding past her.

Everyone else began running too. Chloe held fast to the vessel, not sure if she should set it down or if she should keep carrying it. As light as it was, it did still have some weight, and she would not be able to carry it forever.

The others had rushed, but she stepped carefully, taking her time so she didn't lose grip on the vessel. When she reached the others, they were already huffing in frustration.

"What happened?" Chloe spoke quietly, in case no one was ready to talk yet.

Mishti answered at once, her face in a tight glare. "Someone was digging through our things."

"You didn't catch the person?" Her heart skittered in her chest. Quintus had moved so fast, surely he had caught them.

But Mishti shook her head as her glare deepened.

The news hit Chloe in the gut. Quintus had fae speed. That same speed had allowed him to outrun his mortal father when Julian had tried to take his son's life. Then again, maybe it wasn't Julian himself who had come digging through their things.

They had seen with their own eyes that Julian had fae working for him now. He must have sent one of them.

"We should have known this would happen." Ludo dragged his hands down his face.

Just then, Quintus jogged back into their camp. He must have gone after the person, but his dejected face made it clear it had been fruitless. Even with his fae speed, he still had not caught anyone.

A huff burst from Mishti's nose at the sight of him. She must have been hoping he'd catch up to whoever had entered their camp, but now they all knew he hadn't.

Swallowing, Chloe turned to Ludo. "What do you mean we should have known this would happen? Why would we know?"

Ludo gestured vigorously at the vessel in her arms. "The cloud. It came right to us. That should have been our first clue that King Julian already knew exactly where we were."

Quintus's eyes widened and then he groaned.

It felt like a good moment to reach for Quintus's hand. She wanted to comfort him, but she wanted comfort from him too. How could they not be disturbed by someone, most likely a spy, who had entered their camp?

As least she could dispute Ludo's assumption. "I don't think the cloud came to us because Julian knew where we were. Remember how it followed us when we tried to fly away? I think he must have put magic in it that led it to us."

"So he used it to find us, then. Considering he just snuck into our camp, it is clear King Julian knows exactly where we are now."

"That was not my father," Quintus said. "If it were, I would have caught him."

"Ludo is right." Mishti spoke in a heavy voice, her hand still gripped around her sword. "That wasn't Julian, but *someone* knows where we are now, and that someone probably works for the king. We need to move."

Chloe raised both hands in front of herself, shaking her head. "Wait. Before we go anywhere, we need to figure out why that person was here. What were they looking for? And more importantly, did they find it?"

"Looking for?" Ludo said exasperated. "That spy probably just came to see if the cloud worked the way it was supposed to."

Clenching her jaw, she glared as hard as she could at Ludo. "We are all going to search our things. No arguments."

Stomping past him, she moved to her sleeping area first. Only once she started picking up her blankets and searching around the area did the others finally follow suit. No one spoke while they looked. Instead, the camp was filled with the sounds of shifting and clattering objects.

Ludo and Quintus finished searching the quickest, since they kept nearly all their things in their magical pockets that had infinite space. They soon moved to the weapons stash to see if anything had been tampered with there.

One by one, the Shields began approaching Chloe. Each one said the same thing. "I am not missing anything. Some of my things got moved, but nothing was taken."

And Quintus and Ludo soon reported the weapons stash hadn't even been touched. Mishti had made a mess of her own pile of daggers, bracers, polishing cloths, and other items. It didn't seem like Mishti even carried anything with her, so it was a surprise she'd managed to make such a mess with all of it.

Though Chloe didn't hope any of Mishti's things had gone missing, Chloe did wish to know why that spy had entered their camp. Hopefully this mess meant they finally had an answer.

"Still looking for something?" Chloe asked tentatively.

"No." Mishti wrinkled her nose at the mess, then grabbed her three favorite daggers and her sword and stuffed them into her belt. "I'm going to go check on the dragons. Maybe they were the target."

It wasn't like Mishti to leave a mess anywhere, especially when it included her weapons, but that just proved how shaken they all were.

After everyone had checked their things and found nothing missing, everyone checked a second time. They combed through their items more slowly, each trying desperately to find the reason their camp had been snuck into.

Since their searches still came up empty, Chloe had to admit perhaps Ludo had been right. Maybe the spy had entered their camp just to see if the cloud had worked. And since it hadn't, Mishti was also right that they needed to move.

Now Chloe had to think of a way to transport the large golden table that gave them food. Just as she prepared to stand at the head of camp to make the announcement, she caught sight of Quintus patting the outside of his coat.

Unease sprouted inside her belly. She took a step toward him and whispered, "What is it?"

He continued patting the front of his coat but also turned his gaze downward. "I cannot find my pencil, the one I use to sketch with. I must have dropped it."

"Quintus." She said the word in a rush of breath.

He waved a hand at her worry. "I do not think it was taken. I used the pencil to sketch the vessel. I had it over here, not over where the spy was. I am certain it must be here somewhere."

A ball of golden magic appeared on the palm of his hand. Using its light to see, he got to his knees and began searching the ground. Soon, he was crawling one-handed all across the area he'd been while crafting the vessel.

But he found nothing. By now the other Shields had gathered around him, helping him to search, but most of them stood with the same acceptance Chloe had in her heart.

Whether he wanted to admit it or not, they had finally discovered what the spy had taken from them.

She reached for the leather bag on her shoulder and pulled out her magical book. Opening it, she turned directly to the pages on the sacrificial ritual. She scanned the ingredients again. As she did, one stood out more poignantly than it had on her first reading.

An instrument of creation.

And Quintus had lost his pencil.

Mishti clapped both hands over her mouth. She'd been reading over Chloe's shoulder and must have just found the ingredient list.

"What?" Quintus said absently, still scanning the ground with his ball of golden magic held high.

"Julian has your pencil. He's going to use it in the ritual." Mishti's voice fumbled with fear cracking through it. She shook her head, her jaw clenching tight. "I should have realized we weren't safe. I should have insisted we move to a new location, even with the cloud following us."

"With the cloud following us," Chloe said gently, "that spy could have found us no matter where we went. It was better to destroy the cloud first. But now that we have, I think you're right. We do need to move."

Palpable tension buzzed in the night air. Quintus stared blankly at Chloe, his eyes blinking without emotion. The reality of what he had just lost took all spark from his demeanor. He stood then and glanced at the book in front of her. It only took a moment before his eyes filled with fear.

The golden specks in his dark eyes grew so dim, they seemed to disappear into his brown irises. His hand clamped over a fistful of the fabric at the bottom of his coat. It soon became twisted and tight as he clenched it.

That magical night she had shared with Quintus in the glittering valley seemed almost too far away to remember now. Even with the victory of capturing the cloud that was meant to make them forget everything, it still felt like Julian could never be defeated.

It felt like he would win. No matter how hard they tried.

They moved back to Rubyrise after that, but no one spoke as they did. They gathered their things and packed them onto their dragons. When Chloe pointed to the golden table, Quintus simply nodded and opened a door. He and Ludo then used their fae strength to lift the table and carry it through the door to their camp on Rubyrise.

One thing was certain, Julian was getting closer to accomplishing his goals, and so far, they had done nothing to stop him.

17

ANTICIPATION SURGED IN CHLOE'S VEINS as she rubbed the chill out of her arms. Sparkling mist hung lightly among the golden and ruby peaks of the mountains. The mist usually cleared out as the sun rose in the sky, but today, Mishti insisted they wake early and get started as soon as possible.

They were training the dragons again.

Jagged ruby rocks glinted beneath the sparkling mist. As the sun rose, the flaming rays of the sun would cast breathtaking gold and red hues across the area.

As before, they camped on a wide mountain ledge large enough to fit their camp and the dragons with some extra room to spare. Everyone was careful to stay back from the end of the ledge, where the land dropped off in a steep cliff.

Mishti directed the dragons to line up across the back of the ledge, where it curved upward to rise to a high mountain peak.

Chloe stood on one side of Shadow, her hand resting against the creature's golden neck. Quintus stood on the other side of their dragon, his hand stroking the scales just as Chloe's did. They stood at the very center of the line of dragons.

The other dragons had moved naturally to have Shadow in the center. Perhaps it was because the dragons had finally started truly bonding with their riders, or perhaps it was simply because of her large size, but the other dragons had started treating Shadow as a leader among them.

The bonding had been happening slowly, but since returning to Rubyrise, the Golden Shields had spent several days focused on that alone. Each Shield had a different method.

Mishti liked taking Temper out on long evening flights when the blue-scaled dragon could crackle like lightning against the dark sky. Chloe had a feeling a few of those night rides had brought Mishti to the Forest of the Wraiths to meet up with a certain wraith with blood-orange eyes.

Sofia and her dragon bonded by trying to catch little jeweled insects in the grass meadows at the bottom of Rubyrise. They both seemed happier while staying busy rather than sitting still.

Batu allowed his dragon to fly him to every river, lake, and waterfall in Crystalfall, where he said his dragon rolled and splashed in the sparkling water. The geometric patterns of silver and teal on the dragon's scales must have looked brilliant beneath the waves.

As more bonding occurred, more dragons were named. Sofia named her dragon Fidget. Chloe had expected something more like Crystal or Rainbow, since Sofia's dragon had scales that resembled faceted crystals in pale pinks and yellows, and its translucent wings refracted light, creating dazzling rainbows all around it. But once Sofia declared her dragon's name was Fidget, it suddenly seemed more perfect than any of the names Chloe had thought of.

Mahseer became the name of Batu's water-loving dragon. He named it after a type of teal-and-silver fish he'd seen back when he lived in the mortal realm.

Nearly all the dragons had names now, and when Mishti lined them up, the dragons moved without the same struggle they'd had during their last training sessions.

"First, we will practice aerial maneuvers," Mishti said in her loudest voice. She climbed atop her dragon and shouted again. "I want everyone to practice a loop, a dive, and then a barrel roll. Watch Temper and I do it first."

When she finished speaking, she sat down on Temper's stormy blue scales and grabbed onto the reins made from a blue ribbon. In a flash, Temper soared into the air. The dragon hovered high above for several moments, and then it began flying back toward the ledge with the rest of them.

About halfway down, Temper swooped upward in a tight curl, which then evolved to her back curving and her body flying backward. The backward motion turned even more until the large creature completed a full loop.

Mishti shouted praise for her dragon. After a celebratory yip, Temper then positioned her head downward and shot forward in a sudden dive. Mishti leaned her body close to her dragon's scales while wind whipped through her long, black braid.

Just before Temper slammed against the ground, Mishti directed him to pull upward. Once back high in the sky, the dragon performed an impressive barrel roll. That got an even louder shout of praise from Mishti.

The dragon seemed very pleased as it released a low, rumbling sound like an enormous cat purr.

Soon enough, Temper landed back on the ground. Mishti slid off the dragon's back but kept her hand on the chipped and bent scales. "Everyone onto your dragon's backs. I want to see what you can do."

Fear knotted in Chloe's belly, but it didn't squeeze too tight. She never would have attempted these aerial maneuvers on her own, but since it would help them train for the battle against Julian, she was happy to do it. And even more than that, she trusted Shadow to keep her safe.

Once in the air, she could feel how Shadow loved the rush of each move. The barrel rolls were her favorite, though she also liked the dives. Even though her dragon kept doing more and more dangerous moves, Chloe always felt safe. And she liked how Quintus sat close behind her, holding her tight during each maneuver.

As always, the moves came naturally to Shadow, but the other dragons were getting better too. They moved at impressive speeds and perfected the moves the longer they did them. Mahseer didn't move as fast as Batu wanted him to move. And Sofia's Fidget tended to start a little too fast, causing the dragon to have to re-adjust mid-move. But overall, the training was actually working. Little by little, the dragons were developing skills that would help them in the fight against Julian.

Despite the progress, three dragons and their riders continued to struggle more than the others. Roarke, Hilda, and Devro all fought with their dragons at nearly every turn. These three were also the only Shields who hadn't named their dragons yet.

Whenever those riders directed the dragons, the dragons seemed to take pleasure in doing the opposite of what they asked. They'd growl and whip their bodies, fighting against the commands. Roarke, Hilda, and Devro responded with angry shouts or miserable tears.

When Devro got thrown off his dragon during a barrel roll, Mishti decided it was time for a different exercise.

"Everyone back to the line while I set things up for the next session." Mishti shouted into the air, and then she turned to Ludo. "Go get the golden barrels Quintus crafted the other day."

Ludo scowled at her. "Am I your errand boy now? Why do I have to do it?"

She rolled her eyes at him. "Because I trust you, obviously."

He scoffed and opened his mouth for some retort, but then his head tilted as he touched a hand to his chest. "Wait, really?"

"Yes." A little exasperation filled her tone, probably because she wanted to cover up the sweetness of the moment. But even that exasperation couldn't hide the truthfulness of her words.

"Oh." Ludo stood a little taller and skipped off to gather the large golden barrels that were scattered at the edge of camp.

Once Shadow stood at the center of the line, Chloe and Quintus helped gather the barrels while the other dragons took their time getting into the line.

Chloe only moved a few barrels, but with their fae speed and strength, Quintus got all the others into place fairly quickly.

Now, Mishti stood in front of the line, giving directions once again. "Our next session is for fire breathing. Each of you will have a barrel your dragon will attempt to shoot with fire from above. Our dragons must control the intensity and direction of the fire breath for precise targeting."

As she climbed atop Temper to demonstrate, Chloe looked out at the barrels again. Most of them had been placed away from their sleeping mats and tents, but a few were rather close. Shadow and Temper were meant to aim for the ones closest to camp, but Hilda's dragon was supposed to aim for another close one.

Chloe bit her lip, eyeing Hilda's barrel as she climbed atop her dragon. Shadow needed hardly any direction at all to perfectly breathe fire directly at her barrel. Yellow flames with blue veins erupted from her mouth, hitting the golden barrel so hard it tumbled over to its side.

The sweet scent of lemon and vanilla that usually filled the air around Rubyrise got replaced by the smell of smoke and burnt soil.

At least Roarke's, Hilda's, and Devro's dragons had been pacified by the change in activity. They seemed to appreciate fire breathing much more than loops, dives, and barrel rolls. And the other dragons got better each time they aimed for their golden barrels.

Their improvements could easily be seen, all except for Roarke's, Hilda's, and Devro's dragons. Instead, their dragons seemed to get worse with each attempt. The longer they worked, the more frustrated their riders got. Soon, Roarke, Hilda, and Devro were hot with sweat and hair covering their defeated faces.

Chloe had just directed Shadow to fly back to the ground for a rest. Quintus sat with his legs on either side of Chloe, both of his arms around her waist. As they landed, he leaned in and brought his mouth close to her ear.

"They are getting worse than before. If we bring them to a fight at the castle, they could be more liability than help."

He didn't have to explain who *they* were. The more the dragons trained, the more obvious it was that Roarke, Hilda, and Devro had no bonds with their dragons.

Chloe nodded and started sliding off her dragon. Mishti stood nearby, already off Temper. She eyed the entire ledge where their camp sat.

Moving toward her, Chloe cleared her throat. "I think—"

"I know." Mishti caught her eye for a brief moment and then lifted her gaze to where Roarke's, Hilda's, and Devro's dragons shrieked in the sky. "But I think I have an idea."

Quintus looked at Chloe and shrugged.

In a loud shout, Mishti directed everyone and their dragons to rest. She carefully eyed Roarke's, Hilda's, and Devro's dragons, who all settled on the ledge as far away from camp as they could get.

Before the three of them could slump onto the ground, Mishti waved her arm and told Roarke, Hilda, and Devro to all join her. As they moved toward her, she gave a pointed look toward Chloe and Quintus. "You two stay here."

With a flourish, she turned and stomped toward the three Shields who had yet to bond with their dragons.

"What do you think she is going to do to them?" Ludo said, suddenly appearing at their sides. He wore a smirk like he couldn't wait to see what might unfold.

Quintus released a small chuckle. "She will probably simply tell them they will have to ride with other Shields on the way to the castle and then fight on the ground once we get there."

Instead of coming up with her own guess, Chloe narrowed her eyes at the small group. From this far away, she couldn't hear anything they said to each other.

Mishti wore her same stoic expression as always, but it did look a little tighter than usual. She kept stomping forward, taking the others to the very end of the mountain ledge, right where the cliff began.

The exact location probably wasn't all that important considering Mishti kept speaking intensely and pointing up toward the sky. She had probably only taken them to the edge like that so their conversation couldn't be heard by anyone else.

One by one, Roarke, Hilda, and Devro all looked into the sky where Mishti pointed. And one by one, they nodded with their gazes pointed downward.

Ludo snickered. "I would not want to be chastised by Mishti. Look at how downtrodden they are."

He said the words through a laugh, but just before he finished the sentence, Chloe's entire body froze.

Mishti lifted her arms, and in a movement as quick as a flash, she shoved Roarke, Hilda, and Devro right off the cliff.

Chloe's heart jumped into her throat as the three figures disappeared off the ledge. Each of them screamed in terror, clearly as shocked by Mishti's action as Chloe had been.

"They'll die," Chloe said in a hushed whisper. She whirled around, grabbing onto Shadow's reins. "You have to catch them before they hit the ground."

But even as she said the words, she already knew it was too late. Shadow sensed the fear in Chloe and reacted immediately. But the dragon had been digging in the black soil searching for tiny rubies. Even if she released her wings and started flying at once, it wouldn't be fast enough to catch the three Shields in time.

Just as those harrowing thoughts plagued Chloe's mind, she caught a flash of movement through the corner of her eye.

Dragons.

In the sky.

Her breath hitched as she ran forward to watch three dragons dive over the cliff. Roarke's, Hilda's, and Devro's dragons flew toward their riders. But would they get there in time?

Chloe forced herself to stumble forward until she could see over the edge of the cliff. The three Shields had nearly reached the ground and the dragons still had so far to fly before catching them.

Her stomach seized as she held her breath. What had Mishti been *thinking?* What had she hoped to accomplish with such a needlessly dangerous action?

Curling her fingers into tight fists, Chloe watched helplessly while the three Shields fell closer to the ground.

Hilda was going to hit first. She was mere feet from the bottom.

But then…

Her dragon, with its dark scales and the glints and sparkles on it that made it look like a sky full of stars, swooped in. The magnificent creature with lustrous purple horns just managed to catch Hilda on its back before the woman could smack against the jagged ruby rocks of the mountain.

Roarke's dragon caught him next. Its scales were sky blue now, but once the creature landed and brought its wings close to its back, the scales would turn a mossy green. Roarke held onto the dragon's back, his chest heaving as the dragon brought him higher into the air.

With a sweeping, graceful motion, Devro's dragon caught him last. The dragon's dark scales had sharp, angular features reminiscent of forged steel. Its wings gave off a thunderous sound as it flapped hard enough to catch Devro just in time.

Only once the three dragons came soaring back above the cliff and then landed safely on the ledge could Chloe move again. At once, she marched straight toward Mishti, heat filling her face.

Mishti caught sight of Chloe almost immediately. As soon as she marched close enough for speaking, Mishti gestured toward the three dragons, whose riders still clutched tight to their dragons' scales. "That should help with the bonding, I think."

"The—" Disbelief stopped Chloe from finishing her sentence. She shook her head and then shouted. "Are you crazy?"

Mishti looked at her with a steady gaze, showing no hint of remorse.

Chloe ground her teeth and then spoke even more intensely than before. "You pushed three people, three *fellow* Shields off a *cliff*? Just so they could bond with their dragons?"

Mishti lifted her chin in the air and looked supremely sure of herself. "You put me in charge of the dragon training." She shrugged, still with absolutely no guilt in her eyes. "I won't apologize for my methods."

Quintus and Ludo had joined them by now. When Mishti finished speaking, Ludo chuckled.

Chloe punched him in the arm for it.

His laugh stopped, but it did nothing to alter the amusement on his face.

She almost punched him again. And maybe she should punch Mishti for that matter.

But then Quintus pointed toward the sky. "Look."

They all glanced upward to see Devro's steely dragon completing a perfect barrel roll. That same move had gotten Devro thrown off his dragon and onto the ground earlier, but now dragon and rider seemed to be in perfect sync.

Chloe's mouth dropped in awe.

Mishti folded her arms over her chest and looked far too pleased with herself.

Only then did Chloe remember she was still upset with her friend. "That was insanely dangerous. You put their lives at risk and had no way of knowing their dragons would rescue them in time."

Mishti shrugged, looking less guilty than ever. "You're the one who told me danger is what helped you and Shadow bond.

If we have any chance at all against Julian, we don't have time to waste on slower methods of bonding."

Chloe might have tried to argue more, but it was pretty clear Mishti's plan had worked exactly as she had intended.

Just then, they heard Hilda shout from atop her soaring dragon. "Fly, Nova. Show me what your wings can do."

Raising an eyebrow, Mishti gave a pointed look at the rest of them. "Did you hear her say *Nova?*"

Scrunching up her mouth, Chloe huffed. "Yes, I heard. She finally named her dragon."

Quintus tapped Chloe on the arm twice, suddenly anxious to get her attention.

When she turned and followed his gaze, she found Ludo had a tiny glowing green sprite on the palm of his hand. It started to fly away just as Chloe had turned. It must have just delivered a message to Ludo, but she'd been so distracted, she hadn't noticed.

Ludo turned to her with a harried expression. "It was a message from Revyn."

"Your brother?" Chloe asked. They had met Revyn, and his beloved Clara, but they'd been exploring Faerie to see how it had changed since Clara had been here before. Were they done exploring now?

Ludo gulped. "They need our help."

18

Chloe gripped tight to Shadow's golden scales. They had decided all the Shields would go help Revyn and Clara. After Julian had just found them and used the cloud against them, Chloe thought it would be best if they stuck together. Luckily, Quintus, Mishti, and Ludo had all come to the same conclusion on their own, so she hadn't needed to convince them.

And since Roarke, Hilda, and Devro had finally bonded with and named their dragons, it took no effort at all to fly to their destination.

Ludo sat on Mishti's dragon with her, directing so that Temper could lead the way. Soon they landed in a wide valley near a lush grove of golden and emerald trees. It smelled of vanilla and lilacs and strawberries.

As they slid off their dragons, they were immediately greeted by a mortal, a high fae, and a small flying pixie.

Chloe recognized Plumia, the pixie she and Mishti had met right after Chloe had locked Quintus out of the court. That same pixie and her friends had done a favor for Chloe. The pixies had flown into the mortals' camp and attacked Portia and Julian, giving Chloe a chance to speak to the other mortals and ask them to join her and Mishti.

Of course, none of the other mortals had joined at that time, but that hardly mattered now that nearly all the mortals who still lived were now in the Order of the Golden Shields. In any case, seeing the pixie, Plumia, brought a good memory to Chloe's mind.

Revyn, Ludo's brother, wore a soldier's uniform with silver-and-blue brocade. His face looked brighter and happier than the last time they had seen him, probably due to all the time he'd recently spent with his beloved.

Clara stood in between him and Plumia. She no longer wore the black wedding dress she'd been in the last time they saw her, the dress she was meant to wear when marrying Julian. Luckily, that wedding had never taken place. Now, she wore a full skirt covered in a lovely pattern of white and pink roses on a maroon background. Her top was covered by a loose white blouse with wide sleeves and a fitted maroon vest. A magnificent pink pendant sat at the end of a beautiful necklace. Her dark hair was decorated with silver and pearl adornments.

Her sweet smile grew as she squeezed Revyn's upper arm. He returned the smile and then immediately pulled his brother into a tight bear hug. Ludo beamed as he returned the embrace. As soon as they stepped away from each other, Clara jumped forward to give Ludo a quick hug of her own. "We waited too long to see you again, Ludo" she said as she stepped away.

They all looked far too happy to see each other and seemed to have completely forgotten something was wrong. Considering Chloe knew nothing except that they needed help, she was eager to get more information.

Since the little family reunion had clearly distracted the others, Chloe turned instead to the pixie wearing a dress made of sparkling amethysts. "What was it you needed?"

She managed to finish the question, but the moment it left her lips, her mouth dropped open wide. A stunning tree with a solid gold trunk sat at the center of the valley where they stood. It had glimmering emerald leaves that swayed in the wind. When the emerald leaves clinked together, it created a sound almost like wind chimes.

Having been in Crystalfall as long as she had, Chloe was starting to get used to the excessive beauty of it. But though she had seen many golden trees with emerald leaves, this one immediately struck her as special. It seemed to have more life than the other trees, maybe even more life than her own self. But now that she thought about it, she vaguely remembered seeing this same tree while Quintus was locked out of Crystalfall. Still, it looked so much more magnificent now than it had then.

Plumia flew toward the tree, her wings jingling like tiny bells as she flapped them. "One of the branches from this tree was stolen. We need your help getting it back."

The tree still had Chloe under its trance, but Mishti had remembered to stay focused. She moved closer to the pixie, and asked, "Do you know where it is?"

Plumia let out a little sigh, which ruffled the golden curls cascading down her shoulders. "I assume it is at Crystalfall Castle. King Julian is the one who stole it."

Quintus sputtered at that declaration and took a step back.

"We know," Revyn said, shaking his head. "We have no idea how he became the king. He has always been our enemy, but now he has more power than ever."

All the color from Quintus's face drained at the sound of that. His gaze sank to the ground. "That is not what I…"

Guilt wracked the words, and Chloe wasn't about to let her beloved tell the truth so painful it prevented him from speaking. She'd explain what he couldn't. "It's our fault Julian is the king, but only because he tricked us. And it doesn't matter because we're still going to defeat him. We've been training our dragons, and they're getting so much more skilled. Hopefully it won't be long before we're strong enough to get rid of him."

Delight danced in Plumia's eyes for half a breath before worry overtook it. "If you can defeat him, then we can get into the castle to get the branch." Her eyes narrowed. "But how soon can you go after him? We *need* that branch back. We may need it before you defeat him. Can you help us get it back?"

The pain of remembering they had handed the crown to his father still shimmered in Quintus's eyes. That pain had turned his reaction, which might have been calm in normal circumstances, to one of anger. "Get it back? We have a king to defeat. We cannot waste energy trying to find a simple tree branch."

Plumia flashed her teeth and flew toward him aggressively, her anger matching his. She slammed her hands onto her hips. "It is not a *simple* tree branch."

The pixie flew now toward the incredible tree at the center of the valley. "Lifespark Tree gives life to the pixies." She reached a hand out and touched the golden tree trunk. When she did, both she and the tree gave off a soft golden glow. "If we do not repair this tree, then all pixies will die."

Chloe should have been struck with the weight of all they had to accomplish. Instead, she was struck with confusion. Her head tilted to the side. "Why would he steal a branch from your tree?"

Touching a hand to the pink pendant of her necklace, Clara slipped her hand into Revyn's. Her eyebrows pinched together as she spoke. "Julian knows stealing branches from Lifespark

Tree can destroy it. He has seen it before, back when he very first got to Faerie."

Chloe's eyes narrowed. "But why does he care about the pixies? Why would he want to destroy them?"

Plumia scrunched up her nose. "We have attacked him. You remember, do you not?"

That question was directed at Mishti, who answered with a nod. Of course Chloe also remembered when the pixies had attacked Julian and Portia. But so many things had happened since then. Why would Julian choose to attack them now?

Mishti glanced toward the lush grove of golden and emerald trees that sat above the valley where they stood now. She used her chin to point toward it. "Can you use a branch from another tree to replace the missing one? It doesn't have to be the exact same branch, does it?"

Clara and Revyn shared a knowing look between them. They must have dealt with this tree losing its branches before. Clara touched a branch on the tree, staring at it as she spoke. "The tree branch must go in exactly the right place, and it must be the right size and shape."

"Exactly the right place?" Ludo said with a scoff. Even if you found the branch that was stolen, no one could put it in exactly the same place as before. That is impossible."

"Not for me," Clara said with a shrug. Revyn threw her a wide smile at the sound of those words.

That seemed an impressive claim, but both Revyn and Plumia seemed convinced of her ability.

Touching her hand to the pink pendant on her necklace again, Clara continued. "I might be able to find a branch from another tree that is the right size and shape as well."

When Chloe and the other Shields stared wide-eyed at her, the dark-haired young woman simply shrugged again. "I'm very good with shapes and sizes."

That really did sound impossible, but Revyn and Plumia just nodded as if this sort of thing had already happened before. Shaking the impossibility of it from her mind, Chloe latched onto her earlier question that had still not been answered. "But why would he steal a branch from your tree?"

Plumia touched the tree again, and both she and the tree glowed for a moment. "I already told you. He knows it will destroy us."

Chloe nodded. "I understand that, but why now? Julian is amassing an army. He is preparing for a ritual. Why would he care about attacking you now?"

"Would another branch work?" Quintus asked suddenly. "If it is not the same branch, but it is the right size and shape and it is attached in the exact place, would it save it the tree?"

He stared at Revyn and Clara. Revyn touched a finger to his chin thoughtfully, but Clara just turned and looked at Plumia.

The pixie looked back at Clara and then stared at the tree for several flaps of her bell-like wings. Finally, she answered. "Lifespark would have to draw power from its twin tree. If the twin is at full power, it might work."

The words felt like a punch to Chloe's gut, though it took a moment for her mind to catch up and understand why. Once it did, her head snapped up, and she stared Plumia right in the eyes. "What did you just say?"

Plumia flew a little closer. "It must be at full power. If it is damaged like Lifespark is, then—"

"No, not that." Chloe gulped. "You said its *twin*?

Plumia raised an eyebrow. "Yes, Lifespark is a twin tree. Its match sits at the center of the Forest of the Wraiths."

Chloe already had her hand inside the leather bag hanging on her shoulder. She tore it out as she said the name of the tree

Chandril had brought them to when they were last in the forest. "Undulle Tree?"

Plumia nodded, clearly completely unaware of what she had just revealed.

Furiously flipping through the pages of her magical book, Chloe eventually found the page on the ritual Julian planned to perform. Her finger trailed over one of the ingredients as her stomach sank down, down, down.

She couldn't have guessed what it meant the first time she had read the words, but now, it had all become clear.

Opposing branches of life and death.

She swallowed hard while the realization stabbed at her every nerve. After a heavy breath, she turned her gaze back to the pixie. "I know why he took your branch."

Revyn seemed almost annoyed by the ominous way she had said those words. He lifted one arm as if in a question. "Can you help us find it?"

His beloved stood beside him and leaned ever so slightly forward. "Or perhaps you can help us find a branch from another tree that will work."

"No." Chloe closed her eyes, allowing herself one single moment to grieve. But when she opened her eyes, she was ready to act. "Mishti, get the dragons and the other Shields ready. We have to leave immediately."

Everyone stared at her. Mishti raised an eyebrow, clearly confused, but not enough to ignore the intensity in Chloe's voice. With a nod, Mishti turned and moved toward the other Shields.

Quintus stood at Chloe's side, reading over her shoulder. It only took him a moment to discover what she already had. When he did, he looked at Chloe, his voice wavering. "We need to find out if my father already stole a branch from Undulle Tree."

Chloe nodded. "And if he hasn't yet, then we need to do everything we can to protect it."

Irritation flashed in Plumia's eyes as the little pixie flew closer. She soon hovered on the other side of Chloe where she could see the book clearly. Soon, she sucked in a gasp.

"Bloodstone Convergence." Plumia whispered the words and her face fell. She must have known what power the ritual would give to Julian.

Placing a closed fist over her heart, Plumia's lips pressed into a thin line. "Go. We will find another branch and try to attach it to save our tree. You need to protect Undulle."

Chloe nodded as she stuffed the book back into her bag. She grabbed Ludo by the wrist and dragged him to where the dragons and Shields were waiting. In as few words as possible, she explained that Julian now had yet another ingredient he needed for the ritual.

And they needed to get to the Forest of the Wraiths to stop him from claiming another one.

19

THE HAIR TINGLING CHILL IN the air typical of the Forest of the Wraiths greeted Chloe and the rest of the Golden Shields as their dragons made their way into the small clearing near the front of the forest. Night had already fallen by the time they arrived, and so only the ragged silhouettes of the trees could be seen. Shadow's large body trembled as she landed on the black soil outside the forest. Even though Chloe tried to reassure her by caressing her golden scales, the dragon still did not relax. It was the same for the other dragons and their riders.

Chloe sighed as she climbed off her dragon with Quintus. It was obvious she and the others were not going to enjoy their time in the forest of the undead, but they had no choice but to be here. They had to protect Undulle Tree at all costs.

If they didn't, Julian would be able to steal a branch, putting him one step closer to carrying out the ritual and gaining ultimate power.

They could not let that happen.

The claw-like trees towered into the sky and the branches stretched toward each other, as if protecting the wraiths from the rest of Faerie. Chloe's chest squeezed knowing they would soon walk into a place without the warmth and shine the rest of Crystalfall had. Instead, they'd enter a place of cold and dust After making sure Shadow had calmed slightly, Quintus walked forward to hold Chloe's hand in his own.

She took it gratefully. As her fingers slipped around his, her heart lifted, despite the moody chill permeating the air around them. Unlike the last time they had been to the forest, Quintus acted more like himself. Fire glinted in the golden specks in his eyes, rather than the dim despondent look that had been there on their last visit. He looked ready to fight.

Knowing he did not carry that despairing melancholic air around him now was more than enough to help her move forward into the forlorn forest ahead. She mentally prepared herself to climb between the frightful trees onto the narrow path through them.

"Remember the last time we came here?" She turned to look at the others. Their faces had fallen, looking dismal at the prospect of going into the Forest of the Wraiths. She stood up onto the balls of her feet, raising her voice so all could hear. "We cannot refer to the king by name. The wraiths do not like it when we say his name. Also, no matter what they offer you, no matter what they promise you, do not offer your memories to them. It will cost much more than you realize."

No one spoke, but they nodded fervently. Turning back to the trees, she climbed over branches coated with layers of powdery dust that only enhanced the listlessness in the air. Quintus moved a few steps ahead, watching carefully for anything that might cause harm. He constantly turned back, offering an arm if she ever had to step over a log or a boulder.

Not long after they entered, feathery whispers floated through the air. The wraiths slowly eased through the shadows, climbing across branches and looking out from behind tree trunks and large bushes. Because their translucent bodies blended in easily with the shadows and their small wispy frames made them hard to see, it was their glowing eyes Chloe used to tell them apart.

Chloe waited for them to approach. Unlike before, she had not come here for safety. She needed to tell them why she and the other Shields were here in the forest. About the possible danger.

But still, the wraiths stayed back in their trees and bushes.

Chloe knew what to say to make them come closer. Taking a moment to breathe and steady her breath, she then spoke as lazily as she could. "I suppose this spot is good enough. Let's all rest for a bit, shall we?"

Quintus tilted his head in confusion, but she threw him a look as quickly as she could, hoping he would understand to just play along. The wraiths couldn't know the Golden Shields needed their help finding Undulle Tree again. If the wraiths got any inkling that the Shields needed help, they would immediately demand a memory.

So Chloe did her best to act like everything was going according to plan and that they needed nothing from the wraiths. Quintus gave the slightest nod as understanding lit in his eyes.

The other Shields also started playing along. They moved about quietly, clearing the forest floor in preparation to sleep. No one showed any concern or any attention at all to their undead hosts.

Soon enough, the wraiths left their trees and the bushes to come closer. Their eyes glowed bright in the dark.

Chandril stepped out from behind a gangly tree, and Chloe gasped at the sight of him.

He looked even more different from when they saw him before. His skin was more substantial than the last time, almost as if its sheen was gradually being torn away. But most striking of all, his blood orange eyes did not glow as brightly as the eyes of the wraiths surrounding him. At one time, his eyes had glowed the brightest of all, but now they looked almost like the eyes of a high fae. He walked toward Mishti, reaching out to hold her. His fingers stretched and were clearly not as long as before.

"He has changed so much," Quintus whispered into Chloe's ear.

She nodded. How strange it was. The wraiths had been stealing memories probably since Faerie began, and yet, the memories had never changed any of them. But they had always taken the happiest, most joyful memories. The best days of a person's life. Chandril, of course, had been the only wraith to ever do something different. Mishti had convinced him to take the memory of her worst day. She claimed the pain of that memory would make his joyful memories that much better.

Now the difference was clear to be seen. By only taking happy memories, the other wraiths were translucent and empty. Undead. But Chandril? With each passing day, he looked more and more *alive*.

Would the other wraiths ever desire bad memories like Chandril had taken? Or would they always be content to exist as undead, empty beings?

If they did desire painful memories, they would not get them from the Shields. Chloe would watch her people carefully to stop any exchange. Luckily, none of the Golden Shields had succumbed yet to any of the wraiths' lavish promises in exchange for memories. And Chandril would never share Mishti with any of his kind, not only because she wouldn't agree, but also because he had developed a tender spot for her and had become territorial.

One of the wraiths came forward, wearing a full skirt and silky blouse that were both as substantial as smoke. It was the same wraith who had spoken to them during their first night in the forest, the one who didn't believe they could beat Julian. Chloe glanced toward Chandril. Last time, he'd done most of the talking for the wraiths, but now, he simply moved closer to Mishti and glanced back at the wraith who had stepped forward.

The woman had red glowing eyes and sharp red fingernails at the ends of her extra-long fingers. "We know why you are here." Her barely audible voice was like her body, as light as a feather.

"You know?" Chloe tightened her hand in Quintus's. Were they too late? Had Undulle Tree been violated just as the pixies' Lifespark Tree had? Her stomach writhed, waiting for the bad news.

"You came for Undulle Tree." The wraith's voice did not contain the rise and fall of emotions. It sounded as dead as everything else in the forest.

"How did you know that?" Quintus asked, his eyes narrowing.

The wraith's red eyes glowed brighter. "We have known from the beginning."

Chloe wanted to smack the wraith, although it might not do anything to such a wispy form. Why hadn't they shared the items needed for the ritual if they knew them? Why did they have to be so cryptic? Anger burned in her belly, but nothing could overcome the twisting and curling of fear. She held her breath, waiting for the wraith to deliver bad news.

Tipping her chin into the air, the wraith with glowing red eyes continued. "We know the king needs a branch from our tree for his ritual. We are already using all our resources to guard it heavily. He would not get past us." She snorted before continuing, her lips curling in distaste. "We are not as foolish and careless as the pixies."

Relief washed over Chloe, flooding out both the fear and anger inside her. Perhaps she should have realized the wraiths would be in a better position than the pixies. As undead creatures with memory magic, they had not lost their memories of Crystalfall the way everyone else had. Thanks to Clara and Revyn, the pixies were only just beginning to remember Crystalfall before it had been destroyed.

Just then, Chandril took a step closer to Mishti. "We are right, are we not? You came here because you are worried about Undulle Tree?"

Relieved, Chloe turned to Chandril. She preferred to speak to him than to the other wraith with glowing red eyes. "Yes, that's why we're here. I'm glad you're protecting your tree already, but we came to offer our help too."

Hissing broke out through the forest, loud and harsh before she even finished speaking. Some of the wraiths drifted closer, resentment shining bright in their eyes. Instinctively, Quintus stepped in front of her, blocking her view of the wraiths. His body was poised to defend her. Like she had done countless times, and to his disapproval, she stepped away from his protection so she could see the wraiths. They had not moved any closer, but their eyes were still filled with heat.

Anger vibrated through the wraith with glowing red eyes. "You think we are incapable of protecting what belongs to us?

You insult us with such an implication." She turned to Chandril, as if he was part of the Golden Shields. "Do you see these people you call friends? Do you see the people you choose to defend?"

Chandril's nostrils flared in response.

Before he could say anything, Chloe rushed to speak. "No, I did not mean to imply that at all. I would never want to insult you." She breathed in quickly trying to calm herself. To fix this, she needed just the right words to dispel the anger that had saturated the atmosphere.

"I only offered our help because—" She paused, grateful she had caught herself before she mentioned Julian's name. "The king is not only terrible, he is also very cunning and crafty. He is a master at deception. You remember him from before. Surely you remember just how tricky he can be. If we are to outsmart him, then we must be a thousand steps ahead of him. We cannot ever assume we're safe. We must take even more protective measures than we think are necessary."

Because the wraiths had calmed, she found the courage to say something she had never thought she would say to them. "Most important, we cannot afford to be divided. To stop him, we must be united. Only then do we stand a chance against him. We should do more than just help you protect your tree. We need to create an alliance between your people and mine. From now on, we need to work together to defeat the king."

The wraiths glanced at one another, silently asking each other if anyone agreed with her proposition. Their wraith women, who seemed to be a leader of sorts, swiped a translucent hand across her forehead and then nodded to the other wraiths. Then she turned to Chloe. "We wraiths need to discuss what you have proposed. We will return once we have made a decision."

As she finished speaking, she turned without waiting for a reply. The other wraiths climbed across branches and ducked behind bushes until they had disappeared from view. Chandril reluctantly left Mishti's side and joined the rest of them.

Too exhausted to worry about the wraiths' discussion, Chloe plopped down on the forest floor and stretched her legs out in front of her. Quintus did the same. His gaze held a smile as he lowered his face to kiss her temple. Despite her exhaustion, butterflies fluttered in her belly. She reached close to him. He smelled like parchment and musky vanilla. She deeply inhaled the intoxicating scent.

His nose nuzzled her hair above her ear, and he spoke to her in a gentle tone. "That was impressive you calmed the wraiths enough to consider an alliance, especially when they looked ready to attack. I would not have let them hurt you, but you managed to subdue them on your own. You seem to have a knack for inspiring others to join our cause."

"Even I'm a little surprised I proposed an alliance. It felt right and came out on its own before I even thought about whether it was a good idea or not. I do think it was a good idea now, but it doesn't matter unless they choose to let us help them." Her gaze fixed onto the forest ahead. Hopefully the undead creatures would accept their help.

What if they didn't? Julian must have known the wraiths would try to protect Undulle Tree. He was probably already devising a plan to get past those protections. The only advantage they'd have was if they added even more protections Julian wouldn't expect.

Soon predatory glowing eyes seemed to float in the air around them. The wraiths drifted out from their hiding places, their bodies melting into the shadows. Their expressions looked as frightening as always, giving no indication as to what they had decided.

Chloe turned to Chandril as he walked to Mishti's side, but even *his* face explained nothing. Mishti stared at Chandril, seeming to see much deeper into his eyes than anyone else could.

Turning back to the other wraiths, Chloe got to her feet. The translucent creatures gathered in front of the Shields. She absently dusted soil from her skirt, waiting for the first words to be spoken.

The wraith with glowing red eyes and full skirt came forward.

Unease rolled like a storm in Chloe's gut. Only two outcomes could come of this meeting.

Either the wraiths would accept their help or they would not.

But if Julian got a branch from Undulle Tree, he would have everything he needed for the ritual. Everything except Quintus.

They could not let Julian get the branch. Hopefully the wraiths understood that as deeply as she did.

20

CHLOE'S CHEST ACHED AS SHE waited for the wraith's decision. Her fingers curled into fists as she stared.

Finally, the wraiths' spokesperson had mercy on them. Her red eyes glowed as she cleared her throat. "We have talked amongst ourselves, and we have come to a conclusion."

With her heart pounding in her chest, Chloe leaned forward. Quintus reached for her hand, communicating wordlessly that he had as much tension as her.

The wraith continued. "Even though we are fully confident in our ability to protect Undulle, we know better than to underestimate the king. We want him defeated. After how he violated and stole our magic, we want him destroyed at all costs. We are ready to swallow our pride and accept your help."

In a rushed exhale, Chloe realized she had been holding her breath since the wraith started speaking. Relief trickled through her. But just before she could express her appreciation for their decision, the wraith with glowing red eyes raised her hand.

"On one condition." The words sent a chill through the air.

Chloe froze. What condition could they be asking for now?

Memories. Her blood seemed to stop running as the truth settled in. They couldn't lie, just like any fae creature, so they clearly *did* want Julian destroyed. But it had been naïve to believe that was all they cared about. They must have seen how desperate she and the other Shields were to protect Undulle Tree. Of course the wraiths would use that to their advantage.

She already knew there was no way she could agree to their demands. There was no way she would subject the people trusting *her* with their welfare into giving wraiths their memories, even if it was for a good cause. She'd never be able to look her people in the eyes if she dared to force them into something like this.

Closing her eyes, the bitter taste of defeat spread over her tongue.

Another way, she thought to herself as she tried to remain calm. She would have to find another way.

There had to be another way besides giving memories.

"What is your condition?" Chloe's voice faltered over the words, no matter how she tried to steady it.

The eyes of the wraiths glowed brighter in the dark. It was obvious the translucent beings before them relished this moment.

Finally, the spokesperson steepled her fingers that were twice as long as a mortal's under her chin. "We require that you do not do anything in this forest without our consent. Not a single action. This is our forest, and that must be acknowledged, even while we work with you."

"Of course." Chloe blurted the words out before her brain fully processed what she had said. Relief burst into her chest, filling it with warmth.

Her heart danced in joy and surprise that the wraiths had demanded sovereignty over the forest and not memories. It showed her how calculating they could be. They must have considered asking for memories, the opportunity too great for them to ignore, but they must have realized the Golden Shields would not cooperate with that stipulation.

At least this one thing had worked in their favor. Julian had already gathered many fae to help him, they didn't even know how many, but now the Shields had done something similar. They had forged their first alliance. For the first time since they entered the forest, the other Golden Shields broke into excited chatters. Even Ludo smiled, his grumpiness gone completely.

Chandril turned to Mishti, his lips widened to reveal white teeth. They had once been frighteningly sharp, but now even his teeth looked different too. Mishti leaned closer to him, her shoulder brushing up against his.

Chloe stood tall and addressed the wraiths. "I am certain this alliance will benefit us both. We are glad you chose to partner with us." It was the closest she could get to saying *thank you* without owing a debt to anyone. She looked straight at the wraith with glowing red eyes, then turned her gaze to each wraith around them so they would know they were all included in the appreciation. "And we agree, we will not make a single decision without consulting you as long as we are inside your forest."

"Fine." The wraith nodded her head, her body so translucent she almost seemed like nothing more than a pair of glowing eyes bobbing up and down. "Now we have decided that, what is your plan?"

Quintus answered this question. "We should add a protective barrier around the tree, one created through our bond." He gestured toward Chloe.

They hadn't talked about this, but she instinctively knew this would be the plan. She knew it the same way she knew Faerie sometimes spoke to her. It was a simple feeling in her gut.

"Do you need anything besides your magic?" the wraith asked.

Reaching into her leather bag, Chloe pulled out her magical book. "I'll need some herbs, but I can conjure those. I wonder if I might need a memory elixir though. Since memories are the magic of wraiths, one of your elixirs might help to strengthen the enchantment over the tree."

A sharp hiss released from the wraith's mouth. Several other wraiths hissed too. Even Chandril hissed, stepping forward with a scowl on his face.

They had gained a tenuous trust between their two groups, but this might have pushed things a little too far. Chloe dropped her book back into her bag and raised both hands, as if in surrender. "I will not study the elixir. I won't use it to take a memory, and I won't try to learn how it works or anything."

Only Chandril's expression softened. Every other wraith wore distrust, many of them hissed again.

Taking a breath, she did her best to explain. "When I use magic to conjure things like herbs or tinctures, I must already know everything about the ingredients. In order to conjure a memory elixir, I would have to understand how it is made, how it works, what ingredients are used. Everything."

Several wraiths clenched their hands into tight fists as they stepped forward, closing in around her.

She gulped and raised her hands a little higher. "But if you *give* me an elixir, I don't need to know anything about it. I can use it to strengthen the enchantment around the tree, but I won't know exactly how it works or anything like that."

All around her, translucent wraith fists unclenched, but they continued to glare and breathe through gritted teeth.

Her voice lowered to one just barely louder than a whisper. "I would never try to steal your magic the way the king did."

Only three of the wraiths stepped back. The one with the flowing skirt and the glowing red eyes put her hand on her hip. "But why do you need a memory elixir at all? Can you not protect our tree without it?"

Chloe bit her bottom lip. "Yes, of course we can still protect the tree without it. But memory magic belongs to the wraiths. And Undulle Tree belongs to the wraiths too. I am certain at least some component of your magic will be the most powerful ingredient we can use to protect your tree."

Some of the creatures still looked ready to stab her a dozen times, but at least Chandril nodded.

The wraith with glowing red eyes narrowed them. "What if a wraith is the one to pour the elixir?"

Relief made Chloe's voice husky. "Yes, that should work. I'll tell you when and where to pour it, but that way I don't even have to touch it."

At last, the other wraiths relaxed enough that Chloe could breathe properly.

She gave an awkward nod at them and pulled out her magical book again. She trusted her magic, especially when she'd be using the magic of her bond with Quintus, but it couldn't hurt to read as much as she could about enchantments before they began.

While she read, some of the wraiths disappeared into the thicket of the dusty forest. Others climbed branches and sat on long roots to watch her and the others with her.

More than a few shivers went through the shoulders of the Golden Shields in the area, but they tried to rest on tree trunks and boulders while they waited. Even Quintus had a stiffer back than usual. He came to Chloe's side, reading over her shoulder. But through the corner of her eye, she could see how his gaze kept flicking through the surrounding area, eyeing the wraiths.

Her fingers gripped her book much too tightly. Every time she went to turn a page, she had to stretch out the sore muscles.

The only two people who appeared relaxed were Mishti and Chandril. A light smile sat on her lips. In one hand, she held the end of her long braid where it had been fastened with a leather string. With the other hand, she twirled the tail of the braid over one finger. Her gaze locked onto Chandril, devouring all his words as if they gave her life.

He stood in front of her with his shoulder pressed into the tree trunk at his side. A lopsided grin kept emerging as his arms gestured to punctuate whatever story he currently told. Most telling, he found little ways to reach for Mishti as often as he could. First, he had to fix a strand in her braid, then he had to pluck away a fleck of dust from her shoulder, then he smoothed a wrinkle from her sleeve. Even with his shoulder against the tree trunk, Chandril managed to move a little closer to her with each touch.

"Do you think we should stay here after we create the enchantment?" Quintus had moved close enough to rustle the hair at Chloe's ear with his words.

Her heart skipped as heat stung the tips of her ears. She turned slightly, feeling more than seeing that his face hovered mere inches away from hers. It suddenly seemed like a very good moment to throw the book to the ground and wrap her arms around him. She could envision him pulling her close and dipping her backward as he kissed her passionately.

Closing her eyes and shaking her head, she attempted to expel that thought from her mind. This was definitely not the time for such ideas.

But when she glanced back at his face, the smirk on his lips made it clear he knew exactly what she had envisioned. Or maybe he had simply seen her blush and knew he had caused it.

She cleared her throat before answering, still trying to empty her mind. "I don't know. Part of me wants to stay and watch over Undulle Tree, but part of me wants to go back to our camp in Rubyrise." Her lips twitched with a smile. "You and I might get more privacy back at our camp."

The effect of her words came before she had even finished the sentence. His chest expanded with a heavy breath. Greed filled his eyes. At his sides, his fingers moved almost imperceptibly, but she could feel through their bond how he wanted to reach for her. To do *more* than reach for her.

She might have raised herself onto her tiptoes and stolen a kiss right then.

Except, before she could do anything, strange words tumbled from his mouth in a rush. "I have something I need to…ask…" As quickly as the first words came out, they suddenly stopped again. He shook his head, a crease forming between his eyebrows while he tried to find the right words. "Give you. I have something I need to give you."

Her lips curled upward as she brought her book closer to her chest. This would be a fun conversation.

21

Batting her eyelashes up at Quintus, Chloe asked, "You have something you need to give me? Something more than that magical harp and the twinkling lights? I don't know if you'll ever be able to top those."

It didn't matter that she'd been trying to tease him, he stared at her with such focus that her heart beat faster in her chest. He leaned in closer, his forehead nearly brushing against hers. Reaching out, his hand found her elbow. He stroked his fingers across the back of her arm just once, but that was all it took.

One single touch, a simple one even, and it felt like he had her enveloped in his arms. It felt like his presence owned every part of her. That one tiny touch sent a shiver all through her body. Her fingers faltered, nearly dropping the book in her hands.

But as much as she longed for him, the look in his eyes made it clear he wanted her even more. His body seemed to nearly shake with the effort of keeping only one hand on her. His gaze raked over her, looking at what he could not touch.

His jaw ticked, opening and closing at strange intervals, clearly trying to speak but not having the words to do so.

It hit her then. He hadn't meant to bring this up now. He stumbled over his words, failing to explain. But when she had blushed at him, it had apparently forced the words out of his mouth, even when he wasn't ready to say them.

Was it a good sign he wanted her so badly? Or should she be worried he had worked so carefully to hold this back?

She swallowed hard and looked straight into his eyes. "What is it?"

"We are ready." A wispy voice drifted through the area, acting like a wall between her and Quintus. He jerked his hand away from her elbow and turned toward the voice.

The wraith with glowing red eyes and the flowing skirt stood before them with a wraith on either side of her. She had been the one to speak.

On her right side stood a male with a misty blue vest and glowing purple eyes. He stuffed his hand into his pocket. "We have discussed your idea to use a memory elixir in the enchantment." With a flourish, he retrieved from his pocket a crystal bottle stoppered with a cork. Inside it swirled a teal liquid mixed with a black and glittering liquid that almost looked like stars in a night sky. He lifted the elixir high for all to see. "We agree."

On the left side of the wraith with glowing red eyes stood a male wraith with a shaved head and bronze earrings. His green robe looked as translucent as his skin. The moment the other wraith finished speaking, he stepped forward. "We agree, but only on the condition that a wraith will pour the liquid."

The wraith with glowing red eyes nodded. "Yes, Zael is correct. A wraith must administer the elixir."

"Of course," Chloe responded with a hurried nod.

Considering the last person who had stolen their memory magic was the man who destroyed Crystalfall, and that he had used it to extend his own life, she completely understood their hesitancy to share an elixir. But in this case, they didn't need to worry. Unlike Julian, she had no intention to use the elixir for anything but protecting them.

"Lead the way, Nilyx," the wraith with the green robe—Zael—said to the wraith with glowing red eyes.

Spinning her flowing, wispy skirt, Nilyx turned and gestured down a path. "We will now take you to Undulle Tree."

At the sound of these words, the wraiths lying on tree branches and hidden in the shadows emerged. They formed a circle around the Golden Shields, surrounding them on all sides as they began to traipse down the path with Nilyx leading the way.

The sound of boots hitting the dusty soil filled the air as they moved deeper into the gloomy forest.

Even before they entered the clearing, the smell of decay gradually saturated the air. They were getting close. Just as Lifespark Tree gave life to the pixies, the decrepit Undulle Tree gave undeath to the wraiths.

Only a short while later, Nilyx led them into the clearing with a tree much larger than the others. They had seen Undulle Tree before, but the sight of it was still enough to catch Chloe's breath. Its golden, skeletal branches stretched toward the sky like bony fingers. The emerald leaves were clearly green and glittering like all the other leaves in Crystalfall, but these appeared as translucent as the wraiths themselves. The tree had no movement in its branches or leaves, despite a fluttering wind around them. Instead, it stood lifeless, giving off a slight chill.

She tried to swallow, which didn't work well since her tongue had gone as dry as paper. The tree loomed over the clearing like a dark sentinel. Its gnarled roots pierced through the black soil beneath it. Though the tree trunk was made of gold, it appeared darker than the other golden trees, blending seamlessly into the shadows of the night.

Chloe's hands rubbed over her arms that had been prickled with goosebumps. Of course she had known there was a stark contrast between Lifespark Tree and Undulle Tree, but having visited one after the other, she felt that difference more acutely.

To look at Undulle was to confront the very essence of mortality itself. It was to feel the chill of undeath, how it could not die but how it also lacked life. To be undead was to be neither alive nor dead. It was to be empty. A wispy vessel for an empty soul.

Shivering, she glanced once more at the wraiths around her. No wonder they took memories from others. It was the only way their lifeless beings could feel anything somewhat similar to life. But since they only ever took the best days, and never knew any sort of pain or suffering, they still knew almost nothing about what it meant to be alive.

She forced herself to take a deep breath before removing her leather bag from her shoulder. Even with the magic that made it weightless, she didn't want any distractions while she did this magic.

Without a word, Quintus moved until he stood across from her. They stood near Undulle, but far enough away that they could release an enchantment from their fingertips that would envelope it completely while they stayed outside of the enchantment.

She eyed the area again and then moved her hand in a brushing movement. "Ludo, you, Batu, and Sofia need to back up slightly. We don't want anyone inside the enchantment we're about to create. Undulle Tree should be the only thing inside it."

Turning, she noticed a few wraiths also needed to move. But once she opened her mouth, they immediately stepped back without her having to say a word.

Quintus glanced over the same area, confirming they had enough space. After a short nod, he turned back to the crowd gathered near them. "Where is the memory elixir? Whoever is going to pour it needs to be ready to act on our signal."

"Zael," the wraith with glowing red eyes, Nilyx, said.

With a nod, Zael took a step forward. His feather-thin green robe fluttered around his short and slender frame. His eyes glowed bronze, nearly matching the earrings he wore.

With him awaiting the signal, Chloe and Quintus were finally ready.

Chloe held out both arms. Quintus, standing directly in front of her, took hold of her forearms with his strong, skilled hands. Turning her wrists slightly, she grabbed onto his muscled forearms with her own hands.

It only took a moment of concentration before the tattoos under her eye began to tingle. After another few moments, their joined arms and hands glowed with the warmth of magic. Closing her eyes, she drew from the magic that bound her to Quintus. As it pulsated through her, she then felt it grow inside him.

They didn't have to speak to know what to do. Even with her eyes closed, she could feel glittering golden magic shooting out from Quintus's fingertips. Instinctively, she knew the magic flowed upward, slowly forming a dome over Undulle Tree.

While he worked, her mind began to spin. She envisioned herbs and crystals being crushed into a fine powder, which she then envisioned being sprinkled over the glittery golden dome until the magic and the powder combined. The air crackled with electricity the moment she imagined her concoction combining with Quintus's magic. Energy swirled through the dome inside her mind, turning the golden magic into silver, then blue, then green, pink, bronze. It shifted and pulsed as a spectacular holographic glow.

"Now." Chloe whispered the word, keeping her eyes closed so she could better concentrate. "Pour the elixir at the very base of the dome. My magic will help to combine it with the enchantment."

Her words were followed by a rustling of fabric. She assumed it was Zael unstoppering the crystal bottle. But after several moments, her magic sensed nothing of the memory elixir. Had he poured it?

"Zael!" Nilyx shouted the name, as much as possible with her thin and wispy voice.

Zael muttered something in response, but Chloe couldn't make it out. Had he moved away while their eyes were closed? She reached out with her magic, seeking the elixir through the soil.

Again, Zael muttered quiet words, but she put all her concentration into trying to find the elixir.

Aches burned through her forearms from the exertion. She had squeezed her eyes shut so tight stars appeared behind her eyelids. A few beadlets of sweat began dripping down her temples. Even her knees were starting to knock together.

But then… Was that it? Her magic latched onto something and pulled it in toward the dome. Another droplet of sweat trickled down her face, but it was working. She managed to get bits of the elixir into the dome, though she might not be able to get all of it. The effort of getting just this little bit had nearly drained her.

"Ready." Zael's voice rang out, and soon, she could hear liquid splashing just at the edge of the dome.

Her magic reached for it at once and drew it into the enchantment. It felt… different. The other elixir had felt powerful and vibrant. This one also felt powerful but more like an echo than a sound. Still, she drew it into the enchantment all the same. Since she knew nothing about memory elixirs, she had to assume it only felt different because a different person had created it. Each wraith probably created their own special elixirs that had different looks and feelings.

But she couldn't think about that right now. Instead, she had to finish the enchantment. Her fingers ached from holding onto Quintus so tightly. He probably had red marks on his arms from her hands, but his fae healing would take care of them quickly once they were done.

The holographic dome flowed with magical energy. It breathed, almost like fire, intertwining with the natural energy of Undulle to form a cocoon of protection around the wraiths' tree.

At last, a final pulse vibrated through the enchantment, and Chloe knew it was done. Her eyes flew open as her chest heaved with exertion. Sweat trailed down her hairline, but satisfaction filled her heart. She glanced at Quintus, who appeared just as exhausted as her. Still, a smile creased his lips upward as his gaze locked onto the tree. She smiled too.

They had done well.

Relief burned bright on the face of everyone surrounding them, both wraith and Golden Shield. They had all done this. They had worked together. And maybe, just maybe, if they continued in unity like this, Julian would begin to taste fear.

Maybe he'd begin to feel the heat of the evil things he had done to them.

She, Quintus, the Golden Shields, the wraiths, the pixies, and even the rest of Faerie. They had all been smeared by his treacherous ways.

They had all suffered terribly.

But now it would be different. Now they had protected this tree, putting a stop to his sacrificial ritual forever. They finally had a chance at defeating him.

It was time.

It was time to make Julian suffer too.

22

WHEN CHLOE AND QUINTUS DROPPED their hands away from each other and stepped back, everyone around them cheered. The Golden Shields cheered loud and grateful. The wraiths let out strange whistles that sounded like wind trying to fit through too tight an opening. But even making a strange sound, it was clear the wraiths appreciated this victory.

They had stopped Julian from getting a branch of Undulle Tree. They had stopped the ritual once and for all.

The wraith with a blue vest and glowing purple eyes turned to Chandril. "We are lucky you convinced us to let these Golden Shields into our forest. If we had killed them like we wanted, our tree might be in danger."

A jolt wracked through Chloe's gut at the sound of those words. The wraiths had wanted to *kill* her and the other Shields? He mentioned it so casually too.

For someone who couldn't die, he seemed very flippant about taking a life. Then again, he'd never known how it felt to be alive, so perhaps it seemed trivial to him to lose life.

"Yes." Chandril answered distractedly, his eyes on Mishti. He took her hand and started drawing circles on the back of it. Dark red bloomed across the brown skin of her face. She clearly had no opinion at all about the other wraith mentioning killing anyone.

Perhaps Chloe and the other Shields needed to leave if the wraiths were going to mention killing so casually. The undead creatures had accepted them so far, but maybe that wouldn't last.

Despite that urgency inside her, she slumped onto the black soil and curled into a ball, her favorite sleeping position. A yawn stretched her mouth open wide as she settled her head onto her arm. The urgency left her now, replaced with the deep desire to surrender to the bliss of sleep. Her bones ached, and sweat covered her skin like dew, but nothing could keep her awake any longer.

Quintus dropped to the ground beside her. He positioned himself so he lay on one side and the enchantment lay directly behind her. He clearly wanted to keep her as safe as possible, but in a way that allowed him to sleep too.

His eyelids drooped heavily as he dragged himself into position. He made the final adjustments with his eyes closed.

Just as Chloe closed her own eyes, she caught sight of his chest heaving in deep, slumberous breaths. Sleep overtook her only a moment later.

Hopefully, it would be okay for them to sleep. It was up to the Golden Shields to keep them safe while they did.

She had no idea how long she slept, and maybe it didn't matter since Faerie had no time. She had definitely gotten some decent rest, but soon, strange noises wrested her into consciousness. At first, she simply noticed eerie and mysterious sounds as menacing as the wraiths. But after waking more, she realized the noises strung together to create a haunting melody.

Strange flutes, distant whispers, and eerie chants filled the space. They were punctuated by an occasional discordant note and unsettling sounds like ghostly moans. The rhythm was slow and hypnotic, drawing listeners in like a predator stalking its prey.

It sounded so frightening, it almost didn't seem appropriate to call it music. Then again, considering this was the Forest of the Wraiths, it felt like the perfect music for them.

Her eyes fluttered open then. The subtle glowing green hue of sprites flying above brought light to the night-darkened area. Their glow cast lights of radiant hues across the shadowy ground. After a quick scan, she found the clearing of the dense forest filled with small groups of people mingling.

Many of the wraiths rocked in time to the rhythmic and haunting melody. It seemed to bring smiles to their faces. Nearly all the wraiths held at least one item in their hands. Most were thick, long leaves or large rocks that had been plucked from the ground, but some held other objects like vases or books.

The only similarity between these items was the heavy layer of dust covering each one. Every so often, a wraith would stick out his or her disturbingly long tongue to lick up some of the dust. Seeing it put a shiver through Chloe's spine. Since they had an alliance with the wraiths now, she did her best to hide the shiver.

But then she noticed something she had not noticed before. Many of the Golden Shields sat among the wraiths. The Shields had tensed shoulders that stiffened more each time one of those strange discordant notes rang out. Still, they sat with the wraiths, laughed with them even. They talked and mingled like true friends did.

Her eyes widened at the sight. Ludo sat with Mishti, Chandril, Nilyx, and the other wraith with the blue vest and purple eyes whose name Chloe did not know. Considering how Ludo waved his arms about, he was probably telling some story about how he had nearly died or something as equally dramatic. Mishti chuckled at something Ludo said, and then she dropped her head onto Chandril's shoulder.

In another area of the forest, a wraith with a silver tunic and a bony frame held out a rock toward Batu. "Are you sure you do not want to try some dust? It is delicious to wraiths. I cannot imagine it tastes much different to a mortal like you."

"No." Batu placed a hand over his stomach and made a diligent but ultimately unsuccessful effort at covering up a gag.

"Surely?" the wraith asked. "Are you not hungry?"

Batu's expression warmed as a wide smile covered his face. "It is good of you to offer, but as I already said, we mortals really do need food to eat. *Not* dust."

The wraith shrugged and stuck out a tongue so long it could nearly lick his own neck. He then proceeded to remove all the dust from the surface of the rock with his tongue, all while bouncing his body in time with the music.

Suppressing a gag from her own throat, Chloe sat up to see if Quintus had awoken. Unsurprisingly, he had, though it looked as if he hadn't been awake long. He sat up straight, but he also rubbed the sleep out of one eye.

When he caught her looking at him, he tilted his head toward Batu and the wraith with the silver tunic. "I suppose it makes sense dust is enough to sustain them when their bodies lack so much substance to begin with."

She nodded and leaned a little closer to him. "But I am glad we eat more than dust. It seems the most unexciting thing I can think of to eat."

He leaned in even closer and dropped his voice to the lowest whisper. "It is almost as bad as this music."

A snicker jumped from her mouth before she could stop it, but she managed to clap a hand over her lips and play it off as a cough. With such a low whisper, none of the wraiths could have known Quintus had just insulted their music, but she didn't want them guessing such a thing either.

Training her face to an even expression, she reached for the leather fastening at the top of her wooden foot. The leather itched when she wore it too long, which was why she always took the foot off to sleep. But since she had fallen asleep so quickly, she hadn't thought to remove it. Now awake, she needed to take it off and let her skin breathe for a bit.

Her fingers kneaded over the muscles in her leg, first down one side, across the bottom, and then back up the other side. The soothing massage tended to relieve her muscles after a long day.

It felt so good to relax, to know they had accomplished something that would change their fate. They had formed an alliance with the wraiths, but even more than that, they had stopped Julian. Yes, he was still the king, but this enchantment completely stopped his plans to complete the ritual. Now that Undulle Tree was protected, Julian would never have all the ingredients he needed for the ritual. He had beaten them so many times, Chloe couldn't help herself from basking in the truth that they had finally stopped his plan.

It wasn't over yet, but finally, they had a chance at defeating him for good.

Now she reveled in the sight of her Golden Shields talking and being friendly with the wraiths. When they had first entered the forest, the wraiths looked ready to kill them. According to one wraith, that had been their very intention. The creatures had distrusted and resented the Shields, but now those feelings seemed to have passed.

Perhaps the wraiths might be willing to do more than just let the Shields protect their tree. Perhaps they would be willing to fight in battle against the king. With undead soldiers, ones who couldn't be killed, on their side it could give them a distinct advantage.

Still massaging her leg, she turned back to Quintus and lowered her voice. She didn't want anyone else to hear, but she didn't want anyone thinking they were telling secrets either. "What was it you wanted to tell me before?" she asked him. "You said you had to ask me something."

He began to nod but stopped midway. His voice lowered to a gravelly pitch. "*Give* you something."

Discomfort tied knots in her belly. His face had turned so focused, so determined. "What is it?"

She was almost afraid to ask, but staring at his face while her stomach writhed with worry had to be worse than whatever this *gift* was. She was his beloved, wasn't she? He wouldn't want to give her anything that would hurt her. Right?

His throat bulged with a swallow that looked as painful as the knots inside her. "Not now." He turned away from her as soon as he said it.

"Should I be worried?" She tried to laugh as she said it, just to bring some levity to the conversation. In truth, that laugh was more for herself, to convince herself it was ridiculous to think she should be worried.

But when Quintus turned to look at her again, the fear inside her grew tenfold. His expression looked harrowing. Whatever this was, whatever he had to *give* her, it might be exactly as bad as her deepest fears suggested.

He closed his eyes, rubbing a knuckle across his forehead, as if that might help him think. "I cannot…" He pressed harder against his forehead, then suddenly dropped his hand and shook his head. When he forced his eyes open again, they carried a deep weight inside them.

"I am not sure you will understand." As soon as he spoke, he shook his head harder, staring down at his lap. "Well, I think you *will* understand, but I am not sure you will agree. I…"

"Now I *am* worried." She whispered those words, but only because she couldn't help it. Only a hard gulp allowed her to speak again. "Just tell me what it is, Quintus, or my heart might beat out of my chest."

He turned away from her. "I cannot." He said those same words again, but they seemed like they hurt him more than the first time he had said them. "This is not the place for it."

Scooting her body closer to him, she ducked her head until he looked her straight in the eye. "You still owe me a debt from when you said *I'm sorry* to me. Do I need to use that debt to get you to tell me?"

His expression twisted as he stared back at her, but all he did was stare without uttering a word. He was worried. Or upset. Afraid?

Desperate for any sort of information, she used her bond to reach out for his feelings. But those were as confusing as his face. In a rush, she could feel the love he had for her. It burned as deep as the love she had for him. But something corrupted it. His worry for something she could not guess twisted all through the love, infecting it deeply so it could not burn freely.

In a flash, it hit her. The answer came so clear and obvious, she almost couldn't believe it had taken her so long to realize. Mortality. That was what worried him. *Her* mortality. As they had discussed earlier, he had finally come to understand just how much it would hurt him when she died. He finally understood she *would* die, that nothing could stop it. And now that knowledge gripped the love inside him, doing its best to suffocate it completely.

What had he said? He was not sure she would understand. Or maybe she would understand, but she would not agree.

Her gut curled in on itself while breathing became difficult. What did he have planned?

An ominous foreboding filled her, which was only exacerbated by the haunting music surrounding them.

Still, keeping his gaze away from her, he got to his feet. "Come on." He took a step forward with his back to her. "Now that we are awake, we should join the others. You are our leader, and as such, I am certain the Golden Shields would like to see us being friendly with the wraiths just as they have done while we rested. We need to show we are just as committed to this alliance as the rest of the Shields."

Her nose wrinkled as she stuffed the end of her leg back onto her wooden foot. With trembling fingers, she fixed the leather fastening into place. "You are their leader too. You are heir to Crystalfall, and hopefully soon, the king of it."

He ignored that comment, moving toward Batu and the wraith near him.

She wanted to stomp across the clearing, stand face-to-face with him, and then demand he stop hiding things and talk through the thoughts in his head. But before she could do any of that, Nilyx's red glowing eyes and lithe frame appeared before Chloe.

A chill prickled at the back of her neck, making all the little hairs stand on end. Clearly, the wraith had something to say.

But all Chloe could think about was her beloved... who might not be her beloved if fear managed to wring out the love inside him.

23

CHLOE'S MIND CONTINUED TO WANDER, thinking of Quintus even when he stood several feet away talking to Batu. Nilyx loomed in front of Chloe, but she struggled to give the wraith any more attention than a simple nod.

"Did the enchantment injure you? Is that why you slept?" Nilyx didn't exactly wear concern, but she seemed mildly interested in the information.

"No, I wasn't injured," Chloe answered. "Just exhausted. But I'm better now I've slept."

She did her best to look at the woman, but her gaze kept flicking to the side to catch a glimpse of her beloved.

"We were worried when our first memory elixir got spilled." The first hint of agitation colored the wraith's words.

Chloe still only barely noticed it. "Was that what happened? I am glad Zael conjured another elixir so quickly." She said the words halfheartedly, but then she suddenly remembered how it had felt when the new elixir entered her enchantment.

Snapping her eyes toward the wraith, Chloe said, "Although…"

When she didn't finish right away, Nilyx tilted her head to the side. "What is it?"

Chloe took a step closer, lowering her head to decrease the distance between them. "The new elixir felt different to my magic."

She thought sharing the information might have brought the wraith even closer.

Instead, Nilyx took a step back. Suspicion danced in the red glow of her eyes.

Perhaps it would be better to be more casual. Chloe continued. "I assumed each wraith makes a slightly different elixir, perhaps one that is specific to the individual. If that is the case, then I should not be worried the new elixir felt different, right?"

Nilyx flexed her jaw and narrowed her eyes. "You are trying to learn more about our magic."

"No." Chloe shook her head, as if that might help the situation. "I should have phrased that differently."

The wraith folded her arms over her thin silk blouse.

Chloe lifted one shoulder in a shrug, trying desperately to ease the tension between them "If you are not concerned the second elixir felt different, then I am not concerned. I will not think on it anymore."

Nilyx narrowed her glowing red eyes again, but this time in thought. The fact that she didn't immediately have a response sent all sorts of questions to Chloe's mind.

"*Are* you concerned?" Chloe leaned in, lowering her voice slightly. "Quintus and I might be able to add another elixir to the enchantment now that we've rested."

It took several moments of Nilyx mulling over the offer, but she finally answered. "I am not concerned. I will not explain why, but sometimes our elixirs are different. Never mind the reason."

The wraith was clearly more concerned with keeping information about the elixir away from Chloe than about the difference in the two elixirs. And if Nilyx wasn't concerned, then Chloe could finally relax.

She had no reason to learn anything more about the elixir. As long as the enchantment was strong, she could stop worrying. A warm relief flooded through her, releasing a heavy breath from her lips. "I am glad to hear that." She then smiled at the wraith. "We chose well making an alliance with you. And how lucky for us that we get to hear your beautiful music."

The words left her lips before she thought too much of them, but now she worried Nilyx would be able to tell it was an outright lie for Chloe to call the music beautiful.

Luckily, the wraith's mouth curved into a wide grin. She glanced out at the clearing and touched a hand over her heart as she swayed to the haunting melody. Her face was positively beaming from the compliment.

She had probably completely forgotten mortals could lie. It was for the best though. She didn't need to know the music actually sent chills through Chloe and made her afraid to even blink.

The wraith steepled her extra-long fingers, made even longer by her pointed red fingernails, under her chin. "We are glad for the alliance too. Undulle has never been safer."

With a short nod, she left Chloe and found a boulder to sit on where she then proceeded to lick the dust off a long leaf she had plucked from the ground.

A warm hand slipped across the small of Chloe's back. It might have startled her, but she had felt Quintus creeping up behind her. The magical bond between them continued to grow. It felt especially heightened now after the enchantment they created, making it easier than ever to sense him no matter where he was.

With his hand tugging her closer, he gazed deeply into her eyes. "You are beautiful, do you know that?" The corner of his lips twitched upward. "More beautiful than anyone I have ever seen."

The words sent her heart soaring, the rush of it more powerful than those barrel rolls on Shadow. He only took a few words, and he melted her into a puddle. Her own lips automatically curved upward.

But then she suddenly remembered she was supposed to be upset with him. It took every ounce of energy she had, but she managed to press her lips to a thin line. "You've decided to speak to me again, have you? I thought you might continue to ignore me since you still refuse to tell me what mysterious thing it is you have to give me."

Concern sent a crease between his eyebrows. "I saw Nilyx getting upset while she was talking to you, and…"

Even after he trailed off, Chloe knew exactly what he'd been about to say. She finished the sentence for him. "You wanted to make sure I was safe."

He nodded.

She knew she should have prodded more, but feeling his anxiety through their bond made her more eager to ease that first. "Nilyx thought I was trying to get information about their elixirs, but I just wanted to make sure the memory elixir had protected the tree the way it was supposed to. Zael's new elixir felt so different from the first one he spilled."

"I noticed that too." The crease between Quintus's eyebrows deepened.

Once again, Chloe was struck with the need to ease his anxiety. "Nilyx said it was normal. We have no reason to worry."

He let out a sigh and the crease between his eyebrows disappeared. Now he glanced back at the dome and the tree it protected. "Do you think the pixies managed to save their tree? Undulle is at full strength and completely protected. As long as Ludo's brother or his beloved find a suitable branch, they should be able to save Lifespark."

Chloe bit her bottom lip. "Maybe Ludo can send a message to ask."

"He already did while you and I were sleeping. He told me just before I walked over here, though unfortunately, he has gotten no response yet."

Curling one of her hands into a fist, she moved toward Ludo, who now sat next to Roarke and one of the wraiths.

But as she and Quintus moved, a little sprite flew down from above and landed on Ludo's palm. Chloe moved quicker now, to make sure she got close enough to hear the message the sprite was about to deliver.

Ludo dug into his magical pocket and pulled out a glass vial filled with tiny pink stones. He removed one and gave it to the sprite as an offering for delivering the message.

After the sprite examined it, he stuffed it into his pocket and stood tall. "I have a message for Ludo of Fairfrost from Revyn of Fairfrost. The message is this: It worked. Clara found the perfect branch and helped us get it in the right spot. Plumia had to draw power from Undulle, but just like you said, it was at full strength. Lifespark Tree and all the pixies are saved once again."

With a short nod, the sprite's glowing green wings pulled him high into the air with the other sprites hovering above.

Ludo placed the back of his hand against his forehead and heaved a loud sigh. "I was about to go mad if I had to wait any longer for that message. I have not been able to relax since we left the pixies."

Quintus clapped Ludo on the shoulder while wearing a wide smile. "I am relieved as well. For once, we have truly stopped my father from his plans."

Chloe clapped her hands together and turned to glance around the area. "We should tell Mishti."

A snort erupted from Ludo's throat. "Uh, Mishti is a little...," he cleared his throat pointedly and tilted his head toward a shadowy thicket within eyesight but far from where they stood, "...preoccupied at the moment."

With the area pointed out now, Chloe noticed two figures sitting cross legged across from each other at the base of a gnarled tree. Mishti and Chandril stared into each other's eyes exchanging words no one else could hear. Every few moments, their heads would lean a little bit closer to each other.

Delight filled Chloe's chest at the sight of them.

Quintus shook his head and lowered his voice so none of the other wraiths could hear. "I do not understand what she sees in him. He is a *wraith*. They are so..."

"Frightening," Chloe finished.

Quintus nodded, checking over his shoulder to make sure none of the wraiths had heard.

Ludo snorted again. "Uh, remember the dragon she chose? Are you really that surprised she fell for a wraith? Mishti loves the frightening things everyone else rejects."

Hearing it laid out so simply like that caught Chloe by surprise, but Ludo was right. That's exactly how Mishti had always been, at least for as long as Chloe had known her. Considering Mishti had been forced to be a weapon and kill many people throughout her life, it was possible the young woman had seen herself in the creatures others would call monsters. No one else had compassion for them the way Mishti did, and she did it without thinking.

Chloe's gaze drifted back to the shadowy thicket where Mishti and Chandril sat. Chandril had conjured two memory elixirs and they each held one in their hands. A blood orange and glowing one for Mishti, and a midnight blue shimmery one for Chandril.

They exchanged a few more words and then brought the glass bottles to their lips. Even from a distance, the effect of the memory elixirs was clear at once. Their eyes closed and their shoulders and other muscles slumped. But their faces also lit up with a vibrant life.

It seemed so strange, this unconventional pair, but others probably thought that about Chloe's pairing with Quintus. She had no right to consider it odd. And more than that, Mishti seemed calmer and happier since she'd met Chandril. Maybe helping a monster turn less monstrous had helped her see the positive qualities in herself.

Ludo stared with less acceptance in his expression. He scrunched his nose up and shook his head. "I understand why she fell for Chandril, but I do not understand why she gives him her memories. And what would she ever want with *his* memories in return?"

Quintus nodded, his face as confused as Ludo's. "Especially because Chandril is not giving us any information. Why else would they exchange memories if not for that?"

"Exactly," Ludo said with a hard nod.

Chloe shrugged. "They must be doing it because they like it."

The two fae turned to her with eyebrows high on their forehead. Clearly, they could not conceive of the possibility that anyone would enjoy losing a memory.

Just then, Nylix came stomping forward, her feathery skirt swooshing with each pounding step. "Chandril."

She said the name loudly through her clenched teeth as she got near Chloe, Ludo, and Quintus, but her gaze was fixed entirely on the wraith whose once blood orange glowing eyes now looked a simple amber.

Chandril and Mishti emerged from their shadowy thicket. They walked hand in hand toward Nilyx. The wraith's red eyes glowed bright and fierce. She breathed through her teeth and squeezed her fists at her sides.

The other Golden Shields seem to sense her anger might have consequences. Without speaking, they all casually stood and began gathering closer to Chloe and farther away from the wraiths they'd been mingling with.

When Chandril and Mishti finally reached Nylix, her red eyes looked like fire. She stared straight at Chandril with her jaw still clenched. "You cannot take another one of that mortal's memories. If you do, it will have dire consequences."

Chandril held tighter to Mishti's hand, his eyes filled with determination. "What consequences?"

Nylix huffed and shifted her tone to an ominous one. "Something you would *never* wish for."

In response, Chandril pushed his eyebrows down low. "How do you know what I wish for? Mishti is… she is more important to me than *you*. She is more important to me than anything."

"Important enough to die for?" Nylix asked.

The question managed to snuff out what little conversation still filled the air. Even the music stopped abruptly. In a single moment, every gaze in the area turned onto Nylix.

Die? But wraiths were undead. They *couldn't* die.

Nylix seemed to gain strength from all the gazes fixed on her. She stood a little taller and flashed her black pointed teeth. "If you take another memory from that mortal, you will cease to be a wraith." Her hand lifted, gesturing toward Chandril. "You can already see the change coming over you."

"So he will become high fae?" Ludo asked the question in a low tone, but it was still loud enough for Nylix to hear. "I fail to see how that is a *dire* consequence. It seems much better to me than being a *wraith*."

Nylix jerked her head to the side until she looked straight at Ludo. "I did not say he will turn into a high fae. I said he will cease to be a wraith."

Chloe placed a hand on her collar bone and had to swallow before she could ask the question in her mind. "He will die?"

The glow in Nylix's red eyes turned dark and foreboding. When she spoke, her voice had even more bite. "He will become *mortal*."

Gasps filled the clearing, mostly from wraiths, but a few from Shields as well.

Nylix lifted her chin and turned to look at Chandril again. "You will become mortal just like her." The wraith gestured toward Mishti and then continued. "You will age like her, becoming old, weak, and withered the way only mortals do. And at the end of it all, yes, you will *die*."

Another round of gasps broke out through the clearing, these even sharper than the first. Instead of looking frightening, the wraiths looked frightened. Quintus and Ludo looked aghast. It was clear none of them could imagine a fate worse than becoming mortal.

From the edge of the clearing, Sofia scoffed. "Dying is not so bad. At least we *live*, unlike you wraiths."

The wraiths around her dropped their mouths open in shock. Chloe never would have said it, but Sofia was right. She'd much rather die eventually but still *live* than be like these wraiths who were merely undead. But saying as much right in the center of the Forest of the Wraiths was a terrible insult to the creatures they had just formed an alliance with.

Chloe needed to smooth this over. She wasn't sure how yet, but she'd have to say something and soon.

But just as she stepped forward and opened her mouth to speak, a stick snapped, probably because someone had stepped on it. She would have thought nothing of it, but every wraith, if it was even possible, suddenly looked even more frightened than before.

They were truly and completely afraid. And even worse, they had all turned to look at Undulle Tree.

She whipped around just in time to see the wraith Zael with a tree branch from Undulle in his hand. He had gotten inside. Somehow, he had slipped through the enchantment Quintus and Chloe created. Now he stood inside the holographic dome with a golden branch gripped tight in his hand.

But how? *How* had he gotten past the enchantment? It should have been impossible.

He stared at all of them for a moment, his hand shaking with the golden branch inside it.

And then he ran straight through the dome and away from the clearing, the tree branch from Undulle still in his grip.

24

CHLOE HAD BOTH HANDS OVER her mouth before the truth settled in completely. Undulle Tree still had a powerful barrier enchantment protecting it, but somehow, Zael had gotten through. A wraith had just stolen a branch from the tree. And now his retreating form disappeared through the forest.

Confusion set in, especially among the wraiths. Clearly, not one of them ever considered the possibility that a wraith would betray their own kind to Julian.

Quintus took action first. He started running, then turned back to demand Chloe stay in exactly that spot and to alert him immediately if she was in danger. His fae speed then took him deep into the forest.

But though he had fae speed to carry him, Zael had fae speed too. And because of the shock of his betrayal they'd all been hit with, he'd gotten a decent head start.

Many wraiths and even Golden Shields followed Quintus next. The mortals could not run as fast as Quintus or the wraiths, but that didn't stop them from trying.

Worry marred Chloe's insides. Quintus had told her to stay, but she could do nothing in that clearing. He'd just have to get over it when he found out she ran as well.

She should have known it was too good to last. Things had felt too smooth. They had achieved one small victory, but Julian had managed to snatch it away from them almost as soon as they'd gotten it. Just like he always did.

She should have known better than to relax. She should have known better than to have hope their victory might last.

"Where are you going?" Mishti was suddenly at her side, fear twisting every feature on her face instead of the fierceness that was usually there. Climbing over branches, she shook her head. "Quintus told you to stay. He will kill me if anything happens to you."

Chloe moved so much slower than anyone else. As always, she had fallen far behind the action. It was almost a joke Mishti could be afraid of anything happening to her here. If anything was going to happen to anyone, it would be wherever Zael and Quintus had gone, not here in an empty part of the forest.

Just then, Chandril caught up and came to Mishti's other side. A surprising amount of guilt sat in his eyes. Did the guilt have anything to do with Nylix's revelation that he would turn mortal if he took another one of Mishti's memories? Or perhaps he felt guilty one of his own had been the one to betray them all.

Ignoring that for now, Chloe did her best to climb over fallen logs and duck through the branches of the forest. The sooner she got out and found Shadow, the better. "I do not understand how Zael could have gotten through the enchantment. It should have kept him out."

Chandril coughed uncomfortably. "About that…"

She might have paid more attention to him except a soft golden ray broke through the trees just in front of her. That golden light didn't come from the green sprites above like most of the light inside the forest. No, that light came from something outside and in the sky.

The moon. Through Chloe and Quintus's bond, they had somehow brought a moon and stars to Faerie's sky when it had never been there before. And once again, she was reminded of just how perfectly everything had worked out for Julian. A moon would shine in the sky above Crystalfall Castle when he attempted the ritual, and all because Chloe and Quintus had brought the moon for him.

And now Julian had his opposing branches of life and death.

In her mind, she listed the other ingredients from the ritual. The dragon scale, the instrument of creation, the branches. Now he just needed a sacrificial body or limb as well as blood.

He had everything. Everything except Quintus.

Unless… If Quintus managed to catch Zael, they still had a chance. And if Quintus didn't catch him? Maybe they could still catch Zael, but they needed something faster than fae speed.

Come..

She spoke to Shadow through her bond with her. This was their only chance. Only her dragon could help her catch Zael before he got to Crystalfall Castle.

I am inside the forest, she called to her dragon. She felt the heavy creature stir in response to the call, but she did not move. Chloe called to Shadow again. The creature sent waves of fear in response. She would do anything, anything *except* enter the dark, gloomy forest.

I know you are scared, but I need you. It's the only way, Chloe begged. She closed her eyes briefly, filling her mind with the desperation of their situation so Shadow would understand. Soon, she sensed the flapping of heavy wings, and relief shot through her.

Shadow was coming. She would be there soon.

Chloe stopped mid-stride and moved toward the nearest tree. Her good foot settled onto a low tree branch as she reached for higher branches to pull herself up higher. She'd never been any good at climbing trees, but any little bit would help her dragon get to her.

"What are you doing?" Mishti yelled.

But Shadow had gotten there now. Chloe climbed up two more branches, balanced herself, and then jumped as high as she could.

The golden scales of her dragon's back caught her almost as soon as she jumped away from the tree. She leaned in close, hugging Shadow as she landed.

Mishti went to shout again, but Chloe waved a hand. "Shadow will keep me safe. Jump on. Hopefully we can stop Zael before he gets to the castle."

Mishti and Chandril both jumped onto the dragon just as she started flying higher into the sky.

Chloe pressed her cheek against her dragon's scales. She lay on her stomach, hoping it might help Shadow fly faster. Mishti and Chandril settled behind her, their bodies low as well.

Angling her head up slightly, Chloe managed to catch a glimpse of the landscape below. She could just make out the edge of the Forest of the Wraiths.

Quintus and the others sped across the forest floor, trying their best to catch up with Zael. But the wraith betrayer had just reached the edge of the forest, now running outside it.

From behind him, Quintus pulled two spears from his magical pocket. He shot both with perfect accuracy, but Zael managed to dodge each of them at the last moment.

Turning backward to look at Chandril, Chloe asked, "Will weapons do anything to Zael? He cannot die, right?"

"They will not damage his body," Chandril answered. "But they will still hurt him if they hit. It could slow him down."

Before he had even finished speaking, Mishti pulled daggers from the bracers around her ankles and from the one beneath her tunic. She threw each of the daggers in quick succession with just as accurate of aim as Quintus's spears.

Unlike with the spears, Zael did not notice the daggers until they had come upon him. He clearly hadn't realized a dragon flew above and had only been watching for danger from behind.

He still managed to dodge the first dagger. The second one hit, but it didn't land. It merely sliced across his arm, cutting through his thin green robe. The third dagger landed right in his back, in the lower ribs.

He stumbled. But then he simply gritted his teeth and wrenched the dagger out. After a few more stumbles, he ran just as fast as he had before the daggers had hit.

It *had* slowed him down. A little. It had not slowed him down enough.

But while he got distracted by the daggers, Quintus had been busy with a different attack. Sparkling golden magic crackled all around his hands. With a sharp throw, the magic shot forward. A gut feeling, and probably her bond with Quintus, told Chloe this ball of magic would catch Zael by the ankles. A perfect trap. The magic would wrap around him like shackles, tripping him and stopping him from running any more.

Chloe's chest heaved in relief. She stroked a hand over Shadow's golden scales, reassuring her the flight would be over soon. The traitorous wraith couldn't possibly escape the powerful trap Quintus had conjured.

But Zael glanced back once he pulled the dagger out of his body. He managed to see the golden magic flying toward him. It only gave him a moment to act, but apparently, that was all he needed.

Right before their eyes, Zael grabbed a balance shard from inside his green robe. He squeezed it between his fingers and then threw it toward Quintus and the others coming after him.

If a mortal or a high fae had attempted such an action, they would have died instantly. The balance shards were highly unstable and extremely powerful. A violent whirlwind of magic tore through his whole body when he squeezed the shard. He did more than stumble then. He shook and stopped running completely. But since his body could not be damaged, the shard merely caused pain, nothing more.

Even worse, the fierce convulsion of magic caught Quintus's golden shackles and turned the magic to dust. After a breath, Zael was running once again with nothing left to stop him.

A balance shard? Chloe's gut twisted in shock.

They had already known it the moment the wraith stole the branch from Undulle, but now they knew with even more certainty. Zael had been working for Julian. And it hadn't been some spur-of-the-moment decision. He had clearly conspired with the king long before the Golden Shields got to the forest to protect the tree. Only Julian could have given him that balance shard, which meant he had already made some sort of deal.

Goosebumps broke out across Chloe's neck. They were losing any chance they had of stopping this betrayer. But maybe they could use some of the training they'd done in the past few days. If Shadow could breathe a continuous stream of fire onto Zael, it might cause him enough pain that he would stop running completely. Or at least stop running until Quintus caught up to him. And if it didn't do that, Shadow's fire might at least melt the golden branch from Undulle, making it unusable for the ritual.

Directing her dragon, Chloe sat up a little higher to get a better view of the land below. Pops and snaps sounded at the back of Shadow's throat, and soon, her scales warmed. Another moment later, hot streams of yellow fire with brilliant blue veins twisting through erupted from Shadow's mouth.

The fire would hit Zael soon.

But he grabbed another balance shard from his robe and broke it completely in half. When he threw the exploding pieces over his shoulder, they somehow caught Shadow's flames, as if they were magnetized to the shards.

When the shard touched the yellow flames, Shadow shook violently. Chloe immediately commanded her to close her jaw and stop the fire.

Shadow complied, but judging by the whimper she released, the shard had done something to hurt her. Apparently, fire wouldn't help either.

Zael continued to run, but he grabbed things off the ground too. With each step, he threw glittering stones and broken branches at anyone pursuing him. Such objects would not truly damage anyone behind him, but they did manage to slow several people down.

He pulled out another shard and exploded it in his hand. A cloud of powdery blue smoke and red sparks erupted from the shard. His body was completely enveloped in it, and soon, the smoke grew outward several yards.

It obscured all vision for several long seconds. Chloe held her breath, waiting for it to get cleared away by the air.

But by the time it dissipated enough to see through it again, Zael was *gone*. Chloe gasped and stared hard at the ground below. Shaking her head, she turned back to Chandril. "He is…gone. How could he be gone?"

Chandril turned his gaze downward and shook his head. "He is not gone. He just used the smoke to hide his body. I saw him running toward Emerald Lake, but I lost him once the smoke got too thick."

And then the realization that had already struck Chandril struck Chloe.

Zael had gotten away.

Her heart dropped as she scanned the landscape again. There had to be a sign of him. Somewhere. They couldn't give up yet.

Urging Shadow to fly faster, the dragon soared over the area, everywhere on the way to Emerald Lake. But it was no use.

They had lost him. Everything they had done in the forest had been in vain.

Julian had won again.

With a heavy heart, she directed Shadow to fly back to the clearing at the entrance of the forest where the other dragons and Golden Shields were gathered. She scanned the area quickly, searching for Quintus as Shadow lowered to the ground. It only took a look at his heated face and pinched eyebrows to see anger shook him. He was not happy she had left the forest after he'd told her to stay by Undulle Tree.

But how could she deal with his anger when so much fear shook through every vein in her body? When fear froze her so completely that she could barely breathe?

What were they supposed to do now? What chance did they have at victory?

25

CHLOE'S LIMBS TREMBLED WHILE REALITY settled in. She hadn't been in a battle, so this wasn't the same sort of fear as that. Instead, it hit her entirely just how close Julian was to completing the ritual.

The last thing he needed now was Quintus. And if he got Quintus…

Mishti helped Chloe slide off Shadow's back and onto the ground. Mishti must have done most of it because Chloe couldn't even feel her limbs. Everything inside her felt numb. Skittery. Her heart felt like it might beat so fast that she could no longer breathe.

Quintus marched toward her, his brown eyes storming with anger and fear. "Do not *ever* do that again. You went after him without me? What if he had killed you? What if something had—"

His tirade cut off short when Chloe's trembling body fell into his arms. He must have felt her fear. It evaporated all his anger in an instant. He embraced her, holding her tight and stroking her upper back to comfort her. His hand at her lower back pulled her closer each time she sucked in a shivering breath.

"I am here, Chloe. You are safe." His words managed to slice through the deepest parts of her fear, but they didn't dispel it completely.

Dropping his face into her neck, he spoke in a low, gravelly tone. "When I saw you on Shadow's back, completely exposed… I have never felt fear like that before." He withdrew slightly, forcing her to look at him, forcing her to see the palpable fear of losing her unfold in his eyes. "You cannot do that again. If you care for me even a single bit, do not put yourself in a situation where you might die."

Too broken to speak, she nodded and crawled back to the safety of his arms. Her cheek pressed against his comforting chest where she could feel his heartbeat against her ear. Cold fear gripped her entire body and only his embrace could warm her again.

Quintus quietly rocked her until the trembling inside her calmed. After a tight squeeze, she finally pulled away.

They stood at the clearing outside the Forest of the Wraiths. The entire Order of the Golden Shields had gathered in the area. Most of them comforted their dragons or spoke in small groups to each other. A few wraiths gathered with them, but they stood inside the forest and kept to the shadows.

Mishti, Ludo, and Chandril all stood close, waiting for Chloe or Quintus to say something. When no one did, Ludo broke the silence.

"How did this happen?" His tone had no accusation inside it. He asked the same question inside everyone's mind. And now that he had voiced it, they could attempt to find answers. His blue-and-red eyes pulsed as he continued. "How did Zael get through the enchantment? Was it something wrong with the magic?"

Mishti glanced toward Chandril for a moment and then addressed the rest of their group. "We saw Zael trying to get through the enchantment while Chloe and Quintus were sleeping."

Chandril nodded. "I confronted him immediately. He said he was testing it out to see how strong it was, and I believed him, but looking back…"

Mishti shook her head bitterly. "Zael must have thought he'd be able to walk right through the enchantment and was genuinely surprised when he couldn't. So the enchantment *did* work at first."

Since she had already been suspicious of it, Chloe instinctively knew this had happened because of Zael's elixir. It had to be that. He had conjured that new elixir, which had felt so different from the first. He must have done something to it that allowed him to get through the dome.

Quintus nodded as if he could hear her thoughts through their bond, though he probably just sensed her feelings and came to the same conclusion. She had told him her suspicion about the elixir.

His head tilted in though. "I wonder why Zael could not get through the enchantment at first."

Chloe jumped in immediately, the answer obvious in her mind. "That's because I managed to pull some of the first elixir into the enchantment, the one Nilyx conjured."

Understanding lit in Quintus's eyes with no other explanation needed.

The others, however, were more surprised by this statement.

"Really?" Chandril asked. "You pulled some of that elixir in even when it spilled so far away from the tree?"

Quintus let out a heavy exhale. "It took all her effort. That was what exhausted both of us nearly completely."

Ludo's eyebrows jumped up his forehead. "Is that why you both had to sleep afterward?"

"Yes," Chloe said. "And I did not pull all the original elixir in completely. Once Zael said he was ready and poured the new one, I stopped seeking for more of the original elixir, since that little bit had already taken so much effort. But that extra protection from the first elixir must have stopped him the first time he tried to get through."

Ludo scowled. "So what happened? Did the protection from the first elixir wear off and that is how he got in?"

Chandril swallowed and dropped his gaze to his feet. When he spoke, it was in a low and quiet voice. "Or perhaps when I shared a memory with Mishti, Zael knew it had weakened the enchantment and exploited that."

Mishti's head snapped toward him. "What do you mean giving me a memory weakened the barrier?"

He glanced up long enough to catch her eye, but he dropped his gaze almost immediately. He stared at his feet as the toe of his shoe dug into the black soil beneath it.

Silence hung around them for several breaths, but Chandril finally filled it. "When memory elixirs are used or created…"

He trailed off, glancing toward the other wraiths. They all stood inside the forest, too far to be able to hear any of his words. But seeing them at all had clearly stopped him from speaking. Chloe took a few steps to the side, positioning herself to block him from view of the other wraiths. Quintus and Ludo understood immediately what she was doing and they soon did the same.

Chandril still stayed silent for another moment. But then Mishti reached out and touched his forearm, giving him an encouraging nod.

Only then did he open his mouth again. His voice had dropped to a low whisper. "When memory elixirs are used or created, we all feel it. *All* the wraiths. It weakens us."

Mishti narrowed her eyes. "You knew it would weaken the enchantment when we shared our memories with each other, but you still did it?"

He shook his head. "It weakens us temporarily, but then it strengthens us after the process is finished. And the weakness does not come right away. No one could guess when it happens. It happens so fast, no one else would ever know the right moment to act. Even the quickest fae would not be able to exploit the weakness. No one would." His expression grew dim as he shook his head. "No one except a wraith."

And there was the truth of it. Zael had betrayed his own people. The wraiths had been so suspicious of the Golden Shields, and they had done all they could to protect themselves and their tree against them.

But they had done nothing to protect themselves from one of their own.

Even though she was not a wraith, the truth of it still cut Chloe to her very core. But then another thought burst forward in her mind, more fully explaining the wraiths' hatred for the king.

"That is why it hurts you so much that Julian stole your magic," Chloe said in a rush.

Chandril flinched at the sound of Julian's name. Since they now stood outside the forest, she had forgotten to call him the king. Luckily, none of the other wraiths had heard.

She continued, staring at Chandril to confirm her guess. "It weakens you and the other wraiths when the king uses memory magic to extend his life. Right?"

A scowl wrinkled Chandril's nose. "When *we* wield memory magic, it weakens us temporarily, but then we are strengthened soon after." He craned his neck, searching the area quickly, probably checking to be certain none of the wraiths could hear him exposing these secrets. His head dropped, and he continued. "But when the king uses our magic, it weakens us and strengthens only him."

Chloe glanced over her shoulder at the wraiths inside the forest. She stared at their wispy forms that lacked substance. Their entire bodies, even their clothes, looked translucent. Her eyes narrowed, examining the creatures closely. "When you say it *weakens* you…"

"We have always been undead." Chandril answered abruptly, as if he had guessed what she was trying to imply. He shook his head once. "The weakness does not change our appearance or our nature. Strength to us is not the same as it is to a mortal or a fae. It is simply that we *feel*…emptier. Dust does not satiate us as it once did, no matter how much we consume. The weaker we get, the more we feel like we are missing the very thing that makes us who we are. If the king performs the Bloodstone Convergence, we may never recover."

"Do you think the other wraiths will blame you for what happened?" Mishti's voice came out tight as she dared a glance toward Chandril. "Since it was our sharing of memories that allowed Zael to get through the enchantment?"

Chloe's head went back in shock at the words. "It's not Chandril's fault what happened. It was Zael's fault. He is the one who took the tree branch."

Mishti's eyes scrunched together. "I know that. And you know that." Her gaze flicked toward the forest for a moment before turning back to her friend. "But do you think the wraiths will believe that? When their very existence might change if Julian performs the ritual?"

The sense of dread filling Mishti's eyes now settled deep in Chloe's belly. She turned to Quintus, who wore just as much worry as she felt in her gut.

Ludo's eyes opened as wide as they could go. "What if they force him to give another memory to Mishti, and then he turns mortal, and then they *kill* him?"

Ludo's tendency to find the worst possible scenario often made Chloe chuckle, but this time? This time he might be right.

She gulped and looked at Chandril. "Maybe you better stay with us now. At least for a little while."

Gratitude glimmered in Mishti's eyes as she looked at her friend. A silent *thank you* filled her expression.

From the edge of the forest, Nilyx's voice filled the area. "What is the plan now?" A quiver went through her translucent chin. "You must have a plan, right?"

"We have to protect Quintus." Chloe said the words, but they did nothing to ease the tension knotted in her chest. The answer was so simple and yet it was the most terrifying one she had ever given. Julian only needed one last ingredient to perform the ritual. The fact that the ingredient was her beloved was a truth she almost couldn't bear.

She managed to squeeze her hands into fists and force herself to continue. "Now that the king has gotten the branch, the only thing left he needs is Quintus. We must ensure he is not captured."

"Or we could kill the king," Mishti said with a shrug. "That would stop him from performing the ritual."

"Or we could do both." Ludo's eyes lit with delight at the possibility.

Quintus stepped closer to Chloe, his fierceness from before yet to leave his face completely. "I still think he plans to kill you before he gets to me. He knows nothing will matter to me anymore if he gets to you, and that would make it easier for him to get to me."

A deafening silence filled the clearing after Quintus made that declaration. Though their situation had never been more dire, her heart still leapt hearing him recklessly tell every Golden Shield and wraith just how much she meant to him.

It filled her with a fire that burned hotter than her fear.

They would not let Julian win. No matter how many times he had beaten them, they would not let him win. If they lost every battle so far, it didn't matter because they really only needed to win one battle.

The last one.

Determination bloomed in her chest, igniting a passion that would surely turn the tide in this war. Stepping into the center of the clearing, she spoke in a loud voice for all to hear. "The ritual looms closer. The final battle looms closer. And we must remain united. We must remain focused. Yes, we suffered a huge loss tonight. None of us could have expected Zael would turn on us. But we should not forget we gained something too."

She paused while the weight of her words sank in. Glowing eyes, fae eyes, and mortal eyes stared back at her. She straightened her back and spoke more surely than before. "We formed an alliance. No matter how the king has hurt us, he cannot stop us from working together. And together, we will be strong enough to defeat him once and for all."

A hum of agreement went through the crowd. Hope filled their eyes once more along with the determination that would keep them fighting.

This wasn't over yet.

Julian would regret making enemies of them. Because no matter what he did to them, no matter how many times he beat them, they would never give up.

26

AFTER A QUICK DISCUSSION WITH the wraiths, Chloe managed to convince them to continue their alliance. Nilyx claimed they might be able to sabotage the ritual. It would not stop the ritual or stop Julian from gaining the power he sought, but it could still mess up some of his plans during the ritual itself.

Chloe had no idea what that was supposed to mean. The wraiths would not reveal any more information about it, but they promised to find out all they could and then they would report back once they had learned more.

In return, Chloe promised the Golden Shields would protect Quintus and keep him from Julian's clutches, so the ritual could not be performed.

At last, the Shields left the Forest of the Wraiths, returning back to Rubyrise, where they promptly fell asleep. They had stayed awake all through the night protecting Undulle Tree, and now the lack of rest had caught up to them.

Sleep held Chloe firmly for the rest of the day and into the night. When she finally woke, darkness still filled the sky. It looked somewhat close to dawn, but since there was no time in Faerie, she could never tell for sure.

She pulled herself to a sitting position as quietly as she could. Heavy sleeping breaths filled the area around her. Now sitting up, she scanned their camp, checking every sleeping mat to see if anyone else had awakened yet.

Everyone slept soundly, except one person. Her eyes narrowed at Quintus's sleeping mat, which sat mysteriously empty. If he woke and got up, where did he go?

The answer came when he stepped to her side a moment later. He must have seen her stirring. After donning her wooden foot and a warm cloak, they moved together away from the other sleeping forms.

If she hadn't been afraid Julian might find them, she would've suggested they go to that lovely valley where Quintus gave her the harp and lit the area with floating twinkling lights. Instead, they tiptoed across the black soil filled with rubies to a cluster of rocks near the sleeping dragons.

It was far enough away they could whisper without waking any people or dragons. But since the rocks were in plain view, they'd only have privacy until the others started waking up.

When they finally got settled, sitting on the black soil with their backs against a large golden boulder big enough for them both to rest against, she carefully took off her wooden foot and began massaging her leg.

As she kneaded the sore muscles, Quintus pulled her wooden foot out of her boot. His fingers moved deftly over the striking wood that had been carved from the only remaining piece of his home in Bitter Thorn. Magic shot from his fingertips as he repaired small nicks and scratches in the wood. He even managed to fill a small crack that had been bothering her right at the very top.

Watching him work made her forget to massage her leg. He always had the most serious face when he crafted. It lit his eyes and made him more beautiful than any man she had ever seen.

Suddenly, he glanced up and caught her staring.

Heat tingled across her cheeks as she dropped her gaze to her lap. He'd surely tease her about it, unless she could put him on the defensive first. Glancing back up, she asked, "Are you finally going to tell me what you wanted to give me?"

As she suspected, the words turned him silent. He focused a little too hard on putting her newly repaired foot back into her boot. Then he even took her leg into his hands and began massaging the muscles at the end where her foot had been cut off.

His fingers were gentler and stronger than hers were, making for a much more effective massage. It only took a few moments before the stiffness in her leg had vanished.

Pulling her leg away and putting her foot back on, she looked him in the eye. "Tell me what you wouldn't tell me in the Forest of the Wraiths."

When she caught his eye, he gulped and looked unable to tear his gaze away. But even now, he kept his mouth shut.

She glanced around the area, then gestured toward the sleeping mats and then the dragons. "Everyone is asleep. You have no reason to keep it secret now."

He took a deep breath and opened his mouth. But instead of words coming out, a heavy exhale escaped instead. That was followed by another deep breath, as if to prepare him for what was to come.

"Okay." The word came out crooked and rushed. He lowered his head and pulled a gorgeous pile of white-and-gold fabric from his magical pocket. His breathing increased in speed until he was nearly hyperventilating as he unfolded the fabric.

Its form wasn't clear at first, but then she recognized a collar and then a waistline. A dress. A *beautiful* dress. He must have crafted it for her.

Once unfolded, she could appreciate its beauty even more. The base of the dress was a magnificent shimmery white satin with a brilliant gold flower pattern woven through it. Shiny gold satin adorned the neckline and the tops of the sleeves. The full skirt had a sparkling white chiffon layered over the white-and-gold satin, giving it depth and extra shimmer. That same white chiffon was also sewn into the tops of the sleeves, where it trailed almost like a cape to the bottom hem of the dress.

He had always made red dresses for her before, and she had often requested red. Was there a reason he had chosen gold and white for this dress?

His fingers stroked over the simple golden embroidery that decorated the waistline. Trembling filled his fingers, so he must have been nervous. That was proved even more when he gulped.

"There are so many different customs in the mortal realm, I was not sure exactly what to do. I asked Mishti, Sofia, Hilda, Elora, even Clara. They mentioned rings, dresses, flowers, parties, promises." He swallowed, suddenly poking the dress, as if he couldn't decide whether to tap or stroke it. "I am not certain you will even agree, so I only crafted one item, something you can keep whatever you choose."

His words tumbled out as awkward as the motions with his fingers. He had said so much without actually saying anything. What was he trying to tell her?

She could have asked, but judging by the state he was in, it might lead to broken sentences that gave half answers. Instead, she focused on the moon tattoo under his eye and reached for their bond.

Emotion flooded inside her, and in an instant, she understood.

"This is a wedding dress?" she asked.

He suddenly lifted the dress from his lap and placed it onto hers.

She reached for the shimmery satin fabric of the bodice, which felt thick and luxurious. For clarification, she asked what he had failed to say. "You're asking me to marry you?"

"Yes." He said it in a rush of breath, more heated than any of the others. He looked like he wanted to swallow the word once it was out of his mouth, but knew it was too late now. Staring at her, his throat bobbed like he couldn't decide if he should swallow or breathe.

A relieved chuckle spilled from her lips, and she started to pull herself up to stand. "I thought you were going to do something crazy like try to send me back to the mortal realm. I thought you wanted to get rid of me." She held the dress up, careful to not let it touch the soil while she got to her feet. "I was so frightened."

By now, she stood and held the dress up by the shoulders. With it up like that, she could admire it more fully. Even in the moonlight, the sparkles in the white chiffon of the skirt glimmered and glinted. The gold satin perfectly complemented the stunning flower design in the bodice.

Quintus got to his feet too, still looking a bit like he might throw up. He stared at her and then managed to force husky words from his lips. "Will you?"

Pulling the dress close, she held it against her body and glanced down, trying to picture how it would look when she wore it. She had seen many beautiful dresses and dozens of gorgeous brides, but she was certain this dress would make them all pale in comparison to her. No one could craft the way Quintus could.

Her cheeks filled with warmth as she held the dress against herself and twirled around in a circle. Joy radiated through her body like a song. The love she had for Quintus expanded within her until she was bursting at the seams with it. Her cheeks stretched from the wide smile she wore.

When she finished twirling, she faced him again, ready to agree and make their lives even more perfect. The word sat right there on her tongue. Her mouth was in position to say *yes*. She wanted to, wanted it more than anything.

But then a yank went through her belly. She stared at him and her mind was filled with the same dilemma it had been since she first returned to Faerie. Her tongue soured from the bitter realization.

She couldn't do it. No matter how much she wanted to, she couldn't. They couldn't keep barreling on like they had no problem when they still had done absolutely nothing to address the same problem they'd always had.

As much as it hurt to face that truth, it hurt worse to see how her indecision hit Quintus. His face had been beaming, just like hers. It looked like a weight had been lifted from his shoulders. But slowly, his face fell, dropping with it a new weight that pushed his shoulders down even more.

His gaze jumped from her lips to her eyes, waiting. Expecting. But then he realized the word would not come, and every bit of joy got sucked away from his expression.

Her stomach clenched. Her heart dropped. It felt like she had been turned to stone.

He kept staring at her, anxious and hurt. "You did not say it."

A whimper nearly tore from her throat, but she managed to swallow it first. She lifted the dress, folding it over her arm. "What about my mortality?" Her gaze fixed on the gold-and-white fabric as she asked.

Stepping forward, Quintus spoke in a gravelly tone. "I do not care about that."

She raised both her eyebrows. "You do not care that I will die someday?"

He said nothing.

Folding the dress into fourths, she shook her head. "I *will* die someday, Quintus."

"I know."

She shook her head, folding the dress again until it went back to resembling a pile of fabric rather than a dress. "I *will* die, and before that I will start aging. All fae look young, no matter how long they've been alive. And right now, I look young too, but that will not always be true. I will start changing so much sooner than you expect. I'll become old, weak, and withered."

She spit the sentence out, using the same words Nilyx had used when she described what would happen to Chandril if he became mortal. If Quintus found the possibility of Chandril becoming mortal so offensive, he couldn't possibly claim he didn't care when that same thing would happen to Chloe.

Quintus continued to wear his same lovestruck face that was willfully blinded to the truth. She gestured toward her face. "I am going to look old. Wrinkled."

She would have said *ugly* too, except he started speaking.

"I am aware of what will happen. I have seen other mortals before. I know…" With each of his words, he grew more agitated. He began shifting on his feet and huffing. Soon, he pinched the bridge of his nose and let out a long breath like he couldn't bear this conversation anymore. Finally, he shook his head and took the dress from her, stuffing it back into his magical pocket. "I knew you would not agree."

Her hands suddenly felt cold without the beautiful dress to warm them. Her tone softened. "I never said I disagreed. I just…I want to make sure you understand."

He took a step closer to her, reaching his arms out but not quite touching her. "What I understand is that my heart *aches* to make a deeper commitment to you. I want you to fully be mine and me to fully be yours, by both mortal customs and fae.

I am desperate to do more than just love you. I want to be married to you."

No amount of self-control could have stopped her after hearing those words. They were too beautiful. Too precious. She jumped into his arms and tilted her head up until his lips found hers.

She breathed in the lemon and vanilla scented air while she moved in closer to her beloved. The fear inside her got replaced by something stronger, something that made her restless and greedy. A feeling so romantic it was magical. A feeling only Quintus evoked.

Pressed so close to him, she could feel his heartbeat accelerate. His right arm slipped around her waist, holding her tight. But the fingers of his left hand trailed up her arm. They danced lightly on her skin, causing sensations wild and free to come alive in the wake of his touch.

Fire exploded inside her, memorizing and devouring every feeling he caused within her. He kissed her fiercely, desperately. It was a perfect mirror to how she kissed back. She gave him everything he wanted and more.

She didn't want it to end.

Whenever he slowed down or showed a hint of pulling away, she found a new way to capture him back into the moment again.

The heat between them was rising to a dangerous level, but it couldn't end. Because once it ended, he'd expect an answer. He'd ask her again, and she'd have to decide.

But she couldn't decide. So she couldn't stop.

Even when the other Golden Shields began stirring on their sleeping mats, she didn't slow. Soon, the Shields started sitting up. Through the corner of her eyes, she could see them glance toward her and Quintus.

No matter how she tried to prolong it, the moment had passed. Quintus pulled his lips away from hers. With his arms still around her, he managed to draw her downward until they both sat on the soil with their backs pressed against the large golden boulder once again.

He stroked her hair, combing through the strands gently. She rested her cheek on his chest because then she wouldn't have to look at him. As the Shields began getting up and getting ready, day started dawning.

The moment would have been peaceful and perfect if it weren't for the unanswered question still rocking between them.

It wasn't until half the Shields were awake that Quintus finally spoke. He whispered in a soft and delicate voice. "You still have not given me an answer. You are avoiding it on purpose."

At least he had kept accusation out of his tone. Not that it mattered much, since he stated a fact they both knew to be true.

She sighed and took his free hand in hers. "I *do* want to marry you."

"But?"

Her lips twitched as they tugged downward. "But I don't want to hurt you anymore than I have to. I worry that by marrying you, it will make it that much more painful for you when I die. If there is anything I can do to ease that pain, I will do it, even if it means we never marry."

A sharp huff left his throat. "And yet you have no problem putting me through the pain of rejecting my offer of marriage."

Her heart twisted as she dared to look into his eyes. "Quintus."

The moment her gaze met his, the slightest smile played on his lips. "It is okay." He pulled her close, letting her drop her head onto his chest again. "I can wait until you are ready. I will wait until you recognize how my heart is already far too gone to ease any pain from your death. And once you finally understand, once you ache for it too, I will be ready for our marriage. Just as ready as I am now."

If they weren't in plain sight of all the Golden Shields, she would have kissed him again.

As others began waking and getting ready, Quintus pulled his sketchbook from his coat and turned to a fresh page. She sat up, allowing him to move his arm from around her so he could draw more easily. Still, she dropped her head onto his shoulder as he worked. It didn't take him long to draw a beautiful crown on the parchment.

It was the same crown he had already showed her. The feminine crown.

She watched for a bit as he perfected the more intricate parts of the crown, but then she turned to the soil at her side. Her fingers dug through the black dirt, plucking up small rubies and collecting them into one hand.

"These rubies would make the perfect stones for this crown, especially some of these darker ones that look more like garnets." Her thumb slid over the jewels.

Quintus stopped drawing and jerked his head toward her. "Did I tell you I thought this crown should have red stones instead of green ones?"

"No." In fact, she hadn't thought about it at all until he asked, but now it did seem curious. The other Crystalfall crown—the one Julian wore—had emerald stones. She turned slowly to Quintus. "You also think this feminine crown should have red stones?"

He nodded.

Holding out her hand now filled with rubies, she said, "Here, then. Take these."

His eyebrows flew upward as she dropped the jewels into his hand. "You think I should *make* the crown?"

She shrugged in response. "Why else would you keep getting the urge to sketch it?"

He shook his head. "But only Faerie—"

"I know," she said, cutting him off. "No one can make a crown unless Faerie itself wants it to happen. But that's why you should try it. If Faerie doesn't want the crown, you won't be able to make it. And if you *can* make it, then we'll know Faerie wants this new crown. It might help us understand. Either way, we'll at least find out what Faerie does or doesn't want."

An incredulous expression overtook his face while he stared first at her and then down at the small red stones in his hand. "I never, *ever* would have thought to make this crown." His eyes narrowed. "But I think you might be right. Whatever happens, trying to make it could help us learn something."

She moved closer, expectantly eyeing the rubies and his drawing.

But instead of crafting, he put both the sketchbook and the rubies away. "First, we need to decide what we are going to do. We cannot simply sit here and wait for Julian to try and capture me. We need to get ready for battle."

Now that day had dawned, she was as ready to get to work as him. "I agree. And even better, I have an idea."

They just needed to gather the Golden Shields. Then she could explain what she had in mind.

27

CHLOE'S FEET HIT THE GROUND as she paced back and forth between Shadow and Temper. Her idea had seemed so wonderful in her head, but she hadn't expected the distress of the waiting part. Waiting and waiting and waiting.

She'd done so much waiting, it made her want to scream. They'd sent a select group of Golden Shields out on their dragons. They went to visit the other courts in Faerie to find out if Julian had any influence there and to find out how many fae he had gathered for his army.

With all the defeats they'd suffered, it was clear they needed more information before jumping into any sort of action. But since Quintus was in danger of being captured, he had to stay back at camp, and she had to stay back to be certain he was safe.

And then she'd had to wait. And wait.

Her legs were starting to get sore from all the pacing. The sight of Rubyrise was starting to grate on her nerves.

How had everyone else found things to do so easily? Mishti showed Chandril their stash of weapons. Fascination filled his eyes as he hung on each of her words. Soon, he used his magic to help make more weapons.

Chloe had forgotten wraiths had more magic than just memory magic. But all fae creatures were like that too. The pixies, dryads, trolls, and all the others could open doors, conjure, and create enchantments. They all had magic just like the high fae did.

If Chandril ever gave Mishti another memory, he wouldn't just lose his undeath. He would lose his magic too.

How could he ever make such a choice? He wouldn't. Mishti would never expect him to.

But now they had the same dilemma Chloe and Quintus had. A mortal and a being who would never die. Death for one, and no death for the other.

Her gaze slipped across their camp until it fell on Quintus. His forehead wrinkled as he stared at his sketchbook. His fingers flew across the page as he drew and fixed, then drew some more. He'd been sketching and re-sketching that crown all day. The one that probably belonged to his mother.

For some reason, her heart sank at the thought. His mother, Dyani, would likely be a fine ruler. She had probably been meant to be ruler of Crystalfall from the beginning, and it was only because of Julian's cunning nature he'd managed to steal the crown for himself.

But it suddenly seemed so wrong for Dyani to be ruler of Crystalfall. It should have been Quintus. As sure as she knew how to cure scurpus, Chloe knew Quintus should be the next leader of Crystalfall.

Her head shook hard, attempting to remove those thoughts from her mind. She needed something to *do*. If she stood here waiting any longer, she might lose her mind.

But just as she reached into her leather bag for the magical book inside it, several dragon shadows soared in the sky above. She released a breath of relief. Finally, the others had returned, and she could learn all they had discovered from the other courts.

While they landed, Chloe gathered the other Golden Shields to the center of camp. Once everyone got situated, she realized the six Shields who had left were returning as nine. The Shields had brought three fae with them.

Quintus immediately recognized a fae male named Kai. Judging by his colorful shirt with a large print, the seashell necklace around his neck, and the smell of salt surrounding him, Chloe guessed Kai must have come from the Court of Swiftsea.

After a friendly greeting between them, Quintus turned to Chloe. "Kai is one of the best warriors I have ever known. He has fought beside Queen Lyren of Swiftsea on many occasions. He even helped me acquire the Swiftsea salt I brought back to you in the mortal realm."

A wide smile filled the warrior's face, making him appear more friendly than fearsome. But Chloe had seen Queen Lyren and the other warriors of Swiftsea fight, and she knew Kai would be a great asset in any battle.

Kai offered a short nod at Chloe and then turned to the other two fae. "We understand you mean to defeat King Julian of Crystalfall. We believe him to be a menace that will undoubtedly destroy Faerie as we know it. We have come to offer our help."

He turned now to the other Shields who had brought him there. Sofia nodded at him encouragingly.

After the short exchange, Kai turned back to Chloe. "We wish to join the Order of the Golden Shields."

This was wonderful news, but no one could have beamed brighter than Quintus. He immediately reached into his magical pocket and withdrew the golden chain mail they had each used to mark themselves as Golden Shields.

In only a few moments, Quintus used his crafting to help them attach the small golden circles to their clothing, marking them as Golden Shields too. It was a beautiful sight. Quintus and Ludo had been happy to be Golden Shields, even though they were the only two fae among the group. Now they had three more fae, but they didn't need to number themselves by fae and by mortals. They were simply Golden Shields, one in purpose and in heart.

With the new golden circles in place, Chloe directed everyone to sit. She turned to Sofia, who had led the group who visited the other courts. After a quick nod, Sofia began to explain what they had learned.

"It is worse than we expected." Sofia shook her head and looked down at her lap. "We thought most of the fae would want nothing to do with Julian since they know he was one of the mortal leaders who nearly destroyed Bitter Thorn Castle, and even all of Faerie."

"But?" Chloe prompted.

Roarke shook his head miserably. "But things are different now that he is a king. He offers Crystalfall Castle as a home to anyone who joins him."

A female fae with a long tangerine silk strip of cloth wrapped around her body like a dress sat forward. "You may not understand the significance of that, but fae are granted extra power if they can call a castle home. They must be individually invited by the ruler of that court to gain the power. And they must not be visitors but true residents. Most castles in Faerie have many visitors but very few true residents. It is often only the ruler and a few brownies who call the castle home. But King Julian is offering it to nearly anyone who agrees to join him."

Chloe nodded. "That makes sense. I know there is power in a home. What else?"

Sofia released a short huff. "For those who refuse, he threatens. He vows to come after them and destroy them if they do not join him. Some fae he has even killed."

All five of the fae in their group flinched at the sound of those words. Chloe had seen a battle of fae against fae before. Though they fought viciously, very few actually died. She distinctly remembered when a few fae had been killed by Portia and Julian near Bitter Thorn Castle. The fae had been equally as disturbed at that time.

Mishti scowled. "Bribery and threats. Apparently, he knows the perfect combination every evil ruler has ever used. Wonderful."

The third fae, one with green-and-blue eyes and a smart crimson coat that had polished brass buttons, shook his head. "It is not wonderful, it—"

Ludo raised a hand and threw a pointed look at the fae. "She knows it is not wonderful. Speaking like that is just a thing mortals do sometimes. Do not attempt to understand."

The fae still had his mouth open, but after Ludo's explanation, he shrugged and said nothing.

Quintus had opened his sketchbook to draw a few lines in it. After he tucked it back into his green coat, he turned to Sofia. "How many people have joined him? Dozens?"

"Hundreds." Her face fell as she covered it with both hands.

And Chloe had been so grateful for the *three* fae who had joined them. Meanwhile Julian had gotten hundreds. Did their small group of nearly four dozen Shields have any chance at all?

Mishti scowled. "He has the right incentives. I am not surprised he has convinced so many people."

"How certain are you he has gotten hundreds of followers?" Quintus asked.

Sofia shrugged. "We only know what we've heard from the people we spoke to. Apparently, nearly everyone he meets either joins him or they are injured or killed. The injured ones are often so frightened they won't speak to anyone."

They continued explaining, theorizing. But the more they talked, the more Chloe realized this information wasn't enough. They needed to know the true size of Julian's forces. They needed to know what defenses he had. She sat up straight and spoke in a rush, realizing too late she might have interrupted someone. "We need to go back to Crystalfall Castle."

A beat of silence followed and then Quintus turned on her. "I will not allow you anywhere near the castle."

More silence met his response. Maybe nobody wanted to get in the middle of an argument between them.

But then Chandril lifted one of his wraith eyebrows timidly. "Is that not too dangerous for you?" He glanced around at them and then continued. "For all of you, since you can die?"

Chloe huffed but barreled on anyway. "I'm not saying we should go inside the castle. We just need to figure out how big his army is. We need to find out if he has any special weapons or magic at his disposal. We can sneak through the forests and get close enough to get information but not close enough to get caught. We'll wear glamours and use the whispering stones. We just need to gather as much information as possible."

Ludo wrinkled his nose. "That still sounds dangerous."

Chloe glared at him and then jumped to her feet. Without even trying, conviction filled her tone as determination ignited within her. "We've been playing it safe, only defending ourselves when he attacks us, yet he continues to get the upper hand. If we want to defeat him, *we* need to attack. And we need to learn exactly what we're up against first, since his army has clearly grown since our last visit to the castle. We promised to protect Crystalfall and make it a place of freedom for all, didn't we? How are we supposed to do that unless we rid the court of the stain that is Julian?"

Kai's eyebrows raised, clearly impressed. His friendly face from before had stiffened to a resolute one. The lightest smile covered his mouth, but it did not appear friendly. It appeared ready to fight. "I hear stories about you, Chloe. You and your Golden Shields. I hear stories of bravery and hope from your sister, Queen Elora, and from many others." The light smile turned to a deeper one. "I have only been here for one conversation, and already, you proved those stories are true."

Her heart leapt in her chest. *Elora* had told stories about Chloe? Stories of bravery and of hope? When had Elora ever believed Chloe to have any sort of bravery? Then again, her older sister had recognized Chloe was growing up. After Chloe had healed Faerie from iron poisoning, her older sister had acknowledged that change.

The pair of them had sent a few messages back and forth since Chloe reopened Crystalfall. All this time, she'd wondered why Elora hadn't come crashing into the court with her beloved to save the day. But hearing this from Kai made Chloe think. Was it possible her sister simply believed in her? Was it possible Elora knew Chloe and her Shields were meant to have this story for themselves? That they were the ones meant to save the court?

Sofia nudged Chloe in the side with her elbow. "You promised us our purpose as Golden Shields would be so great the fae would tell stories about us. It sounds like you were right."

Chloe blinked several times before the words sank in. When they did, it felt like hot soup in front of a crackling fire on a cold, blustery day. It was happening already. Julian may have amassed hundreds of followers, maybe even thousands. He may have had a magical army and a terrible ritual that could give him unimaginable power. But all his stories were told through the shadow of fear.

Meanwhile, Chloe and her Golden Shields had their own stories, ones of bravery and hope, just like the epic poems she loved to read. In her effort to simply do the right thing, she had somehow turned into the kind of hero stories would never forget.

All around her, Golden Shields beamed. Pride shimmered in their eyes while a new determination set their jaws. They stared at her, ready to jump into battle. Ready to *win*.

It felt more amazing than she could explain, but it also hurt because she knew one thing the rest of them had apparently forgotten. To be properly immortalized in stories, they had to actually defeat Julian, something they had failed at over and over so far.

To be true heroes, they had to win.

28

Most of the shields had gone to gather weapons and other supplies, strapping them to their dragons' backs using cloth bags. But now they had decided to travel to the castle once again, Chloe had an even more important task to deal with before they left.

She turned her gaze to those still around her, Mishti, Ludo, Sofia, Batu, Roarke, and the three new fae. Of course, Quintus was there too, but she tried to turn away from him slightly before opening her mouth.

"Who is going to stay back here with Quintus while the rest of us go to the castle?"

Quintus whirled around, facing her with more heat in his face than she expected. "What?" He spit the word out and shook his head. "*I* am not staying back. *You* need to stay back. I keep telling you my father will try to capture or kill you before he captures me."

After being restless and waiting all day, she almost wanted the danger. She couldn't bear staying here any longer while waiting on others to take action.

She turned to him, squaring her shoulders as she looked him in the eye. "I'm going."

He must have seen there'd be no changing her mind. But once he accepted she'd be going, worry sent creases across his forehead. His eyes glinted with fear for her safety. When he spoke, it was with just as much resolution as her. "Then I am going too."

It probably wasn't fair to force him to stay back when she refused to do the same. But even hiding as they planned, he needed extra protection around him. Just in case.

Turning toward the others, she said, "I want three guards assigned to stay with Quintus while we're at the castle."

"What?" Quintus scoffed. "That is ridiculous. No."

"Yes." Chloe folded her arms over her chest and glared at him.

He glared back. "Fine, then I want ten guards assigned to Chloe to keep *her* safe."

Chloe dropped her hands to her sides and leaned forward. "Fine, then I want Mishti as your personal bodyguard in addition to the other guards who will be with you."

Narrowing his eyes, he leaned forward too. "Fine, then I want *me* as *your* personal bodyguard."

"Stop." Mishti marched over and stood directly in between the two of them. "Just stop." She pinched the bridge of her nose and sighed like she had just suffered a great atrocity.

After shaking her head, she dropped her hand away and turned to the others. "Sofia, Batu, Roarke, and Kai, you will stay with Quintus and Chloe at all times. Not just on this mission, but from now on. You will move as a single unit, never separating from each other. And no matter where we go, you will stay at the back in the safest spots. Any questions?"

"Uh." Kai raised a finger with his head tilted to the side. "What are *times*?"

Mishti slapped her forehead. "Oh, right, fae don't use time. I just mean you will stay together always. At every moment. At night, you will arrange your sleeping mats around each other. Quintus is in danger of getting captured by Julian, and no matter what, we cannot let that happen."

Kai nodded in understanding.

Ludo turned to Mishti with a signature grumpy expression filling his face. "What about you? You are excusing yourself of bodyguard duties? That hardly seems fair."

Mishti gestured toward Chloe, Quintus, and those she assigned as their guards. "This group will be at the back in the safest spots wherever we go. You, Chandril, and I will be at the front, in the most dangerous spots."

"What?" He dramatically touched a hand to his chest. "Why do *I* have to be in danger? I would rather be a bodyguard."

Scrunching her mouth to the side, she glanced down. "We need your magic."

The grumpy expression fell away when he realized she was serious. All at once, his chest puffed out and he stood a little taller. "I suppose I can help then. If that is what is needed."

With that arranged, they wasted no time setting out. Taking their dragons, they landed in between the hills and the mountains outside of Crystalfall. Quintus passed around the whispering stones, instructing everyone to speak only when using a stone. Ludo, Kai, and the other two fae went around masking everyone with a glamour.

This mission would be easier with everyone visible, so instead of glamours to make them look invisible, they used glamours to make them look like fae. They also changed everyone's appearance slightly, since their faces were known to Julian.

Once ready, they looked like a generic group of fae. Glamoured this way, they would look like nothing more significant than new fae recruits for Julian's army. With any luck, they would stay hidden and the glamours wouldn't even be necessary, but it would be better to err on the side of caution than to not use the glamours at all.

Mishti divided the Golden Shields into small groups and directed them to get closer to different parts of the castle. Chloe, Quintus, and their personal guards had to stay back at the mountains where they had only the slightest view of the castle.

At least they could still mostly see. If Mishti had been in charge, both Chloe and Quintus would probably be back at Rubyrise.

Chloe ducked behind a bush made of jade leaves and silver berries. Sofia and Batu hid with her, all touching the whispering stone so they could hear what they others were saying. Quintus, Kai, and Roarke hid behind a nearby bush doing the same with their whispering stone.

What they saw in the clearing outside the castle had them rooted to the ground in shock. Mishti spoke into her whispering stone, and since Chloe had a stone in her hands, she heard the words directly in her ears.

"It is difficult with them moving, but I'm going to try and count the fae I can outside the castle."

The fae out in the clearing were dressed in gleaming armor and engaged in intense sparring matches, their blades flashing in the sunlight. The air was filled with the sounds of clashing swords, whistling arrows, and grunts from the training warriors. On the roof of the castle and through several small windows inside the castle, archers honed their skills by slicing arrows through the air. With expert precision, they hit small targets that had been placed on the black soil.

Along with the weapons, many fae sparred with magic. They unleashed bursts of glowing and sparkling energy from their fingertips. Some conjured flames, ice, and lightning. The whir of enchantments hitting trees and bushes sent sharp winds through the air.

Hilda's trembling voice drifted into Chloe's ears. "I think their numbers have tripled since the last time we were here."

"Tripled?" Batu huffed at Chloe's side as he spoke into the whispering stone that he, Sofia, and Chloe all held. "That is more than triple. There are twenty times as many people as we saw before."

A pit in Chloe's stomach swallowed up whatever hope or bravery she'd felt back at camp. Now she could only shiver in horror.

Mishti spoke next. "I estimate hundreds of fae soldiers just outside the castle, maybe even a thousand."

"How many fae do you think are inside the castle?" Hilda asked from another stone.

Mishti's voice lowered. "Probably more. A lot more."

The Shields who had visited the other courts were right. Julian had gathered hundreds and hundreds of fae until he now had thousands. None of the other Faerie rulers had convinced so many fae to be their soldiers. Now he had an army so large no one could oppose him. And judging by how these warriors relentlessly trained, Julian clearly planned to win with numbers and strength and skill.

Hilda spoke into her whispering stone again, her voice trembling even harder than before. "Even if we fight night and day for ten years, it would take a miracle to defeat this army. We don't even have a hundred Golden Shields."

A few other voices spoke next, all saying the same sort of thing. This was impossible. They didn't have a chance.

Chloe wanted to pull her hand away from the whispering stone so she couldn't hear their words anymore. Fear and panic gripped her heart, making it hard for it to beat. How could she be the leader the Shields needed? How could she inspire anyone when turbulent thoughts of defeat filled her own mind and squeezed out any chance for hope?

Was it pointless? Did they have any chance at all?

While Chloe wallowed in misery, a short trumpet sounded and the front doors to the castle flew open. Julian strutted out wearing magnificent golden armor that shined over his gleaming green tunic and trousers. An entourage of over a dozen fae dressed in highly impractical but very beautiful armor trailed around him. Their clothing and hair sparkled from the jewels adorning them.

Around the entourage, three dozen fae soldiers held weapons protectively. Julian flipped his hair back as he walked, and he must have told some kind of joke because everyone around him, the entourage, the fae guards, and even the fae in training, all suddenly roared with laughter.

A wide smile spread across Julian's face as he continued to strut until he reached the center of the clearing. Once there, he snapped his fingers.

It must have been a signal because another group of soldiers exited the castle. Nearly twenty fae worked in tandem to carry a large cage that had half a dozen people inside it. Being so far from the castle, Chloe had to squint to see, but soon she recognized the people.

During their last battle at Crystalfall, just before Julian had gotten the crown, many of Julian's followers, the Zeakriesh, had been killed. The few that were left had run away once they realized the Golden Shields would surely defeat them.

But Julian must have found all of them, or at least some of them, and captured them. Now they were stuffed inside this cage with every fae in the clearing jeering and laughing at their slumped forms.

Julian wore a sneering smile as he watched the prisoners. Once the fae had carried the cage out a great distance from the castle, Julian nodded to the fae at the front of the group. With that signal, the cage was set on the ground, opened, and the prisoners were coaxed out of it.

They all wore chains, making it impossible for them to attempt any sort of escape.

Julian nodded again, though Chloe couldn't tell who that particular nod was directed at. A few moments later, Julian spoke to his entourage, who all released raucous laughter once again.

Even so far from the castle, Chloe could still see how a truly evil look seemed to light in Julian's eye. He turned to the head fae with the prisoners and said something she couldn't hear.

With that instruction, the head fae withdrew a spear from a magical pocket and jabbed the spear into the back of the nearest mortal. Two other fae did the same with two of the other mortals, forcing them to walk closer to the castle.

The first mortal yelled something at the fae jabbing the spear into his back, but he continued stepping forward regardless. But in the middle of one of his sentences, a wall of olive-green magic suddenly slammed against the mortal man from the front. His body shook hard while his eyes rolled back into his head. His skin charred as the smell of burnt flesh filled the air. After another moment, the mortal man dropped to the ground, dead and broken.

The other two mortals realized what fate they would soon meet if they continued on their path toward the castle. They tried to stop, but the fae continued to push spears into their backs, forcing them forward.

They both got slammed into the same olive-green magic even though they hadn't taken exactly the same path. After those three had been killed, the fae forced the rest of the mortals to move forward too. Once they hit the magic one by one, it became apparent the wall of magic was actually a barrier that was invisible until a person made contact with it.

Chloe's stomach sank down to her toes.

Sofia spoke into the whispering stone, saying the same thing they had probably all realized. "Julian has a new barrier around his castle. If we or our dragons trying to get past it, we'll all die."

With this new barrier, they wouldn't be able to use the celestine crystals to get their dragons through. It was clearly made of an entirely different magic. They should have known Julian would find a way to block their dragons out again, but it still hurt to see how he had succeeded so completely.

Julian glanced around the area with a wide grin on his face. The fae in his entourage slapped him on the back and rubbed their hands across his arms. One fae woman even kissed him on the cheek. Julian stood taller, rolling his shoulders back as far as they would go. He nodded, again to someone Chloe couldn't see.

He then waved his arms and spoke what was probably some rousing speech. Every fae hung on his words, especially those in his entourage.

"Let's go back to Rubyrise," Batu said into his whispering stone. His voice was deeply strained, showing cracks that revealed the fear inside him.

That same fear swirled inside Chloe and probably inside all the Golden Shields. She couldn't fault him for wanting to leave.

It seemed this mission had accomplished nothing except to squash the little hope they were hanging onto.

As much as she hated it, it probably was best if they returned to camp. They had seen enough. But just before she could tell everyone to return to the hidden dragons, Mishti's voice drifted in from the whispering stone.

"Look at the castle doors. Do you see that golden sphere on the ground to the left of the first spire?"

Ludo responded. "That one surrounded by rows of fae warriors?"

"Yes," said Mishti.

"What *is* that thing?" Hilda asked.

Only then did Chloe find the sphere they discussed. From her vantage point, she could only barely see it through the rows of soldiers surrounding it.

Mishti continued. "You have to look very carefully, but there is a shimmer of color coming out of it that appears every few seconds. It looks like magic flowing out of it and upward."

Squinting her eyes, Chloe concentrated on the area just above the golden sphere. After straining her eyes for several moments, she noticed a tiny shimmer of energy in a light olive-green.

A small gasp escaped Chloe and then she spoke into the whispering stone. "It's the same color as that barrier that killed the Zeakriesh."

Mishti's voice answered almost immediately. "That device is generating the barrier. If you look closely, you can see it flowing upward and forming a dome around the castle that ends right where the dead Zeakriesh lay."

The new female fae Golden Shield asked, "Why would he use a device instead of an enchantment to create a barrier?"

"Because he's mortal," Mishti responded. "I'm sure the barrier is still made of magic, he's just using a device to create the dome because that's how his brain works. It's just like the golden bathtub he had in his quarters in the castle. With his magic as king, he can conjure water into the bathtub. Instead, he created a magical bath that conjures water for him. He may have fae magic, but he still thinks like a mortal."

Chloe nodded to herself, seeing the logic in those words.

Quintus whispered into his stone. "So we know that device generates the barrier. How does that help us?"

Mishti responded. "There's a small opening at the top where the magic is coming out. There must be something inside the sphere that is creating the magic. If we can damage the interior of the device, I'm certain the barrier would come down."

Chloe couldn't see the top of the sphere from where she hid, but other Shields clearly could.

"It's too heavily guarded," a Shield said. "No one could get close enough to get a weapon inside that opening."

Considering rows and rows of soldiers surrounded the sphere, no one could argue with that.

Hilda jumped in next. "Even if we could get close enough, the opening of the device is too small. A weapon would never fit in there."

"A weapon, no," Mishti said slowly. "But dragon fire could."

In a flash, understanding dawned in Chloe's mind.

Roarke spoke into his whispering stone. "What about the archers on the roofs and inside the castle at those windows?"

Another Shield said, "Those archers would attack any dragon who tried to destroy the device."

Mishti had an answer for that too. "We've been practicing flying formation, dives, *and* fire breathing. Our dragons are perfectly trained for destroying that sphere. We could send in two teams. The first will attack those archers. The dragons will use claw strikes and tail sweeps while the Shields on their backs attack with their weapons. The main purpose is to take down as many archers as possible and to draw fire."

"And the second team?" Quintus asked.

"Those dragons will dive in one after the other and breathe fire into the opening until the device is destroyed."

Ludo whined into his stone, "But that will only destroy the *barrier*. What are we supposed to do after that?"

With a calm, unmoved voice, Mishti responded. "That's when the real battle begins."

It would take so much work for only a *chance* to start the battle. Even with all the training their dragons had done, they still needed a great deal more.

With an enemy like Julian, they needed as much preparation as possible. But at least now they had an idea what to do next.

29

THE DRAGONS WERE NEARLY READY. Chloe stood at the back of the ledge on Rubyrise, eyeing the beautiful creatures as they soared above. Mishti walked on the ground below, barking out commands.

They practiced drills over and over consisting of downward dives, fire breathing, then sharp turns upward to fly back into the sky again. Other dragons practiced claw strikes, tail sweeps, and jaw clamps. They did obstacle courses, flying formations, anything and everything Mishti could think of to prepare them.

It had been decided Chloe and Quintus would not be allowed to join the attack on the castle. They would have to stay back with their guards. Quintus and the others still wanted the practice with their dragons, so they participated in the drills, but Chloe stayed on the ground.

When Mishti finished calling out the next set of instructions, Chloe walked over to her friend. She still didn't understand their plan to get rid of the olive-green barrier. Hopefully the young woman had answers to all her questions.

Chloe rocked onto the balls of her feet, hoping her question wouldn't seem silly. "How did Julian's soldiers get in and out of that barrier? Do you think they wore something that protected them from it?"

"No." Mishti answered abruptly, then yelled to a rider above. "You're still too low, Sofia. Fidget needs to pull up faster."

"Are you sure it isn't something they wore?" Chloe asked. "Maybe there are protective crystals or something that—"

"They weren't wearing anything." Mishti's gaze stayed above while she answered. "The device was turned off at first. It wasn't until the soldiers and those prisoners were beyond the reach of the barrier that Julian had the device activated."

Chloe tilted her head. "But the soldiers went back to the castle after they killed the Zeakriesh. We saw them walk straight through the spot the barrier had been."

"Yes." Mishti raised her voice again. "That's better, Batu. Now see if you can shoot twice as many arrows in the same amount of time."

She turned and nearly trampled over Chloe. Throwing her long black braid over her shoulder, Mishti stepped to the side and turned her gaze upward once again. "Before the soldiers outside the barrier tried to return, Julian signaled to another soldier right next to the device. On his signal the device was turned off so the other soldiers could get inside the protected area safely. Then he signaled to have the device turned back on again."

Confusion twisted in Chloe's chest, making it buzz and prickle. "If the dome is above and around the castle, how is the first team of dragons and riders supposed to fly in and attack the archers? The dome won't even let the new Zeakriesh's arrows go through to hit the dragons, and our dragons and riders won't be able to attack them through the barrier either."

Cupping her hands around her mouth, Mishti shouted. "Circles, Roarke, not ovals. Make sure your dragon moves in an even circle."

She kept staring above so long she had probably forgotten to answer Chloe's last question. It took a nudge in the arm to get her talking again.

"The dome doesn't go *above* the castle," Mishti finally answered. "It goes high enough to shield any windows and doors big enough for the dragons to get through, but the barrier stops just below those slit windows the archers use right at the uppermost level of the castle. Those slit windows and the roof are above the barrier, and we'll be able to attack them."

As each question got answered, a new one kept coming to Chloe's mind. "Why would Julian make a barrier that leaves some of his soldiers vulnerable to attack?"

That got Mishti to lower her gaze and actually make eye contact. "Because he doesn't care about his soldiers."

An ache stabbed Chloe's heart, both because it was such a cruel answer and because it was entirely true. She should have realized the same.

Mishti lifted her gaze to the sky once again. "Julian only cares that he has as much protection as possible, which means he needs soldiers both inside *and* outside the barrier."

Nodding, Chloe watched as three dragons dived in perfect formation, each of them blasting the same golden barrel one after the other with perfect precision.

It was too much to hope their plan to destroy the device and take down the barrier would work, but the dragons really were getting better. A lot better. She followed after her friend and spoke again. "That makes sense, but what about fire? How do you know dragon fire will go through the barrier instead of being stopped by it?"

Mishti shrugged, as if this was the most obvious answer of all. "I have seen fire go through enchantments before. If the enchantment barrier only stops solid objects, then fire should be able to get through. It is not solid."

"You don't think the fire will be affected by the barrier at all? You don't think it will spread or get diminished as it goes through the barrier?"

"No." Mishti answered just as surely as before. "But even if it does, we're planning to have several dragons breathe fire on the device. Maybe the first breath won't destroy it, but several of them should. Watch those wings, Ludo. Temper doesn't like her wings touching other dragons."

She shouted the last part and shook her head. "I don't know why I let him fly my dragon, but Temper seems to like him more than the other Golden Shields, besides me obviously. So I guess if I'm not flying him, it has to be Ludo."

After all the explanations, Chloe had no other questions left. "I guess you have an answer for everything."

A tiny smirk graced Mishti's mouth as she turned toward her friend. "If you were worried the dragons might accidentally get too close to the barrier as they fly downward, I have an answer for that too."

Chloe responded with a knowing eyebrow raise. "I didn't think about that, but I do want to know the solution you thought of."

Mishti reached down and grabbed a handful of black soil. "Each Golden Shield brings pocketfuls of dirt and pebbles. When we first get to the castle, all the riders empty their pockets onto the barrier. Since the barrier only becomes visible when something touches it, the dirt and pebbles should land on the top of the barrier and make it seen. Then the second team of dragons can fly down in a sharp dive, but still pull up when they get too close to the barrier."

Pride glimmered in her eyes as she spoke. But as she finished, she put her hands on her hips and turned her gaze to the air again. "We need to train the dragons to not fear the sound of explosions. Julian's new Zeakriesh will probably only use magic and weapons against the dragons, but Julian does love his explosions. If the dragons are used to the noise, they'll be able to continue without getting distracted."

It was clear she said these words mostly to herself, especially because she scurried away looking for a way to create small explosions to practice with.

Chloe dropped to the ground, sitting cross-legged as she watched the flying creatures above. It felt like this would work. It felt like they had thought through every possible setback and had a clear solution for it. But they had felt sure before. They had walked confidently into situations only to be sorely defeated.

And even if this plan did work, it only got the barrier down. They'd still have thousands of soldiers to defeat and a castle to break inside.

Pulling the leather bag off her shoulder, she reached inside for her magical book. She didn't have anything in particular to learn, but hopefully the book would calm her mind and stop her from thinking of all the various ways this plan could go wrong.

The dragon training continued, now with explosions. Chloe focused on her book and read the pages she'd already read many times. Filling her thoughts with familiar words brought her comfort when she'd been so consumed with turmoil.

Soon, she'd been sitting long enough that her legs cramped from the cross-legged position. She moved to another area where her back could rest against a boulder and she could stretch out her legs. After reading a few more pages in her book, she caught sight of the green glow of a tiny sprite.

She dropped the book into her lap at once and held her palm out for the tiny creature to land on. A sprite with velvety green hair and a sparkly pink dress landed. Chloe had seen this same sprite several times before. The tiny creature was a friend to her sister, Elora.

Chloe dug into her leather bag and found a dried leaf from one of her herbs she used to create poultices. She had to give the sprite an offering, something of personal importance, before the sprite would deliver a message.

The tiny creature looked over the leaf extensively with her pink-and-green eyes. She must have deemed it worthy because she soon stuffed the leaf into her pocket and stood up straight. "I have a message for Chloe of Crystalfall from Queen Elora of Bitter Thorn. Here is the message: Tell Quintus to open a door to the Bitter Thorn throne room. Once he does, I am coming through to see you. I need to tell you something."

A knot formed in Chloe's belly. Since the words had been delivered by a sprite, she had no idea how urgent they were. Even though she and her sister had sent a few messages back and forth to each other, Elora had never once tried to enter the Court of Crystalfall. It might have been a bad sign or it might have been fine, but Chloe wasn't going to take the chance.

Waving Quintus and Shadow down, she soon stood at the center of camp surrounded by her and Quintus's personal guards. Only then did Quintus wave his hand and open a door.

In less than a breath, Elora charged through the door, her shiny brown hair whipping behind her with her branch-like crown sitting regal on her head.

Brannick, her beloved and the High King of Faerie himself, traipsed through the door next with his black wolf at his side. He stood tall and eyed the area around him with mild disinterest.

The moment they were through, Elora tackled her sister with a tight hug. "You are not very good at visiting me, you know."

Chloe donned a teasing expression. "You were not very good at visiting me in the mortal realm either, were you?"

Elora snorted at that and launched straight into the reason she had come. "King Julian is having a party at Crystalfall Castle. He has announced it will take place two evenings from now."

Brannick smirked at his beloved while she smirked back.

The smirk remained as Elora turned back to her sister. "Can you believe that? He announced it would take place two evenings from now, as if we have calendars and keep dates."

Brannick nodded with all the majesty a High King could carry as he patted his wolf on the head. "He plans to throw a lavish party to celebrate his impending victory. All fae are invited, even us." He gestured toward himself and Elora. "He also hopes to get other fae to join his army during this party, a fact which he has done nothing to hide."

Mishti's dark brows furrowed in deep thought. "If he throws a party, it will make him appear like he has nothing to fear. It will make those who have yet to join him feel like victory is already secured. It's a good plan. He certainly understands the thoughts of those he is manipulating."

Then Mishti stepped forward, her eyes narrowing. "If he is throwing a party, he might let his guard down."

Both Elora and Brannick nodded. Brushing her hair behind her shoulder, Elora continued, "All his soldiers, Zeakriesh they call themselves, will stop training for that evening and they will also be at the party."

Several Golden Shields raised their eyebrows at that.

Even Quintus could see the opportunity. "Even if some of the guards have weapons, if they are caught up in the party, it will leave the castle vulnerable. It will leave my father vulnerable."

Elora gulped and took her sister by both shoulders. "Do not be so taken with the possibilities. This is surely a trap."

Chloe shrugged her sister's hands off her. "Obviously it's a trap."

A great sigh of relief escaped Elora's lips. "So you will not go?"

"We have to go." Chloe knew this as surely as she knew it was a trap. "They'll only let their guards down if they think we're falling for the trap. Now we just have to figure out how to exploit the fact that we know it's a trap."

Sofia, Roarke, and even Kai slumped, their faces falling.

Ludo groaned miserably. "It would have been an amazing chance if they were not expecting us. But if it is a trap, then they will be expecting us. How could we possibly do anything useful?"

Chloe tapped her fingers against her thigh. "They expect us to start a battle while the soldiers are preoccupied with the party."

Sofia raised an eyebrow. "So what do we do?"

In response, Chloe curved her lips into a grin. "We have to start a battle. That's what they expect."

"But how do we *win* that battle?" Quintus folded his arms over his chest, looking a little more dejected than the rest.

"We don't." Chloe leaned forward, like she was letting them all in on a secret. "We just make them think *all* our forces are involved in that battle. Then the rest of us sneak inside the castle, glamoured to look like fae."

A shocked sputter escaped Batu's mouth. "You want to go *in* the castle? Inside the castle where Julian has an army of thousands?"

Chloe nodded. "They'll be trying to trick us, but that's how we'll trick them. They'd never expect us to take the risk of entering the castle with so many soldiers inside it."

"Because it is crazy," Ludo said, dramatically lifting both arms in a question. "How are a few of us supposed to kill the king when he has an army of thousands?"

Chloe turned to Brannick. "You're very good at barrier enchantments, right? I mean, you're High King of Faerie."

He raised an eyebrow and glanced at his beloved. But then he answered, "Yes."

Leaning in again, Chloe continued. "Then as long as Quintus is willing to kill his father—"

"I am," Quintus added before she could finish.

Flashing him with what was probably a devious smile, she said, "Then my idea should work."

30

WITH THE PARTY STILL TWO days away, they were left with an unnerving amount of time to continue waiting. Chloe kept herself busy planning strategies for every possible scenario. She found strategy after strategy that guaranteed their victory, but fear kept spilling to the front of her mind. It reminded her of how they'd thought so many of their previous strategies would succeed, only to have them fail. Despite that, she kept planning for every possible contingency and then shared the plans with Mishti and Quintus.

Mishti continued training the dragons in drills, but she directed other trainings too. During the party, the dragons and several riders would engage in combat, drawing attention to make Julian think the Shields had fallen for his trap. But since their real plan would happen inside the party, the Golden Shields trained for that too. Quintus directed those drills.

Elora and Brannick stayed, offering their help with the training. Mishti and Elora bonded almost instantly over their sword skills. Brannick offered significant help to the fae in how they could use their magic more effectively. He and Elora would be entering the castle as part of the plan, but they would only be one cog in a series.

Many people would enter the castle during the party, and each of them would have an important role to play.

By evening, sweat glistened on every forehead. They hardly spoke as they gathered around the golden table and ate their evening meal. The large portion sizes everyone devoured offered more proof for how hard they had worked themselves.

Once finished eating, nearly everyone fell onto their sleeping mats and immediately fell asleep. Chloe would have done the same, except Quintus trailed across camp and settled with his back against the golden boulders where he'd been sitting with her earlier.

Deciding sleep could wait, she joined him.

He smiled at her presence and then pulled out his sketchbook. While the Golden Shields were falling asleep, he drew the beautiful feminine crown once again. All his practice had made a difference. His fingers flew across the page, sketching the most perfect version of the crown he had ever drawn. Once he finished the front side, he drew another crown beneath it, this one angled to show the back.

Holding the pencil still for a moment, he glanced over at the camp. Every Golden Shield had fallen asleep, except Mishti and Chandril. But they were too busy whispering to each other to notice anything Quintus did. Elora and Brannick were awake somewhere too, but they had left the camp with the promise they'd be back eventually. But *eventually* probably meant they'd be back in the morning.

Quintus nodded to himself and reached into his pocket. He drew out several golden branches and a few golden rocks that he must have gathered from around their camp. Next, he pulled out the handful of the dark rubies Chloe had collected earlier.

Her eyebrows opened wide as a sense of wonder danced in her heart. "You're going to make the crown?"

"I am going to try." He lifted a golden tree branch and examined it carefully. After setting his sketchbook onto his lap, he released crafting magic from his fingertips. His gaze kept skipping between his sketchbook and the golden branch. He worked slowly at first, but then started moving faster.

Soon, he had a thin circle of gold that would form the bottom of the crown.

Sucking in a sharp breath, she sat a little taller. "It's working."

"Perhaps. Or perhaps it does not look like a crown yet so Faerie has no reason to stop me. I may be stopped as I continue."

He tried to play it off like he didn't care, but he couldn't hide the glint of excitement in his brown eyes. When he began picking up rubies and shaping them to be smaller, perfectly polished and cut stones, a light smile played on his lips. He set the tiny rubies into the bottom circle of the crown, being certain to space them evenly.

She bit her lip in anticipation, watching every move of his fingers with intense concentration. Once the bottom circle had been inlaid with rubies, he took another golden branch and began forming more of the crown. Instead of sharp tines, intricate metalwork formed curvy vines and delicate flowers. Using the small golden rocks he had gathered, he crafted golden flower petals and then inlaid a dark ruby into the center of each of them. These tiny flowers got placed onto the crown, making it more breathtaking with each new piece.

At the tops, he stretched golden tree branches to curve upward like vines, then shaped the ends to look like leaves. Those were inlaid with leaf-shaped rubies. The final golden rock formed a large circle, which he placed at the top front of the crown.

So far, Faerie had not stopped him from crafting. Could it be that Faerie wanted this crown made? Just like they had guessed?

But now Quintus held a large ruby that was clearly meant to cover the large circle at the top of the crown. It was the final piece in this magnificent masterpiece.

He glanced toward her and held his breath. She held her breath too. It was possible this final piece would be the one that got stopped. If Faerie didn't want the crown to be made, the ruby wouldn't stick and the whole thing might fall apart.

The idea of the crown breaking hurt Chloe's heart, but she knew the rules of Faerie as well as Quintus did. *No one* could make a crown. Not unless Faerie itself wanted it to happen. So either Quintus would craft the ruby into place, or else the crown would be torn apart.

Anticipation thrummed through Chloe's veins as her beloved went to set the stone in its spot. Golden and emerald magic sparkled at his fingertips as he crafted. He held the ruby in place as magic surrounded it. The other rubies hadn't needed much magic to stick, but this one hadn't attached yet.

He narrowed his eyes, leaning in closer as more magic flowed from his hands. The ruby shifted slightly, and he had to get it back into position again. One last burst of magic left his fingertips, which may have been his last attempt.

But then a rush of dark red magic sparkled and surrounded the gorgeous crown. It shook the creation, vibrating hard.

Chloe clapped her hands over her mouth and sucked in a gasp. Was it about to be torn apart?

Just as she was ready to give up, the magic appeared to suck back into the crown itself. All vibrating stopped at once, and it sat still on Quintus's palm.

It stopped so suddenly she had to blink several times before it sank in. It had worked.

It had *worked.*

She placed a hand over her heart as her mouth dropped open. Reaching out, she poked the crown with her fingernail, checking that it was as real as it looked.

It was.

A thrill jumped through her heart. She glanced into Quintus's eyes, but his expression did not match hers.

He swallowed slowly, frowning as he stared at the creation. Then he used his other hand to lift the crown up. The frown on his face deepened as he traded the crown from one hand to another. Displeasure continued to grow on his face the more he handled the crown.

"What is it?" she finally asked.

Scowling, he stuffed the crown into his magical pocket. "It did not react to me. A true Faerie crown sparkles and releases magic when the person holding it has been chosen by Faerie to rule. But it did not react to me at all."

He had said nothing about expecting it to react to him before he made the crown. It came as a complete surprise that he'd clearly been hoping for this. But the crown was feminine. Why did he expect that particular crown to react to him?

She shook her head, desperate to ease his fears. "Maybe it's not a real crown."

His scowl only deepened. "Maybe it *is* a real crown, and this means I am not meant to be ruler over Crystalfall."

Gently, she reached for one of his hands, slipping her own inside it. "But don't you think the crown probably belongs to your mother? I thought we both assumed that. If it's her crown, why would it react to you?"

Quintus huffed. "My father's crown reacted to me. Even if my mother is meant to rule, I am still her son. The only reason it would not react to me is if Faerie does not want me as ruler of Crystalfall."

It seemed far more likely the crown *wasn't* in fact meant for Dyani, as they had assumed. But that only brought up more questions than answers, none of which would help ease Quintus's tension at this moment.

Chloe squeezed his hand, leaning her body against his. "Faerie obviously doesn't want Julian as ruler. Let's just focus on that right now."

A heaving breath escaped Quintus as his whole body slumped. When he spoke, it was in a small voice. "I fear my father has more power than I will ever be able to defeat. I may be drawn to this court, but he is ruler over it. What right do I have to fight for the crown?"

"What right?" Chloe sat up, pulling her hand away so she could stare straight into his eyes. "The other crown reacted to you after you made it, remember? It did not make you king because Julian was still alive, but it did claim you as a rightful ruler. We don't know what this new crown is for, but *that* crown is the current crown of Crystalfall. That alone proves you are heir and absolutely have a right to fight for this court."

His shoulders lifted ever so slightly. "I did not think about it like that."

Now that he was starting to remember his birthright, an entirely new question came surging to the front of her mind, one she hadn't expected at all.

He must have seen her thinking because he looked at her a little more closely and asked, "What is it?"

Settling back against the boulder, she prepared herself for what would surely be a revelatory conversation.

31

CHLOE TAPPED HER CHIN, TRYING to find logic where there was none. The fact that Faerie had allowed a new crown to be made was surprising, shocking even. But her mind hadn't stuck on that. Instead, it turned to Quintus's father and his actions of the past. She turned to Quintus, with questions swirling inside her. "I've always wondered why Julian destroyed your home in Bitter Thorn."

A frown dropped Quintus's face. "He knows there is power in a home."

"Yes, but why wouldn't he just kill you? He tried to kill you when you were a child. Why did he bother destroying your home when he could have gotten rid of you for good?"

"In truth, I have wondered the same thing myself." Quintus tilted his head to the side. "Maybe so he could perform the Bloodstone Convergence?"

That didn't seem right. Chloe shook her head. "I doubt that. He probably wouldn't even need the ritual if it wasn't for you. If you were already dead and he didn't have to worry about you stealing his crown, he'd probably get power in less dangerous ways."

"True." Quintus slid a hand through his dark curls. "He may keep defeating us, but our lives still threaten him more than anything else in Faerie."

"Does he have more power over you now because he destroyed your home?"

Quintus turned his gaze downward. "Yes. I will never be able to defeat him on my own because of the power imbalance he created when he burned down my home. But your plan does not require me to defeat him by myself, so I still think it will work."

"I agree." She reached for a lock of hair and started twirling the blonde strand around one finger. "It still doesn't make any sense though. Why would he create a power imbalance just so he could defeat you in some future battle? Even as a mortal and without his magic, he still had Ansel's gemstones, and he still had plenty of weapon experience. And he caught you off guard, right? You weren't expecting him?"

"Correct."

"So why wouldn't he just try to kill you?" She spun the hair faster around her finger, increasingly frustrated with how little sense it made. "Why did he destroy your home instead?"

It took one more moment, but then her heart skittered. Her body went cold as realization set in. Every muscle inside her froze as the truth sent icicles through her heart.

"What?" Quintus stared harder at her now she had gone silent.

Her gaze lifted to his. "When I came to Faerie the first time, back when Elora and Brannick were trying to defeat Queen Alessandra, you felt no pull toward Crystalfall."

"That is true, I did not." He answered without emotion, but once the words were out, a flash of fear lit in his eyes. "So you think I do *not* have a right to claim the crown? Because I was not drawn to this court back then?"

Chloe waved a hand. "No, that's not what I'm saying. You were not drawn to this court because you already had a home in Bitter Thorn. You were safe there and had no need for any other home. There was nothing that would compel you to find a new home."

He sat silent, staring off into the distance as he considered those words. But soon, a crack of understanding broke across his face. "But then my father *destroyed* my home," he said.

A miserable laugh left Chloe's lips. "Julian couldn't find it. He couldn't find *Crystalfall*. Faerie must have hidden it from him when it blocked his magic." She shook her head. "But Julian must have known that as heir to the court, you would be drawn to it once you had no other place to call home."

Confusion pulled Quintus's eyebrows downward. "But when I was drawn to the crystal caves, there was a barrier enchantment that prevented us from getting into this court."

She nodded. "Yes, and Julian wrote a note detailing exactly how to unlock that barrier so we could enter Crystalfall. He wrote it cryptically and stuck it in my magical book, so I thought the note came from Faerie itself. I thought it explained part of the healing process needed to save Faerie from iron poisoning."

Now the same coldness that gripped Chloe's heart tight came over Quintus. His jaw clenched as he curled his hands into fists. "He used me. He used both of us to get back inside the court Faerie had blocked him from." His fists relaxed as he dropped his chin to his chest. "And because he took my home, he has power over me I can never hope to overcome. What if that is why he keeps defeating us?"

Once the words left his lips, Quintus's eyes closed. He put a hand over his forehead and spoke more dejected than ever. "I said your plan would work, but what if it does not? What if he has too much power over me, and we cannot defeat him?"

She reached for his hand and pulled it into her own. "You will not be fighting alone, remember? And he only took your home once. How much power over you can he have?"

His nose wrinkled as he looked into her eyes. "He has taken my home much more than that. He took my childhood home where I lived with my mother. He destroyed my home in Bitter Thorn. He took the castle away from us, he forced us to leave Celestine Meadow near the castle. He took away our camp in the hills near the castle. He took us away from that valley at the bottom of Rubyrise Mountain. I keep being drawn to new places in Crystalfall, and he keeps taking those places away from us too."

The muscles in his hands tightened more with each of his words. She held his hand with both of hers and slid her thumbs across his skin until at least some of the tension released. Then she whispered what she hoped would be comforting words. "Maybe a home is more than just a place."

When she finished speaking, his gaze flicked up to her and golden glints sparked in his eyes. He stared at her in that special way that made her stomach flop over on itself. Heat prickled across her cheeks, warming as he leaned a little closer.

"It *is* more than a place." His free hand reached out until he placed it against her cheek. "It is you. *You* are my home, Chloe."

The heat in her cheeks burned and trailed down her neck. Soon, she'd need to start fanning herself. "There you have it then. He can't take me away from you. I won't let him. So it doesn't matter how many times we've had to move. You still have a home because you have me. And maybe that gives you power over him that he doesn't know how to defeat."

He tugged his hand out of her grip and then dropped both his hands onto her shoulders. A firm, sure grip held her as he stared into her eyes. "I will not let him take you from me. No matter what, that is one home I will protect at all costs."

His lips came down against hers then, just as hot as her own. One hand left her shoulder as it dug into her hair. She found his chest and drew circles over it with her fingers. If she wasn't careful, she'd drop herself into his lap next, and who knew what would happen after that. Especially because the Golden Shields were all asleep now.

But after only a few moments, he pulled away and gazed deeply into her eyes. The hand in her hair moved to her cheek, which he stroked softly. Now he leaned his forehead against hers where he could look at her while speaking. "Are you ready to say *yes* yet?"

Before, she might have done anything to tear her gaze away from his. But after that kiss, she was happy to stare into his eyes. With the lightest smile on her lips, she answered. "Ask me again after we defeat Julian. Maybe by then I will be ready."

The smile he responded with lit his entire face. Any fears remaining in her heart were starting to flutter away. Maybe they didn't have to accept their horrible problem. Revyn and Clara had made their love work even though she was mortal, and he was not. The pixies had gifted her with a pendant that greatly extended her life.

And Julian had found a way to extend his life too. Quintus hadn't found a way to help Chloe yet, but maybe a way still existed. If they could find one, then it would be easy for her to finally give the answer both she and Quintus desired.

"Hello." Elora jumped in front of the two of them wearing a mischievous smile. At once, she used both hands to drag Quintus up and onto his feet.

"When did you get here?" Chloe sat up straight with a start.

"Oh, just now." Elora had gotten Quintus to his feet. Her smile didn't falter as she pushed him, not very gently, away and toward the sleeping Golden Shields. "Goodnight, Quintus, hope you sleep well."

His face turned red as he glanced over his shoulder at Chloe. That got him an extra hard shove from Elora. "Go on. You two have had enough of a moment. Off to sleep now."

He slumped over to his sleeping mat as Elora turned to beam back at her sister.

Chloe glared and folded her arms over her chest. "That was rude."

Ignoring that statement, Elora dropped onto the ground until she sat directly across from Chloe. "You looked like you needed to talk."

Unimpressed, Chloe raised an eyebrow. "Did I? Or did I just look like I was sitting too close to Quintus for your liking?"

Once again, Elora ignored the accusation. Instead, her gaze drifted upward. "Why does Crystalfall have a moon? Has it always been here?"

"No, it happened recently." Chloe turned toward the rest of the sleeping Golden Shields. She should probably head to bed too. But suddenly, her head snapped back to face her sister. "Does Bitter Thorn *not* have a moon?"

"It does not." Elora stared at the sky above her as she answered.

"Are you sure? The moon has not been here long."

Elora's gaze turned to her sister now. "I am certain." She gestured up toward the sky. "That moon only shines in Crystalfall."

Forgetting sleep for a moment, Chloe turned her eyes upward. The moon and stars shined in the sky all because of Chloe and Quintus's bond. Long ago, Quintus had told her a moon and stars were mortal symbols since Faerie had no moon or stars. But Crystalfall did. Perhaps they'd been right in assuming this court, more than any of the others, was meant for both fae and mortals.

Amidst her wonderings, she found her sister staring straight into her eyes with that same mischievous smile on her face. It must have been an older sister thing, because truthfully,

Chloe *did* need to talk. Her recent conversation with Quintus only confirmed it.

It took a long, deep breath before Chloe was ready, but she finally said the words in her heart. "You used a shard to turn yourself fae."

It hadn't been a question, but Elora understood. Her eyes narrowed, but she wasn't surprised in the slightest. She'd probably been expecting this. Her response came out slowly, carefully. "You know what that process entails? You remember how much risk is involved?"

"Yes." Chloe gulped as soon as the word left her mouth.

"Do you think you can do it?" Elora leaned in, awaiting the answer. She didn't doubt. She simply asked genuinely.

But even though her sister hadn't meant to hurt, Chloe's heart still sank. She lowered her gaze to her lap and spoke the painful truth. "No."

"Then you will fail if you try." Elora's answer came flat and unhopeful.

Chloe dropped her chin to her chest. Of course she had long thought the same thing. She knew exactly what it took for her sister to survive the balance shard that turned her fae. She'd never once believed she could do it for herself. But it hurt to confront that knowledge all the same.

Elora's eyebrows pinched together, growing more serious. "You must have the utmost conviction, or you will not survive. Even then, it will be the greatest fight of your life."

Pain etched across Chloe's heart. Why did she have to be right about this? She scowled at the ground. "It's not fair. *You* were strong enough. Why can't I be strong enough?"

"Why do you want to be fae?"

That question caught Chloe off guard. Why would her sister ask such a question. Didn't she already know?

But Elora continued to wait for an answer.

"So I will not die," Chloe finally answered. "I could never ask Quintus to become mortal for me, if that's even possible.

But unless I turn fae, I *will* die someday. I want to save Quintus from that pain."

Elora nodded, as if everything was now clear. "That is the difference then. I turned fae to save my beloved's life, not to spare him from sadness. Without a strong enough reason, no one can survive the process."

"It is hopeless then." Chloe pouted, showing the pain she could never admit to anyone else. "I never should have returned to Faerie. I never should have let him fall for me."

Elora raised an eyebrow and lifted her sister's chin. "You give up so easily? You are the smartest person I know. Perhaps there is *another* way."

It took three blinks before Chloe dared to answer. "You think so?"

Shrugging, Elora got to her feet, wearing a wide smile. "I have no idea. But I know if anyone can figure it out, you can."

She reached a hand out and helped Chloe get to her feet. Then they both tiptoed over to the sleeping mats with everyone else and climbed under their blankets.

Another way.

Chloe had been so stuck trying to get Quintus to accept her mortality that she'd spent almost no effort trying to think of another way. She'd always known a shard wouldn't work, but she also knew others like Clara and Julian had already found other ways to extend their lives. Chloe had to focus on defeating Julian right now, but just as she promised Quintus, maybe after they'd won, she'd be ready.

Ready to find another way.

32

A GLIMMERY OPULENT DRESS OF blue silk and opalescent embroidery covered Chloe's form. Except the dress was only a glamour. Her face had been glamoured too, making her appear as a generic fae with black hair and gold and blue eyes.

Night filled the sky, dotted with twinkling stars and a bright golden moon. She, and the other Shields with her, stepped through the front doors of Crystalfall Castle, heading right into the party they were certain was a trap.

The first test came as they walked past the soldiers lining the entryway. Would the soldiers know they were Shields glamoured to look like fae so they could sneak inside? Each soldier looked over them, just as they looked over the other guests, but they said nothing and they made no reaction.

So far, their presence had not been detected.

They were directed to move into the ballroom, which was filled with music, food, and dancing. Julian sat on the throne, wearing lavish clothes that made him appear taller and stronger than usual. Members of his entourage fed him bits of food and laughed at his jokes like they were the most hilarious ones in the world.

Chloe and Quintus trailed close to the throne, after they'd each gotten a bit of bread from the tables at the edge of the room. They nibbled on their food to blend in with the other guests, but their feet carried them close enough to the throne to hear Julian's words.

Now that they were in position, they just had to wait for the fake battle outside to begin.

Quintus turned casually toward the throne, playing it off like he was simply looking around, but once he caught sight of his father, he flinched. He managed to cover the expression, but he didn't stop his hands from forming loose fists.

This could be a problem. If he gave himself away by looking too angry at the sight of Julian, they might get caught before they could enact their plan.

That fear was soon joined by another. Why hadn't the battle outside started yet? Mishti and the Shields with their dragons should have attacked by now. Julian should have been notified.

Quintus's fists curled tighter while his jaw flexed. Through their bond, Chloe could feel rage filling him. After all their planning, she wouldn't allow them to get caught already. She tore a small piece of bread off the chunk in her hand and held it right against Quintus's lips.

"You must try some of this. I think it is made with hazelnuts."

He turned to the bread and took it into his mouth. He nodded and even ate several bites from his own bread until it was nearly gone. But even those distractions hadn't wiped the anger from his face completely. Hopefully no one was looking at them.

Just then, a soldier rushed into the ballroom and went straight to the king.

The fae soldier dropped his head low. "My king, the Golden Shields and their dragons are attacking outside. We have no forces out there now to protect the castle, except a few archers in the upper floors."

The tiniest smile stretched across Julian's mouth, as if he'd been expecting this. Then his face turned to one of indifference.

Good. So he had been expecting a battle just as Chloe and the others suspected. Hopefully he *hadn't* expected some of them to enter the castle disguised as a group of fae.

Julian lifted a goblet from the arm of his golden throne. "The barrier is in place?"

"Yes," the fae soldier replied.

The Shields wouldn't try to destroy the device creating the barrier. Since that was their best chance at defeating Julian, and since their fight now was only a distraction, they would save that strategy for later, just in case. Just in case this plan didn't work, they'd still have that one to fall back on.

Julian took a long swig from his goblet, then waved his hand through the air. "Go take a dozen soldiers and deal with it, then. The rest of us are busy."

Setting the goblet back onto the arm of his throne, he was immediately taken in by the adoring attention of his entourage.

Chloe's stomach twisted. A dozen soldiers? They had been expecting him to send out much more than that. To Chloe's relief, the retreating soldier made a signal and nearly a hundred soldiers followed him. Perhaps they knew Julian's casual demeanor was a ruse and they'd better protect the castle at all costs or else they'd have consequences.

Meanwhile, Julian's entourage cooed and praised him. They slid hands down his arms and touched his shoulders, as if any sort of contact with him was the greatest thing they had ever experienced.

"That is truly remarkable, my king." A fae woman fanned herself with her hand. "Only a dozen of your soldiers can defeat *dragons*?"

A fae man clapped the king on the back. "The other rulers of Faerie think they have power, but none of them have forces as powerful as yours."

"Only a dozen soldiers," another fae remarked. "It is unbelievable."

No one in his entourage seemed willing to acknowledge it had been more like a hundred soldiers who actually left the ballroom. Each compliment seemed to fill Julian with even more arrogance than before.

Once again, Chloe felt Quintus's anger reach a level so high it threatened to give them away. She could feel through their bond how his emotions surged, but it did seem a little strange this interaction had caused such emotion to boil over. They had seen Julian's arrogance before. Why would it bother Quintus so much now?

And then she saw it.

Ice seemed to trickle down her spine as she caught sight of what had truly caused the rage inside her beloved.

Dyani sat in a chair just next to the throne with her head down. She held her hands in her lap, which was covered in yards of fabric, so it wasn't immediately obvious. But after a longer inspection, Chloe realized Quintus's mother was in chains.

Chains. The blinding rage inside of Quintus grew stronger with each moment that passed.

His mother shifted in her chair and the golden chains made a small noise. It caught the eyes of a few guests, and Julian stood immediately, probably to turn their eyes away from Dyani.

Standing from his throne, Julian stepped in front of her. Her face had looked far from happy, but the mere sight of

Julian made her cringe. Her shoulders lifted as she tried to use one to shield her eyes from his view. Her lip curled in disgust at having to see his face.

When he didn't move, she lifted her chained hands and glared at him. "Take these off."

He shrugged and spoke in a low voice. "I will remove them once you stop threatening to run away."

A fae woman from his entourage slid in close to his side and giggled as she fed him a strawberry. For a few moments, Julian was wholly distracted by it.

To capture his attention again, Dyani spoke in a low, lethal voice. "Let me go."

Julian wrapped his arm tight around the waist of the fae who had fed him the strawberry. Only then did he turn and give a vicious look to Dyani. "I am a man of conquest. I will *not* lose something I have previously won. You least of all."

For all her self-control, even Chloe wanted to throw the plan out the window and smack Julian across the face for that comment. At least she managed to bury the feeling inside herself. Quintus, on the other hand, was losing his mind. She could feel it through their bond.

He was ready to throw a spear into Julian's throat right that moment. But with all the soldiers around, and with Julian's magic back, doing something like that would surely not be enough to kill the king. It *would*, however, get Quintus caught.

They needed to follow their plan. They needed to wait just a little longer, or they wouldn't have the advantage they needed.

She had to distract him before he did something rash. Grabbing onto the muscle of his upper arm, she squeezed gently and tried to turn him away from his mother. "Have you seen the drapes on the windows? Most magnificent, are they not?"

Her effort proved completely ineffective. Quintus made no attempt to hide his rage, which would give him away soon if he wasn't careful. He leaned in until his forehead nearly brushed against Chloe's. Then he whispered in a voice so quiet that no one, not even fae, would be able to hear. "I. Cannot. Wait any longer."

She whispered back. Her voice wasn't as quiet as his, but hopefully it would be quiet enough. "I understand how you feel, but we can rescue her after we take care of Julian. At least wait until the others are in position. They are almost there."

Glancing around casually, she found Elora and Brannick were nearly where they needed to be. Chloe just needed to distract Quintus for a bit longer. With passionate music playing, she grabbed his hands and pulled him into a dance. Maybe that would at least change his expression to one of surprise.

He took one last glance at his mother in chains and clenched his jaw. Nothing about his expression changed, but he allowed Chloe to move his body at least. He danced with her. It wasn't enough. She knew it wasn't enough. His agitation was becoming clear enough the others around them could probably feel it, not just see it. She *had* to calm him down, or they would soon get caught.

She raised an eyebrow and tilted her head until he glanced toward her. "I would look better in a white-and-gold dress, don't you think?"

That did it.

In an instant, his full attention turned to her when she referenced the wedding dress he made for her. The very top corner of his mouth curved up in a smile.

And now Brannick and Elora had moved into position. Even though they had been invited to the party, they still wore glamours hiding their true identities. It would be safer for all of them that way. Brannick's wolf must have been glamoured too because the creature was nowhere in sight.

Chloe dipped her head at Quintus in what was hopefully an imperceptible nod. After seeing it, he released her from his arms and trailed a hand through her hair that currently looked as black as the sparkling soil of Crystalfall. He spoke in a voice loud enough for those around them to hear, but not so loud to draw unnecessary attention. "Hurry and get your drink. I will be waiting anxiously to continue our dance."

She giggled at him and then turned to walk toward the corner of the room where drinks were being served.

Calmly, unsuspiciously, several fae in the crowd began moving into their assigned positions. Ten fae, who were actually all mortals, except for Ludo and the fae woman they had just recruited from Dustdune, moved in around Quintus. They acted as if they were minding their own business, and it was a complete coincidence they had moved so close to each other.

Four fae, who were also Golden Shields glamoured to look like fae, did the same around Chloe. If Quintus had his way, there would have been twenty fae around her, but she managed to convince everyone else that the bulk of the Shields needed to be at his side, not hers.

In only a few short moments, their plan would be enacted. Chloe forced herself to breathe. Either it would work, or it wouldn't. And soon enough, they'd find out.

33

CHLOE SCANNED THE CRYSTALFALL THRONE room. Everyone had moved into the spots previously determined. Glancing upward, she gave a short nod in signal. When she did, Brannick, glamoured to look like a fae from Mistmount, raised his hands high above his head.

Elora, glamoured to look like a nondescript short fae with purple hair, sent a blast of magic from her fingertips. The power from it threw back Julian's entourage and the guards directly around Julian. It even shoved away Dyani in her chains, leaving just the king sitting on his throne. The only people near him now were Quintus and the other Golden Shields.

Before anyone could react, Brannick created a powerful barrier enchantment that surrounded Julian and the other Shields.

Seeing he was trapped, Julian sent a sharp blast at the fae inside the enchantment with him. All at once, their glamours fell away, revealing the Golden Shields. Julian's gaze locked onto Quintus's as a sneer passed over his face.

This time, there was no hint of smile on Julian's face to indicate he had been expecting this. Instead, he said, "I should have known."

Magic and weapons started flying. Julian had been caught off guard and had only a small dagger on him. But now that he wore his crown, he no longer needed a cache of weapons. He had powerful magic and used it to knock down all eleven of his opponents.

They quickly stood but had to catch their breaths as they did so.

Remembering how Quintus nearly got caught by showing emotion for his mother, Chloe worked to keep her face a blank slate. She had promised Quintus she wouldn't get caught. She wasn't about to let even the greatest surge of fear give herself away.

A subtle glance at the fae around her told her casual interest with no hint of concern was how she should view the events before her. She schooled her features and watched while her insides flipped and tumbled. She couldn't see her face to know for sure, but she was determined to keep it neutral.

Julian shouted to his soldiers, who now stood outside the golden dome around him. Many of them slammed weapons and blasts of magic at the enchantment, clearly hoping enough attacks would take it down. Julian's other soldiers went after a glamoured Brannick, who stood outside the barrier. He focused on keeping the barrier enchantment in place, even with the weapons and magic attacking it. Elora, in her glamour, fought off Julian's soldiers using an impressive combination of sword fighting and magic.

Despite there being eleven people against one inside the enchantment, Julian continually got the upper hand against Quintus and the Shields. But they were far from ready to give up. They fought valiantly no matter how often they got knocked down.

Chloe swallowed, reminding herself yet again to not react. She couldn't give herself away.

Across the room, Elora needed more help to fight off the soldiers attacking her and Brannick. It took every ounce of willpower she had for Chloe to stand by and do nothing.

Her heart ached. Her chest squeezed. But her face didn't move.

She couldn't watch much longer. The soldiers were closing in on her sister. This couldn't be over yet.

Quintus and the other Shields needed more time to defeat Julian. They *could* defeat him. They had already started to weaken him. The Golden Shields just need a little longer to wear him down.

Turning her head slowly, in the most disinterested expression she could muster, Chloe made direct eye contact with a fae nearby her. It was Sofia in disguise. With her eyes locked onto her fellow Shield, Chloe dipped her head in the tiniest nod.

Luckily, that look was the only message Sofia needed. She casually moved through the crowd, as if heading toward the table of food on the other side of the room. But when she got close enough to Brannick, she turned and helped Elora fight off the soldiers coming toward them.

It didn't take long before Roarke left Chloe's side and went to help as well.

From inside the enchantment, three weapons rained down on Julian all at once. He managed to block each one, but he had to catch his breath afterward. And his knees looked like they were starting to shake. The Shields were almost there.

Soon, a glamoured Kai left Chloe's side at her instruction and joined Elora and the others fighting to keep Brannick safe. That left only Hilda to guard Chloe. But Chloe didn't need Hilda to keep her safe. She promised Quintus she wouldn't let Julian take her away from him, and she intended to keep that promise.

No matter how difficult, she would hide the turmoil within her so no one could guess how much she cared about the fight. She continued to watch with mild interest and absolutely no concern.

In a flash, Quintus shot a blast of magic at the same moment as throwing his spear. The magic swirled around the spear, combining them into a single weapon. He had aimed perfectly for both to hit Julian in the heart. Her heart skittered in her chest. This could be it. This could be the move that took Julian down.

Just before it hit, someone moving through the crowd bumped into Chloe. The movement caused her to lose her balance, and she had to take a few steps to catch herself. It also forced her head down, causing her to miss the outcome of Quintus's attack. She had to swallow the disappointment as she stood up straight again. She was careful. She was strong. She would not show that she cared.

Her gaze turned to the side. Channeling every fae she had ever seen, she cast the fae who bumped her a sidelong glance like it had inconvenienced her greatly. While staring at him, she quickly and stealthily took in his appearance. She did not recognize him, which was a good sign. His clothes marked him as a party guest, not a soldier, which was an even better sign.

Still, even her relief she would not reveal.

Using her peripheral vision to spot the nearest guards, she found them close enough to see her expression. But she had been careful. She had given nothing away. And luckily, the guards made no reaction to her.

The fae who had bumped her stared back at her with an equally inconvenienced expression.

She managed a quick glance through the corner of her eye and saw Quintus's previous move had not been successful. However, Julian leaned forward, breathing short and hard breaths. He lifted his arms to block attacks, but his arms were visibly shaking. It was working. They were nearly there.

The fae at Chloe's side huffed, his hand still on her shoulder, which he had grabbed to catch his own balance. He lifted his chin into the air, and said, "I did not mean to run into you. I only wanted to see…"

He trailed off as his fingers wrapped around the strap of the leather bag hanging on her shoulder. With her appearance completely glamoured, she'd been able to wear it without anyone knowing it was there. But now the fae could feel the strap to a bag that was invisible.

A wide smirk covered his face. "Found her," the fae said. Before she could react, he grabbed her around the waist and started dragging her backward.

"Finally," said another fae in party clothes who stood nearby. He turned to a third fae. "Send the signal."

Then the second fae grabbed onto her wrists and used magic to bind them in steel shackles.

Her breath caught in her throat, but she wasn't going down without a fight. She had *promised* she wouldn't get caught. Twisting her body, she did her best to wrest herself out of the grasp of the fae holding her.

The third fae pulled something from his pocket and blew into it. A sharp, loud sound reverberated through the ballroom.

Her attempts to get away had so far been feeble, but that wouldn't stop her from trying. She writhed and lifted her feet from the ground, hoping she might slip through the fae's arms and drop onto the ground.

Hilda had noticed Chloe being dragged away. She drew a weapon and immediately went after Chloe. But one person wasn't enough to do much. The third fae fought against Hilda, keeping her back. It was clear if Chloe was going to stop herself from being captured, she would have to do it herself.

Arching her back, she squirmed and twisted as hard as her body would go. Even with that movement, she managed a glance at the enchantment. She'd been trying so hard to be quiet to not attract Quintus's attention. But instead of noticing him, she instead noticed how Julian's face changed at the sound the third fae had made.

His mouth twisted into a wicked grin. A moment later, a door appeared inside Brannick's enchantment. Julian immediately rushed through it and disappeared.

He was gone. Julian had gotten away. They had been so close, but now he was gone. Her body yanked, still trying to free herself from the grasp of the fae holding her. He had tightened his grip significantly. It didn't help that she'd never had much strength. She held her breath, trying to focus all her energy on her good foot. Then she kicked it directly into the shin of the fae carrying her.

It did nothing except anger the fae until he tightened his grip so hard, she had difficulty breathing. The second fae raised his fist threateningly. That was all it took.

Fear gripped her by the throat and didn't let go. Usually this anxiety didn't kick in unless she'd been threatened with a weapon, but a fae fist could do just as much damage as a mortal weapon.

Black spots appeared in her vision while she fought to keep consciousness. She kicked and kicked again, hitting the first fae's shins each time. Maybe once hadn't hurt him, but maybe if she did it enough, he'd be properly injured.

The fear that froze her in battles continued to work down her spine and into her limbs. It took over, slowing her movements, darkening her vision.

The only thing she hadn't done yet was scream. Nearly all her effort went to keeping her mouth shut. She had no idea what was going on with the other Golden Shields now that Julian had disappeared, but she knew one thing for certain. If Quintus saw her being captured, he would lose any ability to think. He would tear after her with no semblance of rational thought in any of his actions. He'd get himself captured and then Julian would perform the ritual, and then it would truly be over. There'd be no hope left.

So no matter how she writhed, no matter how fear froze her body, she kept herself silent. Her desperation to protect Quintus was the only thing strong enough to do it.

The fae dragging her through the ballroom toward the exit turned to the second fae. "She is not screaming."

Her heart sank at the statement. This had been their plan then. She had guessed as much when the fae proclaimed he had *found her*, but now she knew for certain. Chloe and the others knew this party had been a trap, and they thought Julian had been expecting them to start a battle. Maybe he had, but he had also clearly planned for them to enter the castle too.

Apparently, catching her had been his goal all along. Just like Quintus had guessed, Julian went for her before he went for his own son.

The second fae glanced over his shoulder toward the throne and then he shrugged. "Stab her then."

Chloe's heart pounded so hard in her chest, all she could hear were her heartbeats. When the first fae drew a weapon, her body flopped, as if all her muscles had fallen asleep. It was all too much. She had tried so hard, but anxiety pulsed through her too completely now.

After a sharp jab, a small dagger sliced her in the leg.

She tried. She really did. She tried so, so hard, but she couldn't stop a strangled cry from bursting through her throat. She swallowed it as soon as it was released, quieting most of the sound.

But not all of it.

It wouldn't matter for much longer because the world had started falling away around her. Soon she'd pass out and couldn't scream no matter how much they wanted her to.

The last thing she saw was Quintus shoving through the crowd. He locked his gaze onto her and shouted a single word.

"Chloe!"

And then she was gone.

34

CHLOE'S EYES FLUTTERED OPEN, TAKING in the sensation of cold shackles around her wrists first. But once her eyes focused, the sight before her stole every bit of attention from her mind.

Julian stood in front of her with an axe in his hands. He eyed her chest and nearly pulled the axe back. Once he noticed her opened eyes, a slanted smile twisted his mouth.

"Good. I was hoping you'd wake up before I killed you. Now he'll be able to hear you scream."

The slanted smile grew as he pulled the axe back in preparation. He was disgustingly pleased with the prospect of making her scream.

As his axe started coming down, she shouted the first words that came to her mind. "You can't kill me."

Where was she? Did she have any chance of escaping?

Someone like Mishti probably would have taken in details about the room first, but Chloe could do nothing but stare at the axe that was about to end her life. With the polished metal before her, fear threatened to make her pass out again.

Julian chuckled at her plea and prepared to swing the axe again. He was going to do it. He was going to kill her. She only had one chance to say something that would stop him.

"I mean it." Her words came out in a rush, almost too breathy to be heard. "If you kill me, you'll never get Quintus."

The axe hovered in his hands while he raised an eyebrow. That had done it. She had gotten him to pause at least. He hadn't lowered the axe, but he might.

Blood pulsed in her ears. She used her peripheral vision to examine her surroundings as much as possible without making it obvious. She was in a room. It was obviously somewhere in Crystalfall Castle, but she didn't know where. A nearby open door led out to a balcony that opened to a larger room somewhere inside the castle. Julian had probably taken her there so the noise of her screams would travel through the castle.

Even though the axe hovered without movement, a dangerously arrogant expression filled Julian's features. "If I kill you, Quintus will not care about living anymore. He'll make no attempt to protect himself. Capturing him will be easy. He will have nothing left to fight for."

It hurt her heart that Quintus had been so correct in guessing his father's actions. He knew exactly what Julian would do and why. It hurt worse knowing Julian was right.

After a hard swallow, Chloe tried to make him understand the glaring flaw in his plan. "Maybe Quintus won't have anything left to fight for, but the other Golden Shields will. They will protect him at all costs. They'll get him out of here whether he likes it or not. And if he's not trying to rescue me, he'll have no reason to come out from hiding. You will never find him."

Julian's nose twitched and his nostrils flared as he stared at her. The axe gently shook, indicating his muscles were shaking. He probably couldn't decide if he wanted to kill her anyway or if he wanted to accept she was right.

With a sharp exhale, he dropped the axe. "He will only make himself vulnerable to capture if your life is in danger. But not if it is taken away." He shook his head, as if angry with himself for the words he had just spoken. His jaw clenched as he let out a huff. "You are right. I can still kill you before I kill him, but I have to wait until I have him captured."

The anger in his eyes only dissipated when he took a step forward and started eyeing her shoulder. What was he going to do now? Maybe he had decided to injure her instead of plunging the axe into her heart like he had originally planned.

His fingers twitched as he started to lift the axe again, but he lowered them just as quickly. Now his eyes narrowed at her. "Why would you tell me that?"

She couldn't help the shocked chuckle that left her lips. "Because I don't want to die. I want Quintus to rescue me. Everyone knows I could never do it by myself."

She'd taken in more of her surroundings now. A few guards stood throughout the room. Two guards stood on the balcony. Unfortunately, she couldn't see anything past the balcony that would tell her where in the castle this room sat.

The room could tell her nothing more. Now she reached out with her bond for Quintus. Unsurprisingly, he was filled with the hottest rage and was probably attempting to murder anyone who got in his way. If only he could have that same power when fighting against his father.

"Yes." Julian stared down his nose at her. "You are rather pathetic once weapons come out. So easy to manipulate. You would never be able to escape on your own."

She hated the truth in those statements. But maybe just this once she *could* escape on her own. Not by force, but by using her mind.

Julian glanced back at the guards and tapped his foot, probably trying to think of what to do next. After another moment, he dropped the axe into his belt and eyed the balcony.

His gaze gave her an idea. Could she jump off the balcony? If the floor was only one story below, the fall might break a bone or two, but she'd certainly survive. It would be difficult with her hands in chains, but it might work. They'd probably never expect someone as nervous as her to do something so drastic.

"I will draw him out." Julian spoke those words more to himself than to her.

Grabbing onto the chain between her wrist shackles, he dragged her across a stiff rug and over to the balcony.

Good. Maybe now she'd get a chance to jump off it. She just needed to distract him.

"Draw him out?" Chloe asked the question merely to turn his mind away from whatever thoughts were in his head. But as soon as she said it, understanding dawned inside her. She nearly gasped at the realization. "Just like you did with Dyani."

He stumbled over his steps and opened both eyes wide. The moment passed quickly and soon he continued dragging her forward.

Heat pounded in her chest, prickly and angry. "You only brought Dyani here to try and draw Quintus out. I should have realized it as soon as I saw her in chains."

"I am still surprised it did not work." Julian said the words calmly. "Quintus has so little self-control when those he cares for are in danger. But I admit, I had hoped we would catch you first. I want to kill you and watch him suffer before I kill him."

They had gotten to the balcony now. Whatever he was planning, it was going to happen soon. She had to distract him again. She had to say something. Anything.

"How does it feel to have your former lover so disgusted by you? Your very face made her cringe and cower."

Pain shot through his eyes. For once, the determination in him was replaced by an ache. His head dropped and his eyes fell closed. When he opened them to speak, his tone was defensive. "She liked me...once. She was lucky to have me. Any woman was."

"I doubt that," Chloe said under her breath. She shouldn't have let the words slip from her mouth, but it was too late now.

Julian bent and grabbed her by the collar. "What did you just say?"

"Nothing." The word came out too fast to be believable. But by now, he had ripped the pain off his face and replaced it with singular determination.

Her gaze scanned the area now that she had come to the balcony. Short golden poles spaced a hand's width apart formed a railing. Through them, she could see the balcony didn't sit over the ballroom like she'd been hoping. And the floor below was at least two stories down, not one. She could probably still survive the fall, especially if she rolled into a ball for impact.

A sinister look filled Julian's eyes, making her desperate to distract him once again. Dyani was clearly a sore subject, so it would likely work the best.

"I doubt she *ever* liked you. She probably just liked your power and beautiful castle."

Julian's nostrils flared as he lifted his foot into the air. In the next breath, his toe slammed into Chloe's belly, kicking her hard.

A sharp breath escaped her lips as pain exploded through her.

Julian clenched his jaw. "Dyani only cringes now because of what I did to our son. She liked me before that. She was obsessed with me, probably even loved me."

"Loved you?" Chloe laughed, hoping it would distract him and not draw his ire. "Then why did she hide Quintus from you? You think she would have done that if she loved you?"

The words froze him completely. He had no answer. He knew he had no answer.

It gave Chloe the perfect chance to glance around one last time. She'd have to be quick since he stood so close to her. But if she moved fast, she might have just enough time to throw herself over the railing before he could catch her. Then maybe she could use her bond to help Quintus find her.

Julian pulled the axe from his belt again. "For all the healing magic you've done, I know you can do none of it without Quintus. And I've just realized, I don't need you *well* to use you as bait. I just need you alive."

35

If she'd had any more time to prepare, Chloe would have gasped. She might have screamed. But Julian's axe came crashing down on her before she even had a chance to blink. The gleaming metal sliced into her arm, sending waves of pain rushing through her. After that, he sliced her leg, down the calf. The metal broke through layers of skin and tore straight into the muscle.

He aimed for her neck next. He must have known the neck had a vein that, if cut, would make her bleed out almost instantly. Carefully positioning the axe, he sliced vertically through her skin from chin to collar bone, completely avoiding that vein. The cut in her neck was the shallowest one, but it seemed to multiply her pain by ten.

Tears filled her eyes and streamed down her cheeks in sheets. Needles seemed to stab at her every pore. Burning and pounding surged through all her muscles.

Her screams echoed through the large room beneath the balcony. Her throat turned raw from the effort of it.

She couldn't take this. Julian knew exactly how much to injure her without killing her, but this pain was too much. Too much.

What good was it being an apothecary if she couldn't even heal herself while pain sent shocks through her body? She had do *something*.

She had no herbs, no bandages, no healing instruments. She had nothing.

But maybe she could reach through the bond for Quintus. Maybe instead of touching him physically, she could touch him with the bond and still use her magic.

The logical part of her mind shut that theory down almost as soon as she thought of it. That didn't make any sense. She could only touch Quintus with her skin for her magic to work. That had been true from the moment she had first accessed her magic. Touching him with the bond would never be enough. She *knew* it wouldn't be enough.

But the logical part of her mind no longer controlled it. Pain had barreled in and taken all control. It didn't matter if it wouldn't work. She reached out through the bond anyway.

Her breaths turned short and fast as she tried to find him. To *touch* him.

Strings of magic seemed to whip out from her body, stretching down every hallway of the castle, searching. Her body hurt like it never had, but just as deeply, she ached for *him*. She needed to feel his support, his strength. His love. Could the bond reach more of him than just his feelings? The strings of magic had narrowed down to only one now. It reached, tumbling forward with focused resolve.

And then it found him.

The star tattoos under her eyes always tingled when she used her bond magic, but if they were doing so now, she would never know. The explosions of pain blasting through her crowded out every other sensation. She couldn't even see anymore.

Everything was pain.

Still, she reached out as desperate as weakening fingers might cling to the edge of a cliff. Her mind searched, touched. She found Quintus, his emotions, his heart. She wrapped her magic around the sense of him.

And then she tried to use her own magic.

She pictured in her mind stuffing handfuls of pain herbs into her mouth. While chewing them, she carelessly poured tinctures over each of her axe wounds. Even in her mind, the movements came sloppy and disjointed. But it wouldn't matter if it was sloppy. The tinctures would still work if the magic would.

Visualizing more pain herbs, she stuffed those into her mouth and then imagined some honey. It got smeared in globs rather than neat lines. Clean bandages went over the wounds and then she imagined the wounds healing under the bandages. They got yellow and spongy, then they scabbed over. And soon they turned to pink scars, then white, then they faded away completely.

An ache in her jaw brought her back to reality. Her jaw? How could her jaw hurt when she had gashes in her skin? Had the pain made her delirious enough she actually chomped down on the nonexistent herbs she had pictured in her head?

All at once, a sharp twist clenched her stomach. A clench she could feel. And if she could feel anything in her stomach, it meant her wounds no longer pulsed with the same pain they had only moments ago.

Her eyes flew open, examining the wound Julian had left on her arm.

It was gone. It had *worked*. Somehow, reaching out and touching Quintus through their bond had worked as well as touching his skin.

She had healed herself.

And Julian and the other guards had left the balcony. They had gone into the room to prepare to fight off the angry Quintus, who they expected to come charging through the door at any moment. Now she sat alone on the balcony.

Her heart leapt into her throat as she forced herself to her feet. She could do it. Just this once, she'd rescue herself. She'd fling herself over the balcony, curl into a ball, and brace for impact. And if bones broke, then she'd just heal herself again.

A laugh nearly bubbled at her throat. This was going to work.

But just as she got to her feet, the door to the room swung open. Quintus sent a blast of magic into the room that pushed all the guards and even Julian to their backs. Quintus's eyes were wild as he scanned the area.

It took less than a breath for him to find her. He flew across the ground and grabbed onto her before she even registered the movement. She wanted to tell him to jump off the balcony instead of rushing back through the door he had entered, but of course, all rational thought had left him. He moved on pure instinct.

But he moved so fast, she couldn't keep up. Her feet stumbled over each other. With a gasp, she realized her wooden foot had fallen off.

Even moving at incredible speed, Quintus knew the moment she slowed. He swiftly grabbed her foot from the ground and shoved it into her hand. Then he took her into his arms and started running out the door and into the hall.

It had all happened so fast, the room around her looked blurred.

But now Julian and his guards had gotten back to their feet and began attacking. Quintus couldn't do much to defend himself with her in his arms, but he managed to throw a few crushing enchantments behind himself.

It wasn't much, but it didn't matter. Retreating was almost always easier than trying to kill an enemy. And safer too.

He turned a corner, but the way was blocked by hundreds of fae soldiers. Turning on his heel, he went to run in the other direction. The opposite hallway was mostly clear, except Julian blocked it.

Huffing wildly, Quintus set Chloe down and pulled a spear from his pocket.

Julian eyed the weapon. "You think *that* can help you?" He scoffed. "The only thing that can save you now is a home."

Quintus moved to attack, but the words struck Chloe as she looked down at her hands. She held the wooden foot Quintus had crafted for her. The wood had come from the last little piece of his home in Bitter Thorn.

Without thinking, she tore the wooden foot out of the boot covering it. Then she hopped forward.

Quintus gasped at the sight of her moving closer to Julian. Julian raised an eyebrow, more curious than frightened.

Holding the foot tight, she glared at the king. "Unfortunately for you, Quintus has a home."

She swung her arms wildly as she slammed the foot against Julian's chest. He started rolling his eyes and even lifted his hand, as if to bat the foot away. But then the wood made contact with his chest.

He grunted like all the air had been knocked out of him. Then a strangled cry tore through his throat as she slammed the foot against him again. He tried to snatch it out of her hands, but his arms moved too chaotically to find it.

Hissing started erupting from his skin, almost like it was burning. He clutched his chest and gulped as if he couldn't catch any air. A simple piece of wood never would have affected him like this. Her skills at wielding the foot certainly couldn't take credit for his reaction either. No, the fact that this wood hurt him far more than it should have proved one thing.

Using Quintus's home against Julian might be the only thing that could weaken this king.

She smacked the foot against him once more. Julian tried to catch the foot as she did. He managed to get a slight grip on it just as he teetered and fell to the ground.

But the guards from the other side of the hallway had nearly reached them now. She tried to bend and grab the foot. Quintus tried to grab it too. But the other soldiers were too close.

They couldn't waste another moment. While arrows whizzed past, Quintus pulled her into his arms once again and began flying down the hallway. She didn't even get a chance to glance at her foot before they turned the corner.

Another two turns later, they had reached a part of the castle she recognized. Her heart ached at having lost her foot, but hope sprang once she saw familiar surroundings. They were getting close to the front doors.

But then they turned another corner, and a wall of guards blocked their way. Quintus turned on his heel, trying to find someplace else to turn. But there was nowhere. There was no hidden path they could duck into. Soldiers closed in on them from both sides.

This was why she never should have gotten captured. Quintus wasn't thinking. He didn't even have anyone with them. They had no help, and they had reached a blockade they couldn't pass. And even *now* he wasn't thinking. He was blinded completely by his need to get her to safety.

"A door," she whispered to him as the soldiers closed in around them. "Open a door." She hadn't thought of it right away, but she wasn't fae. Quintus *should* have thought to use a door. He should have opened one the moment they left the room he'd found her in. But thought had clearly controlled none of his actions during this entire rescue.

He had to blink before her words sank in, but finally he managed a logical thought. With his hands still holding her tight, he waved a hand and opened a door directly in front of them. Already he stepped toward it.

But the soldiers were too close. He hadn't acted fast enough. A soldier grabbed Quintus by the collar from behind. The soldier yanked him back.

This was why she wasn't supposed to get captured. Because he'd always put her safety above his own. Even if it meant he'd die.

After a deep breath, he launched her out of his hands and through the door. He did it too fast for her to stop him. Magic seemed to envelop her in that moment. And as her body flew through the Faerie door, the hundreds of soldiers filling the hallway closed in and surrounded Quintus.

Her last glimpse before she entered the door was of him being tackled by dozens of soldiers. They'd captured him. They'd won again.

Now Julian had everything he needed for the ritual.

36

BLACK SOIL CAUGHT CHLOE'S SHOULDER as she slammed against the ground. Her chains had disappeared. Quintus must have done some enchantment that removed them just before throwing her through his door. It took her a few blinks to place her location. The door had sent her back to their camp at Rubyrise Mountain. No one else was around, which was no surprise. Everyone else was back at the castle in the fight she'd escaped just moments ago.

She dragged herself to a sitting position. Her hand dug into her leather bag, snatching the whispering stone at the bottom of it. She vaguely noticed the glamour disguising her had fallen away, but it was the least of her concerns at the moment.

"Mishti." Chloe spoke into the whispering stone, hoping her friend held hers in a position where she'd hear the words.

Mishti's anxious voice responded at once. "Where are you? What's going on?"

With a gulp, Chloe shared the words that twisted her heart. "Julian has Quintus."

"He has Quintus?" Mishti said exasperated and nearing panic. "I thought he had *you*."

The other Golden Shields inside the castle must have used their stones to communicate after Chloe got captured by Julian.

Chloe did her best not to sigh or cry. "He *did* have me. Quintus rescued me using exactly no part of his mind. He sent me through a door, but the Zeakriesh captured him before he could go through it."

Now it was Mishti who tried not to cry, but a tiny one still came out as a groan. "Not good. Can you get back to the castle? Shadow is here, but she can come get you. We're going to take the barrier down like we planned. We need to end this now."

Chloe agreed and called for Shadow using their bond. Chloe wouldn't be able to walk, and hopping wouldn't get her far. But even with a missing foot, she could still ride. As she waited for her dragon, her mind spun and twisted. How could this have happened? Of course she knew how, since she'd been there, but it still hurt to see how everything had perfectly fallen into place for Julian.

He'd captured his son. He'd nearly killed her. And now he had everything he needed to do his ritual. If he succeeded, he'd have unimaginable power. The wraiths would be so weak they might never recover.

Quintus would be dead.

She sucked in a sharp breath as her stomach flopped over on itself. *No.* No, no, no. She dropped her head in her hands and shook it back and forth. She wouldn't let it happen. Couldn't. Whatever fears she had in battle, she'd ignore them. Whatever skills she lacked in fights, she'd compensate for by using Shadow.

Maybe Julian had won over and over again, but he wouldn't have this victory. Not *this* one. Whatever it took, Quintus would *live*.

Her heart stammered as Shadow appeared on the ledge beside her. She scrambled up the dragon's back, fierce determination pumping through her. It wasn't over yet. They'd get Quintus. They had to.

Shadow flew them back to Crystalfall Castle, faster than she had ever flown before. And all the while, Chloe's heart thumped wildly.

When they arrived, the other dragons were already diving and blowing fire at the barrier device just as they planned.

The sight of them fighting should have filled her with hope, but another sight filled her with a dread so deep it drowned everything else out. Directly in front of the castle, only two strides outside it, and under the golden moon she and Quintus had brought to Faerie, Julian had already started the Bloodstone Convergence.

Her heart leapt into her throat as Shadow landed in between the hills and mountains in front of the castle. Most of the dragons were breathing fire in order to destroy the barrier device, but the other dragons sat on the ground, waiting. Their riders sat up high on their backs with weapons in their hands.

When the barrier came down, they'd be ready.

Shadow had settled directly next to Mishti and Temper. Ludo sat atop Temper with Mishti, but Chandril was mysteriously absent.

The plan was already working. The olive-green barrier flickered and sputtered, especially each time a new wave of dragon fire hit the device creating it.

From his place in front of the castle, Julian shouted at his guards, waving his arms hysterically to direct them. Row after row of soldiers poured out of the castle, filling all the empty space on the soil inside the barrier. Their bodies formed a thick wall that offered protection for Julian. They would also be ready to fight once the barrier came down.

Julian's blond hair kept getting into his eyes, and he kept pushing both hands through it to hold it back. It led to the hair standing up on his head in haphazard positions, poking through his crown like thorns on a briar. He had an open book on the ground, which he kept bending down to read before acting again.

A large cauldron sat in front of Julian. Smoke drifted up from the vessel, proving he had already begun to mix and prepare ingredients.

The dragons needed to get that barrier down soon if they'd have any chance at stopping Julian before the ritual was over.

Chloe had been so focused on Julian and the Zeakriesh and the cauldron that it took her until then for her gaze to land on Quintus. When it did, her hands clapped against her mouth. A yank through her navel gave her the sudden urge to vomit.

His face was bloodied and bruised. Golden chains around his wrists and ankles held him to the ground. Even worse, his side had been split by a blade and blood poured from the wound. He'd been situated so the blood flowed straight into a large bowl made of emerald. His arms tugged at his chains a few times, but he was clearly far too weakened to move much.

Something about his eyes seemed distant too, like he didn't know where he was or what was happening. Had Julian given him herbs or a potion that impaired his senses? Probably. Otherwise, Quintus probably would have broken through his chains by now. If his senses were impaired, then he'd need all the help he could get to escape.

Her heart clenched as she bit her lip. How much longer? How much longer would it take to get the barrier down?

With her heart thundering, she turned her attention back to the device and dragons blowing fire onto it. It couldn't be much longer now.

Just then, a door appeared on the ground next to Mishti's dragon. A moment later, Chandril stepped through it. He spotted Mishti atop her dragon and called out to her.

"The wraiths are awaiting your signal. They will join us when we are ready."

Mishti swallowed hard before answering. "Can they help?"

On the ground, with the door still swirling behind him, Chandril nodded. "Yes, they have a plan. What about the pixies?"

Ludo answered, gesturing to the left where a large dragon with two riders was surrounded by dozens of flying pixies. "Over there. Clara and Revyn will lead them. They tried opening a door inside the barrier, but there were already too many soldiers on the lawn. Now they must wait for the barrier to come down. They are ready too."

With a nod, Mishti set her jaw. "Okay, the Shields inside the castle are ready too. Have the wraiths start coming through. We'll attack as soon as the barrier is down."

Her head whirled around, focusing on Chloe now. "Why are you still on Shadow? Slide to the ground and go hide in the trees while we fight. We'll need you to run in and heal Quintus once we get past the guards."

A sensation like embers cracking through solid ice stabbed at Chloe's heart. She said nothing in response. She just swung her leg to the side and lifted her skirt. Mishti saw at once that Chloe's wooden foot was missing. Chloe wouldn't be able to go anywhere without her dragon. And anyway, she didn't want to. She wanted to rescue Quintus, no matter what it took.

Mishti's face scrunched into a knot as she let out a sigh. She was probably wondering the same thing as Chloe. *How* did things keep getting worse?

Finally, Mishti nodded. "Okay, stay on Shadow. Just stay low on her back so she can still fight without you getting hit by weapons."

Chloe nodded, putting her leg with the missing foot back to its original position.

Waiting any longer would have been agony, but just then, the last bit of dragon fire destroyed Julian's device.

The barrier came down.

Shadow lifted herself into the air. It would only take moments before she'd be ready to dive down and hopefully snatch Quintus off the lawn before anything could stop her.

The other dragons and riders charged toward the rows of soldiers covering the castle lawn. At the same moment, Shields from inside the castle charged through the doors and into the night air. None of them wore glamours anymore.

The soldiers on the lawn had clearly been prepared for the Shields and dragons that would attack from outside the barrier, but just as clearly, they had not expected forces from inside. Clashing swords and whizzing spears filled the air with their harrowing sounds. Magical bursts and explosions sparked and crackled and slammed.

Nearer to the castle, some of Julian's Zeakriesh suddenly realized they fought against Brannick, the High King of Faerie himself. Many weapons fell to the ground at the sight, and they lifted their hands in surrender. Brannick moved past them deftly and continued to take down anyone who stood in his way. His black wolf fought too, using his sharp teeth as a painful weapon.

But not all the fae cared about engaging in combat against the High King. Brannick and Elora had legendary combat skills. They had defeated the previous high ruler, even though her power had been enormous. Each of their swipes and blasts was perfectly calculated to cause maximum damage.

It helped the Golden Shields. It helped so much. But Julian still had far, far more soldiers than them.

Shadow released a growl from deep in her throat and dove into the crowds of Zeakriesh. Her claws stretched toward Quintus, just as Chloe had directed, but it was obvious right away an easy extraction would not be happening. Too many soldiers surrounded Quintus and Julian. Even worse, the angle of the castle roof just above Quintus made it impossible for Shadow to reach him unless nearly all the soldiers on the lawn had been removed first. At once, Shadow attempted just that. Swooping forward, she clamped her jaw on any Zeakriesh in her path, throwing their broken bodies away as fast as she could.

While she fought, Chloe stayed low, but she turned her attention to Quintus once again. After Julian had sliced her skin, she had healed herself by touching Quintus through their bond instead of touching him physically. Could she do the same to heal him now?

The ritual seemed to require an obscene amount of blood. Maybe if she could heal Quintus's wound, the bleeding would stop and then Julian might not have enough blood for the ritual. And even if he did, at least Quintus would no longer be injured.

Her eyes closed as she concentrated on their bond. Touching him through it came easier now since she had done it before. Soon, images of bandages, herbs, and healing concoctions filled her mind. She could also sense Julian had indeed given Quintus herbs to impair his senses. Quintus's mind had clouded over, making it difficult for him to perceive his surroundings or to use his limbs. When she tried to take away the cloudiness in his mind, it failed. Under normal circumstances, she might have consulted her magical book for a solution. For now, it was probably best to just focus on the physical wound. The impairment would probably fade away on its own anyway, and his fae healing should help it fade faster than it would in a mortal.

Focusing solely on the wound in his side, her healing magic did its work. She wanted to see what was happening in the fight, but she didn't dare break her concentration by lifting her eyelids.

It took too long to heal the wound. She worked slowly and methodically, careful to heal properly without missing anything. She could feel how the celestine crystal still around his neck helped in the process. But all that time with her eyes closed made her afraid to open them again.

When she finally did, she wished she hadn't. Julian stood over the cauldron. Sweat lined his hairline and dripped down his cheeks. His hair had turned even wilder than before, sticking up so high it almost entirely hid his crown. With both his hands, he held the emerald bowl full of Quintus's blood and started pouring it into the cauldron.

Her heart stopped as she held her breath. It was too late to stop his blood from being used. Julian clearly had enough blood already, or he wouldn't be pouring it. Flicking her gaze back to Quintus she saw at least she'd been successful in healing him. His face was still bruised and bloodied, but the wound in his side had vanished. She'd have to heal the bruises later.

Thick red blood splashed out of the bowl and into the cauldron. The ritual called for *blood of the one who wished to converge*. Unfortunately, Julian wasn't stupid enough to use his own blood. The ritual needed so much, a mortal like him would never survive, even with his magic.

Chloe had studied the ritual enough to know Quintus's blood, which had his father's blood in it, should work just as well. It also meant the completed ritual would make it impossible for Julian to kill Quintus, since his blood would be protected too. But since Julian fully intended to kill Quintus *before* finishing the ritual, that obviously didn't matter much to him.

And once Bloodstone Convergence concluded, Julian would become like the fae. His life would go on forever, without aging, unless he was killed. Even worse, he would have more power than any fae had ever known. He would have more power than Brannick. By the rules of Faerie, Julian would automatically become High King, stripping Brannick of his rightful title. And the wraiths would be weakened so much, they might never recover.

More than ever, Chloe needed to rescue her beloved. She couldn't stand by and watch Quintus die. She scanned the area, searching for another way to extract him, since Shadow's body was too large to grab Quintus from his current position.

Wraiths charged across the battlefield, moving closer to the castle than any of the other Shields. The wraiths lacked skill with weapons, but they had something far more powerful than their enemies.

They couldn't die.

When an axe crashed down on one wraith, the creature simply grunted as if she'd been hit by a small rock. The other wraiths charged in similarly, barely hurt from any weapons that hit them. If Chloe couldn't get close enough to Quintus to rescue him, maybe the wraiths could. And considering what would happen to them if the Bloodstone Convergence was completed, they were probably almost as desperate as her to stop it.

They only had one problem. As they charged closer to the castle, they had to weave through soldiers and enchantments. They lacked the visibility Chloe had from the air, and it was clear, they weren't sure exactly where to run to get to Quintus.

When Chloe caught sight of Chandril running at the head of a group of wraiths, she screamed out his name.

He paused for half a moment, looking upward and attempting to find the one who had called his name. When he caught sight of her atop Shadow, she gestured toward Quintus, showing him and the other wraiths exactly which direction to run.

After a quick nod, he looked straight at her and lifted a whispering stone to his lips.

She held her own stone tight, anxious to hear what he'd say.

His voice sounded in her ears a moment later. "Show us the way to go, and I *vow* to you, we will keep Quintus alive."

Her belly clenched. Chandril had made a vow, a proper Faerie vow. A vow like that couldn't be broken. For the first time since Quintus had thrown her through a door and gotten himself captured, she allowed a breath of relief to leave her lips.

The wraiths would save him. No matter what it took, they would keep him alive.

A flash of rage lit in Julian's eyes as the wraiths broke through the walls of soldiers around him. "Hurry!" Julian screamed to the soldiers directly around Quintus.

One Zeakriesh used magic to remove Quintus's chains while half a dozen other Zeakriesh attempted to lift Quintus off the ground and throw his entire body into the cauldron. His body writhed against them.

Using the bond, Chloe reached out for him. His mind was still clouded, making his movements sloppy and disjointed. At least his side had been healed. Julian sneered at the healed skin while a vein in his jaw popped out. He must have wondered how the wound had healed, but he also must have cared far more about getting his son into the cauldron.

Despite Quintus's impairment, he managed to fight off the Zeakriesh holding him. All six of them.

Just then, a group of wraiths with Chandril at the head broke through the last line of Zeakriesh protecting Julian. Knowing this was his last chance, Julian tore his axe from his belt and chopped off Quintus's arm.

The ritual said a body or a limb could be sacrificed. Julian had obviously wanted to sacrifice Quintus's entire body, thereby killing him in the process. But now that wraiths closed in, he had settled for an arm.

Chloe stayed low on Shadow's back as the dragon continued to fight the Zeakriesh on the lawn. Chloe closed her eyes again, reaching for the bond to heal Quintus's wound. She panicked a moment as she considered what to do. She wasn't exactly sure how to approach the healing, since unlike her, his fae body *could* regrow the limb.

Images began to flash in her mind, no doubt provided by Faerie itself. She imagined using celestine crystals to stop the bleeding and then imagined smothering the wound with a tincture of herbs that would promote growth. She had no idea what his body would do after that, since she couldn't even imagine how to regrow a limb. But maybe it didn't matter. She had stopped the bleeding. Hopefully that would be good enough, and his fae healing could take care of the rest.

Steam bubbled above the cauldron, and a frightening grin appeared on Julian's face. Did that mean the ritual had nearly finished? If so, Julian was running out of time to kill his son.

The wraiths closed in around Quintus, each of them touching his hands or his arms. In those positions, Julian wouldn't be able to kill Quintus as easily. The king screamed, telling them to move out of the way. When they refused to move, Julian ordered his archers to fill them with arrows. Their undead bodies withstood the attack easily.

Julian jerked his head back to the cauldron and fear struck in his eyes. Magical sparks and smoky swirls began dancing above the liquid inside. These were the final steps. If he didn't kill Quintus soon, he would lose his chance.

Since the wraiths refused to move, Julian must have decided to ignore them. He clasped his axe tight and prepared to aim it at Quintus's chest.

Shadow swooped down and attacked a soldier just as Chloe's heart dropped down to her toes. She could heal, but she couldn't heal everything. If Julian slammed that axe through Quintus's chest, it wouldn't matter how much healing magic she had. The injury would kill him instantly.

Even though she knew it wouldn't work, she urged Shadow to fly in and use her claws to grab Quintus off the ground. Shadow attempted it without question, but of course it didn't work. The angle of the roof made it impossible to get to him. Could a smaller dragon do it? Now that the Zeakriesh had removed his chains, it might work.

Pressing the whispering stone to her lips, Chloe spoke into it frantically. "We need a smaller dragon. A smaller dragon might be able to—"

Her words got cut off by a scream that jumped from her throat. Julian swung his axe, aiming it at Quintus's chest. When he did, two of the wraiths grabbed onto his arm to stop him. They succeeded, but Julian wasn't about to give up. Julian released a menacing grunt followed by a flash of his teeth. Lifting one hand, he sent a hard blast of magic out of his fingertips.

The magic slammed against the wraiths, knocking them away from Quintus's body. They got to their feet, but Julian moved too fast. He'd be able to swing his axe before they could stop him again. Of all the wraiths, only one managed to keep a hand on Quintus. Chandril stood, staring straight into Julian's eyes as he gripped Quintus's shoulder.

What good was that supposed to do? Chandril needed to tackle Julian or smack his arm away. The wraith had *vowed* he would keep Quintus alive. Chloe had believed him. She had allowed herself to feel relief. But now Chandril did nothing except stand still and grasp Quintus's shoulder tight, as if that could do anything. Gasping, Chloe watched as Julian lifted his axe again.

And when it fell, nothing would stop it.

37

TIME SEEMED TO STOP AS Chloe held her breath and watched Julian's axe come down onto Quintus. It didn't matter that she had healing magic. That strike was too much, even for a fae.

It would crush his rib cage and slice his heart in half. What didn't hit his heart would cut through his lungs. No amount of healing power or healing magic would be enough to save him. He'd die instantly. *Why* had she trusted Chandril? Why hadn't she found a way to save her beloved before it was too late?

A jolt like electricity shook through her when the axe hit its target. Tears stung in her eyes as an ache split through her throat.

Quintus.

Her heart pounded. She had tried so hard, loved him so much. Why couldn't it be enough? *Why?*

But when the axe hit, the air didn't fill with the sound of a cracking rib cage. Instead, Quintus grunted. Was it just a noise that escaped his lips as a result of his lungs being torn apart? But then…

She sucked in a breath, urging Shadow harder than ever to reach him. Quintus glared, his eyes still hazy and unfocused. He stretched out his shoulders and toes. He had *moved*. Was it possible? Had he somehow survived?

She was close enough now that she saw fear send a gulp through Julian's throat as he too caught sight of Quintus's moving, living form.

Still staring straight at Julian, Chandril tightened his grip on Quintus's shoulder. The other wraiths were still recovering from the blast of magic Julian had sent at them, but they would probably join Chandril soon. They might even tackle Julian to the ground. Julian must have known he had to act fast.

Wrinkling his nose, he slammed his axe against Quintus's chest again. This strike came down harder, a move no one should have survived. It should have killed Quintus instantly, but he just grunted again as if someone had done nothing more than punch him.

Sitting up higher, Chloe managed to get an even better view. His skin didn't even look broken from the axe. He moved his body like he'd been hit with a club that had bruised him, but not like an axe had sliced through him.

Confused, Julian touched one finger to the sharpened edge of his axe. Blood immediately beaded at the wound. He scowled at it, since the axe itself clearly wasn't the problem.

Chloe had no idea what was happening, and she didn't really care. Whatever wound Quintus had, she was going to heal it so he could fight off Julian and get away.

Her eyes closed as she reached out with the bond. She found him easily, as she always did, but... It didn't feel like him at all. He felt so different she couldn't begin to find words for it. All she really knew was he didn't feel alive.

As soon as that thought drifted into her mind, her eyes flew open. She stared down at Chandril, a *wraith*, who continued to grip Quintus's shoulder. Was Quintus undead? Had Chandril done something to make him undead?

Flicking her gaze back to Julian, she noticed him staring at Chandril as she must have been. Chandril couldn't have been standing there for nothing but moral support. Clearly, he had done *something* with his hand on Quintus's shoulder like that. He had kept his vow, though Chloe had no idea how.

Forgoing magic, Julian used his hands to shove the wraith away. Chandril stumbled back, his balance unsteady and weak. When the other wraiths tried to come forward, they too seemed unable to walk as they usually did. It seemed like it took them twice as much effort as normal just to stand. Glaring, Julian sent a blast of magic from his fingertips that easily slammed them back onto the ground.

Still reaching through the bond, Chloe could feel the moment Chandril's hand left Quintus's shoulder. In a flash, Quintus's fae nature returned. Now she could feel the bruises on his face, though he had no injury at all where Julian's axe had hit him. Maybe the bruises didn't bother him much, but Chloe healed them anyway. She had to work fast because Julian had nearly stomped up to his side.

He opened his mouth, but the words never came as a sharp flash of crimson magic shot out of the cauldron. A shower of sparks followed it. Soon the glowing magic swirled down until it found Julian. He held his arms out wide, absorbing the great magic.

She didn't want to believe it, but she couldn't deny the truth in front of her. The ritual was over.

Julian had won.

Now she understood why the wraiths had struggled to even walk only moments earlier. With the ritual finished, they had been weakened greatly. According to Chandril, they might never recover. But it also meant, finally, Quintus was safe from his father.

Thumping filled Chloe's chest and blood pounded in her ears as magic flowed and pulsed into Julian's body. It may have been her imagination, but he seemed to grow taller as the magic worked through him. And now, the magic began swirling and sparkling all the way in and through the gold and emerald crown on his head.

The battle stopped completely in that moment. No weapon, no danger, no chance of victory could hold anyone's attention as completely as this display of magic before them.

Every tine on Julian's crown grew taller. The emerald stones sparked and glistened as magic crackled at Julian's fingertips. And then another crown started changing.

Across the lawn, High King Brannick's magnificent crown of branches and vines began shrinking. Each pulse made it appear duller. At his side, Elora's eyes grew wide. She gripped her sword like she was ready to stab someone in the heart with it, except she didn't know who to stab.

As the last of the magic surged, Julian started laughing, a wild laugh that felt like jagged glass across Chloe's nerves. He had done it again. He had beaten them.

And now, because he had more power than any other fae, he became High King of Faerie. He'd stolen the rightful title from Brannick. Brannick's crown had turned to a mere circlet of branches intertwined with a single, unimpressive vine.

Julian's laugh rang through the air, keeping everyone frozen in place. Even his own soldiers seemed to be afraid of him now. With this much power, what would he do next? At first, he merely glanced over the area, staring at it like every being before him was dirt beneath his shoes.

No one dared raise a weapon against him. No one dared to be the first to test his newfound enormous power. Everyone stood in shocked silence. The dragons hovered in place wherever they happened to be in the sky. Would this go on forever? Would no one be the first to challenge him?

Just then, a tiny, jeweled bird chirped above the battlefield. Its delicate presence felt incredibly out of place in this moment. The happy song from its golden beak might have offered a smidgeon of hope. It might have brightened at least a few spirits.

Except as soon as it twittered, Julian had finally found something to test his new powers on. He grinned and shot a blast of magic from his palm. A small glowing orb shot outward, hitting the tiny bird with perfect precision. It exploded into a thousand shards of jewels that fell heavily to the ground.

With another wild grin, Julian used both hands to shoot magic that almost looked like dragon fire from his palms. The hot magic poured over the trees nearest to the castle. It took only a few seconds of the magic streaming against them before the trees dissolved into a puddle on the ground. A few seconds. It had only taken a few seconds. And he had caused so much destruction.

Whirling on his heel, he turned to face his son. Magic burst from his hands. It had just as much power as the blasts that had killed the bird and destroyed the trees, but it had no effect on Quintus.

Julian should have expected it. He had likely studied the ritual just as determinedly as Chloe had. After pouring over the words, one thing was clear. If Julian used Quintus's blood in the ritual, then the magic and power gained could not be used to injure anyone with that blood. By failing to kill Quintus before the ritual had finished, Julian had effectively made it impossible for him to end his son's life.

If only the cloudiness in Quintus's mind would ease. Then he'd be able to get away without any help.

"Can you communicate with Quintus?" Mishti's whispering voice sounded in Chloe's ears. "Don't you have a bond you can talk to him through?"

Chloe gripped her whispering stone tighter, ready to bring it to her lips. She almost answered that no, their bond didn't work that way. But then again, she had healed both herself and Quintus without physically touching him. So…maybe she *could* talk to him through the bond. Even impaired, he'd probably be able to follow a simple direction.

"I can try," she answered into the whispering stone.

Mishti replied right away. "I know he's under that roof, but if he can move to the left just a bit more, Sofia can fly in with Fidget, and they'll be able to reach him."

Nodding to herself, Chloe whispered into the stone again. "I will try to tell him."

She closed her eyes, concentrating on Quintus. On the bond. She waited until she could feel him strongly. Then she spoke careful words in her mind.

Move to the left.

Was it working? Chloe peeked through one eyelid, staring down at Quintus. He continued to stare with unfocused eyes at Julian's magic that flowed over his body like nothing more than a gentle wind. It hadn't worked. He hadn't heard her. She couldn't explain how she knew, she just knew.

With a huff, Julian dropped his hands to his side. He wrinkled his nose, but then his face turned a little softer. "Since I cannot kill you, I will do the next best thing." He raised a single eyebrow that brought a terrifying smirk across his face. "I will recruit you."

So much disgust filled Quintus's eyes, it was a wonder Julian didn't drop dead on the spot. Quintus stared at his father, his lip curling upward. "Never," he said, but his voice came out in a groggy mumble.

Julian rolled his eyes. "Never, hmm? So dramatic. What if you found out your beloved Chloe doesn't even care for you?"

Still hazy, Quintus laughed and tried to stand up. His lack of coordination dropped him as soon as he tried, but at least he was trying. Even in this state, Julian would have to work a lot harder than that if he wanted to manipulate his son.

Chloe closed her eyes again, focusing harder on her bond with Quintus. Again, she spoke words in her mind, hoping he would hear them.

Move your body to the left. Sofia and her dragon can save you if you move to the left.

His head vaguely tilted to the side. It didn't seem like he had heard the words, but maybe he could feel them. Maybe he could tell Chloe wanted to communicate with him.

Julian glanced over one shoulder and looked directly at one the guards nearby. Chloe recognized the guard as one who had been in the room when Julian had tried to kill her. Julian turned back to Quintus with scheming in his eyes.

"When I had your beloved in my clutches, I learned she doesn't care about you at all. She only wanted you to rescue her."

These words hit Quintus a little harder than the others, but he shook them off easily and lifted his chin.

Julian took a step closer, his tone growing colder. "She cared nothing for you. She was happy to explain exactly how to use her as bait so I could capture you. All she cared about was how you could help *her*." He paused for a moment, and then added, "She *used* you."

"No." Quintus shook his head, as if trying to rid his mind of the thoughts his father had placed there. It couldn't help that his senses were also impaired. When he glanced up again, his jaw was clenched. He stumbled over his next words, each as groggy as the last. "You have magic and a crown, but you are still mortal." His eyes turned slightly more focused. "You can *lie*."

Julian touched a hand to his chest. "You don't believe me?" He shrugged, completely unperturbed. "Fine. It is true that I can lie, but this soldier," he gestured behind himself, "is fae. *He* cannot lie."

The fae soldier started at being addressed. He stood a little taller and even took a small step forward.

Julian turned to the fae. "What did she say when I asked why she would tell me how to trap my son? She said, 'I want Quintus to rescue me.' Weren't those her exact words?"

"They were, my king." The fae nodded. "I heard those words too." The fae soldier turned now to Quintus. "King Julian asked why she would tell him to use herself as bait to capture you, and she said, 'Because I do not want to die. I want Quintus to rescue me.'"

A hard puff of air escaped Quintus's mouth, as if he'd been hit in the chest with a boulder. It wasn't fair for Julian to manipulate him like this while his judgment was impaired. Quintus couldn't think straight. How was he supposed to know Julian had twisted the truth? Quintus's cloudy eyes narrowed he glanced between his father and the fae soldier.

Chloe swallowed hard. The fae *was* telling the truth, but he left so much out too. Of course she loved Quintus. Of course she didn't only want him around so he could rescue her. She had even nearly escaped by herself.

One last time, she attempted to speak to Quintus through their bond.

Move to the left. We can get you to safety if you move your body to the left.

He heard it that time. In her heart, she could tell. But it wasn't just about him hearing anymore. Now he had to *trust* her. He had to believe in her love for him more than he doubted it. Trust had never been his strong suit. Considering how he had tried to send her home to the mortal realm not that long ago, just because he believed she *might* betray him someday, trusting her now wouldn't be easy. With his mind impaired, it might be too much.

The face he wore only confirmed that. Quintus's unfocused gaze jumped back and forth between his father and the fae soldier. His eyes scrunched and squinted.

Through their bond, she could feel the turmoil within him.

She should have said *yes* to his marriage proposal. She shouldn't have admitted to Julian she wanted Quintus to rescue her, especially when what she really wanted was for him to be safe. Quintus had too much difficulty trusting. He'd *never* choose her after hearing something like that. How could he?

Her heart dropped as another realization settled deep in her gut. He was going to join Julian.

Quintus shifted, doing his best once again to stand. This time, he managed it. She almost didn't want to hear what he would say.

His face scrunched into a snarl as he stared back at his father. As he did, the first truly focused gaze took hold of his eyes. His voice still came out groggy, but it also had bite. "You think because your fae soldier cannot lie that I believe you? There are other ways to deceive. I do not trust easily, but if there is one thing I do trust, it is her."

With a sweeping motion, he lunged to the left.

The air had been so silent, so still since Julian completed the ritual and gained so much power. But now Quintus had moved, others did too. Sofia swooped in. Fidget flew low and he jumped onto the smaller dragon's back.

In that one single action, the fighting began once again.

38

CHLOE GRIPPED HER DRAGON'S SCALES with her knees as she kept herself low. Shadow swooped down, flying close to Sofia's dragon. Once they were close enough, Quintus jumped off Fidget's back and onto Shadow's. His movements were still disjointed, but he had more coordination than he'd had before.

Sofia and her dragon immediately flew straight back into the fight while Shadow flew away from it. Once Quintus landed on the golden scales of Shadow's back, he shook his head. "He gave me something…"

"That dulled your senses?" Chloe finished for him.

"Yes." He rubbed one hand across his forehead. At least his voice was starting to sound less groggy. "It is finally starting to wear off."

He shook his head again, harder this time. Once finished, he gathered Chloe against him with one arm.

If he had his mind back, then she needed to explain herself immediately. "I didn't *want* them to use me as bait to capture you. I just had to say that so Julian wouldn't kill me."

"Mmm," Quintus replied to acknowledge her words. His actions, however, made it clear he never needed any explanation from her. He tugged her close with one arm. His lips found her neck and left several gentle kisses down it. Then he took in a deep breath, as if inhaling the scent of her hair. With each moment, he pulled her closer.

Even as a war raged beneath them, he managed to steal her breath away. She leaned back into him, nearly sighing at every touch.

But after he had breathed her in, he seemed to turn more serious. His fingers lifted her skirt to reveal the end of her leg. No wooden foot was attached at the end of it.

She could feel his body flinch at the sight. "I will make you a new one." Finally, his words strung together clearly without any grogginess. But his breath also hitched as he spoke, causing him to use more force to get the rest of his words out. "I watched Julian destroy the other."

Her hands flew to her chest, clutching the fabric over her heart. "I shouldn't have used it against him. That was the last piece of—"

"Of course you should have used it. Homes have power in Faerie. You saw how effective it was to use my home against him. I don't need that last piece of my home in Bitter Thorn anyway." His face dropped against her neck again, whispering directly into her ear. "You are my home now."

A blast of gray magic followed by a volley of arrows pierced the air above them. Shadow dove into a tight barrel roll until she reached the ground where she clamped her jaws down on the attackers.

Chloe's muscles squeezed, making it difficult to breathe while her dragon flew. But Quintus used one arm to hold her tight. He even rubbed his fingers against her arm to reassure her.

Once the moment was over and danger no longer threatened them. Quintus tilted so he could look her in the eyes. "Did you heal yourself without touching me? And then heal me during the ritual?"

The corner of her lips twitched into a smile. "You could feel it?"

A matching smile appeared on his face. "Yes. How did you do it?"

She shrugged. "I don't know. When I healed myself, I was in too much pain to worry about if it made sense or not. I just tried and it worked. And since it had worked for me, I tried it on you too during the ritual."

She sucked in a sharp breath then and checked on the other wound she hadn't healed fully. Twisting her body around, she examined the arm Julian had chopped off. Since Quintus's sleeve had been chopped off too, she could see everything clearly.

Quintus's arm had already started to grow back. It looked thinner than usual, but he had an upper arm now, almost down his elbow. The muscles in his arm would probably strengthen once the entire arm had formed. Stretching her fingers over the newly growing arm, she squeezed it gently. It seemed fully substantial and even stronger than expected.

"I had no idea how to regrow an arm, especially since mortals can't do it. So I stopped the bleeding and added a few herbs and hoped your healing abilities would do the rest. It looks like it's already working."

He grinned, squeezing the new muscles with his other hand. "You sped up the healing process somehow. It does not usually happen this fast, but I think it may grow back fully before day dawns."

Such a statement would have filled her with joy except Shadow dove again, even faster than before. Her hair whipped back as shots of spinning magic flew all around her. With a gasp, she dropped her belly against Shadow's back and slammed her eyes closed.

After getting captured, watching Quintus get captured, and then seeing the ritual, her mind was reaching its limit of how much fighting she could handle. If she tried to get involved, she'd pass out. But even without fighting, she could still observe.

Scanning first the skies and then the ground below, she came to an unexpected realization. The Golden Shields defended themselves, but they did not attack outright. Even Shadow only used her combat training when weapons or magic flew at her.

A nagging in Chloe's gut caused her to guess the reason. They had failed to stop Julian from doing the ritual. Maybe the Shields no longer knew what to do.

Biting her lip, she considered the same question. What *should* they do?

Heart beating rapidly in her chest, she scanned the area more carefully. Brannick and Elora continued to dominate the fight with their legendary skills. Even with dozens of fae soldiers attacking, they fought them off easily. Most of the other Shields jumped and swerved to avoid attacks. The fae soldiers had formidable skills, forcing the Shields to fight hard.

But nothing compared to Julian. He hit every target he aimed for. It took him almost no effort to flatten the enemies before him. No one came close to touching him.

Another realization struck Chloe then. The faces of the fae had changed from before the ritual. They continued to fight for Julian, but they kept glancing over their shoulders at him. The very sight of him made them flinch and cower. When they wielded weapons, they fought with fear in their eyes. Did they think he would turn on them as soon as he had defeated the Shields? Would it be so inaccurate of them to fear such a thing?

Her eyes narrowed. Maybe they didn't need to worry so much about every Zeakriesh. Maybe they just needed to get rid of Julian. Without him, the fae soldiers would have nothing left to fight for.

Reaching for the whispering stone in her leather bag, Chloe brought it to her lips. "Who can hear me?"

Mishti responded first, then Sofia, Batu, and several others. Elora responded last of all.

When everyone had finished checking in, Batu spoke next. "Do we have a new plan?"

Ludo chimed almost immediately after. "Should we retreat?"

Chloe glanced back at Quintus, who offered an encouraging nod. With a deep breath, she continued. "I believe if we can kill Julian in this fight right now, then we can win. But we'll only continue if everyone is willing."

Several beats of silence followed her words. She didn't expect them to respond out of obligation. It was important to her that they felt safe enough to share their true feelings. But the prolonged silence still made her stomach squirm.

At last, Sofia spoke into her stone. "I am willing, but..." Her gulp that followed was loud enough to be heard through the stone. "Julian is more powerful than I ever thought possible."

Roarke jumped in next. "And we have lost so many fights against him."

Holding her stone a little tighter, Chloe spoke with a voice that hopefully sounded strong. Determined. "It doesn't matter how many fights we have lost. We only have to win one battle. The last one."

Conviction laced through her words, and when she finished speaking, the air itself seemed to spark with energy. With hope.

She continued. "I know this is the greatest battle yet, but if we can kill him, we can end this now."

"I will fight until my last breath." Mishti spoke with even more conviction than Chloe. "I promised to protect this court, and I intend to keep that promise."

Kai whispered into his stone. "I will fight too. The king may have power, but his soldiers have weakened. If our resolve is strong enough, we can win."

"I will fight too," Hilda responded, her voice strong and sure.

Then others chimed in: Roarke, Sofia, all the other Shields. Elora spoke last, her voice a rush, as if speaking while stabbing someone with a sword. "And we will fight. We will stay with you until the end."

Pride in her people surged in Chloe's chest. For a brief moment, she set the whispering stone down so her words would not be carried to the other stones. Now she looked at Quintus. "If I can use my healing magic without touching you…"

He started nodding and finished her sentence. "Then you can hide in the trees and heal while Shadow and I join the fight."

She smiled. It was nice he'd been thinking the same thing as her. Without a word of command, Shadow started flying to the spot Quintus had mentioned. Chloe picked up her stone again. "I will be hidden in the trees between the hills and the mountains. If anyone is injured, go to that spot, and I'll heal your injuries."

A moment later, Shadow landed on the black soil with sparkling white pebbles that glinted in the moonlight. Quintus helped Chloe down, since she had to do it without her wooden foot. He helped her hop forward until she could settle onto a nice spot of ground. At least she was far more coordinated on one foot now than she'd been immediately after her foot had been chopped off. It took very little effort to bend and sit down, even though she only had one foot to do it with.

Just before standing again, Quintus squeezed her hand. "Be careful."

She squeezed him back, placing her head against his arm. "You too."

His new arm had grown past the elbow now. It wouldn't be much longer until he had a full arm again. After jumping onto Shadow, he flew the dragon back into the thick of the fight. They had all made their choice to continue the fight. And this choice would either save their lives… or end them.

39

Closing her eyes, Chloe imagined pouring a tincture of alcohol and rich healing herbs over a large gash. It took effort not to rush through the healing process, but she did her best. At least half the Shields had already come to her in her spot in the trees.

Touching Quintus with their bond, she healed each one.

Her eyes flew open, and she stared straight at the firm skin on Sofia's forearm. Good as new.

"Excellent," Sofia said, stretching out her fingers. "I love your healing magic."

Chloe smiled but then stopped the woman before she could jump back onto her dragon. "Wait. I have one last thing I need to do."

Chloe's eyes fluttered closed again. Instead of imagining a wound or internal injury, she instead imagined Sofia sleeping. Methodically, she pictured every part of the process, from her settling into her sleeping mat to heavy slumberous breaths to waking up to shining sun rays. For good measure, Chloe even imagined Sofia eating a delicious, filling breakfast.

When Chloe opened her eyes again, Sofia stared at her palms with eyes open wide. "Wow." She shook her head in disbelief, glancing over herself. "I feel *amazing*. I was getting tired, but now I feel like I could fight all through the night."

Warmth spilled into Chloe's chest as she watched the woman fly away on her dragon. Chloe had the idea to use her magic to imagine sleep after watching the fae on the battlefield. It was harder to see the Shields while they flew on their dragons, but her position offered her a clear view of the ground.

She'd started noticing yawns and eyes taking too long to blink around the time the seventh Shield came to be healed. After all the new things she'd tried with her bond, she figured she might as well see if she could give them sleep too. Each time, the Shield she healed jumped back onto their dragon with more energy than they'd started the fight with.

As the night dragged on, nearly all the Shields had come to get healed. She was able to give all of them rest and nutrition. That alone gave them an incredible edge over the sleepy fae on the battlefield. They were finally starting to get the upper hand. Everything was going well, except for one thing.

Julian.

Sitting cross-legged, she absently massaged the smooth end of her leg. Julian never once showed any sign of fatigue. His magic easily blasted away anyone who attempted to fight him. Almost all the injuries she had healed had been at his hands. Even against her instant healing that included rest and food, the man showed no signs of stopping.

With no one to heal, Chloe pushed herself up until she stood on one foot. She leaned against a nearby tree and stared as hard as she could at the battlefield. Her gaze found Quintus first. He shot spears and arrows and more magic than she'd ever seen at his father. Though he fought fiercely and never wavered, not one single attack had any effect on Julian. It never stopped Quintus from the next attack though. He threw and lunged and jabbed, completely forgetting each failure as soon as it had passed.

The other Shields fought hard too, especially since Chloe's healing had given them endurance the Zeakriesh didn't have. All across the battlefield, fae yawned and fought with much less energy than when they'd started. As she stared, one even collapsed, as if from exhaustion.

It soon became clear she was not the only one who had noticed these changes in the Zeakriesh. With a huge blast of magic that soared into the sky and burst into an explosion, Brannick stood tall and shouted, "Stop!"

Even from her distance away from the castle, she could still hear his voice fill the air.

He may not have been High King anymore, but he commanded attention as if he still were. Everyone, both fae and mortal, turned to face him.

Julian shook his messy hair that had grown more chaotic throughout the fight. In a flash, he kept fighting again. Quintus fought back and so did a dozen other Shields. They couldn't stop unless Julian did.

But no one else resumed the fight. Fae across the lawn dropped their hands to their sides. They stared at Brannick, waiting.

Brannick gestured toward Julian. When he spoke, it was in that same booming voice Chloe could hear, even over the sounds of the fight. "This king does not care for you. He would sacrifice every one of your lives if it got him what he wanted."

Several fae in the crowd nodded at those words. The current battle had already taught them just how true it was. And with how much they feared Julian now, they probably cared even less to defend him.

"Go home." Brannick shouted the words and gestured away from the castle. "Leave this court. You have nothing left to fight for."

Would it work? If the other fae left, then all the Shields and pixies could attack Julian at the same time. The wraiths had been greatly weakened by the ritual, but they still did their best to fight too. With no one left to defend Julian, every Shield, wraith, pixie, and dragon fighting against him at once would have to make a difference. But even though the fae had stopped fighting, even though many of them had nodded in agreement, none of them moved. None of them left.

Julian had seeded fear so deep within them that it still controlled their actions. None of them wanted to be the first to make a move.

"How dare you?" Julian shouted in a voice as loud as Brannick's. "You're a pathetic excuse for a ruler."

As usual, Julian tried to make himself look more impressive by tearing down anyone who came close to his level. But his insult had the opposite effect of what he undoubtedly desired.

By speaking about Brannick, the one who had been a revered High King for so long, he had finally spurred the fae soldiers into action.

The first soldier who left was the one standing closest to Julian. From this far away, Chloe couldn't tell for sure, but it seemed to be the same guard Julian had used to try and manipulate Quintus. With a wave of his hand, he opened a swirling iridescent door and jumped through it. As soon as he did, nearly two dozen fae opened their own doors and vanished a moment later.

Julian screamed in an even louder voice than before. "Cowards! I never needed you anyway."

And then Julian did what Chloe probably should have expected but still came as a shock. He turned his magic on his own soldiers. Blasts of magical daggers shot from his palms, which he shot at any fae trying to leave the battlefield.

Unsurprisingly, that last ditch effort to frighten them into staying did the exact opposite. The rest of them left even faster. Very few of them stayed at all. Those who *did* stay now turned on Julian, joining the Golden Shields, pixies, and wraiths in the effort to take him down.

Every Shield charged toward him now, finally able to focus their weapons on their single enemy.

Despite her fear of battles, Chloe almost wanted to hop forward and join them. What could go wrong now? Julian couldn't possibly fight off that many of them forever, especially not when they had Chloe to heal them and rejuvenate them whenever needed.

Julian took a step back. "You think you can defeat me?" As he shouted, the magic erupting from his palms shifted and turned to whipping flames. "I still have ten times as much power as all of you combined."

She wanted to shake her head. Even in the face of a small army against him, he still had enough arrogance to give speeches.

All at once, one of his hands reached upward and clenched into a fist. At the same time, a section of the golden castle wall got torn off and away. He threw his fist forward. When he did, the huge piece of castle wall flew straight for the nearest dragons.

Chloe held her breath as it soared through the air. Mortals and fae she could heal well enough, but dragons were much more difficult. Even now that she had studied dragon anatomy, there was still only so much she could do for the creatures.

Worse, the golden wall crashed straight into Shadow as well as three other dragons. They let out growls as their bodies were slammed backward. Several wings were hit with the crumbled chunks of the castle wall.

But though she'd been nervous, it seemed clear the dragons would be fine. Their strong scales and all their training made them possibly the only ones that had an edge in this fight against Julian. She'd worried Quintus might fall off at the impact, but Shadow managed to keep him upright.

Despite the dragons' impressive ability to dodge and withstand heavy blows, Julian didn't even break a sweat. He moved his arms fast. They never shook or slowed, never showing any sign of weakening.

As he fought, he stumbled over something on the ground. After the stumble, he sent enormous waves of fire toward everyone who attempted to take advantage of his one weak moment. But since she wasn't on the battlefield and she had no reason to pay attention to his attack, she focused on him.

Whatever had made him stumble captured his attention immediately. He used his magic to hide it from the Golden Shields, but *she* saw when he bent down. From her distance, she might not have been able to tell what he lifted into one hand. But since she had been flying over the battlefield earlier, she had seen the object up close and recognized it at once.

He now held the book he had been reading the ritual from. Her shoulders shuddered at the thought. She couldn't even imagine what other information could be in there. With something as horrible as Bloodstone Convergence on the pages, the other pages were likely just as disturbing.

Others moved closer to him, and he sent another blast of magic that shot out as a cloud of fog. It blocked him from view for a moment. She never would have known if she'd been fighting, but from here, she could tell what the other Shields couldn't. He was staring at that book. If he bothered doing it in the middle of the fight, it was likely about something that would help him.

Her stomach squirmed as dread washed over her. He'd probably planned this. He'd found out about Bloodstone Convergence from that book, and he probably had another ritual or spell or concoction earmarked in it to use as a backup plan in case things didn't go according to his plan.

And since he no longer had an army of fae on his side, he must have decided now was time for that backup plan.

He was going to do something. Something horrible.

And no one except her knew it.

40

CHLOE SHOVED HER HAND INTO her pocket and ripped out her whispering stone. She had to tell the others Julian had something horrible planned. Since she had no idea *what* he had planned or how it would change things, she struggled to find the right words to explain.

But before she could say a single word, Julian shot a beacon of light from one palm. He had dropped the book. The fog had cleared, and the book sat next to him on the ground where the Shields would never suspect anything about it.

The beacon of light flowed upward, but all at once, it arced forward. It moved in a blur until it completely encircled Chloe. The round beam of light covered her from head to toe and even shot upward into the air, giving away her location. It proved he'd had this planned even before the party started. All this time, he had a way to find her instantly. He hadn't used it during the party, probably because he correctly assumed Quintus would be too close to her then and could have kept her safe. But Julian knew how she hated battles. He must have known she and Quintus would be separated now, and of course, Julian used that to his advantage.

She had to move. If she could hop out of the beacon of light, maybe Julian wouldn't be able to do whatever he planned But her thoughts never were quick enough for fights.

In an instant, Julian threw another ribbon of magic out. It shot forward and cracked as it straightened, almost like a whip. But it hadn't been created to hit any of the people attempting to fight Julian. Instead, it wrapped itself around Chloe's waist, grabbed her, and carried her directly to Julian's side.

Her heart thundered. Moving so quickly, so unexpectedly, had knocked the wind from her chest. Sputtering coughs and desperate gulps filled her mouth as she tried to capture air again.

The huffing exhales and slumped shoulders on Julian explained another reason he hadn't attempted this move any earlier than now. Nothing else had weakened him at all so far, but this had.

He still recovered quickly. Too quickly.

Quintus was screaming her name, but she couldn't breathe, so she could barely even hear it.

When Quintus tried to swoop in with Shadow and save Chloe, Julian threw up a barrier that knocked Shadow and Quintus to the ground.

No one should have this much power. The only reason Julian hadn't squashed them yet was because every single Golden Shield, dragon, pixie, and wraith simultaneously fought against him. He still managed to keep them back as he looked down at Chloe.

She leaned back with the sudden urge to cover her head with her arms. Using one foot, he nudged the book onto her lap. He used his toe to point at the recipe on the page. Then he brought his foot to the side and shoved an open chest toward her. Herbs, crystals, and a few other items filled the chest, probably providing every ingredient she'd need.

"Make this for me," Julian said harshly. He had turned back to the battlefield again. Quintus's attacks grew more powerful than ever, but Julian continued to fight back. The ritual had made it so Julian's attacks could no longer kill his son, and Quintus took full advantage of that. He charged straight through walls of fire and swatted away magical arrows and heavy axes. It took barriers and hard blasts of magic just to keep him back.

But it didn't bode well that Julian no longer attempted to kill Chloe. How bad could this concoction be if the king cared about it more than he cared about killing the woman his son loved?

Chloe scanned the pages in front of her, trying to determine what the recipe made. All she could really tell was it created a drink. But what would the drink do? Turn him invisible? Make him grow to the size of a giant? Make him undead?

When she tried to turn the page back, hoping it might have more information, Julian slammed his foot down on the book to stop her.

"Make it," he said through his teeth.

She glared back at him. "No."

He kicked her then, right in the ribcage. Once again, she fought to catch her breath. Pain exploded in her side. He had probably cracked a rib inside her, maybe two. As she writhed on the ground, he kicked her again.

"I said, *make it*. I need to drink it immediately."

But she couldn't even tell what it was supposed to do.

Her arms curled around herself, trying to ease some of the pain. Somehow, she managed to sit back up. When she did, Julian used one hand to lift his axe. He raised both eyebrows. "Make it or you die."

In that moment, she realized it didn't matter what the potion was supposed to do. She had all the knowledge she needed right now.

Her side ached as she grabbed a goblet from the chest. After setting it directly in front of her, she eyed the recipe and reached for an herb.

"Chloe!" Quintus shouted her name as he threw spears and daggers and anything else he could pull from his magical pocket.

An ache tore through her throat. If she was the sort of person who could fight, she wouldn't have to bother with this recipe. She could have lunged for one of the daggers on the ground and slammed it into Julian's chest before he had a chance to blink. That's what Elora would have done.

But Chloe wasn't the sort of person who could fight. Any attempt she made to lunge would be sloppy and uneven and would probably get her nowhere near where she meant to land. Not to mention, having only one foot would make it even worse.

Instead, her fingers quivered as she crushed herbs and sprinkled them into the goblet. She held her breath as she checked inside the cup. Her gaze turned to the book next, deliberately eyeing the page.

More. She needed more.

She grabbed another handful of herbs, crushing and sprinkling with hands that were shaking so much she could barely perform her tasks. Each ingredient she needed sat inside the chest, just as she guessed it would. Her heart clenched whenever she dropped something new into the cup. All the while she wondered, what was this recipe meant to create?

As she dropped the last of the final herb into the goblet, Julian kicked her again.

"Hurry."

An audible crack sounded as another one of her ribs broke. Her breaths turned to gasps as she reached for a flask of wine inside the chest. It hurt so much she wanted to curl into a ball and die right there. But she was almost finished. She couldn't stop now.

Tears felt like fingernails scratching down her cheeks. Julian lifted his axe at her again, sending waves of fear through her already shuddering limbs. Tears flowed even faster from her eyes. Wine splashed both in and out of the goblet, but she managed to fill it all the way.

Julian lifted one foot as if to kick her again, but she grabbed the goblet with both hands and lifted it up for him. Her hands shook so much, more wine spilled out the rim.

An uneven and haunting smile covered his mouth. He plucked the goblet from her hands and drained its contents in only a few gulps.

Now she *did* curl into a ball. Black spots had already started appearing in her vision. Her head went fuzzy no matter how she tried to fight it. She almost didn't dare look up to see how she had changed things. It had been impossible to tell what the potion was meant to do.

For a moment, Julian simply blocked attacks as he breathed in deeply. Perhaps he was waiting a moment for the effects of the potion to sink in.

Every muscle in her body tensed. Waiting. Hopefully he would wait longer before he tried to test the potion. Hopefully he would stop, and the fighting could end.

But of course her hopes were dashed almost as soon as she'd thought of them. Sneering down at the battlefield before him, Julian flicked sharp magic from his fingertips.

Quintus managed to get much closer than the others, since he could walk straight through most of the attacks. As such, the sharp magic had been aimed straight at him. Using his fae speed, Quintus dodged to the side, nearly missing the magic completely. Not that it mattered since the ritual had protected him.

But when the magic brushed across Quintus's cheek, Chloe gasped hard. The movement from it stretched her ribcage, bringing burning pain all through her body. But for once, the pain was the last thing on her mind.

Because that little bit of magic had left a mark. It had only brushed across Quintus's cheek, but it left a thin slice across the skin that immediately started bleeding. A superficial wound like that would be easy to heal, but that wasn't the point. The point was, Julian had just *injured* his son.

That wasn't supposed to happen. The ritual was supposed to make it impossible. Chloe swallowed as the harrowing realization settled in. She had just given Julian the very weapon that could end her beloved for good.

She shook her head, not willing to believe it. Quintus was strong. He could fight his father off.

But as she moved, Quintus's gaze turned to hers. He wore a pained expression. No, not pained: *betrayed*. He was hurt because his doom had come at the hands of the one who supposedly loved him.

She couldn't look him in the eye. She couldn't look away.

He blinked at her as his entire face fell. "What have you done?"

She'd already been crying, but now she started sobbing. Weeping. Her insides felt like they'd explode. She shook and quivered and *still* couldn't breathe.

A wild chuckle bubbled in Julian's throat. He reeled his arm back, as if preparing for a final blow. "Now I can end you."

The magic that shot from his fingertips got blocked by every fae among the Golden Shields. But even with all that magic trying to stop it, Julian's blast still knocked Quintus off his feet.

As Quintus fell backward, his gaze caught Chloe's again. Nothing could have prepared her for the question in his eyes.

Why did you help him?

All those times he'd been so afraid she would betray him, and now this. He had finally learned to trust in her and couldn't believe it had come to this.

"I had to." Chloe choked the words out, ignoring how they sent shattering pain through her ribs.

Julian's laugh turned maniacal. "Yes. I told you she never cared for you. I turned your own beloved against you and look how easy it was." His voice turned rough and low, almost like he was losing his voice. After clearing his throat, he continued. "And now I can finally kill you."

The sobs wracking Chloe's body weren't enough. The pain in her heart ached for so much more than just tears. Why did she have to do it like this? Why did she have to stare Quintus in the eye like this while it happened?

Quintus glanced up and saw his father preparing for another attack, but this time, he made no attempt to stop it. He made no attempt to dodge. His gaze simply turned back to Chloe and stared.

She forced herself to look him in the eye. Words sputtered from her lips, and she thanked Faerie itself that her pathetic sniveling self caught Julian's attention. Everyone stared at her now.

She swallowed and spoke in a choppy, uneven tone. "It's like Julian said, the only thing that can save you is your home."

Quintus reached up and touched his heart as pain filled his eyes. "But *you* are my home."

She waited a beat. Just a little longer. The air was quiet all around them. Everyone, even Julian, waited to see what she would say. Julian tugged at his collar, pulling it away from his throat.

One more beat. Now she let her tears slow. She looked at Quintus, staring as intensely as she could. And then she said, "Exactly."

Would he see the look in her eye? Would he understand it? If he used the bond, he'd know her feelings, but even those might not be enough to explain.

Julian lifted his foot like he wanted to kick her again but then decided against it. He tugged at his collar once more. His voice had grown even rougher. "What do you mean *she's* your home? That doesn't…," he had to cough again just to force the final words out, "…make any sense."

The first glint of light sparked in Quintus's eyes. His gaze flicked to Julian, then flicked back to hers almost as fast.

Sputtering coughs tumbled from Julian's throat. His body started shaking after that.

Now Chloe could breathe. She closed her eyes, focusing on her bond with Quintus, her beloved, and then she healed her ribs.

Even with his body shaking, Julian caught sight of his son's face. The lightest smile had started to appear on Quintus's face.

"What did…?" The words sounded more like a croak coming out of Julian's mouth. His eyes widened as he turned to Chloe, finally realizing maybe *she* had something to do with all his coughing.

And then he dropped to the ground.

As soon as he fell, she got up and stood on her one foot. While he continued to shake and cough, she hopped a little closer to him. "You have so much arrogance, and yet it only took one person to defeat you. You only had to underestimate *one* of us."

He shook his head, eyes still wild with disbelief. "But you're…"

"Weak?" Chloe answered. "Scared? Unable to wield a weapon?"

Magic suddenly appeared at his fingertips. He set his hands against his chest, trying to put the magic inside of himself. But it didn't matter. She was a skilled apothecary, and she knew; it was already too late.

Her eyebrow rose as she looked down at him. "I am all those things, but you know what else I am? An expert with poisons, who would do anything to protect her beloved."

She leaned in closer now, making sure he heard every word. "And I know how to play a coward to take down a narcissist."

His body began convulsing as his eyes rolled back into his head. Foam frothed at his mouth. And then…it stopped. His body froze and never moved again. If it had been anyone else, such a sight would have disturbed and hurt her heart. But for him, she almost wanted to laugh.

It was over.

It was truly and completely over.

Quintus lunged toward her, staring first at his father and then at her. "You killed him?"

"Yes." She never expected to answer such a question so completely devoid of guilt.

Mishti came forward next, eyeing Julian's crumpled form. "Are we sure he's dead? Like all the way, completely dead? He can't use magic to come back or anything like that?"

The other Golden Shields closed in, eyeing him as suspiciously as Mishti had. Nearby, a wraith got to his feet. He looked far stronger than he had only moments ago. Hopefully Julian's death had undone whatever weakness the ritual had caused for the wraiths. But just like Mishti and the others, the wraith eyed the king's form, as if unsure he was truly dead.

Gripping her sword tight, Elora plunged it into Julian's chest. She twisted the blade and then yanked it back out. When it escaped his body, Julian's heart sat on the blade of her sword. His body hadn't moved at all as she worked. It hadn't even flinched. He was clearly already dead, but the others seemed happy to not take any chances.

When she finished, Mishti plucked Julian's own axe off the ground and cut his head clean off his shoulders. Apparently, she *really* didn't want to take any chances.

But Chloe had no hint of worry within her, even before his heart and head were removed. She knew exactly how much poison she'd added to that goblet. Even with his magic, no mortal nor fae could have survived the concoction. She merely needed to wait long enough for it to kick in. And she had.

Ludo was the first to laugh. It came out surprised and short, but a harder laugh soon followed it. "*Chloe* killed him. Our greatest enemy and he was taken down by the one he considered the weakest threat."

His laughter was followed by similar chuckles from several Golden Shields.

A wide smile covered Ludo's face as he clapped her hard on the back. "They will certainly tell stories about this. They will make songs, write poems, depictions of it will cover tapestries. You, Chloe, will be a legend Faerie never forgets."

Mishti grinned as wide as Ludo, offering her friend a nod of respect. "Sometimes the greatest hero is the unlikeliest one of all."

Quintus wrapped his arm around her waist and stepped in close enough to hold her tight. He said nothing, but he didn't need to. The look of pride in his eyes, the look of admiration, the look of love, healed every ounce of pain she'd been forced to endure while he'd had to believe she'd betrayed him.

Punching her hand into the air, Sofia shouted, "For freedom."

Batu threw his own fist into the air, and shouted, "For safety."

Every Golden Shield, even Chloe, finished by shouting together, "For home!"

More cheers and laughter filled the air as the first rays of dawn began to shine down on them. Chloe wished the moment could have lasted forever. Joy filled her so completely being surrounded by her Shields, the wraiths, the pixies, and the handful of fae who had turned on Julian.

They had done it. They had needed each of them in this final battle, but they had done it. They had defeated the greatest enemy Faerie had ever known.

While celebrations littered the air, the wraith, Nilyx, stepped forward. She and all the other wraiths looked as wispy as ever, but their strength had clearly returned. Whatever effect the ritual had on them had not lasted beyond Julian's death. Perhaps the cursed wound in Quintus's side would be the same. Chloe had healed it, but it needed a celestine crystal around Quintus's neck to *keep* it healed. Now that Julian was dead, the wound might finally, fully be healed.

Nilyx narrowed her glowing red eyes and used her toe to point at Julian's head. His golden and emerald crown leaned against the messy strands of his hair. Then she looked up. "What do we do with this?"

As soon as she pointed to the crown, magical bursts of green and gold sparkles erupted and enveloped it entirely. It tipped away from Julian's head and fell upside down onto the ground pulsing and glowing.

41

BITING HER LIP, CHLOE WATCHED the crown of Crystalfall spark and crackle. As magic surrounded it, Brannick's crown began to change once again. The two crowns pulsed in unison as the emerald and golden crown shrank to its usual size and Brannick's crown of branches and vines grew to its proper height. Even after the change, the Crystalfall crown still looked magnificent and powerful.

After Brannick's crown changed, reclaiming him as the rightful High King of Faerie, he turned and looked Quintus in the eye. His gaze then trailed back down to the crown on the ground.

Quintus nodded. He released his arm from around Chloe, careful not to move her too much since she still stood on only one foot. In a few strides, he plucked the crown off the ground. Showers of sparks erupted from it, indicating to all present he had been chosen by Faerie as the next ruler of Crystalfall.

Everyone waited for him to set the crown onto his head. When he didn't do it right away, Brannick, with one hand stroking his wolf's head, gave an encouraging nod.

Instead of doing what everyone expected, Quintus reached into his pocket. He withdrew the beautiful golden and ruby crown he had crafted not long ago. The emerald crown in his other hand continued to release stunning showers of sparks, but the feminine crown did nothing in his hands.

He lifted it, looking at Brannick as he spoke. "What do we do with *this*?"

Confusion tipped Brannick's head to the side. "Where did that come from?"

"I made it." Quintus stared at the ground, his toe digging into the soil.

Eyebrows flew high on foreheads and jaws dropped open in shock.

Elora forced out the question everyone wanted to ask. "You *made* it?"

Quintus lifted his hands defensively. Judging by how his eyes widened at the two crowns he held, he had probably forgotten they were still in his hands. "I didn't think it would work, but… it did. I do not know why, but Faerie wants this crown to exist. I thought maybe it was meant for my mother."

No one looked more shocked by that declaration than Dyani herself. She had joined the fight after the Shields had helped her remove her chains. When Quintus went to hand her the crown, she shook her head.

It didn't matter though. Once she had the crown in her hands, it was clear this was not the answer. The crown did nothing, had no reaction to her touch. She handed it back to Quintus who stared at it more confused than ever.

Ludo came to his side and squeezed him by the shoulder like a friend about to deliver bad news. "Not to be rude, but you are an idiot for not assuming this crown is meant for Chloe."

Quintus's head shot up, staring his friend in the face. "What?" As he stared, the slightest glimpse of delight filled his eyes.

Ludo continued. "We all knew this *green* crown was meant for you." He gestured toward the emerald and golden crown, then he gestured toward Quintus's coat and pants that were also green. "Now there is a *red* crown." He gestured at the feminine crown, then turned and pointed straight at Chloe's red dress. "And you could not figure out who it is meant for?"

Mishti nodded. "It's probably the most obvious thing I've ever seen."

"Me?" Chloe sputtered. "But I'm mortal."

No one had any response to that. In fact, no one seemed to think it was an obstacle at all, especially the mortals among their group. Several people shrugged.

Elora narrowed her eyes, contemplating for several moments. Then she turned to her beloved. "Crystalfall is the only court with a moon and stars."

Brannick nodded, apparently knowing exactly what she implied. Standing tall, as only a High King could, he addressed everyone. "This court went with no ruler for longer than any of the other courts. Even when pressed by the citizens of Crystalfall, my mother, the then High Queen of Faerie, refused to crown anyone. She never understood why."

Setting his hand on his wolf's head again, Brannick turned his gaze to the two crowns still in Quintus's hands.. "But I understand now. Crystalfall is a court meant for both mortals and fae. As such, it needs two rulers."

He strode forward until he stood directly in front of Quintus. Brannick nodded at the emerald and green crown. "One fae."

Taking the feminine crown away, he then held it out to Chloe. "And one mortal."

With the crown directly in front of her, Chloe was still a little afraid to touch it. She had poked this crown before, and nothing had happened. But maybe that was because she had only used her fingernail or because she had moved too fast for the crown to react. Or maybe it never reacted because she hadn't held the entire crown in her hands.

Her stomach flopped over on itself. Or maybe everyone was wrong, and she wasn't meant to be the ruler of Crystalfall.

Brannick expectantly pushed the crown closer to her.

Though her insides spun in circles, she reached out. With trembling fingers, she touched the crown that might, somehow, be hers. As soon as she wrapped her fingers around it, and took the crown into her hand, a shower of glimmering sparks released.

Thundering heartbeats filled her chest. It was true. This crown had chosen her as Queen of Crystalfall. She glanced at Quintus and found him already staring at her. Pure joy filled his face as he stood with his own glimmering and sparking crown in his hands.

Elora moved to her beloved's side, smiling even wider at her sister.

With a final nod, Brannick glanced at both Quintus and Chloe. "Go on, wear the crowns. Crystalfall has been waiting for its true rulers. It is ready for you now."

Chloe had to look at Quintus as she did it. Even then, her fingers shook, making it difficult to lift the crown above her head. But soon, she carefully settled it onto her hair. She could feel the moment it became one with her.

Energy surged through her veins. Magic tingled at her fingertips and at the star tattoos under her eye. Warmth grew inside her, giving her a strength she'd never known. As wonderful as the changes felt, she realized another reason she could never use a shard to turn herself fae. This court needed one *mortal* ruler. If she changed her nature, Crystalfall would no longer have the mortal queen it needed.

A mortal. It hardly seemed possible. It had seemed like such an abomination when Julian had worn the crown. She'd thought it was because of his mortal nature, but maybe it was just because he himself was an abomination.

It still seemed too difficult to believe. And part of her seriously questioned Faerie's ability to choose leaders if it had chosen *her*. But one thing she did know.

She would do her absolute best to rule this court as well as it deserved. She would protect it and care for it. And above all, she would offer her people three things.

Freedom. Safety. Home.

More celebratory cheers followed. With his new crown on his head, Quintus, King of Crystalfall, walked over to Chloe and kissed her in front of everyone. That got even more cheers and left her face feeling hot and tingly.

His next act as king was to craft her a new foot. Her wooden one made from the walls of his Bitter Thorn home would always hold a special place in her heart, but the new one was wonderful too.

He crafted it from gold, but altered the metal so it felt soft, almost spongey. When she tested it with a few steps, she found it felt much closer to a real foot than her wooden one had.

After the test walk, Quintus inlaid dark rubies into the gold so it perfectly matched her new crown.

Next, they needed to focus on repairing their castle and making their court open for any and all who desired to make it home.

Plenty of work busied Chloe and the others. When a handful of wraiths and a few fae soldiers asked to become Golden Shields, they were welcomed in with more cheers.

Eventually, Elora and Brannick left to return to their own court with the promise they would all see each other again soon. Crystalfall Castle was nearly repaired now, and the work was nearly finished.

Chloe meandered across the black soil in front of the castle, hoping it wouldn't be obvious she was looking for someone specific. It didn't take her long to find him.

Standing among the trees, away from prying eyes, Mishti and Chandril whispered to each other. Chloe managed to step close enough to hear them before they realized she was there.

Chandril held both of Mishti's hands in his own, speaking in a passionate tone. "I would rather live and die with you than not live at all."

And of course, that was the moment they realized Chloe could hear them. They both turned toward her as her neck filled with heat. She hadn't meant to interrupt what was clearly meant to be a private conversation. But she couldn't pretend she hadn't heard, either.

She offered what was probably the most awkward smile of her life and turned to Chandril. "You're going to turn yourself mortal?"

"Yes." He answered without question, but Mishti gave him a look like they would definitely be talking about it later.

Turning away from her, he looked at Chloe. "But that is not why you are here."

"No." She cleared her throat. "I wanted to ask you about something."

He nodded, as if he'd been expecting this. "About how I made Quintus undead so Julian could not kill him."

"Yes."

She feared he might say he could not or would not answer, but he waited expectantly. He would do it, then. He would tell her what she wanted to know.

With any luck, this conversation would give her the answer she needed.

EPILOGUE

Several days dawned before Chloe and Quintus found themselves alone together. They had spent those days opening their court and castle to all, turning it into the haven it was meant to be. Chloe had checked the wound in Quintus's side, and she'd been right that Julian's death meant it had finally, fully healed. She'd even healed the enchanted wounds some of the Golden Shields had from when they lived with Ansel. Mishti still wouldn't reveal the location of her wound, but Chloe had a feeling it wouldn't be long before her friend was finally ready to have her enchanted wound healed too.

And of course, Chloe and Quintus had to repair the castle and clean up from the battle. Even after all that, they'd still had so much to do. But now their duties were settling into what would be their new normal lives. And with other Shields heading to their own rooms for the night, Chloe and Quintus remained the only two people left in the library of Crystalfall Castle.

A soft glow emanated from the colorful glass-domed ceiling, casting a rainbow of hues across the room. The colors were even more brilliant since a radiant setting sun shone through the gilded windowpanes.

Solid gold bookshelves lined the room from end to end. Chloe had finally deciphered the category coding behind the large colored gemstones embedded into the sides of the bookshelves. The delicious smell of old books mingling with the delicate fragrance of vanilla and lilacs filled the large room.

She nearly plucked a book off a shelf and curled herself up onto one of the velvety armchairs in rich jewel tones scattered around the shelves. But then she noticed Quintus standing at the end of a row, staring at her without releasing his gaze.

At once, she knew they were alone. She had seen the last Golden Shield exit the room, and she had mistakenly thought Quintus had left with the others. But now he stood there, staring. Her stomach flipped as she bit her lip.

When he caught her staring, he smiled. "Did you see Chandril? He gave another memory to Mishti, and he is mortal now. Just like her."

"That is wonderful!" Chloe pressed a hand over her heart. But Quintus said nothing. She stepped closer to him, easing the leather bag off her shoulder and onto the floor. "Do you think he was foolish for doing it?"

"No." Now *he* took a step toward her. "I may have done the same for you, if it were possible. But the only way I know for a fae to turn mortal is with a shard, and…"

A soft chuckle left Chloe's lips before she finished his sentence. "Only Elora has survived that process." It was the same problem she had with the shard.

He nodded.

Chloe swallowed, her nerves suddenly quickening her heartbeat. "Speaking of Chandril…"

Quintus tilted his head to the side, still staring at her like she was life itself. Didn't he know it made it difficult to speak when he stared at her so?

She had to swallow again before she could form any sort of coherent words. "I talked to him about what he did to you in the ritual."

"He made me undead."

"Well." She bit her lip again, trying to find the right words. "That is a simplified explanation, and it doesn't technically explain what happened."

Quintus leaned his shoulder against the bookshelf next to him, clearly having no concept of what she was about to tell him. He looked as casual and calm, as if this were a regular day, while her insides were currently doing cartwheels.

Her fingers twitched to reach for her magical book inside the leather bag she had just set on the ground. She'd written it all out inside the book to help her remember all the details. But she had studied them enough. She didn't need the book to explain it properly.

Taking a deep breath, she did her best to get each aspect correct. "Chandril temporarily shared only that specific part of himself with you, but it did not change your nature. You were still fae the entire time. He just shared the part of his essence that made him impervious to death. And it only worked because he willingly shared it. It's not the kind of thing someone can steal."

Quintus nodded, but she could see how his eyes were glazing over. His gaze turned to her neck, her waist, and then her lips.

If she didn't get to the point immediately, they'd both get lost in each other. She cleared her throat, hoping to distract him. "Part of *your* essence makes it so you never age and can never die of old age."

In a flash, his eyes focused on her. He suddenly seemed to realize what she was saying. "I can share it with you? The part of me that is immortal?"

Her fingers scratched at her dress, still determined to explain things correctly. "If we share in the same way as the wraiths, I will still be mortal, as Crystalfall needs, but I will also never age and die."

He launched himself forward, holding both hands out to her, as if that was how they would share. "I will do it. I will give you anything."

Her gaze trailed downward as she scratched harder at her dress. "From what I understand, I will have to do most of the work. I am certain I can find that part of your essence through our bond, and then I will have to use magic to share some of that part with myself."

Leaning in closer, he tried to catch her eye.

With a sigh, she admitted the part that made her the most afraid. "It will be difficult. It will require me to do that magic almost constantly. And I can do other magic simultaneously as long as I maintain proper concentration. I don't think it takes much concentration or effort to do it for a few moments or possibly even for a whole day." She looked up at him now. "But I would have to do it...forever."

He stared in silence as his chest rose and fell in slow breaths. When he spoke again, it was nearly a whisper. "Do you think you can do it?"

Her fingers stopped scratching. She'd been asking herself this same question ever since she'd learned about the sharing. She knew what answer she wanted to give, and she knew what answer was the truth. They weren't exactly the same, but they *were* close.

When she opened her mouth, she shared what she must. The truth. "Now that I wear a crown, yes, I think I can do it. And if I'm wrong, and I can't, I should know as soon as I try."

Quintus held his hands out to her again, but she shook her head at them. Then she closed her eyes and concentrated. Her bond with Quintus, and her magic, had grown so much in the final battle with Julian. She'd learned to use it in ways she'd never considered before. And once she got the crown of Crystalfall, that magic and power grew tenfold. Her mind had been opened to incredible possibilities, and her power had been able to fulfill them all.

But doing magic constantly, even a tiny bit of it, would test those limits more than anything else. Her heart skipped as she reached out to her beloved. That part was easy. It was like he stood directly next to her in her mind, and when she reached out, he took her hand. Easy. Through the bond, she dove in deeper and found his very essence.

Reading about it on paper was nothing to how it felt doing it for real. She found his essence, and it was like his entire nature enveloped her. Breathing in deeply, her lips curled upward. She'd happily drown in his essence if given the chance. But she knew right now, she had to focus.

Turning her attention, she identified the part of him that made him immortal. She imagined that part of him as a brilliant glowing emerald liquid that pulsed and swirled inside a large golden bowl. Then she imagined conjuring a golden cup, which she dipped into the bowl. Now she had a bit of that glowing emerald liquid with plenty left over for him.

Picturing the cup still in her hands, she trailed back to her own mind. Once there, she imagined another golden bowl, one attached to her essence. With the bowl vivid and steady, she poured the glowing emerald liquid inside. At first it sat plain and unmoving. But with another focus on concentration, the liquid began swirling, it began pulsing.

She could feel the change in her own essence as it trickled down from her head, into limbs, and all the way to her toes. But now she needed to tell her magic to keep the liquid swirling and pulsing, even when she wasn't thinking about it. Even when she was sleeping.

With one last burst of magic, she pictured turning away from the bowl in her mind. She walked away, leaving it to work without any conscious thought. *Hoping* it would work.

In the next moment, it became clear that for once, everything had gone exactly as it should. It had *worked*. The part of Quintus's magic that kept him immortal now swirled and pulsed inside her. And even without her thinking about it, the magic would always continue to work, right at the back of her mind.

Her eyes flew open. She reached out, grabbing onto Quintus's hands that he still held out to her. She squeezed them tight and said words that brought tears to her eyes. "It worked."

He sucked in a breath, clearly afraid to believe it. "Now you will not age or die of old age even though you are still mortal?"

"Yes." Emotion caught in her throat, distorting the word.

But he had still understood. He squeezed her hands tighter and pulled himself just a little closer. "So…you will marry me?"

She should have known he would ask as soon as she finished. But she did not mind. With warm tears slipping down her cheeks and with a wide smile on her face, she said, "Yes!"

He beamed and immediately drew her white wedding dress out from his magical pocket. "I will stand on the other side of the room while you change. And each of us will need a bargain and a vow."

As he pushed the dress into her hands, she blinked at it at least three times before realizing what was happening. "Wait, right now? You want to get married right now?"

His eyebrows pinched together. "You said *yes*."

"And I meant it," she said with a nod. "I just didn't know you meant right *now*."

This had clearly not been in his plans. Frowning, he asked, "How do they do it in the mortal realm?"

She ran her fingers over the sparkling white chiffon and the gorgeous white-and-gold satin of the bodice. "There's usually a long period of waiting. Then, on the day of the wedding, everyone gathers to watch, and that is usually followed by a large celebration with family and friends."

He curled his lip at those words. "They *watch* you? Get married?" He shook his head, as if the idea made him sick. "In Faerie, the bargains and vows of a wedding are meant to be private."

"I know." She said the words soft and gentle. Then she placed a hand on his cheek while looking into his eyes. "I have no problem with that. I just didn't expect us to get married immediately."

"Do you need a few moments to decide on your bargain and vow?" It was pretty clear he would not be willing to wait much longer than a few moments.

"No." She pulled her hand away, putting it back with the other to hold her dress. A twinge of heat prickled across her cheeks. "I may have asked my magical book about Faerie weddings and learned about the bargains and vows. And I may already have a plan."

He must have sensed she still had hesitation. His lip curled again, which he didn't try very hard to hide. "Then you want to wait until we can have a celebration?"

The abruptness of his request had taken her off guard, but now she felt as anxious as him. She leaned in a little closer, touching her shoulder to his. "Maybe we could do the bargain and vow part right now and then do the celebration with our friends and family later."

His lip curl immediately turned to a smirk. He wrapped both his arms around her waist and leaned in as if to kiss her. But just before he did, he shook his head.

She had to suppress a laugh. She loved it when he got so taken with her that he forgot to think.

"I will go…" His voice was husky and low. He shook his head again and pointed across the room. "Over there." Now he coughed. "I'm going over there so you can change."

This time, she did chuckle, but only a soft one. But before he could turn, she grabbed her book from her leather bag and opened it to a page she'd been studying a lot lately.

"About the bargains," she said. "I know most Faerie bargains require both people to agree to something, but marriage bargains are different. For each, only one person agrees to something while there is no requirement at all from the other person."

"That is correct." He had turned away from her to answer, as if the sight of her would make him forget how to think entirely.

Chloe continued. "And since we are king and queen now, I thought it would be appropriate to include our court in our bargains, particularly if we include something about how it is a court for both mortals and fae. I thought these might work."

He leaned forward just enough to read the words she had written, still doing his best to avoid looking at her. As he took in the words, a few tears gleamed in his eyes. He touched a hand to his chest. "That is perfect."

Already he had forgotten himself and went to kiss her again. He stopped himself a little quicker this time and spun on his heel. As he marched across the room, he uttered a husky request. "Hurry."

She threw her other dress off and tugged the white one on faster than she'd ever done so before. Fluffing her hair, she ran her teeth over her lips to make them appear redder. She pinched her cheeks next. Just as she wished for something extra special to put into her hair, she noticed a gorgeous golden and emerald barrette sitting on the shelf next to her. Had it been there before? Or had Faerie itself heard her wish? Wherever it had come from, she slipped it into her hair.

Now, she was ready.

When she declared as much to Quintus, he rushed to her side in a half a breath. Upon seeing her, his mouth dropped open wide. He took her hand and twirled her in a circle, admiring her every curve and feature.

"Magnificent," he whispered under his breath.

When he'd finished twirling her, he kept her hand in his and moved in closer until they nearly stood chest to chest. "I propose a bargain." He spoke slowly, his voice pouring over her like a waterfall. "You will rule Crystalfall well and serve all, but especially the mortals."

Nodding, she said, "I accept." It was her turn now. "I propose a bargain. You will rule Crystalfall well and serve all, but especially the fae."

He squeezed her hand. "I accept."

The air around them shifted, and it almost seemed like little bells chimed to solidify the words they had just spoken.

His lips lifted as he stared deeply into her eyes. "You had the bargains ready, but I have been working on my vow." With a swallow, he spoke again. "To bind this marriage, I make this vow."

Once those words left his lips, the air fluttered more, and the chiming increased. The intoxicating scent of books and vanilla and lilacs intensified, making everything seem more magical than ever. As he continued the vow, it only increased. "I vow to love and protect you, to invoke in you a remembrance of the excellence of your worth, and to forever call your heart my home."

Her lip quivered as his words sank in. Her throat filled with emotion while a tear slid down her cheek. That tear was followed by several more. It was so beautiful she could hardly breathe.

Pinning her with a gentle smile, he used his free hand to wipe away the tears on her cheek. "Do not cry so much that you cannot speak. You still need to say your vow."

She chuckled and tried to swallow the rest of her tears down. Taking several deep breaths, she forced herself to be ready. She could do this.

And then, she spoke her vow to him. "To bind this marriage, I make this vow." Her breath hitched, but she managed to finish without stopping. "I vow to love and heal you, to mend all fractures of doubt within you, and to *forever* call your heart my home."

Once the words left her mouth, he tucked one finger under her chin. His eyes locked onto hers as he brought her lips against his. The smell of him drifted around her, even more intoxicating than the books. It had all happened so fast, she could hardly believe it was already over. But now she was his and he was hers.

And her life had never been more perfect.

She had once promised him she would never return to Faerie with him, no matter how often he asked. She should have known such a promise would be impossible to keep.

Some stories couldn't help but be told.

CRYSTALFALL BEGINNINGS

Get Clara and Revyn's story in the standalone,
Nutcracker of Crystalfall.

The annual Christmas party was going just fine…
until the trolls showed up.
Nutcracker of Crystalfall is available now!

ACKNOWLEDGMENTS

First off, thank you so much for completing this series with me! Chloe and Quintus go through such a journey together, and I'm glad you made it here so you could read their happy ending. If you enjoyed the book, I would be ever so grateful if you left a review. Those help more than you know.

To my excellent editors, Deborah Spencer and Justin Greer, my gratitude for you is unending. As always, you helped to make this book more magnificent than I could have done on my own. You understood my vision and helped me achieve it. I'm not only grateful for your editing skills, but also for your patience in my writing process. It has been an honor to have both of you edit the two series in my Faerie world.

My book cover designer, Angel Leya, deserves all the praise anyone and everyone can offer. She truly made each book in this series special, but this final book cover with the crown required detailed and careful work that turned out unimaginably beautiful. Thank you for being a delight to work with and for making my book covers so much better than I picture.

I must send heaps of gratitude to @pangolin2b, who illustrated the stunning artwork of Chloe and Quintus in the Crystalfall library. The attention to detail was absolutely impeccable, and I love how much emotion the art conveys.

To my family, who were so wonderful for giving me time and space to write this series, especially this last book, I appreciate and love you. And most especially of all, I thank my remarkable husband for believing in me and giving me strength when I needed it the most.

ABOUT THE AUTHOR

Kay L. Moody is proud to be an epic fantasy romance author who gets to create worlds for a living. ;) Her books feature strong female characters, court intrigue, royalty, magic, and slow burn romance with men who fall first.

With 17 romantasy books across 4 complete series, she's no stranger to hidden princesses, deadly competitions, or couples who go from enemies to lovers. Her books have sold more than 100,000 copies worldwide and have earned accolades including *Best Fantasy Book* (Many Books, Dec 2023) and *Bestseller: Fantasy* (BookRaid, Apr 2024).

Her favorite non bookish things are pizza, summertime, the color pink, and having pretty nails. She lives in the western USA with her husband and four sons. Follow her on social media to stay in touch (@kaylmoody).

ALSO BY KAY L. MOODY

Fae and Crystal Thorns
Flame & Crystal Thorns
Shadow & Crystal Thorns
Blade & Crystal Thorns
Curse & Crystal Thorns
Wrath & Crystal Thorns
Standalone: Nutcracker of Crystalfall

The Fae of Bitter Thorn
Heir of Bitter Thorn
Court of Bitter Thorn
Castle of Bitter Thorn
Crown of Bitter Thorn
Queen of Bitter Thorn

The Elements of Kamdaria
The Elements of the Crown
The Elements of the Gate
The Elements of the Storm

Truth Seer Trilogy
Truth Seer
Healer
Truth Changer

Visit **kaylmoody.com/beauty** to download a bonus story,
Bargain of Power and Beauty, for free.

MORE FROM KAY L. MOODY

Don't Miss This Related Series!

Swords first, love later. That was always her rule.

Elora lives for her sword, but her skill can't save her family from ruin. To protect them, she accepts an arranged marriage, only to be stolen away by a broodingly handsome fae prince before she can
say "I do." Now trapped in his cursed court by a magical bargain, she must train him to win a throne, but the greatest battle she faces might be the one for her own heart.

Book 1:
COURT OF BITTER THORN

MORE FROM KAY L. MOODY

You Also Might Like Kay L. Moody's Previous Series!

She's not the only one who will do anything to win…

A girl from the slums with a rare and powerful magic must win a cutthroat competition to save her family. But her greatest rival, a privileged, arrogant, and annoyingly handsome prodigy, is the one person who could expose all her secrets and ruin everything.

Book 1:
THE ELEMENTS OF THE CROWN